To Karen —
you are a
fantastic nurse
I have enjoyed
watching you
grow into an
amazing experienced
nurse.

F. Horton RN

Nov 14. 2012

The Blue-

P.L. Jones

BALBOA.
PRESS
A DIVISION OF HAY HOUSE

ISBN: 978-1-4525-5934-6 (sc)
ISBN: 978-1-4525-5935-3 (e)
ISBN: 978-1-4525-5936-0 (hc)

Library of Congress Control Number: 2012917864

Balboa Press books may be ordered through booksellers or by contacting:

Balboa Press
A Division of Hay House
1663 Liberty Drive
Bloomington, IN 47403
www.balboapress.com
1-(877) 407-4847

Because of the dynamic nature of the Internet, any web addresses or links contained in this book may have changed since publication and may no longer be valid. The views expressed in this work are solely those of the author and do not necessarily reflect the views of the publisher, and the publisher hereby disclaims any responsibility for them.

The author of this book does not dispense medical advice or prescribe the use of any technique as a form of treatment for physical, emotional, or medical problems without the advice of a physician, either directly or indirectly. The intent of the author is only to offer information of a general nature to help you in your quest for emotional and spiritual well-being. In the event you use any of the information in this book for yourself, which is your constitutional right, the author and the publisher assume no responsibility for your actions.

Any people depicted in stock imagery provided by Thinkstock are models, and such images are being used for illustrative purposes only. Certain stock imagery © Thinkstock.

Printed in the United States of America

Balboa Press rev. date: 10/10/12

PROLOGUE:
The End

"Loss is nothing else but change, and nature's delight."
-Marcus Aurelius Antonius (121 AD - 180 AD).

*E*ach generation has its gods.

The advancement and success of a god's myth is directly proportional to the tools responsible for the manifestation of their legend.

Science can deliver the tools—science can make gods of men.

Therefore, even humanity can achieve dominance over all it surveys.

Henceforth, man can become a god.

However, Mother Nature has the power to revoke the usefulness of those tools, in essence erasing all traces of a false god.

Mother Nature's silent reproach descended upon the false gods as effortlessly, as a clock hand struck the hour.

CHAPTER ONE:
The Reaping

"All great change is proceeded by chaos."
-Deepak Chopra (1946 - 2012)

In a crushing blow, a timeless prophecy was satisfied. Nature reclaimed the world, reaping humanity as easily as wild fire could devastate dry kindling.

We as a species were ripe for a pandemic.

We thought we were gods over our domain.

Humanity in its quintessence had become complacent in its science based knowledge and the right to bear arms. The human race festered and corroded the very earth that sustained it.

Mother Nature was due for some retribution.

Deep from her bowels she delivered a microscopic entity of annihilation.

Ninety-nine point nine percent of the world's population ceased to be. Our religious scholars preached the seven days of creation.

Mother Nature proved to be more effective, obliterating homosapiens within three days.

If you left it to a woman—you definitely got efficiency!

Click—as easy as turning a light off.

The seven billion breathing, fighting, breeding homosapiens on planet earth became extinct; it was a sunny winter day in December 2012.

Chapter Two:

The Chaos

"Hell is Empty and All the Devils are Here."
-William Shakespeare (1564 - 1616)

*O*n the evening of Saturday December 22, 2012, case after case began to assault the world's health facilities.

Scientists were bewildered.

There was neither cadence nor reason to who survived and who perished. There were no biases toward race, gender, age, religion or wealth—the viral path showed no restrictions.

The closest the human species came to identifying the manner and rationality of the assailant was through the work of a geneticist. The geneticist claimed the invader was a retrovirus attacking our genes. This retrovirus had become enticed by our genes, compelling them to change into a mutation—as a puppet master would work a finger-puppet, the virus took over the human body.

It killed us, or established permanent altering residence within the body. Our DNA was its playground.

The virus transformed its newly claimed homosapiens terrain into a different version of its former self. Time was unfavorable for the many who tried to identify and combat the plague of our destruction.

The postulation of probabilities through vast technologies procured no results.

The scientific study of processing and delving into the irrationality of the worldwide pandemic was over before specialists could be convened and equipment warmed up.

We were caught, like a deer transfixed by oncoming headlights. Blinded with our pants down—humanity was road kill.

Chaos spread worldwide superseding all artificial borders. The incubation period, by guess, was less than three days. Time was on the germs' side. The infection process was obscure and rapid. It moved with the elusiveness of smoke whilst it delivered its lethal contagious cargo.

Resistance was futile.

We were trying to combat smoke an insubstantial, lethal ghost.

The entire world's vast weaponry sat impotent against a faceless, formless enemy of the people.

No trigger was pulled.

No button was pushed.

Not a single bullet was fired.

We didn't have time to designate neither the mode nor the means of transmission.

We were infected, but how? What was the vehicle of transmission?

The question of transmission weighed heavily on the world's mind.

Our thoughts were encumbered by our vulnerability and defenselessness. Death came quickly; an individual carried the disease symptom free for a couple of days. Then, with impudent abruptness, symptoms incapacitated the sufferer.

The infected human population collapsed into a state a dizzying and waning loss of motor function. The illness ravaged the human body in a matter of a few hours. The onset of symptoms was subtle until death tapped you on your shoulder. Death came quietly to all but the few the virus adapted—those screamed. Pain and terror resonated in their shrieks, a sound that would haunt and reverberate in the dreams of those still living.

CHAPTER THREE:
The Transformation

"Today you are you, that is truer than true.
There is no one alive who is truer than you."
-Dr. Seuss (1904 - 1991)

Ten years as an emergency room nurse, and I was stuck working a night shift. What was I thinking picking up a graveyard shift? I never slept well the next day. Tonight I was no different than a hamster on a wheel. I was running fast, but going nowhere, or so it seemed. My educated hands could not thwart the advancing destruction of the pandemic. Humanity had no time or understanding to take any advanced standard precautions.

Washing your hands or wearing gloves and gowns were impotent endeavors—all of it was a pointless effort.

Everyone was dying.

The beleaguered victims of the virus could not be appeased. The delirious, semi-conscious patients began an endless inward flux into my trauma center. Surge upon surge of the helpless emptied ceaselessly through our doors. It was pandemonium. Uncontrollable bedlam pervaded the conduits of the hospital. Within the first hour of the viral ambush, the tidal wave hurtling down on humanity wordlessly declared a disaster mode.

The beaten staff could not gain their balance against the onslaught. Awash with the profuse numbers of the incapacitated, the hospital was overcome, helpless. Besieged by the unabridged masses of the city's despondent, the numbers crushed our fraught health facility and our moral.

Unbeknownst to our hospital, the virus's lapping flame had jumped borders and was now satiating its hunger globally. Our hospital's macabre scene was reproduced, in all its wretchedness, on the whole of humanity.

We as a species were quickly being annihilated into extinction.

Health institutions were seeing people transition from a state of unconsciousness to critically ill in a matter of hours. These people died quickly, almost peacefully. They just never woke up.

A peaceful demise wasn't always the case. Some, albeit rare cases—appeared to journey through unimaginable torment. They had their own personal view of the gates of hell.

Their screams echoed in the halls of the world's health facilities.

Their cacophony of cries reverberated with varying degrees of wretchedness. Caregivers were helpless to soothe the orchestra of indecent and woeful suffering.

Transmission came like a thief in the night, stealing humanity's heartbeat. An anonymous vector, open to a virus of unknown pedigree, it vied with nothing.

The world's health experts, just didn't know what the virus was and how it was transmitted. Humanity had no resistance, and no clue as to how or what was conquering them. It was a disproportionate war waged on the homosapiens.

A microscopic murderer—a mere virus—laid claim to human existence.

The world had no defense—I had no defense as it turned out. A faceless formless assailant embraced me.

I did not die. Instead, the virus took my hand and dragged me through the doors of an abyss.

My two dogs howled as the assault pervaded within my body.

Echoes of their whines continued to resound throughout my tortured anguish. It was their humble protest to my screams of agony.

A fire and ice storm raged through every cell, simultaneously. I fought poorly against the amassed horror brewing within my being. The virus's attack left no reprieve and no escape. I was circling within Dante's Inferno.

CHAPTER FOUR:

Inventory

"Behind every beautiful thing there is some kind of pain."
-Bob Dylan (1941 - 2012)

I could hear everything and discern nothing. My mind couldn't hold a thought. I twisted in my nightmare. I was unable to process or bring order to Lucifer's divine locker. It was every person's gross under exaggeration of hell.

My screams of terror gave me no reprieve from my plague of pain.

Fear saturated my every breath. I shuddered uncontrollably.

A world of agony enveloped me; my soul adhered to the fire and storm brewing and erupting within me.

When I thought I couldn't stand any more, a fresh cascade of white-hot fire rained down on me. Blessedly, it washed me of consciousness.

I sighed as oblivion stole my existence.

As abruptly as turning a faucet off, the horror faded. I awoke from blankness.

Stillness blossomed around me.

Ensnared in my sheets and blankets, I had mummified myself. The shroud of death and silence pressed with density on my soul while it encased my body.

Sweat layered my skin.

Smells exploded in my sensitive nose. I was overwhelmed with odors.

I stopped breathing through my nose; I couldn't take the sensory overload. I opened my mouth cautiously. The molecules in the air swathed my tongue. I tasted blood, salt and dust.

I was afraid to open my eyes, afraid of what might be waiting for me.

Reaching out tentatively, I felt the fibrous sheets of my bed linen. Pressure was around my neck—the grim reaper had me!

Panic rose from my stomach.

I reached up cautiously to touch my captor. The sheets had encircled my neck as tight as a noose.

I exhaled a shaky breath.

My eyes remained clenched in a shaky vise grip of restraint. Behind my sealed lids, I could see shocks of lightening shooting across my field of vision.

I inhaled gently.

What seemed like an eternity of hell...had just ended? My mind wanted so badly to tilt, to escape the moment, to restart. Where was my control-alt-delete button? I needed to reboot.

"Tick." The hand of the clock struck the hour.

I breathed cautiously.

Although the action felt unnecessary, it gave me relief to perform an involuntary habit. Old habits died-hard. Who knew comfort in the act of breathing could be so soothing.

Was I dead? Where was I?

I must be in hell, purgatory, or heaven—the insane, usually deferred to religious symbolism. Great, I've snapped, cracked and popped.

All right, let's just stop for a moment and take this one step at a time.

I am perfectly capable of handling anything...right?

Right...

I swallowed hard...Getting a grip, getting a grip...I wrestled with my mind.

Hell and purgatory revelations suddenly overwhelmed my thoughts.

In my flabbergasted mind, imaginings of dancing demons, righteous angels and a bearded white haired guy pointing a finger at me replayed. Oh, I am so fuc...!

Get a grip, geesh!

I was not a religious person. Spiritual? Sure. Religious? Definitely not.

Damn, I had to get a grip. Shut the front door.

I took a deep breath. I must have gone a little insane; a little insane is okay, right?

Right?

Michael the Archangel, please come and save me. I vaguely remembered bible studies. Michael was a real tough angel, he could help me.

Great, just great! I've somehow survived a pandemic, only to slip over the edge of sanity. One padded cell and straightjacket needed, stat!

Clean up in aisle two.

Oh and bring some Haldol—lots of Haldol. A good antipsychotic will do nicely right about now.

It finally happened, I was a character in *One Flew Over the Cuckoo's Nest*. None of my bee bees were slipping into their holes; the train had finally left the station and gone off its rails. Oh my God, the excursion through horrendous agony has made me insane.

The surreal insanity of the moment was not lost on me. An abrupt, involuntarily cackle escaped my dry lips—it was the sound of an insane person. I'd heard that involuntary sound in the psych ward—it was a way too familiar sound.

People in the midst of psychotic episodes made that sound. The psychiatric patients made that noise as they pulled their hair out and scanned the room for imaginary foes and aliens.

This single solitary noise quickly scared me straight. My mouth snapped shut with the force of a gale wind.

I bit my tongue and tasted blood.

Ouch, all right…Ok! A deep breath was definitely called for here!

I inhaled slowly and felt rationality and logic surface from the depth of my toes.

I exhaled hesitantly. I didn't want to lose this tenuous moment of clarity. I was still a conscious, sentient being—I was alive. How anyone could survive a trip into the nether regions of hell and live to tell the tale—was beyond me.

Moreover, how, after all that agony, can I be having a rational thought? Much less notice the wet dog smell—coming from the corner of my room.

Ok, so I could still feel my bed linen, and I could smell my dogs—they needed a bath. I was not on some celestial plane, and I had my wits about me.

Breathe in.

I decided this was an excellent foundation to open my eyes. I allowed my eyelids to peel back from my eyes cautiously. A shimmering spectacle of dancing stars exploded in my field of vision—pretty.

No…ah, not stars. My eyes focused on the beige, white and grey starbursts—dust particles?

Geez!

Really!

Movement out the corner of my eye caught my attention. Two shadows lurked— my dogs. Their heads hanging down, they stared at my mummified form.

I heard a whine, a steady thrumming sound and nervous pants. They were cowered in the far corner shaking. A mixture of sweaty paws, musk, urine and hyper-salivating drenched their corner. Is this what fear smelled like?

"Oh girls," I whispered.

I tried to sit up and unravel myself as I continued to talk to them. "Did I scare you? Oh pups! You and me both." I breathed out in a smooth whisper. Hairy confusion overtook their tightly knotted brows.

The sound of my voice caused the two mutts to twitch abruptly in unison.

Apprehension seeped into their taunt muscles as hope and fear played out across their furry faces. It was almost comical if the reason for it wasn't so sad.

Perhaps my voice was not as smooth as I thought.

"Come here girls." The soft invitation slipped from my lips.

They did not move. I could hear their thrumming hearts increase in tempo with the invitation.

"It's okay girls, I'm all right. I think?" They cowered, tighter together. I winced at their response.

Safety in numbers—ah yes. Wild kingdom 101. They didn't move, nor did they look any more convinced then I felt—I wasn't fooling anyone.

I laid my head back onto my sweat-soaked pillow.

Ever vigil, my dogs curled by my bed, their loyalty triumphing over their fear of the unknown.

It was time to unwrap myself from my mummified state. I found a corner and started to untangle my limbs from the sheet. Wow, I did a number on myself.

As I continued to unwrap my self-inflicted bonds, I thought over the circumstances of recent events. I wasn't really ready for personal reflection, so I broadened my ruminating to universal circumstances.

Would we as a species survive this pandemic? Would I?

Nope, don't go there yet. What's happening out there? I gazed outside my window. Darkness shrouded my old window. No street lamps glowed.

It was then I realized a soft blue light illuminated the room.

Did I leave my light on?

The light swayed with my turning head. What the hel..?

Hello.

I instantly became distracted with my own movement. My physical health felt perfect. As a nurse, I was always sore. My whole body presently felt fantastic. My usual aches and pains were gone and my head was clear. In fact, it felt crystal clear. The band, which had plagued my head earlier, was silent.

I flexed my arms. I felt splendid.

I realized when I focused on my hearing the city's usual hum of cars was gone. I concentrated harder on my hearing, hoping to hear some form of human activity. I could hear everything, but differentiate nothing. A strange hum of static penetrated my ears.

I concentrated mentally to focus. My hands inadvertently reached up and clasped my ears.

I had always been excellent at compartmentalizing and multitasking. I was an emergency room nurse, pure and simple.

I focused harder, refusing to be overwhelmed.

My mom always said I was a stubborn child—who knew stubbornness could be such a useful tool?

The noise and smells slowly ebbed—I really needed to give those dogs a bath.

I chuckled. Life and death was playing out in a macabre scene and here I was worrying about the dogs needing a bath. Priceless.

My hairy family was watching me. They blinked with quizzical, cautious eyes.

Released from my cocoon of sheets, I stretched my legs and wiggled my toes. I eased my legs over the edge of the bed.

That bizarre blue light continued to glow around the room with each turn of my head.

Weird!

One thing at a time. If I let too much in my sanity would crumble.

Okay, breathe again.

Excellent, I had no dizziness. I went to push myself up and sprung out of bed. The simple act of standing had caused me to spring five feet from the bed. I hit my plaster and lathe wall face first. I pushed myself away from the wall that had stopped my ungraceful hurtle—it was dented in a perfect mold of my head and chest.

Bedlam erupted behind me.

My dogs scattered, banging, tripping and peeing a little. This melee of fur resulted in a secure hiding place—they squeezed together under my desk.

"Oh, Oakley and Teak, I didn't mean to startle you!" I exclaimed.

They poked their heads out in unison, their ears prickled in recognition. They, however, did not leave the sanctuary of the desk. My best friends did not trust the spectacle before them.

Ok, so everything was working better than ever. I felt light but solid.

Time for a mirror—yes, vanity called to me.

I had been unmercifully subjected to intense burning and freezing—I must be freezer burnt.

I made my way to the bathroom and hit the bedroom light—nothing, zilch, nada and zip. I flicked the light switch again. No light.

"Humpff."

I made my way to the bathroom mirror anyway preparing to squint. I did not need light.

Everything surrounding me was illuminated like a blue cell phone light.

Where's that blue light coming from?

I put my hand to my face and saw it gleam blue.

I jumped and turned, expecting someone with a blue light to be standing behind me.

Nothing!

I rubbed my head in confusion.

"Humpff." I said again. It was the best I could do; that's all I had in me.

That blue light illuminated my path down my hallway to the bathroom.

I approached the sink. Gripping the pedestal basin, I faced the mirror and slowly lifted my head.

Techno blue eyes danced in the mirror.

I gasped and fell back onto the toilet. I stood up slowly and peeked in the mirror again. The eerie vision before me—instantly captivated me.

Like a mockingbird, a shiny blue object engrossed me.

"Wow, I've never seen…what the?" I reached up to touch my face. My eyes, once a vivid blueberry color—courtesy of both parents were now radiating incandescent blue.

My irises were swirling molten blue lava.

After thirty years of life all, my laugh lines were gone, as were the chickenpox mark on my nose and the subtle scar on my forehead. My convenient, streaked short-blonde hair—was disjointly sticking up in all directions; punk rockers had nothing on me. My hands warily glided over my relatively athletic body. Years of weightlifting human carnage beat out any workout regimen.

I felt for excess fur, fangs or weird alien protuberances. I wanted to make sure nothing was amiss and everything was intact. My breath caught in my throat and my gaze swept back to the mirror to the chief spectacle—my eyes.

I stared, I couldn't help myself. They were mesmerizing. I got lost for a moment in the wild, swirling blue magma.

Changed? Into what? Panic rose as I reached down and clenched the sides of the pedestal sink with a rigid grip. I flexed my arms in my panic as I tried to hold onto my sanity.

My severe grip inadvertently broke both sides of the sink off with an ear-piercing groan and crunch. The high-pitched sound muffled my gulp of shock.

Dumbfounded, I just stood there holding the broken sink pieces in my hands, with my mouth hanging open. A small maniacal laugh involuntarily escaped once again, from my chest.

My god—what the hell had happened to me?

Panic started to rise again. I fought it down with a dose of logic. The last day of work, I remember. The pandemic sweeping the world—did I get it? Nevertheless, why am I not dead?

The virus, yes the virus, it must be...?

What...?

What has it done to me?

Infested, parasitic bodies must be coursing through me. I trembled at the image. It must have altered my physiology somehow, to fit its own requirements.

I must have been appropriated and transformed, but into what and how?

I stood in the blue swathed darkness of my bathroom, holding the remnants of the sink in both hands while a bewildered expression grew on my face.

Flurries of firecrackers were exploding in my head. I was lost in the terror and magnificence of the moment.

A shuddering breath hiccupped into my quiet blue bathroom.

CHAPTER FIVE:
Default to Logic

"Reality is merely an illusion, albeit a very persistent one."
-Albert Einstein (1879 - 1955)

I know a little about science; a Bachelor's Degree in Nursing has some benefits. Pathophysiology was one of my favorite subjects. Viruses could invade any domain through the body's numerous and varying orifices. An unsuspecting body may well become the hapless residence for these trespassers. Once inside the host's body, these immigrants started attacking the body's immune system so that it can set up residence to start replicating and transforming the host's genes. The new residents could thus reap the controls of the host's natural homeostasis. It could literally redecorate your body to suit its needs. You could either die from the infection or be a carrier—like herpes or HIV.

Contracting the influenza virus, for instance, could spread either by direct contact or airborne hitchhikers. A simple cough could transmit either a virus or bacteria to a whole nursing home in a few days. The perpetuated myth, that exposure to the cold caused illness, was just untrue. You needed a nasty bacteria or virus to infiltrate a body. The cold could however, weaken your immune system.

Once inside the safe domain of the body, the germ could corrupt and shape the host's body for its own unnatural and greedy purposes.

The mouth is a primary festering ground for nasty germs—it's warm and moist. You'd be surprised at how often our fingers ended up in our mouths. Touch a handrail and end up with someone's urine in your mouth because they didn't wash their hands. I read that a person touched their face an average of three thousand times in a day. Nurses often joked that their version of a diet was licking the handrail of someone who had C-diff. Explosive diarrhea for a month could shed a few unwanted pounds.

Crap, focus.

So, how did this virus get in? Which orfice? What was the vehicle of transmission? Did I inhale it, ingest it—osmosis? What the hell? Did I lick a rail and not know it?

I knew all the various ways the little buggers could gain entry into the body, but the hospital staff had worn gloves, gowns and masks—we had taken precautions.

I remembered my last shift. I suddenly felt very tired, frightened, stunned and confused. It had been pandemonium.

This quartet of unharmonious feelings enveloped me; I could not form any more coherent thoughts.

I was beyond stunned!

Just keep going!

I could only hear static!

Focus, yes, just keep focusing on logic.

The world had no time to react. There was a moment of panic, and then it was over. It was hardly sufficient time to take a breath or regroup. Damn, we didn't even have time to form a group.

A death-rattling gasp exhaled from the human race.

The ticking of a clock resounded in my head.

Click.

Cuckoo, cuckoo…

A door slamming shut—we were done. Our goose was cooked, tilt—game over.

All our vast technologies, vaccines and intellect were rendered useless in the end. The virus that attacked the genes—a minuscule trespasser—we had no defense against.

All we had was a flimsy "do not trespass" sign, toothless and ineffective.

The status quo of all health care workers was "wash your hands." It did not help us.

I remember passing through the waiting room on my last shift and hearing vague reports on the television. Groups of scientists had formulated the gene hypothesis. The virus was attacking our genes. They had only a small framework of time allotted to them. Time, as it turned out was not on our side. The virus was taking us one by one—dominos falling, quicker and quicker. Soon more reports that the whole world was infected filled the channels.

People had died in their homes, on the street, in their cars. Holding a hand, reaching out to the empty air—humanity had over reached. We trusted in our technology and our science. Death's hand had seized the world, overwhelming and incapacitating by simple dizziness and stupor.

The world stopped, a pounding heart stilled with no chance of resuscitation.

I listened to the city's echoed stillness; a bird's flutter of beating wings, a gentle gust of wind that rustled my wind chimes, a dog's haunted howl.

A dog's howl?

"What the...?" I turned in the direction of the distant noise. It rebounded indiscriminately up through the staircase.

It was coming from my house.

It was coming from downstairs.

I snapped to attention, crunching the basin into porcelain fragments. I turned and ran toward the source of the howl. I flew down the stairs. A special effects expert would have been proud—I scarcely touched the stairs.

Teak, my scrappy wolf terrier, was staring intently out the back patio door. Another howl was endeavoring to form on her hairy grey and black lips, when she startled at my approach. She back peddled and curled in on herself simultaneously, almost hitting the wall.

"What's the matter girl?" I whispered.

She regained some semblance of composure, sneezed, and—with the fortitude only a terrier could muster—approached the door. She attentively refocused her stare into the evening light. Anxiety rippled my spine. Teak was not prone to howl unnecessarily.

Through the patio window, I scrutinized the scene. At that moment, I realized I could easily scan the nocturnal yard with as much ease as blinking.

My keen eyesight gathered an exuberant amount of information in one glance into the dark night. I filtered and processed the flight of a gliding bird circling my back yard, the neighbor's cat sitting on a fence with raised hackles, the rustle of winter's brittle leaves, and my hammock catching in the late evening breeze.

Exposed by my perfect vision, the darkness was mine.

My nose flared. I inhaled deeply and tasted the night. I sensed it. I tasted...what was that smell?

A sharp distinctive odor assaulted my experienced nose. I had never smelled this alien odor in my life. Then again, I never smelled the business end of a horse and I was okay with that.

I focused harder. I absorbed the sight, smell and sound, but was having difficulty processing this overwhelming information.

I felt dizzy, like standing in front of a stadium speaker while wave after wave of pounding noise pummeled my body.

I shook my head, trying to clear out some of the overload.

So I focused on Teak's breathing, then on the mongrel's heartbeat. Thump, thump, thump...

I returned my attention to the backyard. The tidal wave of stimulus slowly subsided. I felt the hairs on the back of my neck bristle. An overwhelming sense of *danger* rose from deep inside my core. I swallowed hard. My base animal instincts had been activated. I didn't even know I had base animal instincts! What was I, some deer caught in the headlights—prey?

I clenched my hands into fists and breathed deeply. I narrowed my eyes.

I was no prey.

Something was here.

CHAPTER SIX:

Saturday, the Day of Oblivion

"For every dark night, there's a brighter day."
-Tupac Amaru Shakur (1971 - 1996)

Three days earlier they kept coming, a horde amassing toward empty hope. We had none; the hospital was a cul-de-sac for the dead.

It was well into my twelfth hour of my shift, and my buttocks had not even come close to grazing a chair. I was beyond exhaustion.

If I had actually dared to sit, I feared I wouldn't have the strength to rise again. What did I know of fear?

Presently, I was attempting to hold a man down on his stretcher.

Yes, a university degree utilized to its fullest. I was terrified that Mr. John Doe would flip himself off the too narrow stretcher he was presently tied to.

I steeled my grip on Mr. Doe's shoulders. The anonymous man had been found unconscious—barely alive—slumped over his steering wheel. The poor fellow had been less than a block from the hospital, and the ambulance crew had nearly run into him.

My weary eyes, cast an exhausted gaze over the main area of the emergency room. I sighed heavily as I viewed pure mayhem. Screaming and crying people dashed to and fro. Fatigue was seeping deeper into my tired bones. I hung my head in defeat. No help would be forthcoming. I was on my own. Meanwhile Mr. Doe was screaming and thrashing like a man possessed.

The four point restraints lashed to each battering limb was barely holding, dental floss flailed with his lashing limbs. I wrestled my ward with a waning grip as I surveyed the emergency department with resolute eyes. I sought anyone with a free pair of hands to help me.

I spotted Dr. Rosenblum, who was trying to hold her section of the ER together. I could see she was losing the battle. I felt helpless, and saw it mirrored in her eyes. Dr. Rosenblum was a scrappy little doc, but the circumstances were taking its toll on her. She needed a chair to keep her stance righted. As I watched, she wavered and slid down the wall, the chair skirting out and banging feebly into an unconscious patient in a wheelchair.

I attempted to get up, but John Doe bucked, and we almost toppled the stretcher over.

Glenda, my charge nurse, came staggering around the corner and tripped on Dr. Rosenblum's still form. Glenda was a very distinguished nurse retiring this year. She carried herself with grace and strength. I could never have imagined her splayed out in such an undignified manner. I watched as she realigned her world. She pulled herself to a sitting position beside the doc, adjusted her uniform and attempted to focus her attention.

Squinting, Glenda caught sight of the violent movement of Mr. Doe and me, as I clung to his bucking form. Glenda raised her hand and waved.

Just then, Jo-Jo, one of our unit clerks, came around the corner and almost tripped on the two immobile downed people.

It was almost a three-car pileup in aisle four. I gasped. Fortunately, Jo-Jo recovered himself—albeit awkwardly and came to Glenda's aide. With his assistance, Glenda and Jo-Jo got Dr. Rosenblum into a chair and rolled her in the direction of a trauma room.

I breathed a small sigh of relief. I took a moment and absorbed my surroundings. Tears, wails, sobs, stressed voices and the occasional scream resounded off the pale yellow walls.

My fellow staff members and I had no gaping wounds to convene upon; we were helpless hamsters on a wheel. We weren't making a difference. No lives were being saved.

People just passively exhaled their last breath. We were destitute to prevent the submissive surrender of their lives. Abandoned, despondent and directionless, the limited remaining staff toiled in vain.

Sustained on life support, a few patients circled the drain. Mechanical ventilators forced the unwilling infected bodies to breathe. The virus ignored the effort and continued to eat away at their existence. We were participating in a pointless endeavor.

You didn't have to be, a seasoned nurse, to recognize this judgment. One breath and then one heartbeat ceased unceremoniously at a time. The absence of a heartbeat caused many of the monitors to flatline, beckoning someone— anyone to heed its cry for help. The machines cries went unnoticed. Their alarmed bequests wouldn't be soothed. No life would return. Moreover, no caring hand would still the alarm. These lifeless entities would be our only heralded mourners.

A swaying man approached me: he looked haired, unkempt and crumpled. Dr. Berdusco, one of my favorite docs, navigated his way through the obstacle of bodies, to my stretcher.

Berdusco's usual confident stride had degraded to an exhausted shuffle. He made his way to the side of my stretcher and stood for a moment, bloodshot eyes stared unseeing off into the unknown. John bucked on the stretcher, which pulled the Berdusco's attention to my beleaguered face.

"Jones!" he whispered.

"Berdusco," I replied.

Our usual exchange did not elicit a smile from either of us.

"Sam, give him morphine if you want, if ah, um…if you think it'll help." He glanced at the exit sign, and then sighed quietly. He turned hastily and walked away, mumbling incoherent words while rubbing his tired stubbly face.

John had stopped screaming but continued to buck. I knew the narcotic would not make a difference in hell in calming my human bull. As I was considering the pros and cons of the narcotic, John's screams began again. I tried to sooth his pain with calm words, but it made no impact. I was unable to rebuff John's cries of horror. He screamed for all he was worth and I hung on for all I was worth. I wasn't worth much…

Individuals suffering from a head injury can initially present as sedate, then erupt into violent behavior. As was the case with John, when he initially presented to the ER, the doctor had been concerned he might have suffered a head injury. The staff had tried in vain to totally sedate and intubate him. He had fought through the anesthetizing effects of numerous drugs. No medications at our disposal touched his tortured psyche. John had bucked our intubating attempts like a pissed off bull bucking its rider off.

I did not attempt to leave his side. Relegated to my designated position, I draped my body over his rearing restrained form. One hundred and twenty pounds of raw authority, I was reduced to a bag of inconsequential feathers.

I didn't know how long I could continue to keep him on the stretcher. Who was I kidding? I was failing. I was sweating and my whole body ached. I had muscles from ten years of emergency nursing, who needed a gym? They quivered.

Most days my young body was tortured with an eighty-year's old stiffness. It never fully betrayed me. However, if I stayed still for too long, my joints tended to snap, crackle and pop. A hot mess, my niece used to say.

Ah…the joys of nursing! Decrepit at thirty, life of a well exploited caregiver. Damn, where was security when you needed them? They were probably securing his vehicle with a big fat ticket.

I continued to fatigue. I felt shaky, and I couldn't remember when I ate last. I had some bottled water I think, like a decade ago. I tried to distract from my waning strength, I decided to reflect on the scene before my eyes. I realized just then, that If you hear or see something long enough, it will become commonplace even melt into the background. The scene and noises weren't melding. We were losing control of the ER. I've never seen that happen before. Glenda my charge nurse wouldn't let that happen…couldn't let that happ…! I quickly looked away. The thought caused panic to rise. I shook my head and looked towards John's rising chest. I needed a little denial.

I felt fatigue war against, the residual adrenaline I had left in my system. The exhaustion won.

Somehow, I fell asleep. The weight of my body pressed into John. The stillness should have been my first clue that something was wrong. I floated, lost in the darkness. The thrumming of his heart tethered me gently to reality. Rising and falling with his rhythmic breathing, I floated away.

It was then that I noticed the silence! It was too quiet.

I awoke startled. I wiped the drool off my cheek and looked down at the young man that had been my mattress. He was awake and staring up at me. No breath raised his chest.

A nurse could assess a vast amount of physical information in a quick glance: the level of consciousness, the quality of respirations, the color of the skin, and the color of the sclera. All these said volumes about the patient's condition.

John's eyes pierced me. Thoughts tumbled through my mind like a heavy unbalanced load turning in a dryer, my brain rocked with no rhythm. I stared into incandescent amber eyes. "What the hell are you?" I cried out.

Conflicting emotions played out across his face. The silent range of emotions that orchestrated his facial features, changed radically from fear to confusion to sadness then anger. The swift slideshow of facial expressions almost seemed hilarious, comical even, except…

Fear was growing inside me. I'm not a screamer, but I felt one blonde bimbo slasher scream rising from my shaking chest.

I did not scream. Instead, I attempted to heave myself off his still chest. A shadow descended toward my right eye and a lightning bolt shot through my vision in almost the same instant.

Damn, not fast enough. The punch viciously propelled my body through the air.

Huh…

Crap, damn…shi…! That stung really bad. I'd never been punched in the head before. Note to self: I don't need that experience again.

Stars blinded my vision.

In midair, I realized that time and space really does slow down during a traumatic event. I flew through the air with the greatest of ease. Feeling helpless was a new experience. Uncontrolled weightlessness was also a new experience. I wasn't enjoying any of these new experiences.

During my in-flight dialogue, I noticed that the hospital really needed to paint the emergency room—it was so bland, no color.

Then I abruptly collided with and rolled onto, an inanimate object. Yes, an inanimate, inert, and unmoving, however you want to say it—object that did not give an inch to soften my trajectory.

I had flown fifteen feet through the air from my original site of takeoff. Thoughts of impressive momentum, with amazing airtime went through my mind. It's weird, how things can go through a person's head, during a stressful moment. Being an ER nurse, I thought I was immune to stress but apparently not.

Damn, once again.

The stretcher was the inanimate object that caught the end of my wingless flying escapade. The damn stupid impressive brakes held—this time. Half the time, the brakes never worked and in those situations, the stretcher would roll over my toes or slam into a wall.

Nevertheless, I caught wicked airtime. That just doesn't happen every day. Without warning, my head hit something very solid. Unfortunately, my head did not get the in-flight instructions to tuck and roll. I've seen enough Bruce Lee movies, that honestly my head should have known better. Instead, it cracked against the top of the stretcher with a sickly thud.

And for a second time that day I slept. Blackness enveloped me into sweet oblivion.

I returned to consciousness sluggishly. This was partially due to the very loud band playing rudely around me. I reached for my alarm clock.

During this ritual habit of reaching for the alarm clock I realized, well, I was hanging off my bed in a very contorted and unladylike manner.

I managed to lift my head with the dawning realization—I was not in Kansas anymore. I was still in the nightmare.

Damn.

Chapter Seven:
Check Out Time

**"Tell the negative committee that meets
in our head to sit down and shut up."
- Kathy Kendall (1956 - 2012)**

I wrangled with my miserable and uncooperative eyes. The drumming in my head made it difficult to focus. Would someone turn the bass down—please! The pounding in my head was starting to make my eyes water.

I finally managed to control my vision, and I steeled my focus on the opposite stretcher.

Huh, empty of my bucking assailant.

Scanning the rest of the ER, I noted it was devoid of any movement. There were bodies on stretchers, on the floor and lying at the desk. I gripped my pounding head and closed my eyes to the stillness of my beloved ER. I could hear machines beeping and whirling with their alarms sounding off. A phone rang in the background—but no movement.

The band played on with nauseating emphasis on the drum section. How long was I out?

I picked myself up painfully, gaging down some rising gorge. I gripped the mattress steadying my spinning carousel world and moved gingerly forward. Ugh, the gorge peaked just a little, and I think I tasted lunch. Cafeteria food should never be tasted once, let alone twice.

Managing my nausea and the spinning room, I gripped the bed and stood unsteadily. Thank God, I was great at multi-tasking. I stretched out my arms to gain some semblance of balance while I returned my attention to the sight before me.

Through hazy vision, I could make out many still bodies. The survey proved to be a mind dumbing experience. Please, I needed a delete button. My mind could not comprehend the information my eyes were sending it.

Delete, delete, delete…

I couldn't believe what I was really seeing. People were really everywhere. All were lying motionless.

I proceeded to projectile vomit rudely, a steady stream of puke that hit the wall. I was amazed at the extraordinary force of the projectiled regurgitation.

Corn, when did I eat corn?

Huh! Magic Johnson would have been proud of the arc of spew. Clean up in isle five, please.

Huh. Head injured and my sense of humor didn't get any better! As a nurse, I wasn't moved really by vomit but the sight surrounding me—well, I gagged again. No projectile mess this time, just a little dry heaving that made my head pound harder.

My eyes continued their flabbergasted inventory of my environment. I felt my heart lurch with a deafening thud. Co-workers and patients were ubiquitously scattered everywhere. Instant bone numbing remorse encased my shattered existence.

I mourned openly. I wrapped my arms tightly around my torso gripping myself tightly. Devastated, by the resolution that I had to breathe, I inhaled another choking sob. My sobs echoed through the ER corridors in solitary agony. Blood from my head injury mingled with my tears. My sobs trailed into whimpers, and then slowly hiccupped to a close.

I was physically, emotionally, mentally and spiritually— spent. I unwillingly began to compartmentalized reality into a jack in the box. I stuffed it deep into the wind up box in my mind.

The clown in the box wanted to pop.

Somewhere I found the mental fortitude to shove the clown deep into the recesses of my soul. Sheer determination swelled in me; there would be no popping of the clown today.

I painfully pushed off the floor and I took a few experimental steps. I began a series of slow, drunken dance maneuvers. Swaying willy-nilly back and forth, I staggered forward—nope sideways. Where did that wall come from? That, damn band was still playing so extremely loud.

I decided the Parkinson shuffle would suit my needs. Where's a walker when you need one? And they call this is a hospital.

I slipped and slided, then slipped and skidded. I stumbled pelvis first, into the main desk, such an elegant display of my fine motor control skills. Refinement was my middle name.

I felt something warm, trickle down to my chin. I wiped it away without a thought. My drunken gait ensued. I tripped over someone's hunched form and flew into a spread eagle, skidding face first along the floor. I was not a pretty sight.

I rested a moment. I couldn't believe I was laying on the floor. There was no five-second rule in a hospital setting. Once something hit the floor, it was history. Blood, guts, germs and of course poo has touched a hospital floor at one time or another. As I said, there was no five-second rule.

Blood pooled around my face…ah, finally a halo. Mom would be so proud. That was going to leave a mark.

Housekeeping, paging housekeeping—spill in aisle nine— clean up! Nurses have, what's been called black humor. In reality, it is a coping mechanism. It's the ability to find amusement in the sick, disgusting or strange aspects of the everyday life of a nurse. My humor was a default setting. I wasn't feeling very amused.

I cautiously righted myself and stood somewhat straight. Well, if you tilted your head I was standing straight. I took a step.

The crooked floor mandated a lunging uncontrolled dance. I was an ape on ice. The floor must have been tilted—I am sure that was the issue. I think I was standing straight. I made it halfway across the room, before I grabbed onto a stretcher to catch my breath.

I thought that went smoothly. Next, I'll enter America's got talent. No really, no applause, please! Please don't stand... You're so kind. All right, I'll take a bow.

I bowed and without an ounce of grace, my center of gravity propelled me to head-butt the nurses' station. I slept again that day. So many naps! How lucky was I?

My unconscious bliss didn't last long. I awoke to find myself in the fetal position. The pounding headache had returned with fervor. I had to get up, go home. I had to move. The insanity of the circumstances would find me, grasp me, shake me and shred me if I didn't keep moving.

I wanted to check for survivors, but it was all I could do to keep myself moving forward. Safety, I needed safety. I had to get out of this graveyard with its cacophony of echoing alarms. I tried desperately to keep the reemerging revelation of the circumstances out of my mind. I needed to be in denial.

Therefore, I coerced myself forward—one drunken sailor coming up.

I managed to find my Jeep and crawl inside. Sometimes God, Allah, Buddha or the universe takes care of the little things. I found my keys, and after numerous attempts keyed the ignition.

Taking a moment to clear my head, I took a few deep breaths and started the engine. Home, I needed to get home.

Slowly I drove my beaten, battered soul home.

Home is where the heart is, home is where the heart is... All right, I knew I was defaulting to a hallmark card...

I gawked.

The streets were remarkably clear of traffic. I think I saw two bodies lying on the sidewalk, but I chose to focus on what lay before me. I drove listening to the radio hum static. The news got out quickly—remain in your homes.

People were not necessarily prone to listening to the government's directions, yet the compelling news broadcasts changed people's attitudes. Vivid footage of the chaos on the streets, the rising violent riots and the brimming body bags stacked outside hospitals swept through the networks. People were afraid.

The need for information and the growing fear of the pandemic prevailed in gluing the public to their televisions. The reports simply repeated urgent directions to remain in your homes and additional information would be forthcoming. The emergency broadband warning was the additional information. I had no idea what day it was—my shift had started Saturday night.

I lived about twenty blocks from the hospital in a century old house I was currently renovating. Ah, to be frustrated with the chore of stripping hundred year old wood. What I wouldn't give for that trivial torture. The house was a labor of love. Eight years later after buying it—it still wasn't painted. How I longed to be in my bed waking up with the realization that this had been a bad dream, a Chinese food-induced hallucination. It's the small things really that can keep you hoping.

I pulled into my driveway and killed the engine. I just sat there breathing deeply. I sighed softly. It was a beautiful winter day—both sunny and warm—and I was home. Everything looked exactly as I had left it. I focused on this, and felt artificially comforted. I clung to my steering wheel and fought down my rising nausea as reality fought with my weak denial. Apprehension rose with my gorge. Life as we know it had callously changed. I did not get the memo.

With some deep breathing and an intoxicated stagger, I managed to spill out of my Jeep and blunder to my back door. My two dogs were going ballistic hitting the patio doors with the ferocity of a linebacker.

I slowly eased opened the door. My caution was rewarded with the door sledgehammering me in my forehead. My dogs wanted out—now! The swinging door to my head and chest sent me reeling backwards into the barbeque.

Their greeting included a barrage of whining, barking and their idea of body slamming displays of love. This proved unfortunate. I buckled under their onslaught, my tenuous stance crumbled. I was a beaten mess. I was easy puppy fodder.

The dogs were all too eager to take advantage of my delicate state. They decided I was to be adorned with kisses, whines and barks of joy. Two very hairy, fifty-pound dogs were attempting to become lap dogs. They succeeded. In a show of solidarity, they showered me with love, verifying I was theirs and I was home.

I managed to extricate myself from the furry linebackers. I pushed and held onto a tail and pulled myself to my feet.

I was home. I left the back door open, tossed some food and water down for my assailants, then tentatively climbed the stairs.

As I ascended the stairs, I could feel death's hand trying to seize my sanity once again. Exhaustion and dismay was trying to crush me. Fatigue, was winning the war against my anxiety and rising panic. I had to lie down.

I crumpled onto my bed. I could feel coldness seep up my spine. I grabbed a blanket and rolled, cocooning myself.

My whole body throbbed and an ensemble of drums began to crescendo in my head. My resolve gone, I tried to surrender to unconsciousness. I felt the darkness steadily approach and descend upon me. I closed my eyes tighter. Fatigue and a combination of fear and horror deflated my soul. With a trembling sigh I issued my white flag of surrender.

My consciousness slipped away to what may.

CHAPTER EIGHT:
The Enemy at my Gate

"Never interrupt your enemy when he's making mistakes."
- Napoleon Bonaparte (1769 - 1821)

Something or someone was making the hairs on my neck stand at attention. I could smell it, a potent bag of oranges that had been left in a sunbaked garage for too long. The odor was simultaneously sweet and sharp. Then I saw it out the corner of my right eye. A flash of blue—baby blue of all things.

Teak actually came to my side, pressed into my leg and growled. I was outside and leaping over my six-foot fence before I realized what I was doing. My pervading thought was "Danger! Danger Will Robinson. Danger!"

I stopped for a moment, skidding to a halt. Danger. A conflicting battle waged within.

I must act.

What the hell? *NO* I shouldn't! What am I thinking?

Damn.

I should be running the other way with a dog tucked under each arm, while I screamed like a banshee into the night.

All this action should be occurring in the very, very opposite direction, that I was heading in. Apparently, I felt I could somehow manage to channel *Rambo* with ninja skills. What the hell was I thinking? I knew I was thinking hell a lot. My inner vocabulary was fast becoming stunted. All this end of the world stuff was kicking my ass. Honestly! For the love of...!

Thirty feet from the safety of my house, I must have looked absurd, glancing one way then another while standing in the middle of an alley. Fortunately, only Teak witnessed this comical expression of my internal conflict. I looked back at her still form and noticed not a drop of confidence graced her hairy face. Superb, fantastic, I couldn't even convince a dog I have things in hand!

Then I heard it. My head whipped around. The crack of a twig to my left, a hushed curse, then the weight of a locomotive hit me square in the chest. Taunt arms locked around my gasping chest.

Air rushed out of my lungs in a whoosh. Hairy male arms had me in a death grip, throwing me along with him off my feet and through the air. During my propulsion through the air, I realized I was aware of everything happening around me. My mind processed the rapid swirling environment as if it was happening in slow motion. I changed my focus and started to struggle, punch, pull, and kick my attacker. My efforts were in vain.

I was just about to sink my teeth into my foe's neck when we—hit a tree. I had no air to expel—the impact didn't slow the fight down. For Pete's sake, I almost went all vampire on my assailant. Edward would have been so proud—team Edward all the way.

The small tree that had interrupted our flight plan bent at its base and together we bounced and rolled off the limb.

Rolling in the alley, we exchanged rib-breaking punches. I did not relent. I was not going to be prey. I could feel a distant pain but I ignored it. A knee came up and clipped my chin—I tasted blood, huh. It tasted like licking an iron rail.

Mutual lightening quick blows ensued. An elbow to the shoulder—not my shoulder and yes, a few bites. I think I got part of an ear. We were two tomcats in an alley scrap. Apparently, this was my alley. I think I even peed a little. Yeah, was marking my territory. Sure.

I felt the strength and conviction of Ripley in *Aliens* and Demi Moore in *GI Jane*. I was strong. I was invincible. In addition, I was going crazy.

With this pervasive thought, I jumped and perched myself fifteen feet up a nearby telephone pole. It was time to disengage myself from this delusion of grandeur. I needed to catch a thought.

We had both paused in our bobcat fight. I yelled down to my attacker. "What the hell are you? Hell, what the hell am I?" Too many hells—I know. Normally I am not much of a swearer—my mom use to say swearing showed a lack of education.

The interloper was bent over looking ready to pounce and my roost was his target.

"Stop!" I ordered.

The man actually hesitated at my command, but only for a second. His muscles tensed. I saw the tension build and ripple down his back like a panther ready to pounce. Then he sprang.

I threw myself into my backyard a good thirty feet from the pole. I rolled, turned and coiled myself into a readying stance. I looked like a racer at the starting line, muscles taunt, nerves strung. I quivered. Fear and anger battled within me.

My attacker, I noted, was presently perched in the exact position I had just vacated on the pole.

I cocked my head to the side and stared into the eyes of my accoster. Incandescent amber lava held my gaze.

A grin played across his face. "Nice jump," he said.

With an unsure, cocky grin, I returned the appraisal "I owned that GI Jane impersonation!"

He guffawed.

Yes, even I was impressed with my jump and GI Jane roll. My grin turned serious.

"Have you snapped yet? Is that it? I mean, ah…I understand if you have, but could you give me a second to collect my dogs and clear out of here? I'll leave you in peace!" I stared at the perched man hanging fifteen feet up the telephone pole. I scrunched my forehead. I needed a moment to process everything.

I just wanted to curl up somewhere safe with my dogs. I really needed a moment.

I paused.

He was listening to my question. Conflict and confusion crossed his determined face. Perhaps, he wasn't too far gone yet. Perhaps! Maybe reasoning with him was still a possibility.

Without warning, he started laughing, full out belly laughter. He dropped like a rock, falling the fifteen feet ungracefully with a landed thud to the ground.

"Humpff." He issued a slow groan, muffled by the fence. There was a long pause in the laughter fest, then the laughing, continued.

"Pffst!" I spit. "Really, seriously, what are you laughing at?"

Geez, someone had snapped like a baby bird's wing.

Gonzoed! I need to call the people with the strait jackets, so they could load him into a nice, safe, *medicated* paddy wagon. It was time to call 911.

Saddening comprehension goaded my hope. There was no one left to call. I was on my own except for this here lost cause. So I mustered a little GI Jane, Ripley and, of course, Bruce Lee and approached the fence tentatively.

I peered carefully over the fence. My mama didn't raise no fool— I wasn't about to put my head into a hornet's nest.

Searching the ground at the bottom of the telephone pole, I spied his shaking form. Yep, he was still laughing, curled in a fetal position and holding his stomach.

I was not impressed. At least he hadn't peed himself—
yet!

The laughter dissipated all of a sudden—it slowly dissolved into soft sobs. During a break in the sobs, I heard a semi muted, "It's just so normal, you concerned about your dogs' welfare."

I rubbed my face. What was I going to do with a mentally crushed man? I mean, I am a nurse, and I've seen grown men sob before, but this was just pure sadness, flowing out through the man's broken being.

Reality had set in; the facts were crushing this poor soul. The heart, mind and soul cried out through his wretched tears. We couldn't check out of this horrifying reality.

The man's body continued to release some of his grief. He held himself in a tight embrace, rocking and sobbing, rocking and sobbing.

I eased myself closer, opening my gate slowly. I didn't want to startle him.

I held my hand out, "Hi, my name is Sam. Do you want to meet the dogs? You see, I don't care too much about myself, but if you hurt them I will have to…well— it's just that they're innocents. Please don't mess with them." I paused, "also, there all I got, and I think they're what's keeping me sane." My voice trailed off in a whisper.

He looked up at me and wiped his snotty face. A boyish grin of twelve transformed his forty-something face.

It was then that I saw his eyes in full splendor— iridescent molten amber eyes.

I gasped. "You! You're—John Doe," I stuttered out.

He stammered to explain. "I smelled you! You're smell from before, that is. Your smell has changed. I uh…followed you home." He pulled down the hospital gown. Something was winking at me and it wasn't his eye.

I turned and looked at the house. "You hit me and disappeared." How he could still be alive was beyond me. Wow, may wonders never cease!

I turned back to movement. He was attempting to stand up. He wiped blood off his right ear that was beginning to trickle down his neck. I knew I got a piece of that ear! Ha!

A soft chuckle slipped from my throat. I grinned in his direction. His glowing amber eyes met mine. He gasped and stared, mouth agape. He stammered, "Your eyes. You've changed too." He was staring unabashed, mesmerized by my disco eyes.

I felt red creep up my neck and I started fidgeting with my hair.

He cleared his throat and turned his gaze to my back door. Rubbing his stubbly chin and running his hands through his graying black hair, he stood and tentatively approached me.

"I followed your smell here. I'm sorry about lashing out at you at the hospital. You were kind. I uh…was overwhelmed." He turned his head to my neighbor's fence. It suddenly drew his intense focus. He fussed with his gown.

"Please don't lift that thing!" I pointed at his rising gown that he was bunching in his hands.

I saw his neck redden and color creep to his face. He dropped his gown. "Err, sorry."

"You're not going to hurt us now are you?" I cautiously asked. My eyes narrowed. I was not prey. I watched too many wild kingdom shows to know it never ended well—for the prey that is.

He turned his molten gaze back to me. His eyes smiled and he swallowed. "No I, um…just didn't know what your intentions were." He looked sheepish.

"Hello, you're in my alley, stalking me," I barked.

He grinned and nodded toward the tree by the telephone pole, "Yes, I also think you peed over by that tree and marked it, after we ahh, debilitated it." I stared at the dilapidated tree, blinking quickly—stunned. My mouth remained open.

I was speechless! My work mates would have been surprised by that turn of events. Me speechless, it's never been witnessed.

Dr. Sharma used to say that I had a story for everything. I responded to her statement matter of factly. "I've lived is all!"

The man chuckled and returned my narrowed gaze. I could feel heat and probably redness leaching up my neck. We both burst out laughing. I sat down hard on the ground. Together our eyes watered with tears. We were a pair of loons—crazies who shared a psychotic episode. Great, now I needed the nice, safe paddy wagon.

I held my stomach; it hurt from laughing. I never thought I'd laugh again. Sometimes you just *have* to laugh at the stupidest things. We wiped our tears away.

The gowned man held out his hand. I reached up and clasped it. I nodded toward my house.

He followed me inside the yard hesitantly. My brave terrier was growling steadily at the back door. Oakley was hiding somewhere in the house—it was all too much for her sensitive demeanor. I could hear her jump off the bed upstairs and pad in a steady lope toward our vicinity. Since the entire disturbing racket was over, a thorough investigation was called for. Besides, her sister was in need of back up—she would lick the assailant to death if need be.

John was staring up at the moonlit sky. No planes marred the grey sky. He turned and rubbed his now healed ear. "What are we, what happened, is everyone dead?" John whispered. With that one sentence, he had stated everything that mattered—stated it within a simple breath.

I had no answers. My head hung. In the stillness, I heard it before I felt it. My heart beat—just once. I hadn't even realized I missed it, until it thumped in my chest—just one solitary beat. *Thad ump* echoed in the silence.

Memories, realizations, hopes and dreams came together and then dispensed with one beat of a muscle. "Oh my God, we're still alive." I stuttered. "Are we monsters then? Good God, we're not vampires or the walking dead—I refuse to be a zombie!"

"Alive, monsters—what's the difference now? I mean look around. The world is done. Our hearts can't even bother to make much of an effort. What's the point?" Pain and anger simultaneously erupted onto John's face.

"But maybe if it beats..." I could not bring myself to finish articulating the thought. I couldn't imagine a future. I couldn't even imagine what tomorrow would bring.

John sighed and rubbed at the drying blood around his ear. "The heart beats a few times a day." He said while he played with his regenerated ear. "We don't need sleep. We need a lot of food, mostly protein. I think to fuel what is going on inside us. If you don't, you start to feel really fatigued fast and die or something—I don't know for sure." John was still busy playing with his ear, distracted.

"Focus, man!" Geesh. I blinked quickly. "What—what else?"

The distracted man slowly continued in a whisper. "We're strong, fast, and we heal quickly but I think we can be killed."

This man could have been a reporter—just the facts ma'am. He was so matter of fact, without the hint of emotion. Maybe he just couldn't go there yet.

I looked quizzically at him. "How do you know this stuff? Where are you getting your information? Did you meet our maker and get the hand book?"

He looked cynically at me. "I have been out and about for the last two days since I Rockyed you in the hospital, remember?"

Wow, I'd been out for almost two days.

"Ahh" I rubbed my elbow. A two-inch gash was healing—blood had stained the side of my scrubs. I tightened my eyes and nodded toward his apparel. "And what—you never bothered changing out of your hospital gown?" I raised my right eyebrow and gave him a hairy eyeball.

I considered his apparel. He was still dressed in a baby blue hospital gown open in the back.

John's eyes tightened. "As I've said, I've been overwhelmed." And he left it at that.

He looked away.

We sat on the deck and quietly discussed recent events. We wordlessly agreed not to talk about family or friends, at this point anyway. It was an open wound, and neither one of us wanted to poke around in it. We instead decided to venture to the topic of what happened to humankind.

"Have you seen anyone else who's alive?" I asked, not really wanting to hear the answer.

"No" he said flatly. "What do you think happened? I mean you are in the medical profession aren't you? You're wearing scrubs!"

I sighed and rubbed my head. "I have no idea. Everything happened so fast. It was like an avalanche, and we were all swept up in it! I don't know how or why I survived, or how I was exposed to the virus!" I lifted my face and stared at the bright moon. There were no answers up there—damn planet didn't even wink at me as if to say "the jokes on you!" I was gathered up in an avalanche, and I didn't even know from which direction it had originated. All I knew was that it had crashed down on my head.

John's glowing eyes pulled me from the bland moon. "A virus?" he whispered quietly.

"Yeah, and something to do with our genes. The scientists had never seen anything like it—that's as far as they got before... everything um, ended."

We turned our discussion to the virus's origin. Our postulating got us nowhere. We had too few fact-based premises to form any hypothesizes. We speculated on such possibilities as terrorist germ warfare, Mother Nature revolting and my favorite. Martian intercessions—I loved the *X-FILES*.

We had no information to base any conclusions on except that the world has gone to shit in a handbag, and we were left holding the handbag. Our only response to the circumstances was wondering, "What is that stink and how did it get into my hands?"

We sat in silence, taking comfort in the quiet dawn that was approaching on the horizon.

I heard the click of nails. Teak made her way out to us. She was not impressed with either of us. Regardless of my strange smell and foreign mannerisms, her love for me won out. She sat and nuzzled my dangling hand. John of course, made even less of an impression on the hairy mongrel.

She snubbed John, but her hairy gaze continued to peak over my knees and proceeded to glare menacingly at the bloodied strange man. A deep rumble flowed from her chest. John had some of my blood on his sleeve. Teak stared at it suspiciously. John merely ignored her. However, I did see that he kept a cautious eye angled toward her tense glare.

Oakley on the other hand, pranced out onto the deck; her concern for her sister overpowered her need for serenity. She nosed John's hand. The investigation—produced a bout of sneezing. My curious little border collie was *sooo* vicious.

John's real name turned out to be Christin. He was a forty-year-old architect, single, no kids, and his only family was out east.

He had just moved here to start a huge contract. He was tall, lean muscled, had black hair, that was going gray around the temples, and he carried himself quietly.

I was comfortable around him almost immediately. Strange really, he rather reminded me of an older brother. I wasn't apt to feeling easy around most people—emergency nursing had kind of jaded me. I often saw the selfishness and stupidity in people.

It moved me when people surprised me with unnecessary acts of kindness and patience. I enjoyed those surprises. Those occasions, unfortunately, were rare.

Christin needed a new wardrobe—the blue hospital gown was wearing thin in a few places. Christin also felt the need to moon me on the way over to the neighbors. Whether it was intentional or not this encouraged me to break and enter. Hospital gowns were neither flattering, nor did they insure privacy. I reached my limit and decided it was time for a little excursion.

We ransacked my neighbor's house. We said our thanks aloud that they weren't home, for they had two young children—a vision we didn't need.

Wading through other people's belongings felt creepy—we agreed stores would be a more appropriate venue for resupplying in the future.

The power was off, for who knew how long? The phones and Internet conveyed similar versions of static as the TV did.

We showered, ate and settled in the living room, a fire warming the cool winter afternoon. Over steaming cups of hot chocolate and Baileys, we contemplated our next move.

"The mountains along the coast seem logical. The weather tends to be mild, lots of wildlife and fresh water—you could build us a house up there," I surmised.

"Humph, there are enough houses in the world. I don't think we need to build any new ones." Christin was a warm and fuzzy kind of guy. I could tell immediately. Not. Geesh.

Oakley was passed out and twitching on his lap—whore through and through. Christin rubbed the dog's scuff. I could see her eyes rolled back into her head and her breathing sounded like a purr. Can dogs purr?

"My point being—the cities are going to start to stink. We need food, but there won't be much left of anything fresh. Plus eating out of cans for any amount of time won't be met with enthusiasm on my part." My stomach growled. For Pete's sake I just fed the damn thing. Christin was right about needing to eat a lot. "And who knows? Maybe we'll meet some people and start a Hari Krishna commune." I said this while laughing.

Hot chocolate sprayed out of Christin's nose.

"You could be the head Krishna, Christin." He rolled his eyes while wiping the growing hot chocolate stain off the front of his shirt.

"We'll have to gear up. Get tents, supplies, maybe weapons—don't know what we'll run into out there. Plus if we find a place to hole up, we'll need to hunt eventually…" I deduced, trailing my thought off to a whisper. The future found us.

CHAPTER NINE:
The Road Less Travelled

**"Do what you feel in your heart to be right
because you'll be criticized for it anyway."
-Eleanor Roosevelt (1984 - 1962)**

The next day we decided to take Christin's Land Rover, because it was bigger than my Jeep. I grabbed what I needed from the house—a few clothes, dog food and an antique brass surgeon's lantern—not very practical, but it had sentimental value.

We headed to a sporting goods store about ten blocks from my place. The streets were eerily quiet, no movement except for the occasional cat, wild hares and a scrambling dog—survivors making their way in a new world.

Our keen senses already detected the faint fetid odor of the city's dead rising with the wind.

We made it to the store without incident—getting in was another matter.

Chris shook the heavy metal doors. The doors appeared to be securely locked. A sign hung in the window.

CLOSED UNTIL FURTHER NOTICE!
NO TRESPASSING
TRESPASSERS WILL BE PROSECUTED
WITH MY SHOTGUN!

Not an issue, I had a little lawbreaker in my blood. A Jones through and through—my daddy would be proud. I had no idea if my family endured or succumbed to the end of days—they were out east, where Christin's family was.

We focused on the task at hand, and my task was to get into the store.

I grabbed part of Christin's jack assembly from his Rover and rectified the issue of "CLOSED TILL FURTHER NOTICE."

Our keen senses checked for the prosecutor with the shotgun. The store was empty.

Teak and Oakley stayed in the air-conditioned Rover, furry car alarms.

We found high-grade supplies: camping rations, a little stove, propane, sleeping bags, air mattresses and my new favorite—cross bows. I have never held or used one in my life—but I thought it was a better alternative than a gun. Guns are loud and occasionally unreliable. The bow would be silent, and we could always figure out how to make more arrows—bullets were not so easy to make.

So, a bonus to our infection was our ability to aim—it was not a problem to hit a target hundreds of yards away. This day and age bows had admirable range.

I loaded and released an arrow—a stuffed bear on the other side of the store sported a newfound projectile in its left eye.

A satisfied "humpff" escaped from Christin. I grinned. I didn't know if I could actually kill anything.

Christin was checking the sight of a rifle. He grinned mischievously—apparently killing something wouldn't be an issue for him.

I encouraged him into taking a crossbow and he talked me into a shotgun. I was a nurse and Christin, an architect—neither of us had hunted in our lives. Supermarkets were our friends. We were just finishing loading up the Rover with our stolen goods—when Teak started to growl. Both dogs were staring out the driver's window.

The hair on the back of my neck bristled. We smelled rancid fruit, before we saw them.

They were coming up the off ramp—fast. A horde of men and women, fifteen at least, eyes blazing green. I think I peed a little—no, I don't have a bladder problem. I was petrified.

Chris and I were stunned, with our mouths hanging gaped in horror. What in God's name...?

We scrambled to the Rover's doors. The dogs were barking ferociously.

Before Chris could key the ignition, the Rover started shaking and rocking as something overtook our vehicle. A plague of locust had descended, blocking the light out.

Chris and I both screamed in unison. The dogs went berserk, howling and barking.

"Drive now," I yelled.

Chris turned over the engine and put it in reverse. As we backed out, a sickly crunching and popping noise broke through the shrieking. Yes, I was shrieking. So was Chris. The Rover swayed turbulently as our assailants rocked the Rover into a swerving flight.

Christin drove like a mad man fighting for control of the Rover's trajectory while trying to unhand us from our attackers. He was not successful. The assailants held tight. At one point, I thought they were going to tip us over—a Rover is very boxy.

I was intently staring out the front window while bracing myself with the holy shit handle. The turbulent ride was slamming me around the inside of the Rover. Therefore, I didn't see the shadow descend to my right and block out the sun, until the passenger's window smashed inward scattering broken glass everywhere. A hand was reaching for me. I screamed and tried to duck out of its reach. But it was too late; the noose had closed in on my throat.

Teak lunged and sank her teeth in the assailant's mid-arm. The attacker retracted his arm, pulling Teak's wiggling body with it. I grabbed Teak and hung on to her tense hairy body--she yelped. The hand released my throat.

I had squeezed Teak too tight, and she let go of the offending arm mid—yelp.

I heard a howl resound from atop of the Rover. A shadow flew off the side. I yelled for Chris to keep driving as I climbed into the back—Oakley was shaking and panting heavily. I hugged and shooed her out of the way, grabbed the cross bow, loaded it and turned.

Someone or something was attempting to crawl in through my busted window. I aimed and fired. A simple prayer followed. "Please let my aim be true." Now firing a cross bow into a very cramped chaotic area is never going to end well.

The string and I sighed as I released the lethal projectile. It found its mark—the center forehead of one of our assailants. It was then as my arrow hit its mark I saw something, which chilled me to my bones. It was only for a fraction of a second but a swirling green incandescent eye flashed angrily at me—then it was gone. There was pure insanity in that green eye. Over the years, I have come to recognize that evil could be seen in the eyes. I've seen it twice in my life-time, up close and personal. I shuddered for I had just seen it again.

I reloaded quickly as a body slipped off the roof and tumbled down the highway. Something was moving on the roof. I looked up and decided to grab the shotgun instead. I loaded it and aimed where I saw the roof dent in.

I pulled the trigger of a gun for the first time in my life. The shot was loud in the cramped quarters. Everyone in the Rover blanched in unison. I've never seen a dog blanche before.

"Humpff" I blew out of my pursed lips. "Sorry, sorry, everyone!" I yelled apologetically.

"Get them off us Sam!" Chris yelled, not hiding his startled expression well.

Oakley peed herself a little.

Channeling my GI Jane, I grabbed the crossbow, and climbed to the front seat and stuck my head out—genius I was not.

A hand swiped down at me and I felt something sharp rake across my face. I almost dropped the crossbow, but luckily, the strap had wrapped itself around my wrist during my muddled crawl for the front seat.

I swung it up and stared into the eyes of insanity perched on the Rover's roof. I swallowed my fear and aimed at the pair of green swirling eyes in front of me. I released the trigger as the Rover lurched and swerved. I heard glass shattering from inside the Rover.

My released arrow had missed its mark.

Feathers fluttered in the wind, the business end of my arrow protruded from the assailants shoulder. A giant of a man, he stood up, stumbled backwards, reached for the arrow and dropped off the back of the Rover.

I could hear Oakley growling loudly inside the Rover—the sound of tearing cloth accompanied her snarling. Oakley wasn't a growler, unless someone stole her ball. I pulled myself back into the Rover.

Christin was waging and losing his own battle. An arm was wrapped tightly around his throat. Oakley's teeth were grinding in a tug of war battle with the arm.

I gawked; I was momentarily stunned by the scene. When Oakley and Teak grappled for a toy, Oakley rarely won— she was too passive and easy going—so not like her sister.

The lanky Border collie didn't carry a lot of weight on her frame, yet she was somehow managing to pull the jacket and its owner into the Rover.

Christin was fighting to maintain control of the Rover whilst avoiding obstacles on the highway—impressive. I'll have to tell him that if we made it through this madness.

I snapped out of my ill-timed reverie and grabbed the steering wheel. "I got it!" I bellowed.

I fought for control of the wheel amidst the shrieks, growls, roaring winds and our breakneck speed. It was pure unaltered mayhem.

I managed to steady the steering wheel, which in turn, freed Christin's hands. Christin and Oakley both began to heave their assailant off the roof and into the Rover. With each tug, Oakley was gaining a firmer clutch on the jacket-wearing arm.

Without warning, Oakley's trajectory reversed and her body slid toward the smashed window. Chris was still struggling to liberate his throat from the unwanted accessory. Chris pushed and pulled the dirty hand that gripped his straining throat. Oakley's clenched jaws started to follow the path of the retracting arm. I quickly wedged my shoulder against Oakley's shaking frame and stopped her from being pulled out the window. We both almost ended up on Christin's lap.

The sound of shredding fabric preceded the man's plunge to the speeding road below. I managed to look back at the collie. A generous portion of a beige jacket was flapping in Oakley's closed jaws. I did a double take—I could've sworn she had a self-satisfied grin on her face.

"I got it!" Christin yelled into the brash wind. He was rubbing his neck and trying not to look like he soiled his pants. I warily released control of the Rover to Christin's shaky hands.

Dog seat belts, I decided—might be a good idea to invest in. Chris and I looked at each other—stunned disbelief permeated our mirrored expressions. We simultaneously burst out laughing—hysterical, a—giant—hairy—tarantula—just—went—down—the—front—of—your—shirt laughter.

Tears were streaming down both our faces. Oakley and Teak were mugging me with kisses. I praised, hugged and kissed them back. Christin even got a lick from Oakley. The little collie has always been a bit of a whore with her kisses.

We cleared the city without any further incident. With some anxiety, we agreed to stop in order to check the Rover, consult the map and let the dogs stretch their legs. Personally, I needed to walk off my shaking.

We stood back from the scene of the crime and appraised the Rover for damage. We were both surprised that it had sustained so little damage and had survived the onslaught. I gingerly fingered the holes in the roof—we now had new air conditioning. Things could have ended far worse.

The dogs were playfully chasing an elusive gopher. They seemed unfazed by the recent horrifying incident. Christin and I both turned and looked at the road before us. So, this is what it had come down to—green eyed monsters who roamed the world in packs. Great. Just friggin fantastic. I'm in a friggin *Twilight Zone* episode, and I've never seen this friggin episode before. Shut the front door. Geez.

I leaned against the Rover, bent over and placed my hands on my knees. I took a few deep gulps of air—the hollow act wasn't helping. I prayed for Steven Spielberg to jump out and yell "Cut and print."

I turned my head slowly and looked up at Chris. His still quiet form was eyeballing my hunched shaking stance.

"Say it isn't so. Are we dreaming together?" My description of recent events was not received well—he did a lot of wincing. "Really green eyes? All of them?"

His long fingers swept through his hair. "How much more of this maddening world could we take before we both just snapped?" He used both hands to clasp his head. Maybe to keep it from exploding.

I raised my hand to tap out and told Chris I was done. Staring at me, he quietly admitted he had been done the day he took flight from the hospital.

We drove in silence for a while. My face healed with every mile we put behind us. I cleaned off the dried blood from my face.

I stared out into the growing night. With my keen vision, I caught glimpses of animals grazing in the trees. The world belonged to the beasts now; Mother Nature had beaten man.

Having no recourse to alleviate our questions or ally our fears we drove onward towards the unknown. This was most definitely the road less travelled.

CHAPTER TEN:
The Color of Night

"When one door closes, another opens; but we often look so long and regretfully upon the closed door that we do not see the one that has open for us."
-Alexander Graham Bell (1847 - 1922)

The highway proved to be an insignificant source of concern. We maneuvered easily, going off road when necessary. People didn't have the time or interest to flee their homes—they had trusted that the world would keep on turning.

As we headed west, the south of us drew our attention. Looming smoke trails ascended to the heavens. The hazy sky before us instilled a new sense of apprehension and foreboding. Ah, how the gifts kept on coming—life was so good. My internal sarcasm hadn't floundered since the world ended. Good to know.

I wondered how close we were to any unmanned fires. I imagine, since we had no fire brigades the fires could blaze throughout the country unchecked free to consume anything in their path. This winter had been a dry one—minimal snow falls nationwide. Remnants of humankind were going to be burnt off planet earth. Mother Nature was free to do as she pleased.

A deer jumping in front of the Rover broke my musing. Christin's fast reflexes kept us and the deer from becoming road kill. We continued to see a variety of wild animals.

This variety of outlandish species, alien to this part of North America, paraded around us. They sprinted across the highway, unafraid—we saw lions, tigers and bears, oh my! I ogled out my smashed window at a grazing giraffe. Chris and I exchanged a puzzled look.

"Zoos maybe? Someone freed the animals to give them a chance maybe." It was not a confident answer. Chris just shrugged a response. I never did like zoos—what with keeping wild animals locked up for our viewing pleasure.

Drooling, the dogs stared raptly at their surroundings. They had no idea what their sightings could do to them. I spotted a mammoth grizzly stripping bark off a tree twenty feet from the road. It glanced lazily in our direction. The road conditions caused me great anxiety, but my body didn't react with the trepidation I felt. My heart should have been thrumming like a hummingbird—it remained silent. The experience was unsettling like leaving your house without your pants on. A block latter you realized you were missing something. I looked in the back of the Rover at two wagging tails. The dogs were happy with the strange animal sightings. Chris and I were not.

Chris slowed down. We didn't want to push our enhanced reflexes or test our newly acquired healing abilities, not to mention harming our furry gladiators.

The wild fires were far south of us, but the wind was blowing the smoky cloud toward us. We drove through a soupy haze for days. Christin and I remained unaffected when we inhaled the smoke. Our newly enhanced vision proved useless—we didn't have x ray vision so we couldn't see through the murky curtain.

My furry family however was struggling miserably. A lot of sneezing and coughing from the back seat jarred our quiet drive. At one point, we were tempted to pull over. The smoke had gotten so thick we were rolling at a snail's pace. It was slow going. On the fourth day of driving, a gaggle of animals made us stop abruptly. Bears, cougars and bouncy deer sprinted in front of the Rover. They were heading in the exact opposite direction from where the smoke was originating. We decided not to stop. A few hours later the smoke started to clear, soothing the assault on the dog's watery eyes and throat.

"What do you think is with all the animals? It's so weird." Christin asked. I was staring at a lioness and her two cubs drinking out of a farmer's pond. We inched around a small five-car pile-up. "Zoos. Private animal reserves. Circuses? I don't know it's so weird seeing them. Like we're driving through a game park. They're not really scared." I whispered as I pushed Teak off my lap—she wanted to get a better look at the big cats.

The dogs complained. They were city dogs, and all the new smells were causing them to struggle against their usual calm demeanor.

Indicators of civilizations shot by my window, town names immortalizing dead villages. We decided against voluntarily entering any towns unless it was extremely necessary. Green-eyed monsters could be anywhere. We just couldn't take another radical experience. A sign that read "Population: 561, Newton" rolled past us.

We stopped along the side of the road, got our bows and guns and set them at the ready. We eased our way back onto the road. We needed gas.

On this stretch of highway, the roads were clear. Unlike the major highways that were a congested maze of people and cars who had fled the cities. Stalled out cars had blocked our way when we were near cities or towns. Apparently, not everyone heeded the warnings to stay in your homes.

We had chosen instead to use the less travelled back routes. The back routes were mostly clear of traffic, which made for clear roads, but they didn't afford us an opportunity to pilfer gas.

Chris and I had been syphoning from vehicles along the way. Most gas pumps at the filling stations didn't work. The power was out everywhere. The grisly bodies in various states of decay always accompanied our looting of gas from stalled cars. After the fifth car, we preferred a state of ignorance and stopped looking inside the cars—the last one had a baby in the back seat. Those were memories you don't want.

Travelling the back routes, we hadn't seen any stalled vehicles for a while—that should have told us that something was amiss. I mean the back roads were clear of blocking vehicles, but we still came upon intermittent cars. We were just so happy to have an obstacle free stretch of road. We didn't think it meant anything.

Pushing vehicles out of the way was fairly easy, what with our new strength. The chore was kind of like pushing your couch around the living room. There was risk involved when we left the Rover. The possibility of another green attacking us, or the accidental stumbling across a carnivorous animal concerned us. I did not want to attempt to wrestle a bear or be catnip for a lion. We were in the middle of a frightening new world, and we only had each other. Since we didn't have back up, excursions away from the Rover made for a nerve wracking ordeal. The dogs alleviated our anxiety somewhat, but they sounded many false alarms, whenever meandering animals strayed too near our work sites. Once when we were clearing a wreck of three vehicles, we had to chase off a large black bear. Mostly unafraid, it sat and stared at us, as we disturbed its feeding grounds. I pushed passing thoughts of what it was feeding on to the very rear of my mind.

Our newly emerging skills piqued our curiosity. It's not every day you become super hero—like. We had to push a semi-truck and trailer in neutral once—the driver had taken the keys. We did break a bit of a sweat, lifting and angling that massive load clear of the road.

We were fast too. A deer ambled up to our parked Rover as we were discussing our route. The deer snagged my bag of chips off the hood of the Rover and took off. I ran after it without thinking. Twenty yards from the Rover, I caught up with it and smacked it on its rump. It kicked me in the shin and dropped my bag of chips. The kick broke my lower leg. It was incredibly painful, I cried a little. With a lot of encouragement, I got Chris to straighten my leg and splint it. Poor guy almost threw up. I ate my reclaimed chips while I watched my leg heal within a couple of hours. They were really good chips.

Our vision was impressive—it had to be at least twenty times stronger than the average human's eyesight, especially with concentration.

Whereas we weren't concentrating when two pick-up trucks swung in behind us. Damn.

Chris uttered some excellent and colorful profanity while I concentrated on getting a better look at our pursuers. No green eyes met my tense scrutiny—regular homosapiens now trailed us. There were eight men in total all armed, looking dangerous and very unhappy.

We put our sunglasses on and slowed. A truck pulled alongside us. A hairy man with a gun and wearing a surgical mask instructed us to slow down.

What? The redneck police had survived.

I've seen *Mad Max* and other apocalyptic movies. I was afraid of being killed or worse. Chris and I must have been, long lost twins— because when we turned and looked at each other, the exact same panicked expression was written on our faces.

"What do you want to do Chris…?" I had barely finished my sentence when, abruptly a large red dump truck pulled out in front of us.

By a nose, is not just for horse races. Dump trucks had enormously large tires, something you couldn't really appreciate until you were really up close. The two pick-up trucks pulled in behind us. Cut off.

Chris and I looked at each other, exchanging another panicked look. "We'll be okay. Do you think they're Hari Krishna?" Chris asked, and grinned.

I didn't grin back.

As it turned out they were not Hari Krishna's—weird I know, but a town of loggers. Mountain men to the bone—they bled plaid flannel.

One of the hairy masked bandits, pointed at us. "We knew you were coming."

"And where is the red carpet, then?" I intoned dryly, bored. In reality, I was scared. Chris hissed a warning.

"Follow us," the plaid man directed, dry and bored—he was scared too. He issued a loud whistle. With a surge and roar, the great red beast that blocked our passage lurched forward into an alcove of trees. Then one of the pick-up trucks moved ahead. The other one remained behind us.

No escape. We were being herded like cattle—but toward what?

The winding mountain pass sloped us toward a picturesque road and a magnificent log cabin. Mansion actually— since it was massive. Its proportions blended into the forested greenery. It was an entity manufactured from the trees, still of the forest.

A quaint, cobble stoned Main Street, strewn with pleasing blends of color, drew the eye to its gentle artisanship. We drove with deliberate care. If not for the circumstances, I would have embraced this haven.

Camouflaged subtly amid closed windows and doors, twenty or more pair of eyes surveyed our approach. I lost count.

We were directed to stop outside a bed and breakfast. It was an old rustic house. I had an appreciation for old houses—this one was aging with grace. Made of pure hand milled wood, it held stories in its wrap around porch and worn stairs. I could see myself, sitting on the porch swing, nursing an ice-cold lemonade—spiked with something strong of course while swatting away large mosquitos. A hand scrawled sign in the front yard read, "NO ROOMS AVAILABLE."

"Think the manger is available?" I stared, at the ancient house. "We could try running," I whispered.

Chris eyed the house. "I think bullets are not our friends. We wouldn't make it ten feet—I'm sure hunting is second nature to these folks." Chris had mastered talking without moving his lips— noteworthy.

The hairy man was standing beside my door. Teak growled. "Follow me. Leave any weapons you have with you. You won't need them." He grunted.

We leashed the dogs and entered the house through a double arched doorway. Our masked entourage surrounded our entrance into a well-lit hallway. Hmmm, they had electricity.

"Remove your glasses." Another polite, grunted request ensued. Guns of varying calibers were trained on us. We raised our sunglass to our foreheads.

There were eight simultaneous intakes of breath.

"Breathe boys. We don't bite. Well Oakley does." Eight sets of eyes followed my gaze. Oakley chose this particular moment, to groom her nether regions. I rolled my eyes. A few exhaled quiet chuckles escaped. This was a really tense group.

"An amber and a blue. Like the old woman said." A terse sigh from the big hairy guy accompanied this declaration. Chris and I exchanged a quick worried glance.

We were escorted unceremoniously to *our* rooms. The dogs came with me. I didn't like being separated from Chris, but the hairy man, assured us that the rooms connected.

The door closed behind me with a deafening click.

The hand of a clock struck the hour.

Teak and Oakley bounded onto the bed. They were happy and oblivious, excited just to lay on something that didn't move.

We were all served a hardy and delicious home cooked dinner-- Chris joined me, and we ate in silence.

The steak, potato and salad were devoured with haste—at least these people weren't starving. Perhaps this was to be our last meal—very civilized of them. I felt my throat tighten, and I choked a little on my last bite.

The dogs growled at each other over a femur bone. Any remnants of meat had been scoured, gnawed and licked clean. There bulging bellies showed exactly where the meat had gone. The girls loved each other, but they liked to pretend contention over bones. If they were human sisters, they would be playing with Barbie's, haggling over which Barbie's head looked best on which body. Rest assured, giggling would be involved.

A knock to the door stopped the bone challenge. "Come to the main room downstairs in an hour." More instructions with a smile supervened—not.

"Yes, fine. We'll be there with bells on." A chuckle escaped my lips.

Christin eyed me as if I'd totally lost my mind.

Okay, maybe I get overly self-confident when my nerves were strung too tight. A banjo could be played with mine right now. The theme for the movie *Deliverance* crossed my mind. Well, we were in hillbilly country.

It was decided we wouldn't run. Everyone in that room would die if we didn't like what we were hearing. Vicious I know—who was I kidding. We went down the creaky old stairs with our four legged hairy counterparts. We were not going to sneak up on them in this house. They had light, gas and plumbing—their town must have been able to sustain life independent to that of the rest of the world.

The main seating area was roomy yet homey. Overstuffed chairs and couches were holding plaid wearing lumberjacks' hostage.

The large men looked very out of place. One lumberjack was trying in vain to get his large callused finger into a teacup handle—it broke. Red color fanned up his neck, getting lost in his hairy facial features. He pocketed the broken handle.

"It's okay Randy, my mama gave me that set, but I never really liked it." I spotted the origin of the voice. An old black woman rocked slowly in a chair, sipping from a petite teacup. I noticed her fingers fit easily into the handle.

Someone was playing a piano in the background. It was a familiar melody, but the title didn't come to mind.

Twelve heads turned in unison as we descended the bottom stairs. We entered the parlor to eleven gasps—the piano player stopped mid-note.

CHAPTER ELEVEN:
Little Ant Answers

"Everyone wants some magical solution for their
problems and everyone refuses to believe in magic."
-The Mad Hatter

Yeah, Teak and Oakley often received that kind of response when they entered a room. The end of the world and my sense of humor remained intact.

Six men and six women of varying ages, sizes and ethnicities stared openly at us. An elderly woman with dark glasses on waved us to two chairs beside her. "Good evening my dears we were expecting you" she had a soft soothing rasp, "my name is Mae, welcome." Everyone in the room started talking at once, in anxious hushed whispers—apparently, not everyone felt welcoming. Mae hushed up the murmuring then asked for two cups of tea.

"You do like tea my dears—don't you?" She asked in a conspiratorial whisper.

"I don't know. I've never had a 'teamydears.' What does it taste like?" I smiled my best shit-eating grin.

Chris rolled his eyes.

Ha-ha, playing with an old lady—nice.

A hoot escaped Mae's openly grinning mouth. She smacked her legs and stomped her feet all the while, whacking her cane on the ground. Thump, thump, whoot.

Dignity returned to Mae's face.

She said. "Nice to see the spark of life still warms your cockles, but you're not that funny."

A very unhappy looking man thrust two cups of hot tea curtly into our hands. He backed away from our vicinity quickly.

"Please sit down youngins, it's all right. I have things to tell you. Please sit!" The old woman gestured to a couple floral overstuffed chairs.

We sat, with our teas in hand, pretending we were visiting grandma on a Sunday afternoon. I took a sip of tea—peppermint, hmm…not my favorite.

The old woman took a sip of her tea and placed it gently on her saucer. She turned her head to the smoldering fire. "I went down south to visit some kin." She began in a composed tone. "I thought it might be my last trip. I ain't no spring chicken no more, I'll be ninety-four next month God willing. Though, I don't know if God has anything to do with it anymore."

A deep sigh escaped her chest. She looked sixty-five, but she was wearing dark glasses, so I couldn't see her eyes. Age is so often reflected in the eyes—windows to the soul and all that.

"Nasty going-ons down there just about kilt me. But you both know that, you two went through the same suffering I did. My southern kin are all dead." With that statement hanging in the air, she lifted her glasses. The fire illuminated pink incandescent swirling eyes. Two gasps echoed in the room.

"Been waiting on you a long time children—my mind's eye showed me, you was coming!"

I waved my hand in front of her face—Chris slapped it away.

Mae cackled a warm laugh. "Yep, been blind since I was six. Some kind of fever left me blind as a bat. Killed me for a bit too. I've made out all right though—sixteen kids and thirty-two grandchildren, two husbands safe in the grave." Her voice trailed off as she tilted her head down to the floor with a forlorn expression.

"Well, enough about me, this isn't the biography channel. I need to tell you two a story. I used to watch those discovery channels, only thing worth watching on the television, what with all those reality shows.

So...there are these ants in Africa—fire ants—tough little suckers that build their homes near the water.

Now every year the damn things get flooded out, everything lost." Mae sighed and poked at the fire.

"Now, you'd think they learn, but nope. Stubborn critters. You'd think they'd all just drown too. Nope. Some little ant clings to another little ant and hangs on. Then another little ant grabs on, and well, hundreds of them started floating on the water, life rafts hanging on to each other." My mouth was hanging open as I listened.

"Hell, it turns out those little critters could float that way for months, till the flooding receded—damnest thing. Community can be a lifesaving entity."

It was all I could do to sit still and not breathe a word.

Mae took another sip of her tea and continued. "Now Sam, Chris, our community needs your help to stay afloat."

I heard guffaws in the background. Apparently, some people didn't want this little blue ant to help them stay afloat.

Mae tsked at the grumbling crowd. "We're having problems with the greens picking at our raft."

Silence echoed in that packed room—I think everyone was holding their breath.

Mae's words troubled me. I just stared quietly in her direction. My eyes narrowed as I said, "I thought I smelled something funky going on here, but I just thought it was Christin. Showers have been a little scarce as of late."

"Humpff. You should talk!" Christin wrinkled his nose, then sipped his tea

I looked at Christin our glowing eyes caught each other. I'm sure no rainbow contained our eyes' hue.

Chris nodded a slight gesture that indicated I should take the lead. He sat back and stretched his legs, getting comfortable for a show. He figured they needed something; which meant we had something to haggle with.

"So you must realize Ms. Mae," I began. "This has all been a little overwhelming to say the least, and I have no idea or intention to play GI Jane for you and your towns-people." Actually, I wanted to get the hell out of here.

Hairy guy piped in. "I told you Mae, this was a bad idea, and we don't need these other versions of humanity to do our bidding. Let a crew of us flush out the greens ourselves—it's our problem." He said this with distaste, contorting his hairy features toward our area. The very tall plaid-clad, hairy man pressed on. "We don't need outside help. We're fine on our own. Next thing you know, vexations of all kinds will be traipsing through our woods—we'll be infested with no exterminators to turn to." Eyes downcast, he didn't address me directly.

I jumped in. "So you see, no need for Chris and I to go all GI Jane and Rambo on your greens. We can just go on our merry way—parting ways, knowing we both exist and survived the apocalypse." An innocent smile played at the corners of my lips.

"Now Randy, we all as the human race need each other. There are not many of us left. We need to pick up the pieces of what Mother Nature left us…" Mae whispered. The room fell into a contemplative silence.

Staring straight at me, Randy glared. He lost whatever inhibition he had. "They are not part of the human race. They're abominations." Randy was not a man who minced words. I decided I liked him, redneck and all.

Mae sighed and sat a spell, the firelight making her pink eyes dance. She bent down and beckoned Teak over. Teak looked at me. A small whine escaped her throat. I gestured toward the old woman, and encouraged her on.

Teak walked over to the old woman, slipping her head under the extended wrinkled, gnarled hand. "It seems like there's always something wanting to harm your loved ones."

I swallowed. Teak was in the old woman's hands. My eyes tightened. I swallowed louder.

"Heavens no child, I would never harm this innocent little creature. But the greens don't have the same predilections. Three littlins got taken and their parent slaughtered." She rubbed Teak's head, mushing up her face and hair. My hairy dog was a mess. Teak was in heaven.

Mae paused and let us chew on that little tidbit of information before she continued. "You two want to help, you're good people—I see it in you. You're a healer, and he's a builder." Mae was grinning and making smoochy faces at Teak.

"How do you know so much about us? We haven't even been formally introduced." I couldn't contain myself any longer I was getting frustrated. I didn't do well when people hung a carrot just out of my reach.

Mae chuckled. "The virus not only changed me but gave me visions as well." I choked on my tea mid-sip. A person shouldn't suddenly inhale when drinking. Mae ignored my aspiration of tea and continued. "I did have the sight before the virus changed me. Though not as strong, as I experience now." The old black woman took a sip of tea and didn't continue. Damn carrot was just hanging there. Just that. Nothing more. Nothing less. Just that vague hanging statement. Damn.

I think begging is going to have to be involved. I initiated the groveling process for information. "Mae you…" The old woman cut me off mid-sentence.

"So, you'd like some education on the where-with all of things. Shall we do a little horse-trading?" Her pink eyes twinkled with mischief. "So, how about some information? Say, in exchange for an extermination job. Are you two interested?" Another chuckle escaped from Mae's smug grin. She started rocking again. "You two go ahead and take a moment. I'll be here when you're ready to talk."

Chris and I looked at each other got up and retired to our rooms to discuss the turn of events. The crazy, wrinkly conniving old woman wanted us to hunt down some greens and rescue three children. At which point she'd answer all our questions. Apparently, she had answers.

We could leave in peace either way—she made it clear they were not barbarians. The crazy old woman knew exactly how to manipulate us and push our buttons. We needed answers more than air.

Discussion over we headed back down stairs. We interrupted a semi-muted conversation as we descended the stairs. We found our chairs.

"Tell us everything," I said gently.

Old Mae smiled. "Took you long enough."

Christin and I rolled our eyes in tandem.

For two hours we sat there and listened, finally dragging ourselves back upstairs to let the knowledge sink in. I sat on the bed and petted Oakley; Chris sat in the chair and looked out the window. "What do you think? Are you up for this?" I asked.

Chris just kept staring out at the greenery and without turning whispered. "This is crazy. I don't know how much more of this I can take." I nodded and sighed. "I know. I feel the same way."

Ω Ω Ω

The townspeople figured there were five greens left, best they could tell. They had come down on the town about a week ago—making a ruckus, breaking and destroying things. The greens had a particular taste. They liked using cattle as playthings. Mutilated carcasses were left strewn in the fields for the townspeople to find.

The residents had excellent sharpshooters. They killed and burned six of the original pack. The townsfolk found they could move about freely during the day—the greens preferred to move around mostly at night. Mae thought mostly because their prey hunted or foraged at night. Reinforced doors and shutters kept the greens at bay during the twilight hours. After exterminating and burning the shot pests, the town hadn't encountered any greens for over two weeks. They thought the greens had moved on.

Everyone was craving fresh meat and getting cabin fever. The Corbet family decided a mile hike to the lake was a reasonably safe endeavor.

The children were fishing with their armed father in a boat on a serene lake. It was late afternoon. Seemed safe, right?

The family didn't notice, that the birds had suddenly gone silent. They were laughing and having fun.

The towns-people found the family's empty boat capsized the next morning. The father's body had washed up on the shore. His neck had been broken. There was no sign of the girls. That was a day ago.

No one knew that the greens had migrated up from the south, following the migration of game. Unrestrained by human needs they released their hunting instincts. Predator became their prey.

The virus had defaulted their befuddled minds to pure instinct. They had no memory of their humanity. And now they were the newest member on the top of the food chain.

Basic survival instinct, spiced with the increasing need to challenge their hunting skills, drove them to track and kill challenging prey. Eat and sleep that's all the instinct they had within them. Grizzlies were their favorite. However, the big bears were becoming increasingly more difficult to find. Man had over hunted the great bears. The greens were driving them to extinction. Now the greens were growing bored.

Eager to migrate and follow the big game, they were quenching their thirst with fresh water from the lake when distant laughter caught there sensitive hearing.

Turning, a green spotted the source of the laughter floating in the middle of the lake. It cocked its head, and then entered the water without a conscious thought. The green was irrevocably drawn, to a bright and loud new toy. The rest of the pack followed.

The five heads emerged from the serene lake, encircling the girl's laughter. The floating greens puzzled over the sound, for they had never heard that mesmerizing din in their newly transformed lives.

Screams erupted, dashing their puzzled trance. Their response to the shrieking was to collectively pick up the boat and throw it fifteen feet from where they were treading water.

They immediately surrounded the floundering people. They snapped the neck of the male easily and without a thought. They turned their attention to the young females, dragging the sputtering, flailing girls to the shore. There they took their new toys to the recesses of a nearby cave. Migration could wait, they had a new amusement—they wanted to hear that puzzling noise again.

CHAPTER TWELVE:
See Spot Run

**"The happiest people don't necessarily have the best of everything;
they just make the most of everything that comes along their way."
-Unknown**

Mae had assured us they were still alive and in a cave somewhere. The three Corbet girls were all in their early teens. What were the greens doing with them? No one wanted to speculate out loud his or her trepidations; it would make it too real. Chris and I headed downstairs.

"So, how are we supposed to find them? This is a mountainous region with a vast and unlimited supply of caves. Needle in a mountaintop comes to mind." I said as we descended the stairs." Chris shrugged. He frowned and said. "Hopefully Mae has some ideas. I haven't rescued anything in my life unless you count saving my whites from my colors." I chuckled at Chris. I often ended up with blue t-shirts that had been white.

Mae was standing with Randy looking down at a dining room table littered with papers. Chris and I approached them. "Where would we even start?" I asked.

"There by the lake." Mae stated matter of factly, pointing to a spot on a map. I looked down at the spot Mae's black wrinkly finger was indicating.

"How do you do that?" I pressed.

Mae tapped her head. "I can see it."

I nodded my head in fake understanding. "We'll need our weapons. I'll need to leave the dogs here and be assured of their safety." I glanced to the overstuffed couch and saw that both dogs were unconscious on their backs, feet splayed in the air.

We agreed to leave the dogs in Mae's care. The big hairy guy was to be our escort. Randy was the uncle of the girls and was an excellent hunter and outdoorsman. He lost his two daughters, wife and sister-in-law to the reaping. His brother's family was all he had left in the world. Allowing Randy to partake in the hunt alleviated some of the big man's frustration. Truth be told, he could have it, I had no idea how to track, hunt or ambush anything but a hamburger.

Mae could only be as specific with her visions as the south side of the lake. The sun's positioning over the lake helped pinpoint the general location of the greens whereabouts. We had a starting point.

The three of us headed toward the lake, we decided walking was the most inconspicuous mode of transportation. We wanted to avoid having the greens stalk us. We left town in the wake of a chorus of howls—the dogs were expressing their betrayal at being left behind.

We had a healthy store of weaponry lashed to our bodies. I didn't feel the weight.

Randy slowed us down, but he was more agile and quiet then one would expect from a man his size. He could also make his way around these woods blindfolded.

The day was growing dusky—it wasn't to be an issue for us. Chris and I should be able to smell and see the greens before they detected us since we were downwind of the south caves.

If they were in the caves, it would be a difficult and dangerous undertaking to get at them cleanly. Outnumbered by beings with the same abilities as we had… hopefully our weapons would even those odds.

We needed to scout out the caves. I chose myself. The guys argued with me vehemently. I told them they were being sexist and that quickly ended the disagreement.

We agreed going across the lake and scouting from the water was the safest and most subtle route. I wanted to walk up to the cave's entrance and ring their doorbell. Avon calling. Kidding, of course I was quite frightened.

I kept feeling GI Jane surge up in me. I was hoping this wasn't just a transient instinct but would consistently rise when I needed it. The lake was cold, but I couldn't really feel it. I only knew it was cold, because I could see wisps of my breath rising.

Christin said he'd keep his concentration focused on my crossing, so he could watch my back. We both could almost distinguish the south bank from our vantage point on the north shore—neither of us however, could see any dancing green lights.

Inside the cave, the five greens just stood encircling the huddled girls. There rapt attention focused, waiting, listening for the sound that caused yearning in them. The sound of the laughter triggered a longing deep within their simple psyche. Happiness, contentment, and joy, the sound of laughter, evoked mysterious emotions in them. The alien emotions dazed and puzzled the greens.

The three girls clung to each other and intermittently released soft exhausted mewing sounds. The three kept their eyes closed tight against the sickly green iridescent light that illuminated the walls of the caves. The girls were in hell. If they survived this reality, green light will forever haunt their nightmares.

I decided to go underwater until I got to the shallows. Night was pressing over the horizon. My damn eyes were giving off a distinct blue light that reflected on the dark waters. I didn't want to broadcast my presence unnecessarily. Note to self, bring dark goggles to suppress my not-so-subtle eyes.

Hello, a big neon sign flashed—gawk here.

I had just made it to the shallows and was about to scan the shore when I felt it before I heard it. Damn.

The greens were getting bored; restlessness was taking hold of them.

The delicious sound that had enraptured them earlier was not forthcoming. The sound's enlightening rapture was fading from their souls.

Thad ump.

Their heads turned in unison—they leaped for the cave entrance.

My heart beat once loudly. My breath seized into a sharp knot, mid-throat. I uttered a lot of profanities in the shallows. Fear seized my spine.

A moment later, I saw ten bobbing green lights emerge into the night. I pulled out my bow and aimed it at the two closest bobbing green lights. I released my wet arrow and heard it whiz to the shoreline. The twin lights flickered and faded as they plunged to the ground.

I reloaded swiftly and took aim. The array of green lights had already halved the distance between us. A shot rang out and another set of green eyes faded and dropped.

The remaining greens split up and scattered in three different directions. Randy and Christin came running down the beach. I yelled hasty directions at them, and we all split up. Randy ran to entrance of the cave while Christin and I set out after the two closest greens we saw duck into the brush.

GI Jane was in raw attendance I felt the urgency to hunt course through me. I could smell him; it was a male green. I followed the scent.

The trail weaved from mid tree to the ground to mid tree—I could almost see a green vapor in my mind's eye. It was erratic. I postulated trajectories—yes, postulated—and changed direction. I leaped onto a rocky outcropping and spotted two bobbing green orbs, racing toward my location. Sweet!

I raised the crossbow and took aim. Poor thing wouldn't know what hit him.

A force equal to a speeding car toppled me off my rocky perch and sent me flying through the air. Totally focused on my approaching quarry, I failed to hear or smell the additional green that had turned from his escape route and had stalked me.

We went flying through the air. I noticed that my surroundings remained in focus. Cool. Until, that is, we hit a rather large tree with an ear-splitting crunch. If I had any air in my lungs, it had been forced down to my toes and out my nose. I dropped my empty crossbow. It must have discharged when I got hit. We slid down to the base of the tree and rolled into a small clearing.

The green had me in a constricting bear hug—I now respected the notion of the hourglass figure. My arms had been up to shoot, so they were free. I'm glad I watched my share of Jackie Chan and Brue Lee movies during my insomniac nights, because I now went all ninja on this green. Move over GI Jane, Jet Li has arrived.

I released a barrage of elbows and punches. The steel cables of the greens arms were securely wrapped around my chest—good thing I didn't need to breathe. Under the rain of my fists and teeth, the cables minutely relented in their steeled grip.

Something was really starting to jut into my lower back. What now? The wrestling lock hold had become increasingly uncomfortable, what with the jutting and squeezing.

Then I remembered Randy had given me a rather large Bowring knife, and I had stuffed it into my belt at the small of my back. Okay, so I'm new at this arming of the body with all kinds of weaponry.

I felt the greens hand squirming around where the hilt of the knife would be. I reached back and twisted the greens fingers for access to the blade, and then. Yes, I felt the hilt expose to my probing fingers. My hand encircled the handle, and I pulled. The green screamed as I sliced through a few wayward fingers.

I pulled the knife free and drove the blade to the handle deep into his shoulder. The green wailed in protest. It finally released its compressing arms from around my chest. Its empty grasping hands sought to pull my blade free of its lodging.

The green collapsed to its knees, weakening, screaming and flailing. Its frantic seeking hands went unrewarded. It slumped to the ground, one of its hands continuing to grope empty air.

The hairs on my neck bristled. A gust of wind lapped at my face. Sweet breeze—the green stunk badly. My fleeting sense of peace was interrupted as I was thrust, once again, winglessly through the air.

My swift midair journey didn't last long. I hit an outcropping of rock with such force the fresh air residing in my lungs rushed out.

"UGHHHH!"

The sound echoed dully off the small canyon walls. The green I had previously been hunting had found me. Damn! I was hoping it had headed to Kansas.

I was struggling to regain my footing when a sturdy weight knocked me back to the ground. The greens angry contorted face was drooling over me. Its hands enclosed around my vulnerable throat. Where was GI Jane now?

Temperamental bitch.

I reached out and up for his throat—he must have been a foot taller and probably had a hundred pounds on me. His breath reeked of decaying flesh.

I found purchase around his slimy neck and squeezed. Somehow, we found ourselves in a stalemate, locked throat to throat in a deadly embrace. We breathed heavier, wagering for a better grip. Rancid drool dripped onto my cheek. I gagged and turned my head. Flickering lights to my right pulled a fraction of my attention away from the grunting green. Green lights weaved in place not ten feet from my position.

"Mother fu…"

Further profanity crossed my mind, but my airway clenched off so I didn't even get the satisfaction of voicing my frustrations.

I'm done. At least I went out of this world fighting, not laying in a bed, wheezing my last breath—or finger painting with my own poo. I just hoped it'd be fast.

A quick black movement out of the corner of my eye caught my distracted attention. Teak hit my accoster in the back of the neck, growling and twisting as her teeth clamped down and dug in. The indecisive greens eyes bugged open, the predator had probably, never been attacked before. Predator had become prey.

Meanwhile, the other green had managed to dislodge my knife and was unsteadily getting to his feet. My deadly weapon was now in his control. He was waving my knife in my direction—in Teak's direction. I felt my heart beat.

THA DUMP.

Teak turned her attention to the armed green and jumped to put herself between my second attacker and me. My house pet had found her inner animal…

She held her head low and growled menacingly. Wow, you go girl! I was a little shocked. I had never seen this side of her.

Teak was in danger. For a moment, both greens attentions had been distracted by my heartbeat but their attention quickly returned to the task at hand. The green I was grappling with stared at my blazing eyes and grimaced as he renewed his efforts to break my neck. I heard growling and a scuffle a few feet from my head. Followed by a thud, a yelp and a scream piercing the night.

Oh my God Teak! A surge of anger and fear whelmed up inside me. I focused all of being on the green straddling me and twisted my grip on his throat. It was then that I heard two simultaneous sounds, bone crunching and another yelp.

TEAK!

Ω Ω Ω

I was out on an EMS ride-along. It was a scorching day and the crew was inside a trailer on a call. I had no interest to go into that stifling tin box. I stood outside and surveyed the native's reservation. It was such a shame to see, a once proud people reduced to living in squalor in trailers.

I sipped my warm water and noticed about ten crows hopping and flapping in the distance. I walked over and saw a handful of puppies scattered about the dry scrub—they were dead. The crows were decimating the carcasses.

The mother dog fought the badgering murder of crows. I shooed the resolute birds from the mother. She growled in pain. The mama dog held up her matted dirty and emaciated body with shaking courage. I tried to offer her water, but she limped away and crawled into an abandoned car.

Tears touched my hot eyes. Should I bury them? I prepared to dig a hole with my bare hands, when I heard a soft cry behind me. I glanced at a pile of old tires a few feet away.

I got up from my kneeling position and brushed dust from my knees. I slowly walked over to the pile of tires, afraid of what I'd see. I didn't want any more brutality lodged within my memory bank.

The water bottle dropped to my feet, as I absorbed the scene before me. I fought against a sob that sought to rise and choke me. A little matted, black, dirty body was nestled in a tire. Blinking eyes stared up at me. It mouthed a weak mewling sound.

It's siblings were dead and its mama was on her last legs. I scooped the survivor from the scorching tire and ran for all I was worth.

It was touch and go for a week—the vet was surprised she lived. The little puppy was malnourished, dehydrated and had a bad case of worms and fleas.

The sweet little puppy grew to eat my cell phone, my two hundred dollar glasses, my couch, and of course, the day I picked up my brand new Jeep—she ate my emergency brake handle. One night I had come home late after an arduous shift to find a massacre had transpired in my house. Pieces of my red flip-flops were scattered everywhere. I was not impressed.

My little scrappy terrier owned me. I was the alpha of the house, but Teak was my beta and she ran it with an iron paw. She's not a guard dog by nature, but she can hold her own at the dog park. A large husky had been a bit too invasive with his sniffing, so Teak had sent him packing back to his owner with his tail between his legs.

Teak kept everyone in the house in line. She'd whine for me to open the door when the cat was outside for too long, and would let me know when Oakley was causing issues. I'm surprised the rest of her charges weren't lined up for inspection when I came home from work.

When we were training Oakley—and I mean us—I would try to verbally discipline the unruly Oakley. Teak however would put herself between Oakley and me and try to take the berating on. Teak would stretch and yawn to distract me. Oakley would see her opportunity for escape, and toddle off to chew on the cat. Oakley did turn out all right though—mostly. Teak was my second in command.

Ω Ω Ω

I pushed the stinking green with the twisted neck off me and got to my feet. Immediately I spied Teak's body lying immobile twenty feet from me. The armed green had turned away from the motionless grey and black pile of hair and was approaching my position. It still hadn't recovered from its shoulder wound.

I stood stock still, overwhelmed by the spectacle of Teak's lifeless form. Anger swelled inside me. I screamed and lunged at the stumbling green.

I flew the distance between me and the green in one leap. I was the pilot of this flight. I straddled the greens neck with my legs, scissoring its throat while I twisted midair. It had only a moment to paw at my sinewy thighs. I felt something slice into my calf before I heard a satisfying crunch.

Releasing and rolling, I landed in a ready crouch. Both greens were down in the dirt. The knife was imbeded through my right calf. When

I pulled the knife free, blood began to flow. The pain of my calf was overshadowed by the ache that radiated from deep in my heart.

I moved gingerly to Teak's lifeless body, my heartache growing stronger with every step. A quietly thrumming heartbeat and slow breathing caught my attention. I dove to my dog's side.

She was alive but bleeding a lot. A gash to her left flank and head oozed blood. I tore my shirt and I applied pressure to the wounds and checked her for any other obvious injuries. My expert fingers felt nothing deformed. She whined and tried to sit up. I picked her light body up and ran so swiftly it was exhilarating. My thoughts sobered brusquely—the reason for my pace punched me in the stomach.

I made it back to the bed and breakfast in a swift blur. I almost kicked the Inn's solid door down. Well actually, I did but the large wooden door stayed on its hinges. Christin was standing in the middle of the stairs with an astonished expression on his face.

I heard him yell. "Sam!"

Ω Ω Ω

After leaving Sam and Randy, Christin had hunted his green with ease. The smell alone was ripe and pungent. The greens apparently didn't believe in bathing. He spotted the green perched in a tree. It looked as if was surveying the forest. Christin pulled an arrow and loaded it quietly. He aimed between the two glowing green orbs and released the singing arrow. The green fell to the forest's dense floor with a thud. Standing over the green, he pulled the machete Randy had given him and hacked the female green's head off. He kicked the head away from the body. Mae had said the townspeople had been decapitating and burning the greens bodies. Apparently the infected could heal themselves unless finished off this way. Chris took note of the location of the dismembered body in order to tell the townsfolk where they could find it. He headed back in the direction of the cave.

He saw Randy exiting the cave with the girls tucked under his arms.

"Have you seen Sam, Randy?" Chris asked.

"No not since she took off after one of the greens." The three young girls were whimpering quietly and glancing around furtively. Chris eyed the girl's state and thought that the girls were going to need some heavy-duty therapy after this experience.

"I'm sure she's okay that girl seems like she can hold her own." Randy started ushering the girls toward the town. Chris realized he couldn't leave the quartet unprotected. He reloaded his bow and with a wary glance over his shoulder, he escorted the group home.

The girls couldn't get into the Inn fast enough as they pushed and twisted the doorknob in haste. Christin felt something push past his leg as the door swung open. He caught a quick glance of a black form racing into the forest. Damn he thought. That furtive shadow might have been Teak. His attention was pulled to the wailing mass of young girls, who had collapsed on the hallway floor. Chris bent to help Randy with the howling girls. The men slowly helped the traumatized girls upstairs. Chris urgently wanted to get back to the forest and look for Sam. She could need him.

Mae was following the group as they were heading upstairs. "Just put them in the first bedroom Randy. I'm right behind you."

Thank God, Mae was here. Christin turned around and headed downstairs as the front door burst open. Sam was standing in the doorway covered in blood. Teak's limp body hung in her arms.

"Sam," he yelled.

"Oh my... Shit Sam are you all right? Is Teak? She got past us as we were bringing in the girls." Christin stuttered out in shock.

Ω Ω Ω

"Come on I need your help." I pushed passed Christin and headed for my bedroom.

"Chris, go ask Mae where we can get some medical supplies." I gave a list to Chris and he sprinted from the room.

Teak was still groggy from her head injury, so I took the time to thoroughly investigate her wounds. Oakley watched from the foot of the bed.

I looked at Oakley's solemn demeanor. "She'll be all right girl we'll fix her up." With that, I set to work. Teak had a laceration to her forehead and a deep gash to her left thigh. A few bumps and bruises were starting to discolor. I was extremely concerned about her head injury. I checked her pupils and neurovital signs. She moved all her limbs independently, but remained dazed.

Chris returned a short time later with a drug store cache of supplies. He mentioned quietly he had raided the town's veterinarian office for the supplies.

It was dawn before I finished cleaning, suturing and bandaging Teak's wounds. Chris and Oakley sat quietly by the bed in case I needed something. All we could do was wait to see how she responded to treatment.

Meanwhile, Chris told me the townspeople had collected and disposed of the greens remains and were now milling about taking care of their daily chores. We had taken care of their problem. I looked out my bedroom window and watched the passing people eye the Inn with wayward glances. Mae came into check on all of us, to make sure we had enough to eat and to see how Teak was doing.

I continued to stare out the window and murmured. "Mae, why is everyone looking at the Inn like our septic tank has overflowed into the neighborhood?"

Mae was sitting by Teak's still body. I had medicated my traumatized dog with some sedation. "Oh child, don't fret none. They're afraid is all and they don't understand things." The old woman stroked Teak's sleeping face.

"Afraid of what? We killed the greens." I turned and eyed Mae.

She sighed and said. "Ah child they are afraid of us."

My eyes tightened, "But...why? We're not going to hurt them!" I huffed.

Mae grinned. "I know that and you know that but we're different since the transformation. And well, we could infect them with the virus."

"Ha! I'm not planning on getting that close to anyone!" I grunted and turned back to the window.

Mae chuckled. "They just don't understand things. They need time is all." The room turned silent except for Teak's steady breathing and the soft thrum of her heartbeat.

A little while later Christin and Oakley returned to the bedroom quietly. Chris had dinner for both Teak and I. The war torn dog lifted her head to the smells that now permeated the room. I decided to let her stand and have some water and soup. She eyed my roast dinner with hope.

"Not yet Teak. We have to take it slow hun." My dogs didn't beg but Teak came slowly up beside me and gave me the most pathetic look I've ever seen in my life. I caved and gave her a piece of my roast. It was a good sign she was eating.

After dinner, I took her outside to do her business. We returned to our room where my scrappy terrier surrendered to nestling in my arms. The sedation wasn't quite out of her system yet, she needed to rest.

Her cold nose sought my hand. I heaved a sigh of relief. We had saved each other. I squeezed her gently to my still heart and closed my eyes. I listened to the beat of her steady heart all night long.

The next morning was sunny with a slight chill in the air. Christin and Oakley escorted us outside so Teak could pee and stretch her legs. Oakley nosed Teak's new apparel and sneezed. Teak was swathed in bandages from head to tail and was a little unsteady on her feet. Teak, I think was out of the woods so to speak.

I glanced around the town and noted it was alive with activity. For them it was a new day; their resilience left me in awe. Christin informed me, that the girls were traumatized but physically okay. The three teen girls had slept fitfully with the aid of some chemical tranquilizers.

Mae wanted to meet with Christin and I this evening. This plan suited me fine. That gave me all day to shower, eat and stay with Oakley and Teak. I wasn't tired but my mind felt fatigued.

I eyed Teak and she returned the stare. It was time for her morning dressing change. Neither one of us enjoyed ripping off old bandages.

"Time to change your bandages Teak." I rubbed her face gently, then we headed back to the Inn.

I saw Chris note our exchange. We had stayed in denial for long enough. It was time to let some light and air in—to heal our wounds.

CHAPTER THIRTEEN:
Meeting the Wizard Behind the Curtain

"The pessimist sees the difficulty in every opportunity;
an optimist sees the opportunity in every difficulty."
-Winston Churchill (1874 - 1965)

Mae invited Christin, my dogs and me to her house for dinner. To Teak's dismay, I carried her. Oakley seemed to enjoy this. She was in fine form trotting beside us.

Mae's house was a cottage nestled in the corner of town. It was something right out of a fairy tale. Stone structure interlaced with planks of old wood. Potted plants and a small garden sat nestled beside a small creek. An apple tree winked from behind the house. The seven dwarfs did not answer the front door—a squat black, silver haired, goggle-wearing woman did.

"Come in Teak, my little hairy hero. I have a place set up for her on the couch, Sam. You two can make your-selves comfortable anywhere. Oakley honey, there is room for you on the couch too. Come in. Make yourself comfortable—mi casa es su casa. Dinner with be ready shortly. We'll be having rabbit, wild greens and homemade apple pie with whip cream." With that, we entered fantasyland.

We all made ourselves comfortable after dinner. Mae came into the living room and handed us each a cup of tea.

Mae began after taking a sip of her tea. "We have to burn them because they're still contagious." We gathered around the fireplace, nursing our cups of tea. Yep, peppermint again.

"In fact, all three of us carry the virus still—it can be transmitted through body fluids. We have been burning anything you've used or I've used. You just learn to become aware of your habits is all. They haven't banished me because I've helped the townspeople out in the past—they're tolerant of me. Some, I feel are warming up to my old bones. I don't take it personally. They're just scared." Mae paused and sipped her tea.

"I was down south, as I said before with my New Orleans kin when all this mess started. The virus ate away at my family quickly. We eventually didn't bother going to the hospital. After the youngest fell ill, the hospitals just seemed like wastelands. The medical establishment was no help in the end. My nephew said he saw piles of bodies stacked out back of the hospital."

Teak yawned I rubbed her belly.

Mae continued spinning her tale of woe. "So, with my dead family surrounding me, I fell ill, and went through the gates of hell. I returned as this pink eyed monster you see before you. I had to get out of that stinking, rotting city. I didn't feel safe driving. I mean I am blind, and everything, so I found me a mount." Mae chuckled and smiled softly.

"Ah, she was a fine steed, a big Clydesdale—a monster of a horse." She sighed and smiled again, and then her expression turned serious. "An infernal green eye got her while I was in a grocer getting a few supplies—ripped her throat out. Damn green didn't even have the decency to finish her off. I had to do it. Poor thing."

The old woman tsked a couple of times and then continued. "I managed to find me another plain old farming horse. He's out back. He's a stubborn old work horse, not used to being rode. We however, came to an understanding."

She stopped and chewed on her lower lip. "Yep, he got me here. I didn't stop at no grocers after that. His name is Bob because he made me bob up and down all the way home."

Mae got up and stoked the fire, while she rubbed her backside. "That damn horse gave me calluses on my behind. I know we heal, but my behind has a memory. We can get injured, but heal quickly, another reason why we burn the infected. There ain't nothing that seems to put 'em down for good except a good burning.

The men decided to do a little experimenting with one of the greens they had killed. They found that bullets slowed em down—if you left the bullets in—and a good decapitation seemed to stop them in their tracks. No one wanted to wait around to see if the separated body parts would reunite and reanimate."

Mae scratched at her wrinkly chin. Chris and I simultaneously gulped on our teas. I thought they mentioned the townspeople weren't barbarians.

The old woman held her cup steady, and we could see Mae was remembering the incident. The old woman told her tale slowly, staring off at the memory.

"The green was restrained with a lot of chains and a few bullets lodged in his kneecaps. The investigators were well dressed in full welder's garb. Some thought to use medical gear, but the nearest hospital was over one hundred miles away. The townspeople agreed it wasn't worth the trip—apparently the protective medical garb didn't help the doctors and nurses live anyway," Mae said.

"So the task of the investigation fell to a cattle rancher—he was good at butchering. Originally, the task fell to the town butcher, but after a few swipes with a very sharp, mean looking knife, the town butcher found he had to take a moment. He didn't have the stomach for it. After all, these were once humans. The rancher didn't have such a ah… delicate disposition. He had killed people before. He had also seen his friends tortured in the war. He was a Vietnam vet. Human gore did not startle this man anymore."

Mae sighed deeply. "I couldn't stay for the rest of the experimentation but the men told me what happened.

Ω Ω Ω

The rancher had appraised the bloody gore left by the butcher. The wizened man was a cautious sure fellow, perhaps an aspect of his personality that allowed him to survive Vietnam. The rancher noticed a blue and white, plastic band on the greens wrist. It read "Wakefield Mental Institution."

During his inspection of the bracelet, he heard a couple of his ranch hands come in to check on his progress. They were laughing about something. The older cowhand was telling his friend about his family.

"Damnest thing, she got up took a few steps, grabbed the table cloth off the kitchen table to brace herself. She fell onto her backside and pulled the whole dinner onto of her lap. Little thing just sat there with a big old turkey in front of her. Then she patted the basted bird, looked up at us with an expression of 'I didn't do that.' Then she shrugged her shoulders and crawled off. Oh my God—it was priceless. Oh and we abided by the five second rule. We still ate the dinner." Tears were streaming down the storyteller's face softening the haggard scar running lengthwise on his cheek. He removed his sweat-stained cowboy hat and wiped the battle-etched wrinkles that caught his salty tears. He struggled to maintain the moment of happiness. The cowboy had lost his wife and two-year old granddaughter to the reaping. He had been out of town helping some friends load up some lumber equipment when the world had changed.

The greens sorrowful moaning ceased the instant the laughing men approached his bound and bleeding form. The green attempted to reach out with longing, beckoning the men closer.

During the remainder of the investigation, the green didn't utter a single iota of protest. Instead, he just stared at the two men, a dumb-founded expression stamped onto his face. That is, until the rancher detached his head.

The rancher told Mae what had happened. Mae visualized the scene in her mind's eye. With a knowing clarity, she made the connection—it made her frown.

Ω Ω Ω

"What's the connection Mae? I don't understand." I asked in a choked whisper.

Mae sadly shook her head. "Well you see, the greens must have had severe mental issues as humans. We found other greens with similar bracelets. I think the virus didn't know what to do with that type of brain chemistry and just erred on hitting the default setting. Basic animal instinct, not much better than a rabid dog really. I believe some humanity still lingers deep within their original psych—they seem to crave the sound of laughter. Maybe it's the joy, which was missing in their lives before the change that they crave. I don't know really know for certain, it's just a hunch." Mae heaved a sigh and started rocking.

I found myself suddenly blinking incessantly, after Mae had weaved her tale. "So the greens are all, ah…mental patients? Or were?" I could barely articulate the question. I just kind of stuttered it out.

"So far as I been able to deduct, yes." Mae looked distracted. She too had a deep sense of what was humane, and killing anything troubled her.

"So what about Chris? Or me or even you. Are we going to snap and go green on everyone? I mean, I would really feel comfortable checking into some nice padded cell right about now!" I could see Chris beside me nodding agreement. "No child, you are what you are. The soul can be seen through the eyes!"

"Hogwash, this is ridiculous! Why us? There were a lot of blue and brown eyed people, out there. Why did we survive and change?" I was getting exasperated. This didn't make sense.

"You died" Mae stared me straight in the eyes and held her blind gaze. "You both died!"

I sat back into the couch and started chewing my lower lip. "Well the transformation was hard, and I guess I could be one of those walking dead zombie things, but my heart beats." I was reaching—I didn't want to be a zombie.

"No child, you are alive now, a different physical version of yourself, but alive"

I exhaled. I hadn't realized I wasn't breathing.

"No child, you died when you were a littlin. So did Chris here, and so did I."

How did she know that?

I didn't share that with anyone. It's one of the reasons I became a nurse. As I stared at Mae, my mind wondered to the past…

Ω Ω Ω

It had been a beautiful summer's day. Summer break was here, yippee! I was ten.

The world was mine to do with as I pleased. I had awoken early. Still in my pajamas, I sprinted to my brother's bedroom and jumped full force onto his sleeping form. "Come on, get up! Let's go swimming and fishing!" I exclaimed. Containing my enthusiasm was not yet in my handbook.

"Ahh Sam, get off me. You're crushing my balls!" Air escaped through his clenched teeth in a high pitched groan.

Kevin's voice was changing, and he was getting weird tufts of hair on his body. Ick, hairy beast.

I adored him. He always let me tag along with him. He could dispense a roughing up to anyone that gave him or me a hard time. After all, he was letting his little sister tail him most days like a ninja shadow.

Kevin taught me to fish, hike, swim, ride a bike and fight. My own personal sensei and I was his grasshopper.

"Sam, go ahead, get ready. I'll meet you there. I have to ice my balls." He mumbled sleepily, pulling his blanket over his head.

He loved saying "balls." He could turn any phrase to include balls.

My mother was praying for the day he would grow out of it. Do men actually grow out of their fascination with their balls? I don't think so.

"Ok, I'll meet you there. Hurry up, I got the Samwiches." I made the best sandwiches so Kevin renamed them. I dashed from the room holding my pajama bottoms up. I was dressed, stocked and racing to the quarry on my bike, peddling my scabby knees off.

The quarry was abandoned forever ago. It had filled with water and now housed the biggest catfish in the county. Damn ugly fish in my opinion, but they made for delicious fixings. Yummy, life was good.

I baited and wedged my pole in between some rocks and threw the line out. Time for a morning dip.

The morning sunshine warmed the still water. It was only a minor shock to the system when I dove in. I floated face up into the sky and watched a pair of hawks do aerial dances for my pleasure—mating season.

I was starting to prune up, so I decided it was time to get out and check my line. I had to do one more thing before I got out. I had to practice my swan dive off the edge of the quarry. Kevin would want to see my progress.

I started to climb the twelve-foot, jutting rock wall. I made my way up easily. I'd been doing it like forever—okay, the last two years, fine. Kevin didn't want me climbing it alone. When I was little, he made me go around to the lower embankments.

Boring.

The sun was hot on my back, and my tan skin was already drying out from the delicious heat. I was almost to the top, thinking about arching my back and getting a longer running start when my grip on a protruding rock disintegrated.

I scrambled to regain my hold and pulled a larger rock loose. It hit me right between the eyes. I saw stars as I plummeted through warm air.

I hit the cool water's surface with a stinging splat. Water rushed over and enveloped my stunned body. I felt myself begin to sink.

I attempted to inhale a last shocked breath of air. Instead, musty water spilled into my lungs. The impact of my landing had made me dole out my air supply. I had nothing to work with but a lungful of water.

I struggled to the surface, my strength and focus dissipating rapidly. I looked toward the surface as the murky green sun was fading. I saw a few bubbles rise above me, then darkness swallowed my vision. I gulped another lungful of water. I felt my weightless body creep toward the quarry's depth. Shadows swathed my insubstantial frame.

I was drowning in the dark.

"But…" was the last thing I thought as I was overtaken with nothingness.

Searing pain engulfed my chest. Firecrackers exploded with each intake of air. I awoke choking and gagging. Light blinded me as I fought to clear my vision. Kevin's face was leaning over me, yelling.

What was he saying? Why was he yelling and shaking me? The sound was a fuzzy din. I couldn't hear any better than I could see. It was like trying to understand someone while you were underwater.

Duh, I must have water in my ears. My head throbbed and my chest felt like an elephant had sunk in for a nap. Breathing made it feel like the napping elephant had porcupine quills coming out of its rear.

I groaned and attempted to hug myself.

"Sam, Sam are you okay? Breathe, that's it breathe. Oh, my God Sam, I thought you were dead. You weren't breathing. I couldn't find a pulse." He hugged me with a ferocity I've never seen in him.

I felt his salty tears drip into my eye—I couldn't breathe.

I coughed quills and my throat burned.

"Ouch, that hurts. Ugh, did I get any fish?" I whimpered. He squeezed me even tighter and rocked me.

For two years my brother had been a junior life guard. This year he'd been practicing to take the senior level exams. Lucky for me he took his propensities to save drowning damsels seriously.

Ω Ω Ω

My focus returned to Mae's living room. I rubbed my forehead. The faint scar I had earned that day had been erased with my transformation. I rather missed it. "Yes I died. What does that have to do with anything? Chris did you?" I looked toward Chris.

His head hung. "I died too," he whispered.

"So you figured this theory out based on us three? I mean is that all the empirical data you have?" A little indignation reared itself.

"Now child, settle yourself down now. I got more to tell you!" Her scolding tone banked my indignation.

"Now, you know I got the sight. I can see things, but I don't have no real control over it, unless I focus real hard. It's mentally exhausting. I ain't no spring chicken no more!" Mae rocked a little faster and straightened out her apron.

I eyed Mae, and thought about this spring chicken. I decided I needed to know something. "Mae, are you fast and strong and have GI Jane instincts and skills?" I inquired.

Chris and Mae both started laughing.

I felt my cheeks redden. "Humpff!" I crossed my arms and sank deeper into the couch.

"Now child, I am ninety-four. The poor virus didn't have much to work with, but yes, I feel like a sixty year old. I can move fast, and I am strong. Nothing like you two though!" She stopped rocking, and pointed her wrinkled finger at me. "But I suppose I got a little Chuck Norris in me." She grinned, and with that, we all erupted into laughter.

"I always did like a man who could pull off a moustache!" Mae smacked her knee and kind of cackled, her pink eyes dancing molten pink in the firelight.

We refreshed our teas, and I checked on Teak and Oakley. Neither had left my side since the ill-fated return to the bed and breakfast.

Christin refreshed and stoked the fire. He joined me as we resettled into the overstuffed couch. I felt a little more relaxed. I needed a good laugh—it soothed the room. Teak and Oakley were snoring and farting, on either side of me—too much protein, geesh.

Mae continued her story. "So when I returned home here, the townspeople where uncertain what to make of me and what to do with me. They placed me in "quarantine" for a few days. They treated me fair under the circumstances. I was all alone with nothing really to do, so I decided I needed to delve into this "gift" and see what would happen. Three days later, after intense focusing, I had found a few answers.

The townspeople were grateful for at least some explanations. They let me live here in peace and seek me out from time to time and to make small inquires. They are simple folk who just want to live in peace and well, umm, I scare them. I had already earned their respect over the years. That respect is returning slowly, along with their trust."

"So what did you see, Mae?" I was leaning in her direction.

"My child, you shook your Christmas presents in the middle of the night, didn't you?"

Once again, I felt heat growing up my neck and spread to my ears. Chris chuckled to himself and nodded.

"It's okay hun, I shook 'em too." Then there was more chuckling from all of us. We agreed all nodding.

Mae explained how she saw the world come to its decimated end.

"There were two principal players in the tragedy, big oil and a global water company. A big oil company drills down into the earth. No big surprise, humanity has been drilling all over the world for decades, that's just what they do. They ever seek the liquid black gold. This time they just happened to bring up a little something extra. The problem started when this little something extra got flushed into the water table."

Mae sighed and continued.

"Now I'm sure that human civilizations around the world had been introducing a lot of things into the water tables. Hell, you could've Goggled it. I love Google my grandkids showed me the wonders of it. Anyway, if you had, you may never have wanted to drink water again. Hmmff!

Most individuals choose to believe blindly in the government monitoring balancing and checks to keep us safe. What we put into our bodies usually accompanies swallowing ignorance peppered with a lot of denial.

So, in comes a nice big water company—humanitarian's through and through. They give free water to third world countries and provide much needed water during catastrophes.

Such a noble and giving company—concerned for the people." Mae smacked her lips in disgust.

"Water marketing and sales had become the fastest growing industry in the world. Competition soared. I listened to the Discovery Channel. I loved that station.

"The people wanted water, and they needed water. This particular water company couldn't keep up with the supply and demand of the global market. Pressure was intense. If they didn't meet the demand, their competitors would happily step in. The contracts were worth billions of dollar. By constitutional law, water companies had safety standards to follow, specific minimal health codes.

"Many government agencies were friends with the water companies though. These agencies had to meet the people's needs, and they needed to get re-elected, hence the *minimal* legislation issued pertaining to water purification and distribution. The water companies were not tyrants. They weren't wringing their hands while cackling diabolically and intentionally trying to cause harm to their customers. No, they were just greedy bastards looking at the bottom line. Profit was the bottom line.

"They met the minimal health code requirements and sent their water around the globe. Their bottom line was looking fat. Water was being turned into gold.

"The water company was innocently ignorant to a very new organism saturating their product, a virus without the usual markers. It could survive just about any temperature and wasn't detected by their minimal filters.

"Now, the microscopic entities must have been cackling when they went through all the staging processes at the water plants. The minimal safety requirements governing their products for public consumption actually stimulated more replication and virulence within the virus. The damn virus was prehistoric. It could take any heat and chemical treatment.

"Within a week most of the world's population was chugging down a refreshing bottle of pure clean water—who didn't drink bottled water in this day and age? Who didn't kiss someone who drank bottled water?

"The end started with a virus maybe millions of years old."

Chris and I were silent, not breathing, our faces in our hands.

We did it to ourselves.

"People were all so worried we'd blow ourselves up, or screw up the planet's eco-system with global warming. But no, we drank ourselves to death." Mae sipped her tea.

Damn, I was hoping for germ warfare. That at least meant that maybe some organized people were hiding out somewhere.

"How did most of the people here in the town, manage to survive?" A whisper escaped my dry lips.

Mae shrugged. "They for some reason or another didn't drink bottled water. Hell, we have the purist, sweetest water here, a beautiful, untainted glacial lake in our backyard pumping through our pipes. Who needed bottled crap from somewhere unknown with God knows what in it? The water companies we're always knocking on this town's door to get at its water rights."

Disgust, accented Mae's punctuated words. "We lost almost nine tenths of the town though. They were vacationing or working out of town. Some used the bottle water as a convenience. I've seen crates of bottled water at the grocer. It usually had a layer of dust on it."

I stared at my knotted hands while Mae continued. "Once I figured out that it was the bottled water, we scoured the town for any remnants of that plastic-packaged garbage. We used an empty gas truck that now holds all the bottled water we found. We thought it was the best way to contain any possible viral contaminants, intentional or accidental." Mae's quiet voice trailed off. The catastrophe was hard on everyone that had survived.

I wanted to slap myself silly to wake up from this horrendous nightmare. "What do we do now?" I breathed out unsteadily.

"Live." Mae whispered into the crackling fire.

For the first time in this conversation, Chris found his voice. "What about people like us?" His voice trembled.

"Well child, it's your life to do as you please, but I hope you'll choose to live." Mae started to rock rhythmically again, her rocker creaking in the silent room.

"Live for what? The way I see it, I think we age slowly. A natural death is not around the corner, and it's not a wonderful state of affairs out in the world!" I yelled, feeling afraid.

"You're correct Sam, and you're not welcome here to top it off. The citizens here won't want to risk infection. I also have no idea how other uninfected communities will treat you, if they're out there. However, I do think you two are wonderful" Mae shifted her gaze toward the fire. Molten pink reflected the dancing flames.

Feeling unwanted did not come easy to me. I was always welcomed, unless I had to give someone an enema.

Mae's soothing voice pulled me out of my stupor. "Child you'll find your place, but in the mean-time I have an idea, a direction for you."

Mischief played in the crinkle of her eyes. I didn't like the sound of that. The last time Mae had an idea my neck was almost broken clean off my shoulders.

I reached down and stroked Teak's mane. Oakley noted this outwardly lopsided display of preferential treatment, so she decided to climb onto my lap. Now, a fifty pound, gangly, brown border-collie taking residence on your lap might not be so bad but… Unfortunately, I must have had some remnants of dinner on my face, because she insisted that my face needed a thorough scouring.

"Oakley, I think you got it all, geesh!" I heaved her insistent weight off my lap. She pranced away. Can dogs wear a self-satisfying grin on their faces? Because I do believe that dog has mastered it.

I raised my eyebrow towards Mae's distracted gaze. With nerves of steel, I asked *the* question. "What did you have in mind?" An exasperated sigh punctuated the question. I have mastered the exasperated sigh.

Mae smiled. "It's your life, but I see the both of you heading west towards the coast."

"That was, well, is our plan Mae." I stuttered, turning my attention to Christin's puzzled expression.

"Yes, well there's someone you have to find and bring with you." Mae looked guilty.

"*Oh,* Mae, what did you see!" Exasperation was coming second nature to me.

Mae busied herself, fixing her apron. "Only fragments really. I just know you have to find someone special. She's a yellow."

"What the hell is a yellow? Are they cowardly or something?"

Mae was petting Oakley's smooth head. "Or something…"

I rolled my eyes at Christin. "Okay, why are we going hunting for this yellow? Is she a genie, and if we rub her the right way, she'll make the world right again?"

"Yes, but not that rubbing bit." Oakley was sitting now.

"I felt her when I was coming home. I would of tracked her down, but there was something dangerous associated with her. I've been chewing on it ever since I got home." Oakley was pawing Mae's massaging hands.

I leaned further toward Mae. "Okay, just so I'm clear. You want us to, I presume, go out of our way, track some unknown entity, bump up against something ominous and load her up—possibly against her will—and bring her out west, because she's going to save the world!" I surrendered and stared into the fire. "Did I miss anything, Chris, chime in anytime?"

"No you're doing fine" I did a double take at him. He gestured for me to continue.

I turned toward Mae and gesticulated that she had the floor. "No really, go ahead Mae"

Mae nodded and said. "Well yes, that about sums it up." Oakley, was lying on the floor, all of her legs were reaching for the ceiling. How could a ninety-four year old woman look so innocent?

Sweet even?

Mae asked. "Do you two have something better to do? Wouldn't you like GI Jane to come out and play again? She sounds like fun." Mischief, I realized lived in this woman's eyes.

I sensed I was in the presence of a master manipulator. I only hoped she used her powers for good. I didn't want to be on the business end of her manipulations.

She was impossible. I could not be mad at her but I did wonder if I could deck a geriatric variant. Yes, I think I could.

Just a small punch.

Chris and I had had enough. We needed a break.

We thanked Mae for a delicious dinner and said we'll talk with her later. We took Oakley for a walk around the town with Teak snoozing in my arms. It was dusk. This place is so beautiful, serene, I could almost live in a place like this, but I knew I would get bored and restless eventually.

Chris and I agreed if there was something we could do to make the world right again, we ought to try. Like Mae said, we weren't doing anything anyway. Saving the world seemed like a good enough reason to keep breathing, so to speak.

My best friend Jill and I used to talk about the mysteries of the universe. Why things happened to good people. We decided that everything happened for a reason. Sometimes the reasoning is obvious; sometimes you don't see the reasoning for a long time; or, the worst, you're just a little ant in this big old universe, and you don't need to see all the workings of this wonder.

I hated when that happened. Welcome to the now. I always wanted to know everything. Jill thought my head would explode as I tried to grapple the riddles of life. I missed my friend—she was in Las Vegas when the *Twilight zone* hit. I couldn't contemplate further on the notion she wasn't walking around on this planet anymore. It was still too soon to let my mind wonder too much.

Jill and I had surmised that all a person could really do is be in the present, go with what feels right and do your best. The rest will work itself out, and the answers might be forthcoming or not. A person just had to have a little faith.

Well, we've been thrown into the present with minimal information. Mae's "proposals" didn't feel wrong and I could see that Christin and I were equipped to do our best. The only thing left then was to come up with a name for Chris's alter ego—*The Terminator*. I started laughing my ass off as we walked.

Chris looked at me as if I had lost my mind—again.

"What?" He asked.

I looked at him. He was becoming a master of incredulous looks. "Nothing Arnold." I replied.

"Huh!"

I laughed again and wiped the tears that were streaming down my face. I told him. "I'll explain later Lucy!"

Chris looked flabbergasted. I think that expression could get stuck on his face. He used it enough, especially when he was around me.

We met with Mae one more time before we left. We needed a general direction to head in. Then we packed, said good bye to a few of the residents and drove off.

Randy gave me the Bowring knife and wished us well. The rescued girls were slowly coming around but they still didn't want to go outside. They were doing the best they could, mourning and coping. Their nightmares were riddled with green monsters, and they couldn't escape their past. I wished them warm and happy dreams—one day soon I hope. It was hard to watch the pale twitchy teenage girls, as their eyes furtively glanced around their environment. It broke my heart, but at least they had each other to cling to. And their uncle Randy hardly left their side.

I was waiting in the Rover and had seen Christin talking to Mae. Chris had his head hanging and was nodding, mumbling responses. I could have listened in if I focused, but I felt that would be intrusive. I knew Chris would tell me what I needed to know. We agreed early on to be honest with one another.

I trusted him to my core he felt like my brother. We were in this together. Whatever *this,* turned out to be.

Mae had seen us off with a warning, listen for the bell chime and you'll find friends.

Once we were in the Rover it immediately started raining. The roads were slick and full of debris. We were happy to get off the mountain pass. The highway heading south had a bit more vehicular obstacles. We had to stop numerous times to push vehicles out of the way. The dogs enjoyed stretching their legs and barking instructions to us. Mae had given us some landmarks and roads to follow. Hopefully our noses would do the rest.

Paging GI Jane, report to the information desk as soon as possible, please. Christin and I hadn't decided on his alter ego's name yet, so I just called him Arnold. We joked that I was his DC and he was my AC—we were electric together.

Baaha—sad humor, we knew it.

We travelled mostly in silence as we privately processed what lay ahead of us. The landscape was hypnotic and the tires on the asphalt struck a rhythmic cadence. Our hearts thudded intermittently letting us know we were still alive. One breath at a time we headed for hope into the unknown.

"Oakley get in the back. Your nails are digging into my crotch. Move your little hairy behind." I pushed her butt into the back seat.

Teak was now wearing her characteristic innocent grin. This translated to her being perfect.

Teak was starting to move easier, her wounds were healing nicely. And she no longer looked like a mummy.

We were all getting bored. We needed something to do. I decided to check the dogs for fleas. Yes I was that bored. My enhanced vision made short work of the annoyances. The dogs appeared grateful and enjoyed the grooming. Super powers maximized to their fullest.

We didn't need to hunt. The townspeople had loaded us up with a variety of fresh meats and jerky. The dogs were currently haggling over a large piece of the smoked meat.

Christin pulled my attention away from the wrangling jerky dispute, pointing to the front of the Rover.

A looming dark city opened up ahead of us. I swallowed dryly. We settled on a course of action: drive until we couldn't, keep our senses on alert and pray we don't get jumped by a pack of greens.

Simple right?

Chapter Fourteen:
Off to the Ruby City

"Thinking is the hardest work there is, which is probably the reason why so few engage in it."
-Henry Ford (1863 - 1947)

As we entered the city, we were surprised there weren't a lot of vehicles on the road. If people had gotten suspicious or panicked, they would have been heading out of the city—not into it. People always left big cities whenever panic set in. Our lane into the city was pretty clear. The lane heading out of the city was moderately clear as well. Some cities didn't have time to panic.

We didn't see any unexpected movement. There was a bird circling an empty parking lot, a dog knocking a trash can over and the largest lion I had ever seen was watching the dog scavenge. I presume someone let the zoo animals out of their cages in this city as well—gave them a fighting chance. That was decent of them. I like it when people surprised me.

We heard the bells in a big clock tower chime in the distance. I wonder what that clock runs on? Weird. Hearing a clock in the silence.

Silence. Clock.

"Chris the cl..!" I stammered.

"Oh my God Christin, the clock it's chiming!" I screamed while grabbing for "the holy shit" hand-rail.

Something flew out in front of us. Then we heard it—a discord of fast beating hearts. Simultaneously, all four tires suddenly blew. The Rover rocked noisily.

For a moment, Christin struggled to regain control over the careening Rover. The choppy ride eased to a lurching stop.

Guns were immediately thrust into our faces. Come on, not again!

A gruff voice told us to get out and put our faces to the ground—original. Sweaty hands held guns that were pointed at our heads. It was all I could do to focus on the hands and gun barrels. We held our hands up and exited the vehicle.

Chris was escorted to my side of the vehicle. "Arnold," I said.

"Jane," he responded. Chris's heart beat chose that moment to thump. A reminder he was close helped me relax and use my enhanced senses to broaden my view.

There were three of them. I listened hard and heard one more heartbeat on the roof. We were easing ourselves onto the ground when Teak and Oakley thought they were missing out on something and jumped out the window. Teak didn't land gracefully she was still healing. I winced at her pain. Damn. We have got to get those windows fixed.

The men turned at the sudden movement and raised their guns in the dog's direction. The raw essence of GI Jane surged through me. I leapt.

I hit one of the guys in the chest with a left-sided leg kick and quickly nabbed the other one by his throat. Christin had his forearm snuggly wrapped around the third man's throat, gagging him.

I grinned in my cohort's direction. He wiggled his eyebrows which accented his mischievous grin. I winked. Let the games begin.

I directed my voice to the roof looming over us. "Don't even think about shooting at us. We won't hurt your friends—much!" A self-satisfying grin fixed on my face.

"You had to say 'much,' didn't you?" Chris rolled his eyes. I shrugged and turned my attention back to the business at hand. I'd spent too much time with the dogs. I think I had to get out more.

"Come on dude, this is getting old. If we meant you guys any harm, we would have already ended your friends' lives!" I yelled up to the roof.

Teak started sniffing intently at my hostage's crotch. Ah… girl, where are your manners?

The guy in my vise-like grip murmured, "Can I talk please?"

"You're talking, have at it." I was growing bored. I felt very exposed. The last guy was tucked in on the roof, just above us and he could easily start to open fire. I tucked my head behind my hostage.

"Can you please, call your dog off my nuts?" Teak had found something really interesting in this guy's crotch, and she was digging in.

"Teak, sit." She did as she was told, but look longingly at the poor man's crotch.

Guys—go figure—were ever so consistent in their protection of the family jewels. This was nothing if not predictable—priceless.

"Im going to yell up to my friend. Don't get startled." My hostage didn't dare twitch, but he was involuntarily starting to shake.

Teaks intensive scrutiny in the direction of the guy's crotch didn't waver.

"If you tell him to do anything other than come down here, I will twist your neck off—even if he shoots me. Do you understand?" The sandy haired man nodded vigorously. "And I will let Teak continue her unfinished mission of exploring your crotch." The guy gulped dryly. Impressive. The power of the hairy testicles.

Christin rolled his eyes while he poorly attempted to stifle his not so-subtle guffaws. He gave me a "You are so going to burn in hell for torturing that poor man" look. I shot him a dirty look. I was trying to work it here.

My hostage cleared his throat nervously, then yelled to the roof. "Ready, ok…ah Corey come down here. It's okay!" he yelled unimpressively. I still had a tight grip on his vocal cords.

I could see a serious sniper rifle barrel pointed at Christin.

A deep businesslike baritone resounded from the roof. "Are you sure Gil? I have one of 'em in my sights."

I growled in response to the snipers assessment.

Gil began to tremble. "Yes, we'll be fine. Right?" His voice trailed off, so only I could hear the last word. He tried in vain to turn his head to look at me.

I stared at the rooftop. "Yes, but hurry up Teak is getting hungry." He couldn't see my smirk.

I didn't need to look at Christin. He squeaked a small sound as he tried to restrain his laughter. I shot him a dirty look. He was not helping. I was trying to look and sound tough.

"Hurry up Cory. It's fine!" Gil's body strained with urgency. He glanced down at Teak. The perfectly behaved dog licked her lips and edged closer, all the while maintaining her sitting posture. Gil shuddered. Never underestimate the power of the nuts.

The rifle barrel retracted and I heard quick footsteps descend the noisy fire escape. I'm glad the sniper was off his perch, so there wouldn't be any witnesses to my smirk—it didn't instill fear.

Cory exited the building with his rifle trained on my head. He was pure army, looming at least six-five with a shaved head and fatigues. He has killed before. Death is always reflected in the eyes—I've cared for enough soldiers in my time to see it.

"Are we going to have to do this dance all over again? Geesh Cory, you don't have to put your gun down, just lower it and sling it as a sign of good faith," I directed dryly. This violence was all new to me. My mouth was getting dry.

He didn't change his aim. I continued. "Then, the moment I see it slung on your shoulder, I'll release Gil here. Arnold over there is going to hang onto…What's your name?"

"Adam" A strained squeak escaped the sweat-suit wearing guy. Fear was making Adam's eyes bulge, not a good situation. I could feel the man's blood pressure rising. His head might pop from sheer stress.

"Okay, now Arnold is going to hang onto Adam, until we get a little more comfortable. Okay?" I was using my sweet voice.

It was the voice I used when you need to reassure the psych patient that the imagined purple monster in the corner was not going to hurt them, and that this nice pill will make it go away.

Corey looked intently at Gil. Gil nodded acquiescence. Corey reluctantly slung his rifle, and I released Gil. Parley successful.

The three guys picked up their unconscious friend and put him on the bed of a pick-up. Gil kept absently rubbing his neck while his other hand absently drifted to the vicinity of his crotch—poor thing had been defiled. Teak trailed after Gil with a sheepish grin.

They took us to an old brownstone ten blocks from where we left the Rover. It was a beautiful place, except for the thick steel shutters on the windows and a .50 calibre rifle sticking out a gun hole. Home sweet home.

The place was full of supplies, guns, medical gear and maps. I checked on their unconscious friend. I assessed a probable concussion. I didn't really leave any marks you'd notice. I attempted to apologize numerous times, but they waved my gesture off. They busied themselves putting the maps away.

I watched Gil clean up a dining room table full of maps. I crossed my arms and leaned against the living room wall. I tried not to narrow my eyes at his actions as I said.

"We're looking for someone—a girl. She has yellow eyes." The three men, exchanged knowing glances—I thought easy breezy so can read you. "Come on now, boys. You help us, and we'll help you." I heard groaning from the unconscious guy. I stepped over to check him out while I lifted my glasses.

I leaned over his moaning form to check his pupils. A long chorus of screams ensued. Gil slipped into the screaming guy's line of vision and tried to reassure him that it was all right. The screaming guy became unconscious guy again.

Christin decided to go scavenge for tires just in case we had to make a hasty retreat out of here. I wasn't happy with his decision. We didn't know what had these boys so jumpy yet.

I was left with the task of information gathering—it must've been my sunny disposition shining through again. "So, start talking Gil. What's been happening since the end of the world?" I was sitting down petting Teak. Non-threatening—right?

He looked over at me, then down at Teak and shuddered. "Sit." Teak sat so did Gil. "Good girl, but I wasn't talking to you Gil?"

Gil was running his shaky hands through his hair and nervously glancing through one of the open shutters. "I've never seen you or Arnold's colours before—only greens and reds." He crossed his legs and averted his gaze to check unconscious man's still form.

Wow, reds? This is going to be interesting. "What about a yellow?" I asked.

"Once, I think. A few days ago, we were dropping off a couple of greens, when I saw this young girl of about fifteen, maybe seventeen, being escorted out of the office where I meet the reds. I only caught a glimpse of her eyes when she turned her head in my direction." Gil now continued to stare at one of the gun holes.

I glared at Gil. "You got some 'splaining to do Lucy—start explaining!" I did my best impersonation of Marlon Brando's gruff voice. I scratched my chin like he did in the *Godfather*. Gil turned to look in my direction and an involuntarily tremble swept over his body.

Wow I'm scary. I'm sure it had nothing to do with my intense burning eyes, staring him down.

Oakley came over to get her quota of love while Gil started twisting his knotted hands. "After everything changed eight of us came together. Grouping up, trying to figure out how to survive, and you know, deciding what to do next.

"We were in agreement that we should head to the coast on account of the equable weather out there. We were almost loaded and had picked a route when the reds showed up. This pact of reds made it perfectly clear what they wanted and they expected our full cooperation in acquiring it," Gil spit out, his rendition of events distorted his facial features.

"They killed two of our group just to illustrate their degree of seriousness." Pain wrestled the disgust on Gil's face. He continued his story. A sigh cleared his face of the internal war being waged. "They wanted us, to…to hunt colours. They explained how it should be done and where to bring them when they were caught."

Great, just super! Excellent. We had a new world and there were still racists and slave traders. Real rednecks, wanting their quota of colors—geez, really!

"They came here with directions and instructions. The instructions divulged the greens' location and approximately how many we would encounter."

Gil continued in a shaky voice. "Anyway, we now hunt the colours and bring them to the office. What happens, to them after that I have no idea. We never see the greens again. Barbaric, I know, but it's them or us." He released another deep sigh and rubbed his face vigorously. He didn't look at me.

It was slave trading, in a sense. I shook my head in disgust. No amount of rubbing would erase what he had done or witnessed. The greens had been humans once and now they were being hunted and their lives traded away.

"Only greens though—you're the first blue I've seen."

I think I was scowling at Gil. "What about the yellow? Have you seen anything after that initial sighting?" I turned my gaze to Teak.

I was scaring poor Gil. "No, mm—sorry" Gil suddenly busied himself picking some lint off his pants.

"Jesus Gil, what are you doing, we have to take them in— you want to get us killed?" Unconscious man had spoken up.

"Would you like to become unconscious again? What's your name?" I prefer to threaten people using their Christian names.

Unconscious man—well, now conscious—man turned from my molten blue eyes. They were not sparkling with happiness. "Trevor Whittaker." he stuttered to the wall.

"Well, Trevor Whittaker, the adults are talking here—go back to sleep!" I glared at the soon to-be unconscious Trevor.

Gil groaned. "He's right. If the reds find out you're here, and we're in cahoots with you, we're all as good as dead." He jerked his chin at me.

"I need that yellow, and you fellas are going to help us, one way or another. You're going to earn your freedom!" I bent down to give Oakley her share of love. The two men were now talking, and I didn't want to intimidate them with my glare.

Mr. Whittaker snivelled and attempted to get to his feet. "We already tried an escape and we lost two more. They'll hunt us down for sport. We have no chance in hell of getting out of this dead city. Why do you think we stay? They mostly leave us alone, except when they want a color."

His stance wavered, and faltered. He wasn't successful in remaining in an upright position. Trevor grabbed his head, threw up and collapsed on the sofa. A small grin, tickled my lips.

Gil looked very tired. Actually, defeated would be a better word.

"Listen guys, I'm not talking about an escape. I'm talking a hunt and a rescue." Oakley's pathetic face was receiving my full attention. Her eyes rolled to heaven. She then lost all composure, and rolled onto her back. I heard Gil give a little chuckle.

I looked up and made eye contact with Gil, and he held my gaze but lost his chuckle. I liked this man. He was trying to reclaim his strength. "That's impossible. We'll be fodder for their pleasure." Trevor's whine broke our moment, again.

I stared at Trevor. "We will hunt them down and get the yellow. You can help us or hide in your snivelling hole. Rest assured, when we leave town, we won't be stopping by to pick you up." Trevor averted his gaze from mine.

My blue eyes felt heated as I glowered in Trevor's direction. Brutal, I know. He was just scared, but he had to choose life over servitude. "Besides, you now have two special weapons at your disposal. I'm sure we're no different physically than the greens or the reds." How I tended to assume so much lately is beyond me.

We laid out our plan. There were four of them and six of us, descent odds. Gil, as it turned out, had been designated the human director by the reds, so he had full access into their inner sanctum.

He drew a map, illustrating the layout of the large office. The room had two doors that opened to an office with an enormous panoramic window, which exposed a dark city. Gil reported seeing a lot of religious icons strewn about the office suite. A substantial wooden desk usually held a sitting red, and a nearby couch allowed two reds to lounge, while a fully stocked bar drew the reds to intermittently fill their bottomless glasses.

Alcohol didn't do much for the transformed. Chris and I knew this first hand because we tried in vain to get drunk one night. Three bottles of scotch and five bottles of white wine didn't touch our mental alertness. We weren't impressed.

Everyone was preparing for the insurgence—even Trevor. Gil was explaining the location and layout of the office. Cory was looking out the window with his rifle clasped in his arms, a pure soldier. I never saw him put the large rifle down. I'm sure he slept with it cradled in his arms. I should ask if he'd named it.

Adam was trying to figure out how to fit one more handgun onto his body.

"Your ankle," I suggested. "Mm...thanks." He mumbled distracted. He attached a gun to each ankle.

Gil was standing upright, his hands on his back, stretching.

"We could go for a direct assault, go in with guns a-blaz..." His head exploded in front of me.

Have you ever seen a melon shot with a high velocity rifle only to have the camera man slow it down for you? Probably not, but Gil's head did an excellent impression.

The gun's retort echoed in the distance.

Glass showered the floor, jingling as they cascaded around Gil's still form. Damn, amazing shot.

Only someone with extraordinary eyesight could make that shot. The shooter had put it through one of the gun holes. They were only about six inches wide.

Everyone in the room was dumbfounded, jaws agape.

Suddenly, four stunned bodies drove to the floorboards. Two hairy ones hunkered down, unmoving.

"Teak, Oakley, come here." I commanded. They crawled hesitantly to me—an excellent combat crawl. I noticed a trail of darkness followed Teak's skulk. Damn bastard, scared the pee out of her. Poor thing was going to have bladder problems if this damn chaos kept up.

"Come out. Come out. Wherever you are!" A cajoling male voice echoed out front of the brownstone. When would the bad guys come up with better lines?

"Come on, come out and meet my little friend!" A louder male voice made the announcement this time. It was followed by a maniacal laugh.

Really? We're going for an Al Pacino impression? Frick and Frack watched too much television.

The seconds ticked by, and I heard Cory chamber a round. He stood up and fired through the shattered window and gun hole. He was repositioned on the ground before the echoing din of his shot finished reverberating through the living room.

I heard a satisfying thump hit the asphalt outside the brownstone; it was followed by a ballistic scream. Someone was pissed.

I stifled a small giggle. Cory looked over and grinned. He held up one finger. One down, and three to go. I peeked out the window and saw red bobbing lights. Outstanding, the sun was going down. They'd be easy to track.

Abruptly, I caught sight caught of twin amber lights. They belonged to Christin who had just had his goggles removed.

During our travels, we had come across a fine Harley shop. There we equipped ourselves with dark biker goggles. Our eyes were not inconspicuous, but our new accessories remedied that.

Damn, damn, damn. If they hurt Christin...

"Arnold, are you okay?" I spoke in a normal tone; I knew he could hear me.

"Jane, I'm fi..." Something or someone choked him off.

Behind Christin's amber eyes, red eyes peeked out.

"Boys, send out your new friend and we'll go back to business as usual!" The speaker didn't need a bullhorn. It was silent in the house. Trevor scrambled to the door and threw himself over the threshold.

Coward.

"Please, please, I wanted no part of this. I'm here to serve you!" he cried. Then he bowed on his knees. I'm sure his head scraped the cement stairs from bowing so low.

Shared sounds of disgust slipped out of my and Cory's mouths.

Trevor was shot in the back of his head mid-bow. Free at last.

I assumed the necessity for peons was finished. Cory swore underneath his breath and Adam threw up.

I stood up, aimed and fired my crossbow at the closet pair of glowing red orbs. Christin's amber eyes swirled beside the red spheres. Feathers now protruded from between the dimming red circles. I heard a whizzing sound just before I felt the pain slicing through my right side. The area just below my liver burned. Darn, that was going to leave a mark, and I really liked this shirt.

As I fell, I heard the rifle retort resound in the distance. Son of a...!

Man that wound burned—didn't really hurt that much though. Cory scurried over to my side while conflicting emotions played out on his face. He wanted to help but was afraid of getting infected by my blood. His hand reached out but I stopped it mid-way. "Shit, are you okay?" he asked in a hushed whisper.

I felt blood trickle down my back. Hmm... a penetrating gun-shot wound had exited out my back. "It's okay. It just burns. Let's move!" I hissed a little through clenched teeth as I applied pressure to the seeping wound.

We hit the back door at a sprint. I heard another whizzing noise as the wall a few inches beside the back door exploded into a plaster cloud.

I heard another whizzing noise as Cory's body was flung backwards, shattering the kitchen table in a loud crash.

Crap, Cory...

Adam started to fire aimlessly in all directions outside the back door. He had his eyes clenched shut. Mumbling, "I can't give up I'm no bitch."

Inaudible to the average human ear, soft thumffs whistled above our heads. The thumffs shattered the room. Pieces of glass, plaster and furniture exploded in the kitchen and living room. A tornado of flying debris swallowed the room.

I dove onto Cory's moaning form and rolled him behind a kitchen island. I heard one of Adam's shots hit its mark.

An unmistakeable scream pierced the night. The barrage of gunfire stopped sharply.

Adam however, did not get the memo, so he continued to fire, unaware that one of his careening shots had been successful.

I peered around the island to find Adam, who had only now stopped firing, reaching for his ankle holster.

"Adam," I whispered. No good, he was a man on a mission.

"Adam," I yelled a little louder. He had the handgun off his ankle now and was deciding on which direction he was going to release his next volley of careening shots.

I threw a can of chicken soup at his head. Adam's head bounced off the cabinet door. Oops, a little too hard.

"Ouch, what the hell was that for?" He sat rubbing the sweet spot I targeted. "You got him Mr. Sniper!" I smiled at him.

"What? Really?" A large grin replaced his grimace.

The reprieve in the assault allowed me to breathe a sigh of relief. I turned my attention to Cory. He was still breathing. Actually, he had started a long string of curses that didn't appear to be ending any-time soon. That boy sure had a mouth on him.

I checked his shoulder. It was bleeding in the front and back from matching holes. The bullet had penetrated and exited. Thank goodness it didn't lodge in his shoulder. I grabbed a dishtowel and wrapped the wound as best I could. I put my ear to his chest and heard air fill his lung. Good it hadn't caused his lung to collapse. I smiled. He tried to smile in return but grimaced when I pushed his hand to his wound. I didn't have to tell him to put pressure on the wound—he had been schooled in the art of war.

I turned back to crazy-eyed Adam. He was searching everywhere for movement but not processing much.

"Adam, stay here and protect Cory," Cory rolled his eyes.

"You can't Sam. You're out numbered. I can come with you..." The big man winced when he reached for the gun strapped to his leg.

"Relax Cory, I got this. There's only two left and one is injured. Adam stay with Cory and shoot anything that moves, all right? I'll be right back" I tentatively stood up.

Neither man looked convinced. I had to learn to lie better.

The three of us exited through the back door. No, not the boys. The girls left the building. The boys stayed in the house. Ah, woman's lib organizations would be so proud. I was really scared. Once again, I really wanted to run in the opposite direction—what was I thinking?

My hairy cohorts were coming with me. Short of restraining them, I knew they'd follow.

I slipped down the alley and doubled back after I crossed the street. I jumped to the roof of the house where I thought I had heard the red's gunfire. I looked down at the dogs. They stared up at me unhappily. The experience of being this high up so easily and quickly was both cool and terrifying simultaneously. I had jumped fifty feet straight up.

I found a blood trail and started hunting across the roof. There was a substantial amount of blood. Adam's careening bullet had nicked an artery. Adam would have been so proud—or thrown up.

I grinned. The vision of Adam tossing his cookies made me laugh out loud and the weight of my fear slipped off me like a cloak.

Jane was in the building. I quickly scanned the rest of the roof. The red wasn't in sight; the clear blood trail was. The trail exited off the opposite side of the roof where it then continued down onto the alley floor below.

I jumped without fear to the alley behind the house and called the dogs. They came bounding down the alley, good dogs. They looked happy, again.

With deliberate silence, we advanced cautiously down the alley, predators this time, not prey. The red path of blood beckoned me to follow.

Ω Ω Ω

Christin knew Sam would be okay, so he hunted the red that had orchestrated the other reds. The reds had to be put down. No one was safe while they existed.

He felt sorry for the greens—they appeared to be mindless creatures that were dangerous and needed to be put down—but humanely. He had watched *Old Yeller* and cried. They were just innocent humans who had been turned into rabid beasts. It wasn't their fault. Their deaths should be humane.

The reds however were intentional killers. They knew exactly what they were doing. Before he left to get the tires, Gil had mentioned a few things. Gil thought they were religious fanatics. In his dealings with the reds, Gil had heard them mention cleansing the world of abominations. Their office housed a lot of religious icons that were strewn about their headquarters. Christin surmised it wasn't a big leap to assume their motive was to hunt for some perverse religious satisfaction.

The smell of the red was easy to track. It was richer and sweeter than the greens. He wondered what their diet consisted of.

Tracking and dispatching the greens back at the lake, had not been a moral or physical issue. Catching the elusive green monster had proven to be a mildly interesting endeavor. He picked up the trick of jumping from tree to tree. This turned into a useful skill, especially when the target liked to weave a lot. The height of the treetops offered a panoramic view of the quarry.

At present, he had no trees to utilize, but the city was full of mammoth buildings. Christin was currently perched atop a five-story building. His keen eyesight enabled him to spot the fleeing red; it was entering a third floor balcony in an office building.

Jumping from his perch, he pondered midflight that maybe he'd get lucky and the yellow would be in the vicinity. Christin leaped to the fifth floor of the red's office building.

The building was dark. He grabbed the patio door lock and gave it a slight jerk. A satisfying crack echoed loudly into the night. The noise was too loud. Panic coursed through Christin's body.

Damn. Wait a minute. He realized he had been concentrating so hard, listening for any alien sound that his hearing was amplified.

"Haaaaa, Sam would have laughed at that! Honestly I almost gave myself a heart attack. Jeepers!" He pushed in through the open patio door.

Arnold was in attendance.

Ω Ω Ω

CHAPTER THIRTEEN:
Lambs Turn into Lions

"To me every hour of the light and dark is a miracle, every cubic inch is a miracle."
-Walt Whitman (1819 - 1892)

My wounded quarry swayed unsteadily as he pushed through the glass door of an office building. Note to self: extreme blood loss is an impediment.

I scouted out the area and determined that no other reds were near. I would've smelled them if they had been. A strong catlike odor lingered in the breeze. Huh, a zoo must be near.

My perch was eight stories up. I could see the dogs anxiously waiting for me down in the alley. I did a flip in the air, aiming for a large dumpster that had been shoved into the corner of the alleyway.

I went straight through the metal lid of the trash container and hit the bottom hard. Damn. So much for this imagined grace and stealth.

I could hear my dog's whining and sniffing outside of the dumpster. How humiliating. I was just starting to get a little cocky with my jumps.

"Just a minute you guys!" I started pulling cardboard out of my ass. More whines and sniffing ensued outside the object of my shame. "I'm coming, hang on!" I startled when I grabbed a handful of newspapers that read, "THE END OF THE WORLD IS HERE!"

"No shit Sherlock," I said to myself. I threw the paper aside.

The sound of metallic thunder shuddered a few feet above my head. Damn, I hope that's Christin.

Brilliant red light irradiated the inside of the dumpster.

Damn, not Christin!

Behind the red glow came an excited voice.

"Hi pretty, it's time for dinner. I haven't eaten blue before." A guttural breath escaped my lips, betraying me.

"Don't worry pretty, I'll make it fast. Did you know Jesus's eyes were blue? God will love me when I take you into my body!" I could almost hear him salivate.

Great, a religious cannibal wants me to be his commune wafer. Flesh of Jesus—tastes like chicken.

"So are you going to come up here, or do you want to die in the garbage?"

"Is that anyway to treat your last meal?" I yelled. I didn't wait for a response and jumped out through my man made hole.

A cement truck slammed into my chest, I didn't travel but a few feet when a brick building stopped my flight—at least it felt like a brick building. My thoughts were slowing down. I grated gently down the wall—Wile E Coyote style.

The dogs found my crumpled form, and started licking my face. My vision was blurry. I could see the red standing atop the dumpster gloating. His red haze lit up the dark alley.

I hope he doesn't kill the dogs. They could survive, I think if left alone.

My dogs turned and started growling. Ah, bless the little creatures. They were going to get slaughtered.

I attempted to push myself up, but the world spun. GI Jane could not answer now—please leave a message.

I reached my hand around to the back of my head and felt my skull. It had been caved into a half-moon crescent.

My vision was fading and I felt weakness creeping up my limbs. I paused in my neurological assessment. I could smell that strong catlike odour again. Huh, poor zoo animals. Or maybe the smell was a figment of my imagination. Perhaps the smell was a symptom of a head injury.

The red laughed. "Lunch time Father, see how I honor you!" He turned his pleased face up to the heavens, arms outstretched.

Holy crap, I couldn't believe I was going to die at the hands of this religious shmuck! I tried hard to focus on his revering form; I almost had him in focus. Man he was proud of himself, standing there all self-righteous.

I'm not a religious person as I said. I find man so often corrupts religion for his own selfish purposes. I spit out some blood and reached up to paw at the side of the dumpster. I kept my eyes on the glowing red. I really hadn't travelled far. I almost had a grip on the dumpster's bracket when a dark blur swooped the red away.

I blinked frantically. Did I really just see that? What happened? What the hel…

In the darkness, I heard a lion roar—a sickly moist cracking sound followed.

Soft silver light danced into my foggy vision—pretty.

The appealing light began to fade as I passed into oblivion. Who knew I could pass out?

Huh…

Ω Ω Ω

Christin worked his way up the stairs silently. He had never hunted a day in his life but this new stalking instinct had somehow become second nature now.

The reds had ambushed him, while he was taking the tires off another Rover. A smelly dark bag had been thrown over his head. He was then roped like a calf, beaten to near unconsciousness and thrown into a trunk. Their numbers had overwhelmed him.

Blood caked his clothes. The bastards had ruined his favorite pair of jeans. He finished his quick self-assessment. All his wounds had mostly healed.

He checked the floor number and was pleased to see he had made it to the sixteenth floor without incident. Cracking the emergency exit door, he glanced through the opening.

Taken aback by what he saw, he scratched his bloody scalp. He had never seen so much religious paraphernalia stuffed into one room in his life, short of a basement in a church.

Raised Catholic, he never had much use for religion. Most followers of organized religion were persecuting, judgemental bastards—to each their own. He wanted no part of the association. If he wanted to speak with God—he did just that, cutting out the middlemen and going to the top.

Ω Ω Ω

When Christin was fourteen he was social enough, but had kept to himself. He had a passion for building models. Cars, boats, planes and houses; any kit he could get his hands on, he had built it. He did his best work when he used his own imagination, building projects from scavenged scraps.

The Catholic school Christin attended enforced rigidity and a conformist mentality. He did what was expected but escaped back to his model building world whenever he could.

Avery, a popular student, had shown an interest in Christin's models, and they had become fast friends. Other students noted their close relationship and decided it would be sporting to hound them, calling them faggots, mama's boys—any name that elicited a reaction.

Christin and his friend were ostracized and bullied at every turn. This behavior went on for a month. One day Christin found the contents of his locker strewn in the hallway. The contents of the locker had been ransacked and destroyed. The debris included a prize model he had been laboring over for months.

Deflated, he stooped to pick up the pieces of his model. His best friend's shoes were crushing a significant piece of his model, grinding the piece further into obscurity.

Christin raised his head slowly to meet scowling eyes. A gaggle of boys stood behind his friend. They started laughing and pointing at the wreckage that surrounded Christin's shrunken form. Then his best friend stepped on the one remaining piece of intact model, grinding his foot dramatically. The boy grinned, turned and left with the group of boys.

Christin was heartbroken. He did care for his friend. The betrayal cut deep. Religion preached that homosexuality was a sin and they would be punished in hell—he was an abomination. That night he died.

He raided his mom's medicine cabinet, finding many colourful pills. They slipped down his throat easily.

There was no place for an abomination—all the religious experts said so. Even his parents voiced their judgement about homosexuality.

His parents found him asleep—too late?

The paramedics brought him back from the dead. The emergency staff brought him back again. People had fought for his life. Christin's nurse had said he was a lucky boy—he wasn't meant to leave this mortal plane yet. He heard that he had horse shoes up his ass. Apparently that meant he was lucky. He didn't feel lucky. Christin felt a horse had kicked the crap out of him and maybe left his shoes behind.

Spending time on a pediatric psychiatric ward saved and changed his life—a caring nurse guessed his situation. The nurse listened and nodded, letting Chris know that God in his infinite wisdom loves all his creations and that he didn't make mistakes.

The nurse encouraged him to find his way. One day he would understand that most people acted out of fear when faced with that which they don't understand. Christin didn't know if he was acting out of fear, or if the people that surrounded him were.

Chris left the hospital with a small amount of hope and a little understanding. That little bit of hope bolstered him into realizing he did not want to live in fear. He quietly sought out gay and lesbian organizations, which helped him to understand he wasn't an abomination.

His family was not supportive. They made him transfer schools and refused to acknowledge the incident. He had his models and a few friends. He was all right. He made it through, he found his way.

Religion he didn't have a lot of patience for. It preached too much hate when it feared something. He chose not to live with, nor associate with, anything that propagated such fear-fuelled hate.

A red glow ebbed from beneath the far door. How the hell would he get at the red?

A distraction was called for.

Removing his goggles, he released his amber light. The architect had renovating to do. He hurled an enormous ornate wooden cross out the large picturesque window. Other religious icons soon followed. He was a professional, and a complete remodeling of the devil's alter was called for. Christin was a very proficient worker.

The two large wooden doors violently swung open. A barrage of gunfire sprayed his now vacated spot. He was also very fast—the bullets didn't find him. He dove behind a large wooden cross that was lying on its side. Damn, he really wanted to toss this monstrosity.

Christin's crossbow found the shooter's knee. The red fell over, screaming blasphemous rhetoric.

Christin reloaded his bow, got up and stood over the red. The arrow was pointed at the red's head.

Sweating the red spit out, "you are a mutation of the devil, don't you understand! We are ministers of God doing his work, removing the abominations. We must cleanse any trace and every detail of them."

"The devil is into the details. Remember that when you meet him." Christin smiled and released his arrow.

The machete he carried was kept razor sharp for just such occasions. He promptly separated the red's head from its body. He kicked the head through the smashed window like a pro football player.

Touch down. The crowd goes wild. He never bothered with sports in his life and now he'd gone pro. He danced around the room with his hands over his head. He mimicked the sounds a crowd would make. He hissed, "Waaaaaaaa…." in a loud hushed whisper.

Okay, it was official. He had to get out more. Sam was wearing on him. Go figure.

There was light clapping over his shoulder. He turned with his crossbow at the ready and pulled the trigger.

Click.

Empty.

Oops.

A young girl of about seventeen stood clapping, a smirk playing on her lips.

Drying blood caked her face and hair.

Swollen and dark, her right eye looked like it oozed pain.

"Well done hero. Would you like to take a bow?" Christin's solitary fan, pulled her goggles down, and the room lit up with an iridescent yellow glow.

Christin's mouth plummeted open, "*Oh* shit, what happened to you? Are you okay?"

She looked like she had gone three rounds with Mike Tyson—and lost badly.

"You happened to me!" She whispered.

Christin was dumbfounded into momentary silence.

Pause…

He cleared his throat. "Ah… err…What did I do?" He gulped air and hiccupped.

The yellow smirked. "It's about time you got here," she scolded.

Chris felt abashed so stammered. "I've been umm, ahh... We've been, looking for you! Mae sent us. She said we're supposed to find you." The explanation came tumbling out. He felt twelve.

"Well you found me. Now, what are you going to do to me?"

Christin stuttered again. "We're not going to do anything *to* you. We were just going to give you a ride out west!"

He continued quickly. "Mae, this old lady, said you needed our help 'getting somewhere,' that's all." He used his fingers to illustrate quotation marks.

"So you don't want to eat me like the reds?"

She nodded in the direction of the decapitated red—it was staining the carpet.

"Sorry, but you're not to my taste. I was a vegetarian before the change. I can barely stomach eating animals. I'm not interested in human dinner."

Christin rolled his eyes.

Changing the subject would be a good idea. "What did the reds want you for anyway?"

The yellow-eyed girl frowned. "Eventually lunch, I'm sure. In the meantime, I was their lojack to find greens for their religious communion."

"Huh?" Confusion was deepening on Christin's face.

Exasperated the young girl threw her hands up into the air and walked over to the smashed window. "I can see and locate other colors. Can we leave here? This place gives me the creeps."

The girl stood still for a moment and looked out the smashed window.

Christin stood mesmerized. The girl's appearance reminded him of a searching light house's beam that could easily pierce the night. The wind caught her long sandy hair. She turned and her eyes pierced the darkened room.

He shook his head. "Ah yeah...sure. This way"

"What's your name?" She asked.

"Christin. And what's yours?"

"Griffin."

"Pleased to meet you Griffin," he bowed. He loved Shakespeare.

"Are they all dead?" Griffin looked around. "I don't see any colors anywhere in the building, but two are outside. Are they with you?"

Christin felt alarm course through his body. "One might be. My friend is probably out tracking another red!"

"Come on. Let's go see—she may need help." Chris headed for the door.

Ω Ω Ω

The thrumming drums in my head were receding. The damn red must have doubled back.

Ah, my head. The stupid band was back, and it stank like a cat on steroids. Where was that cat smell coming from?

Wait, my head wasn't strumming. It was…heartbeats—three of them. Yes. A really large heart resounded like a deep bass drum. A silver haze shrouded my slowly improving vision.

"Hey, are you all right, can you sit up?" It was a boy's voice, speaking from above me. He sounded like he was in his late teens. My hand reached out and found my two dogs standing beside my outstretched legs.

"Come on, wake up. Your dogs won't let me get near you." The boy's request was becoming more intense. I could hear the dogs growling.

My eyes opened wider and I slowly focused.

Two silver orbs stared at me. Oh brightness. "Turn your eyes down!" Arggh… I raised my hand up to shield my eyes.

I heard more growling and shuffling, then a large sniffing and huffing noise.

"Oh, sure—sorry. One second…."

The light disappeared. I blinked again. Better. I could focus unfettered. I twisted my gaze up and blinked at a tall scruffy boy of about seventeen who was standing casually by a very robust male lion.

I squeaked and back-pedaled in between the wall and dumpster. The dogs followed. I don't think I had ever squeaked in my life.

"It's okay, it's okay. This is Bruno. He's with me, and he saved your life by the way!"

I think I sensed a little indignation over my reaction. The boy was petting the scruffy mane, which was attached to a majestic great cat.

At the mention of his name Bruno sat on his hunches with a thud and licked his massive lips.

"Your lion needs a bath! Whew…" I pinched my nose.

"Yeah, well so do your dogs!" We both laughed. Mine was a nervous titter. I've never tittered in my life. I always liked to experience new things but these weird noises coming out of me was an experience I could do without. The boy held his hand out. Teak growled.

Bruno growled deeper in response. In comparison to Bruno's size, Teak's dwarfed body pushed deeper into my side and continued to growl. She tried to appear unfazed by Bruno's brutish size and growl.

Sort of. She tried, poor hairy thing.

I tried to reassure Teak with some comforting strokes. "What the hell are you doing with a lion anyway?" I was trying to recover some semblance of control over my conduct. It wasn't working—the question came out harsher then I meant.

"Well hello, my name is Garrick, pleased to meet you. And you are?" He reached out with his right hand again.

Teak growled, then Bruno growled. Teak and Oakley both ended up in my lap shaking.

"Sorry, my name is Sam. Pleased to meet you." I painfully attempted to push the dogs off my lap. A wave of nausea surfed over my body.

I felt for the crescent moon in the back of my head—its rigged outline had disappeared. Dried blood caked my matted hair. I felt my right side where I had been shot. More dried blood, but the penetrating hole in my abdomen had healed. This viral mutation had its advantages.

"You okay?" Garrick looked concerned. I was literally covered in blood, a gruesome sight. "You know. The virus is helping by the minute."

The dogs had reclaimed my lap. I pushed the nervous dogs off and made to stand. I felt a little dizzy.

The dizziness and nausea was passing quickly. I was almost back to my old GI Jane self. "So Garrick, where did you come from?"

"Idaho!"

"Oh geez Garrick, I mean, why are you here?"

"Well, I ran into an old, blind black woman a little while back, and she told me to find the yellow," he said nonchalantly, like that happened every day. "Well, I said 'sure,' because I felt bad—Bruno almost ate her horse Bob." He grinned sheepishly at his *pet* lion. "And well, I wasn't doing much. I was heading west anyway." He continued to eye his big cat affectionately.

"You met Mae? Honestly, she sent the second string—that woman!" The dirt and dried blood on my clothes got a furious brushing.

He shuffled his feet in the gravel, his head down, hands in the back of his pants. "Um, excuse me ma'am, but by all accounts I think you're the second string. We saved you!"

I chuckled. I had offended his manhood. "Yes, you're right Garrick. You are my hero!"

"Actually Bruno is." He reached over and proudly scratched Bruno behind his ear. Bruno huffed a couple times and started purring.

"May, I thank him?" Holding my hand up indicating I wanted to pet him.

"Oh sure. If you're with me, he thinks you're part of his pride." Garrick's chest pushed out a little.

"Pride, hey?" I looked at Bruno's large teeth then looked at my hand and wondered just how attached to it I was. I stretched my hand out tentatively and let Bruno sniff it—his teeth were huge. I had never been this close to a lion in my life but always secretly wanted to be.

Bruno sniffed and sneezed on my hand. Great, cat snot.

The big cat gave his big mane a shake. We started laughing. Bruno looked at Garrick with an admonishing side-long glance that said, "She smells weird!"

I reached for Bruno's ear. He pushed his head against my hand. A step behind me, Teak whined.

I turned to look at Teak. She looked nervous. "You wanna meet the big kitty Teak, Oakley?"

They cocked their heads. Kitty, did you say kitty?

Then they sneezed, and Teak stretched. What was with all the sneezing? Did we smell that bad?

Oakley leaned toward Bruno and stretched, sniffed then yawned out a squeak. Teak pushed against my legs and eyed the big kitty.

Chewing my lower lip I asked, "Garrick how did you avoid the reds?"

"Oh we just got to town, in fact we saw you drive by us."

I remembered the lion lying on a parked car. "I think I saw Bruno. But I thought he was just a fugitive from a local zoo."

"Yes he does have that fugitive hint about him." Garrick laughed at his lion. I was scratching the lion's forehead. I think I hit his sweet spot because he was starting to purr.

I was enraptured. I was actually petting a lion. "When I saw him, I thought he was the biggest lion I had ever seen."

Garrick looked satisfied. "Yes he eats well, he is spoiled."

I turned my attention to Garrick. "I have friends. I have to check on a couple of them and find a couple more—wanna come?"

"Sure. As I said, I wasn't doing anything, and I still have to find the yellow. I promised the old lady I would try!" He smiled a boyish grin and said. "Let's go, you lead."

We made it back to the house in no time. Adam had a panicked expression on his face and almost shot us as we came through the door.

I did tell him to shoot at anything that moved. The boys both looked a little haggard and twitchy when my new friends and I walked through the kitchen door. I wondered whether that was in reaction to the lion, the silver or the expectation of being killed by a red?

Probably all of the above—poor Adam, he was kind of delicate. At least he didn't throw up. He was looking a little pale though.

Adam gave me a pair of latex gloves pulled from their medical cache of supplies. I put the gloves on and helped Cory take care of his shoulder. Fortunately the bullet made a clean path through his shoulder. Time will tell how well it would heal and what kind of range of motion he'd have. I was no surgeon.

Their house was well stocked with everything you'd need for any kind of end of the world scenario. A little dose of antibiotics, a shot of morphine and Cory was passed out on the couch. His tetanus shot was up to date—ah, the joys of nursing. It felt good to make a genuine difference. I could work with blood and guts.

Once Cory started snoring logs I heard Christin pull up in the Rover. I hadn't realized how tensely I was wound until relief flooded my body, knowing Christin was safely pulling up in the Rover. I realized my relief was directionally proportional to having Christin nearby.

The lion stayed out on the porch as 'look out' as Garrick put it. I think the lion didn't like being cooped up in a house. Garrick heard the Rover and went out to make sure Christin didn't become lunch. When he walked through the door, Christin and I embraced with enthusiasm. That was too close I could of lost him.

"Arnold."

"Jane."

We started laughing as we separated from our embrace but continued to hold each other's hands.

"I thought your name was Sam?" We both turned to look at Garrick with smiles on our faces.

"And I thought your name was Christin?" A young pretty blond teenage girl peeked from around the open door.

"It's a long story!" Christin smirked.

I eyed the new face. "And who might you be?"

"Oh this is Griffin—she prefers Griff!" Christin piped in, smiling. "Oh and she's the yellow" he announced proudly.

Griff pulled her goggles off and the room was cast in a soft yellow light.

"Cool, nice job," I murmured. Everyone just stared at the yellow, including me.

We almost had a rainbow going on, as the room danced with colorful light. We decided to keep our goggles on. The light was distracting.

CHAPTER SIXTEEN:
The Yellow Brick Road

"A dreamer is one who can only find his way by moonlight, and his punishment is that he sees the dawn before the rest of the world."
-Oscar Wilde (1854 - 1900)

We packed up the vehicles and our newly adopted traveling companions. Another Rover was appropriated. Yeah, we could make a commercial. "What vehicle would you choose to drive if the world ended? Land Rover—what else?"

We also grabbed a big blue Chevy Hemi, Garrick and Bruno's new ride—the cat liked lying in the open truck bed. Cory and Adam took the new Rover. Griff came with us.

In actuality, she kind of bounced around visiting everyone—even Bruno. She talked freely, and it was easy to be in her company. We inquired if she had ever met Mae or knew why Mae would send hunting parties to recover her. She had no clue.

We asked after Griff's life, hoping to get any inkling as to why Mae designated her as essential element to the future of mankind. Griffin grew up in a rural farming town. Her parents were hippies and they liked to protest. It was during one of these protests that Griff got shot in the head.

The incident occurred during a peaceful protest against the big oil companies who wanted to invade the Bering Sea. The bullet was still lodged in her brain. She had died twice on the operating table. The bullet had caused swelling and bleeding in her brain. Several emergency surgeries had saved her life. She had remained in a medically induced coma for a month. A year of rehab had eliminated the atrophy in her muscles and her inability to speak. She had just turned twelve when she started walking again. Only two years had passed since the bullet had pierced her innocent world as she was taking her first unaided steps. She continued to walk with a limp and had limited strength in her right arm. It wasn't until the virus infected and transformed her that it erased any remnants of being brain injured. This would have been a joyous moment for the young girl, except her family and the world had been erased as well.

Since the reaping she'd been inclined to just wander unsure what to do next. She had lost everyone and everything she had ever known. Griff had watched the greens from a distance but chose not to approach them since they appeared erratic and violent—sound choice. The reds found her instead.

Surrounded and outnumbered she surrendered to their will. Their will revolved around religion. They were religious extremists who had come together under a common goal, to do God's work. Jones Town converts. They somehow decided hunting and eating colors would bring them closer to God's grace. The flock always finds each other. Flocking moron!

They believed they were cleansing the world of abominations—too bad they didn't start with themselves. God's so-called-tools ate the evil. In their confused minds, communing daily brought them closer to their God. They liked to eat the eyes first.

The only reason Griff was still alive was her ability to track colors. Fortunately, she only directed them to the greens. She couldn't differentiate between colors. Griff had seen our blips on her radar since we entered the city. She had kept the reds busy in their insane quest for greens.

The reds had no idea there were other colors out there. We asked her why she hadn't set the reds on us. Her answer was matter-of-fact: it had seemed wrong. Negative experiences with the greens cemented her resolve, that it wasn't a horrendous crime to set the reds on them.

Her sense of us, made her hesitate. She had watched us moving around and thought our movement was particular. She said that our blips on her radar had purpose.

Something was different about the two blips so she had continued to watch our activity but didn't let the reds in on it. Griff couldn't distinguish between colors—"I can sense a color like a spot on a radar screen." On the day of our arrival into the city, the reds knew she had been holding back. They had beaten her badly.

Our trip back to Newton was slower. We couldn't drive night and day like we had prior to the adoption of our human cohorts. Then there was Bruno. He needed to eat, and so did we. My God we ate so much. I think we ate as much as the big cat.

Garrick told us late one night while we were gathered around a fire that Bruno had been rescued from the circus. He had been born in captivity. He apparently didn't know how to hunt. His antics could have fooled me. The big cat had dispatched my red easily enough. As a trained performer, he did as he was directed. Garrick could command him with slight hand gestures. Bruno was just an actor. He wasn't a real lion; he only played one. The lion hadn't killed the red, Garrick had. Bruno had distracted and discombobulated the red while Garrick separated the red from his head.

Garrick came from a family of animal trainers.

The family trained big cats. Their services helped zoo and circus animals earn their keep. The occasional movie role added work for the family's own pride of big cats. When Garrick was a boy, Bruno had accidently knocked him over during a training exercise. The young male lion had dashed the boy's head into a training stool. Garrick's family, a sturdy lot, always told the story laughing and grinning. Garrick's mother never failed to blanche during the retelling.

After the initial mishap, the boy had stood up, brushed himself off and hugged the cat, telling the upset lion he was okay.

A moment later the boy swayed and fell over onto the lion mid-hug. He was unconscious and barely breathing. Bruno loved the boy and so protected Garrick in his vulnerable state. He wouldn't let anyone come near the boy. Garrick's dad didn't give him a choice—he quickly sedated the lion. The lion curled around the young boy as he closed his heavy lids. His immature mane shielded the boy.

Garrick died on the operating table. An emergency craniotomy released the pressure that a cerebral bleed was exerting on his brain. This drastic procedure saved his life.

Garrick lost all his family to the reaping. All he had left in the world was the lion. Bruno and Garrick were best friends—he couldn't leave him on the ranch. Bruno would have eventually died of starvation. Male lions didn't really hunt. Bruno had been hand fed all his life so never had any training in order to hunt for his survival

When Garrick and Bruno met Mae, Bruno was just "attempting to ride Bob."

"Really, he wouldn't have hurt that horse." Garrick crossed his heart. My and Christin's eyes bugged out a bit before Garrick could explain. Bruno used to ride the horses in the circus—he loved it. Poor Bob had almost had a heart attack.

It seemed that during their chance meeting old Mae hadn't been any more forthcoming with information with Garrick than she had been with us. The only declaration the old black woman made to team one and team two was—save the girl.

That old lady had some explaining to do.

CHAPTER SEVENTEEN:
Lady Sings the Blues

"Life is what we make of it, always has been, always will be."
-Grandma Moses (1860 - 1961)

Mae had said we weren't welcome in Newton but Cory needed a break from all the driving we were doing and we had questions for Ms. Mae. We'd get in and get out. So what if we weren't welcome? We'd make our own welcome mat.

We were standing in the middle of a field and Bruno's roaring was pulling me from my internal conflict about going back to Newton. The lion was standing over the deer we had just killed. He was looking around and huffing. My thought exactly. I felt huffy. We were going to see Mae.

Our little caravan took the same route back as Chris and I had come. I doubted new cars would magically appear. Christin and I had already cleared the route. Griffin reported no colours around for miles.

It was an uneventful trip until we got to the big red dump truck's valet parking site. The monster that had previously made us stop and park was on its side—hanging half in and half out of a ditch.

I craned my head out my broken window and asked Chris. "What do you think happened to it?" Chris just shook his head as we drove on cautiously.

Griffin sat in the back seat concentrating. She confirmed that she didn't detect any colors in the area. So we drove our caravan into town. The once naturally majestic town of Newton smouldered before our eyes.

We found quite a few bodies, but no Mae. I felt simultaneously relieved and anxious. What happened here? Where was everyone? We saw a lot of horse tracks. I didn't remember the town really using horses.

Griffin sensed something east—it was moving away from us. None of the group wanted to linger around the devastated town. We turned ourselves west.

"Did you smell it? Back in town" I asked Christin, my eyes focused forward. A rotting, unnatural odour had permeated the town center.

"Yes," Christin answered doggedly. "What do you think it was?"

"I really don't want to find out." I felt chilled—weird.

Queue the eerie music. The hell with that, I popped in the Beach Boys. I would love to be a California girl right about now. We made it to the coast without incident. Griff suggested we head south from here.

The ocean was fantastic. I had forgotten how it smelled, how the sound of the ocean equalled peace. I inhaled deeply and forgot for just a moment the horror of the end of days.

I didn't know lions could swim. Teak and Oakley joined Bruno as he sprinted up and down the beach. Teak kept trying to climb up Bruno's back when the lion ventured into the surf. Personally, I think she was trying to drown him. To no avail—the terrier did not succeed. The cat and dogs were warming up to each other, but Teak's memory was long.

It was great having Griffin on board because she let us know if there were any colors around. No colors meant safety. Assumption was going to be the death of me.

It was a beautiful starry night, and we had decided to camp out on the beach. The colors found they could close their eyes and rest. We didn't need to, but it gave us the much-needed opportunity to process. Tonight I was in the tent concentrating on the rhythmic crash of the ocean's waves. My own personal wave machine pulsated as a heart thumped, crash, roar, crash, snore and crash. Teak snored.

The rumble of several truck engines, gunned at full throttle interrupted and superseded my wave machine. I sat up so fast; I almost went through the roof of the tent. Bruno roared as I scrambled out of my cocoon of sanctuary.

Three pairs of white truck lights were bouncing haphazardly down the beach. Numerous green orbs—too many to count—flashed behind the bouncing trucks.

Everyone sprang into action. Our gear was mostly loaded already. We were always prepared for anything. Christin had been a boy scout.

Chris and I leaped into the Rover, the dogs on our heels. Chris pulled out and readied the rifle while I drove. We headed directly toward the bounding array of lights, both white and green.

The other Rover and Hemi trailed behind us. I'm sure they thought we were crazy. We were steering straight into trouble. All right, I was steering straight into trouble.

"Do you know what you're doing Sam?" Christin looked skeptical. He was deciding between the rifle and crossbow.

The dogs were hanging out the windows, enjoying the unexpected car ride and cool beach air. It's all fun and games until someone loses an eye. "Teak, Oakley, lay down now!" I yelled. Begrudgingly they complied.

"What are you doing Sam?" Chris was gripping the "holy shit" handle with fervor.

"I'm aiming us into the torpedo. In the movie, *The Hunt for Red October*, they did it!" I screamed over the roar of the wind. I was grinning. Chris wasn't.

I glanced at Christin's cynical face. Huh. What no faith? We had to get these windows fixed. They were so distracting.

"Sam, have you finally lost your grip? That was a submarine and a movie!" He gave me that, you've-lost-your-mind look again.

"Hmmff!" I glowered.

"Sam, you watched too much television, honestly. You have to be kidding me!" His head kept darting from me to the scene unfolding before us and back at me again.

"You're going to get us killed!" He screamed now white knuckling the broken window.

"Nah, it worked in the movie." I turned to him and smiled my best, devil-may-care grin.

Chris looked at me, then out the front window, and then shrugged. A devil-may-care grin started to spread on his face as well. "Okay Jane!" We're getting to know each other so well! I could feel Chris surrender to the crazy and bizarre course his life was now on.

The three trucks parted to our oncoming approach. We hit the pack of greens full on. Rovers have amazing high and hardy suspensions. We heard a couple of solid thumps pass under the Rover. We didn't slow down. They also got great traction as well.

I checked my mirror and saw the rest of our group, headlights bobbing along behind us. A male green landed on our hood—he looked pissed. He was wearing a tattered suit and tie.

"Arnold, clean the windshield please!"

"Yes, Jane! My pleasure!" Chris leaned out with the rifle and cleaned my windshield. He was an excellent co-pilot.

I saw the Hemi behind me tilt to the right. I bet Garrick didn't have bug issues, what with his jacked up Hemi. I heard a lion's roar—he also had an excellent co-pilot to boot.

My Rover was aimed for another green. She jumped the length of our Rover. Wow. Superb air time—agile even. She landed on the hood of the Hemi. It swerved and sped up to us. Garrick and Griff pulled up alongside us, waving and smiling. Kids. Wow again, they were very well adjusted, considering. Teak and Oakley started barking at Bruno. He roared back.

Garrick pointed to the female green. A gesture that said, "Could you rectify that please?"

We looked at the female green. She was splayed out on the hood of their truck, attempting to surf. She looked petrified.

A lion's roar can be an intimidating sound. Or maybe it was the breakneck speed we doing down the beach. Weird, I know.

Christin aimed his rifle at the green. She pushed off the hood and rolled. The following Rover's headlights jabbed upward into the darkness after hitting a sand bar colliding with the escaping green. Rovers, all-terrain vehicles, green speed bumps were not an issue.

I turned the Rover to face the flattened chaos and idled. The Hemi pulled alongside us.

"You're friggin crazzzzy Sam!" Griff was smiling and checking her shoulder.

"Apparently I watch too many movies." I rolled my eyes and motioned to Christin.

"I didn't have cable growing up. You're so lucky," she gushed.

I think I had a fan club. One member, it's a start.

"What happened, why didn't you sense them?" I asked Griff.

"I…we…um…" she was starting to flush and looked to Garrick for help.

He had his hands clenched to the steering wheel and was focused straight ahead, a red flush was creeping up his chin. He cleared his throat, "We, umm…were making, ah…out. I guess, ah…well, I distracted her. It won't happen again." The young man didn't turn his head to look at us, as the red hue finished overtaking his pale complexion.

"Well, umm…yeah, carry on. Try to stay focused. Um, let's keep driving for a while." And with that brilliant response I sped off. Christin's laughter echoed in the Rover.

We pulled alongside Adam and Cory's Rover. "You guys okay?" I assessed Cory's grimacing face. He removed his hand that had been pressing against his shoulder wound. Fresh blood had seeped into the white bandages I had applied less then an hour ago.

"Yeah, but sandbars, greens and air time don't mix with healing bullet holes." He smiled weakly. Amazing, my new hearing allowed me to hear his statement perfectly even though he was clenching his teeth and mumbling.

"Adam, can you give Cory another shot of morphine, or do you want me to do it?" I lifted my chin and nodded to the front of the Rover.

"Ah you have green stuck in your grill!" I said.

Chris leaped out the passenger side. "I'll get it Sam go help Adam." Teak growled, her sniffing nose pointed steadfastly at the lush khaki border lining the beach.

A green suddenly burst through the underbrush, it was targeting Chris's open door. I pulled out the loaded crossbow and aimed toward the Rover's open passenger door. Teak leaped out of the exposed door just as the Hemi's front bumper obliterated the charging greens approach.

I froze. Teak was…"Oh my God Teak!" I shrieked and made to lunge for the open door. The hairy good-for-nothing love of my life jumped back into the passenger seat. My heart beat once.

She was sitting, panting and shooting sporadic glances at me. "What are you yelling for?" This question was smeared on her long hairy, grey and black face. I dove for her, fervent hugs and kisses were exchanged. Oakley couldn't resist the love bomb and joined in. It was a pure display of unconditional love, tears and kisses.

The walkie-talkie buzzed to life. I grabbed it.

In the last town we decided to refresh our ammo and ended up absconding with a new means of communication—an armload of walkie-talkies. This simple means of communication made it easier to convey information between vehicles without stopping. Very important things like bathroom breaks, dinner breaks and, "Hey, did you see that giraffe?" Were conveyed.

Garrick's voice artificially buzzed in the Rover. "Sorry if I startled you, the green came out of nowhere. It wasn't in the pack that we ran over on the beach—over."

He had no clue that I'd almost had a heart attack and nervous breakdown—simultaneously.

I allowed a sigh of relief to escape my chest. I freed the dogs from my death grip before I keyed the radio. "No problem, see any sign of the trucks or colors?"

"Yeah, Griff says one color but it's heading away from us. Just one—over."

"Be right there!" I started to shake. That was too close, almost losing Teak again.

"Ah—over! You gotta say over Sam." Griff brusquely informed me about radio etiquette. Kids. They were going to be the death of me.

I gave Cory a shot of morphine and checked his bandage. Then I shakily got into the passenger seat with Teak perched on my lap. Christin wordlessly took the wheel. We continued our southerly course.

The walkie-talkie buzzed to life, breaking the silence. My now steady hand reached for it. The walkie crackled again. It was Cory, "Hey guys, should we go after the trucks? They could need help."

"They could be trouble! They might not like Varian's." Garrick's two cents piped in. We had become a democracy. Geez, Varians—aliens from Venus. Only a teenage boy could come up with our new title. Geez.

"Garrick did you get cable growing up"

"Yes."

"Carry on." I said. Christin and I were grinning. "Kids—got to love them."

"They might not like lions" Adam, piped in. "Or, tigers or bears." Griff's added her two cents.

"Oh my!" Christin finished.

The radio crackled with intermittent laughter. We were all so losing it.

"I don't care either way. I just don't want anyone to get hurt." I chewed on my bottom lip. I could see Christin nodding.

"Anyone feel strongly about going after the strangers?"

"We were all strangers once," Cory's voice quietly chirped in.

We turned around and tried to track the path of the fleeing trucks.

It didn't take long to locate the source of our search. We pulled alongside a new red truck. It was upside down, no heartbeats were heard. We didn't stop, just rolled by. Remember, certain images you didn't want to keep.

The next truck was blue and laying on its side, no heartbeats again. We slowly eased by the carnage. A bloodied arm protruded through the front windshield.

The walkie-talkies were quiet. We drove on in silence. A disheartened weight filled our hearts.

A green truck was heading toward us.

"Sam! Color!" Griff exclaimed in a static haze.

"Sooner, would have been better!" I responded and braced myself.

"Sorry, new at this thing!"

"It's okay, I know. Sorry sweets."

I gripped the walkie-talkie. "Be cautious, hang back!"

Christin and I advanced and pulled up beside the truck.

I didn't hear a heartbeat.

"Christin?"

"I know. I don't hear it either."

Orange light spewed from the truck's cab. A middle-aged looking guy, probably fortyish, with short brown hair pulled his eye coverings free as we pulled alongside his truck. "Hi, didn't want to surprise you. Sorry to have brought those green-eyes down on you." He regarded his steering wheel and fumbled with a dark pair of goggles.

Good beginning—we used the same lingo.

"We got ambushed going through the city. My name is Ray Danylak." He extended his right hand.

"Amazing, some color. Could you put your shades back on, please?" I raised my hand to shield my eyes. I noticed Chris didn't draw his gaze away. Ah, ever watchful my Christin. We didn't need any unwanted attention drawn to us. The greens or ill-disposed uninfected could be around.

"Oh sure, absolutely. Sorry." Ray quickly replaced his goggles.

"Hi Ray, nice to meet you. Ah, you okay?" I eyed his shaking hands. "Where did the greens go?" I asked more gently.

Ray was scanning the area in a quirky, jerky motion. He stuttered, "Well, I lost the few that were tracking me." Ray started looking over his shoulder.

His movements were contagious. Chris and I both checked over our shoulders. I grabbed the walkie-talkie. "Griff, any colors around?"

"Just the one sitting beside you!" Sass, they start so young.

"Ray, take a breath. You're going to give me a heart attack. It's okay, we're all right." I took my glasses off. Blue light flared in the Rover's cabin.

I smiled in Ray's direction. "Do you think we're like in a group acid trip and we all somehow got trapped in a *Twilight Zone* rerun?"

Christin took his goggles off. "See safe!"

Chris turned to me and gave me a dirty look and said, "Don't pick on the poor man Sam. Geesh!"

Just then, Garrick, Griff and Bruno pulled up saving me from further dirty looks from Christin. The lion did not go over well with Ray. Once we managed to peel Ray off the roof of his truck the questioning resumed.

Ray was leaning on his open truck door. "The other trucks, did you find my friends?" Ray asked while keeping an eye on Bruno, who decided at this very moment to clean his large claws. Do these animals do these things on purpose? I should have paid more attention to animal planet. I shook my head and stared straight ahead.

Ray gawked intently, his gaze bouncing between mine, Christin's and Bruno's quiet forms. He continued. "The three people in the other trucks were descent folks. They let me tag along," he turned away from our glowing stares and muttered to himself absently. He stopped scanning for a moment and looked down at his hands.

"We we're going to grab a boat and find an island somewhere." Ray decided to turn his back on Bruno. I raised my eyebrows. If he was going to die, he didn't want to be tortured by the vision of it.

Bruno yawned behind him.

Ray shivered and continued. "Since the change and well, the world, ending, I didn't know what to do with myself." His shivering seemed unrelenting.

"I was just wandering around, going from city to city looking for survivors, when I came across Merrick, Logan and Janic. They were from Canada, vacationing in Montana. We didn't have a lot of time to bond. They were real civil with me. They weren't infected…"

He rested his head in his open palms.

"On our way to the coast we were trying to figure out what had happened to the world and see if we could find anyone else alive…" his story railed off into a whisper.

"You find any answers or anyone?" I asked.

"Some. Is it okay if we start driving and talk later? The greens make me nervous." Ray eyed Bruno again. The large cat stretched, displaying his unsheathed claws. Honestly Bruno was going to cause the man to stroke out. Garrick looked at Bruno and chuckled softly.

Garrick's not a mean spirited person. He just knew Bruno would never harm anyone—unless of course he was asking for it. Garrick would be the deciding factor.

Ray had already climbed into his truck and was turning the engine over. "Oh, I take it you want to come with us? You don't even know where were going or who we are?" I looked at Ray with a little surprise.

He sighed heavily and said, "Well I'm all alone in this world. I could use the company, and I'd like that lion to be on my side. If it's all right with your group I'd like to come."

Christin and I looked at each other and shrugged. "Sure, we'll talk later. I'm Sam and this is Christin. We'll do further introductions later." I tossed him a walkie-talkie.

"Okay, I look forward to chatting with you guys. By the way, which direction are you guys going?" He flipped the walkie-talkie on. Static erupted.

"South. We're heading along the coast!"

"Okay, thanks." He waved. We smiled. With that we added another member to our group.

Life on the road was uneventful. We ate, sort of slept and hunted. We took it slow and avoided any civilization bigger than a town. Even then we stayed on the outskirts of the towns. We needed a break from marauding greens or encounters with unfriendly humans. Town after town passed us by. Our rear view mirrors reflected distant civilizations devoid of the living.

We found the roads were a little more obstructed as our caravan progressed further south. A little auto rearranging was called for.

"Ray, can you put that Toyota over by the crushed Ford truck?" I was a nurse, not a firefighter. What did I know of clearing a major collision? The pile of cars we had ummm… *arranged,* teetered precariously.

"Ahh, Sam…" Chris was eyeing, my pyramid of steel a little sceptically.

Distracted, I answered, "Yes Christin…?" The tall man stood with one hand on his hip and the other scratching his grey temple, "Why are you stacking the cars?" I noticed Garrick was adding a grey Subaru to the pile.

"Ummm, in case someone comes by. They'll know someone is still alive…"

"Sure, I guess that makes sense, but couldn't we just leave a note or a sign?" Christin sighed and kicked the dirt.

"Sure I guess, but this pile would get anyone's attention!" I stood back and eyed my steel traffic sign. A stacked pile of cars led to an arrow that pointed south. The arrow was made of blue cars. Apparently that was the number one color selected by American auto buyers. "Plus everyone was bored being cooped up, driving and all that!"

Chris grinned. "Ahh…yeah. It was kind of fun tossing those cars around. We needed a good stretching!"

"Life feels so surreal, like we're in a dream. Is this really real? I keep expecting to wake up and find out that I slept in, that I'll be late for work and that my biggest concern would be deciding what color to paint my living room!" Tears started to stream down my face, my arms hugged my shaking body.

Christin grabbed me and held me tight. "It's okay Sam. We'll be all right. Just breathe hun. Just breathe one breath at a time. I got you!" I cried intensely into his solid shoulder. After a few choking sobs, I started hiccupping. I pulled away. A darkening stain on his red jacket revealed my melt down. I wiped snot away and apologized.

"You can't apologize. I'm due for my melt down, in say…" He looked at his watch. "Can I use your shoulder in three days?" We laughed quietly.

I stared at his serious face. "What are we going to do Christin?"

He rubbed his square jaw. "Let's take this one day at a time. We'll figure it out. Who knows what the next turn of the road will bring? Maybe we'll find some sort of occupied civilization, and we can start that Hari Krishna commune!"

I punched him in the stomach. Ass.

He started laughing, then fell and curled on the ground, clenching his stomach.

"You big hairy donkey's ass!" I groaned.

In a choked whispering laugh he replied, "Not as hairy though!"

I stood over him with my hands on my hips. "I beg to diff—"

His leg shot out and knocked me to the ground. "Be careful, donkeys kick!" We started to laugh loudly.

"Hey you guys, a little help here? This is hard work!" Ray stood with his hands on his hips, dirty and sweaty, his shirt hanging out the back. We just started laughing harder, tears intermingling with our raucous laughter.

We spent more time taking breaks than we did driving. We didn't push ourselves hard. Subconsciously, maybe we didn't want to see what was around the next corner.

Our caravan had gone around the outskirts of a small town we had come upon—we camped by a small lake. It was a serene cool night. A breeze barely ruffled the tent flaps. Crickets chirped, frogs sang their garbled mating call—spring had arrived.

We were huddled around a small campfire. The remnants of a venison roast sizzled lazily on the spit. Individual conversations melted away as Ray started talking about how he had escaped New York.

Ray had barely made it out of New York—a long journey to the coast by anyone's standards. He described a few green encounters and meeting a woman who had white eyes. The white-eyed woman had proven to be very unstable and fled when Ray attempted to approach her. Perhaps she had gone over the edge of sanity and wasn't returning any time soon.

The elderly woman had run off screaming. "The sun, the sun. It's burning me!" when Ray had tried speaking to her. So sad. Ray was shaking his head while twisting his ever-moving hands.

"I just wanted to help her!" He frowned and stared into the crackling fire.

Ray had skirted the outer rim of most cities. Too nervous to investigate any traces of human activity. His infrequent detection of humans resulted with them scurrying off like rats hiding in the shadows. Ray decided it was pointless to try and make contact with uninfected humans. He now knew fear when he smelled it.

Fear was running rampant—it even cloyed to his own skin. Ray was a man of science, a molecular biologist. The scientist was having a hard time wrapping his logic around the chaos of the times. He had no answers to alleviate his anxiety of the unknown.

We helped him out with what information we had. We retold Mae's tale. He nodded his agreement with the newly articulated facts. "Dead? We had to have died sometime in our lives?"

"Yes. Have you ever died Ray?" I quietly asked.

Ray stared into the fire. After a few moments of silence, he said. 'Yes I have died three times, so they told me."

"They?" Christin softly continued, "Who are they Ray?"

"The emergency room physicians."

Chris stared at Ray then asked patiently. "And? What happened?"

Ray took a deep sigh and began his tale of his demise.

Ω Ω Ω

It was a rainy dark Sunday morning as I walked into the emergency department. The department was empty, except for a couple of nurses at the triage desk. They had a student nurse shadowing that day. They were all so very pleasant and informative. They showed the student how to triage a patient with my symptoms.

I felt weak and dizzy. The nurses said "I looked a little grey." They did a full preliminary work up on me: vital signs, a sugar level test, electrocardiogram, blood work and put an IV lock in my arm. They were very thorough. I dropped dead in their waiting room five minutes later.

I woke up freezing and had a tube in my lungs. I could hear beeping alarms all around me.

I groggily looked around the room. A nurse with a soft concerned face leaned over me and told me I was going to be okay and that they were getting the doctor. I must have looked panicked because she put her hand on my forehead and shhhed me gently. I closed my eyes until I heard my name.

A stocky bespectacled bald man stood beside my bed. "Hello Mr. Danylak. I'm Dr. Haager. You gave us quite a scare. We found that you have some heart issues. I'll keep this short and we'll talk more later when you're stronger. Your heart stopped three times. The electrical activity in your heart was blocked. So we inserted a pacemaker to help your heart keep beating."

I attempted to reach for my chest, but my hands were tied to the bed.

"It's okay sir, we applied those restraints so you wouldn't accidently pull any wires or tubes out." I put my hands down and looked at the doctor. I wanted to hug him. He saved my life.

"We're going to take you to the operating room to insert a permanent pacemaker into your chest."

I nodded understanding.

"If everything goes as planned, you'll have this pacemaker for the rest of your life and you should be okay."

I nodded again.

"It's a good thing your uncle made you come in to get checked out. Your aunt and uncle are in the quiet room. I'll go get them so you can have a quick visit before you go for surgery.

Dr. Haager smiled and patted me on the shoulder. "You're a lucky man."

I did not feel like a lucky man. I quess it was all about perspective.

Ω Ω Ω

Ray pulled his shirt open and exposed the left side of his chest. A small bulge the size of a silver dollar pushed up from under his skin.

Ray tapped it and said. "I think it still works, but I haven't felt any electrical zaps since I transformed. Maybe the virus fixed my heart. I guess the virus can't have a defective host carrying it around." He chuckled at the irony.

I didn't see anything amusing in his story. It must be his way of coping. "How old were you when this happened Ray?"

"Twenty-two."

I looked surprised. "Crap, you are lucky they caught it. If there are powers that be, someone was definitely looking out for you. If you weren't in the hospital when your heart became fully blocked, you would never have survived." I said.

Sarcastically he said. "Yes, I'm so lucky to have survived."

We were all quiet for a moment. I decided to change the subject. "What do you think of the pandemic Ray?"

"Yes, well what you told me makes perfect sense. I've just never seen a virus alter a host to this degree. I mean, we were finding new viruses every week. Most unidentifiable, but this one somehow managed an ideal mode of transmission!" Ray's stubbly chin was apparently very itchy, for he scratched at it vigorously as he stared off in a contemplative gaze.

A virus of unknown pedigree and mechanisms had found a mode of transmission akin to a Ferrari to expose the world. "That's what's so unusual. We've never had a combination of a virus with such virulence be able to find such an effective mode of transmission. Say Ebola for example, it was virulent but wasn't as easy to contract and it had a long incubation period. So we always had time to react to an outbreak. This virus was ingested by so many around the world and was easy to contract. Not to mention it has a short incubation period before onset of symptoms."

Damn. It was an unspoken law by all in the scientific community that nature couldn't move *that* fast, for Pete's sake.

Ray continued. "It was totally manmade. We did it. We gave it a vehicle, and then opened the world for it to drive on."

I choked a little on that piece of information. Everything wanted to survive and we were the virus's lifeboat, its nirvana. It mutated some of us, into different variations of ourselves. We became a host for its survival—we had become a Varian.

The voracious contaminant continued to circumvent any hindrance to its propagation. It would survive. The vicious circle would not end, unless we variations were ended. I winced at the thought.

"What hypothesis would explain the varying colors of our irises?" I directed my question to the quiet Ray.

"I'm not sure about that. I can only guess really. I haven't really been able to study the…phenomenon." There was something strangely private about his expression—Ray was lost in his thoughts.

I rolled my eyes. Ray was a pure scientist. He must have felt uncomfortable speculating. A solid hypothesis required empirical facts, and Ray hesitated to hazard at a simple deduction. A guess—was beyond his capabilities.

"Your best guess Ray," I urged gently. He scratched his stubbly face again. He was painfully forming an educated guess. Painful was putting it mildly. Imagine someone in a dentist chair weighing the pain in his teeth against the inconvenience of putting the procedure off. Ray looked like that.

"Well, from what you and I've gathered, the change could only happen in someone who has died….right?" I nodded.

"The color seems to reflect something in a person's psyche. The virus transmutes it to the eyes, maybe for mating purposes. You know—maybe likeminded people are attracted to each other. Or it's like a peacock the colors are there to draw potential mates in." Chris and I both looked at Garrick and Griff. They were holding hands.

Ray sighed heavily—tooth pulled.

Might as well pull the other tooth, while he's here, Ray continued. "Perhaps it has something to do with hormones? It's just conjecture. I'm no expert on the virus. I don't think anyone could be…an expert…" He coughed and drew his full attention back to the fire. Everyone listening to Ray followed suit. "It would take years of study. We had only days… before…" Ray whispered.

The tension of the group sung loudly in the quiet night. As if in response to the surrounding energy, the campfire crackled noisily, punctuating the end of the discussion. We all retired to our tents. Garrick and Bruno took first watch in the back of the Hemi.

The next morning we hunted deer. We had a group of hungry beasts to feed, and—oh yeah—Bruno ate a lot too. Bruno was fast becoming a hunting machine. He'd attempted to run down a lone deer, but because he was alone without a pride of lionesses, his endurance waned. We stood back, watched and encouraged his solitary attempt. Poor guy—just didn't have the back up to bring his quarry down.

We Varians became his special pride of lionesses, corralling the deer so the big cat could be crowned the king of the forest. This simple act increased his confidence tenfold. Now every time we hunted we often had to playfully wrestle the deer from his clenched jaws. The king insisted on dragging the deer between his front legs, parading his dominance over all he surveyed. He often tripped on the carcass and got a face full of deer. Ah the King of Beasts in all his glory. The big cat was pretending he hadn't tripped and was casually chewing on the hump of the deer. We decided to take our share before it became Purina Cat Chow.

The needs of the animals and humans alike eased the monotony of the trip. If the situation wasn't so macabre, it could almost be deemed enjoyable—almost. Variations of humanity or not, our mutation connected us to our remaining humanity. We were living, and we had found a community.

Griffin came to my side. "We're moving closer to something, I can feel it. We should be careful." A furtive look accompanied her whisper.

"How many do you think?" I scanned the horizon.

"I don't know. It's hard to get a lock on the source. It's fragmented..." I could sense her frustration. Her forehead was knotted, and she rubbed her temples. Urgency laced her apprehension. Griff wanted to keep her pack safe. The young girl had managed on numerous occasions to steer us away from encounters with colors. It appeared humans and colors were rare, mostly. "Maybe, ah...limit your make out sessions with Garrick. Which might help you know...ah...find some balance." I grimaced as I saw her face darken with concentration. I witnessed the beauty of her innocence. Her expression changed as the night changed light into dark. She so badly, wanted to help.

"Garrick is really sweet! You guys are so cute together!" I said uncomfortably, while I played with my jean holes. Her dark expression changed back to the light of a soft grinning monkey. I should write hallmark cards. Geez my inner cheese ball was seeping through.

"Sure." Griff bowed her head as redness crept up her neck. "It's just… well, he's just so yummy, and I don't feel so alone when I'm with him." The young woman lifted her head and a full out smile erupted.

I smiled in return. "You're not alone hun, we've got you. In fact, you need a break. Go hang with Garrick. I don't want you to focus on anything but some fun, all right!" I pressed her hand.

I'm-a-hapless-fool- in-love grin spread further over her face.

The infectious grin made my smile grow. "I'm sure—you'll find ahh…balance." I eyed Garrick leaning on Bruno not far from us. I could tell he was subtly watching us. Well, watching Griff.

"Now get going." I pulled her arm and propelled her into Garrick's beaming line of vision.

Ah, young love.

During the course of our travels along the coast, we all decided to stay on the beach route. Hell, we might us well enjoy ourselves. The ocean waves washed away some of the anxiety and the trepidation we all felt. The horror that coated us could be voluntarily placed into the denial bin once our bare feet hit the sand. It would of course have to be picked up at the end of the day, but with each passing period of time, our coat of pain lessened. We attempted to abandon the weight, which had been placed on our souls. The past was so heavy and the future so unimaginable that we chose to live in the present.

Processing the recent events the best we could, we gathered close to each other for solace. We were becoming a nuclear family—well, viral family maybe.

Time for dinner! A debate rose—which fisherperson or animal would get the biggest fish? I knew Bruno would make the biggest mess, and Teak would attempt to steal his fish. Ah seafood, so refreshing. We were deered-out.

Fishing had become a not-so-friendly competition amongst us. We had raided a sporting goods store, mostly to stock up on supplies and ammunition, and we had found a little something extra. Garrick and Cory came out of the store carrying fishing poles, good old boys through and through.

"I caught one this big." Garrick was illustrating the size of his fish with both his hands spread wide.

"Yeah, well mine was this big." Cory's of course was much bigger.

Men and their obsession with size! Will it never end? There was a joke in there somewhere, but I just leaned back on the dusty Rover's hood and crossed my arms while grinning. The scene playing out in front of me was so normal, I savoured it. Humans could find the fortitude to overcome any obstacle. Throw a little fishing into the mix, and well, it increases the odds of fortitude substantially.

Catching fish wasn't a difficult task. Keeping them whole and intact, well, that was another matter. Bruno, the king of beasts, thought we were fishing specifically for him. The struggling fish on the line became a giant cat toy.

Bruno ended up smelling quite fishy for my tastes at the end of the day. The king lounged by the fire, a deep rumbling purr emulating from his throat. Cleaning time—his large rough tongue started cleaning his tawny fur coat. I'd actually got a lick from him once—I don't think I'll ever have to exfoliate that side of my face again.

Teak and Oakley found a kinship with Bruno—fish. See, cats and dogs can get along, especially when the cat has bigger teeth and outweighs them significantly. Bruno stole the fish from the men and the dogs stole the fish from the cat. A new food chain was established.

"Bruno ate a boat load of fish today. He stole most of them—I don't think he caught one!" I said.

Playfully defensive, Garrick patted Bruno and said, "That's because the dogs kept stealing them from him, right poor guy?" Bruno rolled onto his back in a helpless posture. Ham! Poor Bruno.

"Yeah he looks really hard done by!" I laughed and eyed the contented cat.

"Yeah, but your dogs are faster and sneakier!" Garrick said. I laughed. It was true the dogs managed to bait and trick Bruno. Tricking him into dropping the fish, in order to give chase to one or another of the two dogs.

"Garrick, your cat needs a bath he smells really fishy." I pinched my nostrils—super smell had its drawbacks.

"Yeah, so do your dogs. And they have fish scales stuck to their fur." He half turned to look at the dogs. He was focused on barbequing the remaining fish. My nose wrinkled as I noted the wet fishy dog odor. "Hmm, yeah your right, I'll get on that—good point." There was no way I was going to let that smell in my tent tonight. I turned and looked at my hairy bed mates. The dogs were both chewing on a fish head in the cool sand. You could almost see the odor drifting off of them. I really wrinkled my face up with the prospect of having that curled up beside me. My expression was rewarded with laughter from the group.

Teak innocently looked up from her fish head, her muzzle covered in scales. "What, I'm innocent," was written all over her face. She returned back to her prize.

"My fish was bigger than yours Cory!" Garrick exclaimed with a smug grin.

Cory was whittling a piece of driftwood, its shape was amorphous. It was just his idea of physiotherapy for his healing shoulder. "Yeah, but Griffin owns the supreme title!" A grin played at the corner of his mouth. He opened his arms wide. "Hers was this big!"

Beaming, Garrick chuckled. "Yeah but she didn't do it the traditional way!" Cory turned and winked at Griff. She was grinning and braiding her long blonde hair, staring off at the memory of her first fishing trip.

Griffin and I had decided to try our hand at scuba diving and deep-sea fishing, minus the gear. We did tie knives onto hardy sticks then splashed out and then plunged into the bluish depths. The cold didn't bother our newly insulated skin. Who needed scuba gear when you had a virus running rampant through your blood? Our special sight allowed us to see clearly in the mildly murky water. We could go for long periods under the water. We kept bobbing up to the surface, but only because we were so excited and needed to share what we were seeing.

The ocean's waters held an array of colourful fish, rock formations and waving vegetation. A beautiful coral formation housed a multitude of colourful residents. Enamoured, we both just sat floating in the current. The silence of the water soothed our souls. Everything in the water was very busy and oblivious to the trivial affairs beyond the borders of their world.

A dark torpedo sliced through the foggy stillness. The swift and calculating grey missile came from the other side of the coral bed. It was heading straight for Griff's head with its rough jaws opened wide. I didn't think—I threw my spear.

The resistance of the water reduced the force of my plunging motion. Nevertheless, the spear lurched into its gaping grey and white jaws. Half the spear protruded from its gullet. White jagged teeth tried to clamp down on the wooden protrusion. It tried to turn its trajectory, but Griff turned and thrust her small frame at the shark. The petite girl would finish the beast off, easy. I swallowed a little salt water as her small form neared the shark's massive torso.

I was struck dumb. Submerged, mouth agape, I stared into the ocean's silence and witnessed a spectacle of unbelievable proportions.

Griff had encircled the beast's head with her arms—hugging it. Then she swam quickly to the surface with the shark in tow.

Have you ever seen one of those documentaries where the killer whale breaks the water's surface catches airtime with a seal locked in its jaws, then lands with a tidal wave splash? No? Well, Griff did a perfect impression of a killer whale. Fortunately no one was in anyone's jaws.

The beached fishermen witnessed the whole spectacle from afar. They dropped their poles in stupefaction. Bruno, a genetically inherited opportunist, grabbed their two fish and ran. The two surprised fishermen didn't notice there poles being dragged down the beach. Stunned recognition crept from Garrick's stomach. It ignited a response. He dropped his net and dove in.

Bruno's great escapade was thwarted when he noticed Garrick's sudden flight into the water. He turned his sinewy body, dropped the fish and attempted to follow Garrick. It was a sad splashy effort. Big cats like Bruno don't swim well—he was no tiger.

Garrick reached Griffin as she was yanking the spear out of the slippery, thrashing beast. A gentle pat and push on the shark's gritty skin sent the troubled shark deeper into the ocean.

A large smirk was plastered across Griff's face. "He's okay. It's not his fault. We invaded his hunting grounds."

Mine and Garrick's faces reflected puzzlement. Garrick and I both swallowed a mouthful of sea-water.

Your mouth shouldn't be ajar, when wading in water. We turned and gawked after Griffin as she casually flipped in the air and backstroked, spitting an arc of water in our direction.

Garrick and I looked at each other, and then mutually shrugged. Our echo of incredulous laughter kept pace with our swift front strokes.

We ate with gusto that night. We had caught a lot of fish—and a shark.

CHAPTER SIXTEEN:
Home is Where the Heart Is

"The basis of optimism is sheer terror."
-Oscar Wilde (1854 - 1900)

The next day we took to the road, apprehension churning in all our stomachs. Griffin was sensing more colors. We drove cautiously. Thoughts of an ambush lurked behind every blind corner.

Jane and Arnold were in the building.

Fear and trepidation ground our nerves to dust with each turn of the wheel. Now, imagine the most unlikely sound you'd expect to hear. Have you thought of it? Good.

You'd be wrong.

Maniacal Laughter saturated our sensitive ears.

At least that's what I thought I was hearing. Queue the villain standing in the middle of the road with arms outstretched, welcoming us to die. I shouldn't have watched so much television. The surgeon general had warned against television rotting your...

The loud, artificially produced laughter cut my thought off. The unnatural sound was intensifying with each inch of asphalt our tires battered.

The walkie-talkies droned crackling static. Everyone was trying to talk at once. I pulled over and idled the Rover. The other vehicles pulled alongside us. "Anyone have any idea how we should proceed? Cory?"

The dogs tried to jump to the front. Pee time already—excellent!

"I'd say to send a scout in, but the scout could be overwhelmed by numbers of whoever is responsible for that ah—noise. I'd go but..." Cory flinched with pain when he tried to sit up.

"No, I don't feel numbers. More like some, not many," Griffin chimed in.

I think Cory was right. A scouting party would be the safest. I wouldn't put anyone at risk for something I could do.

"Griff, Garrick—could you take the dogs please?" I grabbed the dogs' harnesses and directed them into the Hemi. "Christin and I are going to go on foot. Stealth and all that." Christin crossed his arms and looked at his feet. "Cory, get everyone out of here and find safety! If we don't come back here, we'll find you up the coast. Okay?" I said, shutting the Hemi's door.

A chorus of unanimous no's resounded.

"Why just you guys?" Garrick protested. "We shouldn't separate!"

"Listen, we're uglier and faster. Besides I have to make sure the animals, Cory and Adam are safe. I need you to take care of my girls!"

"I'm not a girl." Adam said with an indignant scowl.

"I'll sound like one if I have to move." I looked over and saw Cory grinning, no wait grimacing. No that was a grin.

"Speak for yourself." Christin whispered and smirked.

Sheesh… "All right, I'm uglier and you're faster. Plus someone has to stay with the *boys*!" I sighed and went to open my door.

Christin looked contemplative for a second and then nodded. "Just trust me guys—we'll be fine!" I said and climbed into the back of the Rover.

I rolled my eyes. My eyes are going to get stuck that way one day. Chris and I grabbed our gear. "Just give us an hour, okay? Keep your walkie-talkies on. We'll call you. Just keep your eyes sharp. Griff watch out for colors. It'll be okay!" I lied. I think I was getting better at this lying business. No one argued.

Loaded with our weapons, we dashed into the trees. The dogs howled as our heels left the asphalt. I shook my head, so much for our surprise encounter. We used the trees to propel ourselves silently off the ground, the action felt safer. Glad I watched *Tarzan* movies when I was young.

The laughter was eerie—fake happiness. It was dusk, and the horizon ahead of us held a sickly green haze. The fake laughter was originating from the docks. We caught glimpses of the masts of ships, swaying in the twilight hue. We could smell the greens. We decided to creep high in the trees, enabling us to gain a high vantage point. We could see if any greens were tracking our way. It didn't hurt we were downwind. We crept in for a closer look.

There were eight of them. They stared straight ahead, stock still, drooling. Their attention was focused on an array of large strung up speakers. Pulsing green light saturated the marina. The greens were like deer caught in headlights. They didn't notice our presence.

An assortment of shots rang out in the night. Someone was shooting fish in a barrel. The greens yielded there stoic stance and collapsed to the hard packed ground. Heartbeats, at least fifteen, descended upon the greens' incapacitated forms. The erratic drum roll of so many human heartbeats was alien to my enhanced hearing. It had been so long, since I heard that many heartbeats.

The execution squad, adorned in identical medical suits, masks and gloves, proceeded to decapitate the still, lifeless greens. There were women and men in the melee of decapitators. They pushed the headless torsos into a heap. A guy with a flame-thrower doused the greens with liquid fire. The heap of dismembered greens belched burnt black smoke. They were efficient—almost tactical.

One of the hermetically clad individual's walked over to a severed greens head and kicked it into the inferno of bodies.

Punctuation. Exclamation mark!

No question about it—those greens were not going to heal. I swallowed a dry gulp. It left a lump in my throat. Then I smelled her. Mae.

"Get your butts down here children. I know your there. It's okay, these folk won't hurt you none!" She didn't have to speak loudly. We heard her clearly even though she was over two hundred yards away from our hiding spots.

I spied Mae in the background, leaning nonchalantly on her handmade cane. Mae was chewing on a stick of something. Christin and I exchanged looks, shrugged and jumped.

The men didn't raise their guns. They just continued chipping away at the task at hand. "About time you got here, been waiting on you a spell now. Come on, give old Mae a hug!" We embraced peppermint.

Our attention was momentarily distracted as the roar of a bulldozer turned over. It exhaled smoky diesel breath. In the din of the roaring beast, I turned my attention back toward Mae.

"Mae?" I said. The old woman winked and smiled at the mention of her name. I grimaced.

"Ah, kids it sure is good to see you!" The old woman grabbed my arm and pulled me toward a loping figure heading in our direction. A tall, lanky man was making haste toward Mae as he unzipped his medical suit. "Wow, Mae—that contraption works phenomenal. It was as easy as baking a pie!"

Mae interrupted the approaching man. "Doc, what do you know of baking a pie, I don't think you ever been in a kitchen 'cept to eat a piece of my pie!" Her voice chortled against the rumble of the bulldozer.

The man was grinning distractedly, fighting to take off his rumpled paper suit. The suit was winning.

"You make baking a pie look so easy though!" He smiled at us. He walked toward us with his right hand stretched out in the customary welcoming gesture; he tripped and fell on his face. I winced. Ouch, that was going hurt. The man, who looked like he was wrestling a straightjacket off, recovered quickly. He did however; continue to gingerly rub a growing lump on his forehead.

"It seems humane Doc." Mae smiled at the ruffled man. "I'd like you to meet a couple of friends of mine—Arnold and Jane." Mae motioned for us to come to closer to her. She started laughing at her witty introduction. Now I knew where the recording of the laughter originated….

The doctor checked his fly, then looked quizzically at the laughing woman. He hadn't been able to wrap his head around the old woman's humor yet. "What? Did I miss something?" The doc seemed comfortable in his puzzlement. It was probably the result of hanging around Mae too long.

"Hi, I'm Sam. This is Christin. Mae thinks she's funny." I grinned and shook the doc's hand.

"Funnier than you think you are, child!" More chuckled laughter from Mae. She was having a ripe old time of it. Geez wasn't she the comedian. Christin went over and shook the doc's hand while the bulldozer started pushing the smoldering greens into a hole.

"Is it safe Mae?" Both our expressions turned serious. "Yes hun. Call the others."

I made a call.

Ω Ω Ω

Mae leaned on her old wooden cane, her blank stare drifting off into the night.

The gift was always so foggy. She was always waiting for decisions to be made. Mae already knew she would meet the kids again. The vision was vague though. They hadn't made all their decisions yet

The wrinkled old woman had wrestled with the haze for some time. She missed her porch and old rocker. The peppermint stick, was almost whittled away as she remembered the first time she had felt pure horror.

Mae, shuffled to her favorite rocking chair and settled in—the creak, creak, creak of her rocker helped her focus. Taking time every day, was important to practice focusing through the haziness of her special sight. The sight had always been with her—the virus had simply enhanced it. It was like ESPN on steroids. She had a quiet giggle. ESPN—some network she was linked to. No sports here.

The vision had cleared. She reeled from the shock as a feeling of getting hit upside the head with a baseball bat stole over her. Fear then pounced on her very being.

A small smile had been playing on her withered lips. The smirk upended itself brusquely—shifting into an expression of revulsion and utter alarm.

Black eyes loomed in her vision. They were devoid of emotion, vacant of sense. Such anger and hate plagued this man. The stench emulating off him filled her nose. She could feel her eyes water. The image and stench of him was growing stronger. Nausea swelled up her throat, threatening to suffocate her. He was coming. He was coming here now!

Mae stood up too quickly and fell over. The virus did nothing for fake joints. Mae was a walking robot; the replacement of her bilateral hips and knees weakened the virus's abilities during its remodeling process. Humbled on her knees and gripping her rocker, she hoped she could convince the townspeople to go southwest. The rest of the vision was still so foggy, so she wouldn't be able to explain her reasoning.

The townsfolk needed to have a little blind faith. Hahaha, blind faith—Mae loved that.

Regrettably, only about half the town had blind faith. Perhaps their decision was only a result of the stark terror she exuded when she spoke of the need for the town's exodus.

The emigrant group of believers left with their heads hung. Newton was the only home this group had known. On their journey west they lost a few souls. The greens were hard to predict. They were rabid dogs in essence. Basic animal instinct ruled their choices. It was like trying to predict the wind—impossible.

Mae's despondent group had stopped to rest and resupply. They sat around a fire retelling stories of home. Quiet laughter floated in the night.

The greens approached, stealthily and lethal. The people shot first and asked questions later. The onslaught manifested pure chaos. Mae saw the approach of the greens too late. They lost three of their own and killed twelve putrid greens.

The nomadic travellers had been out in the open and vulnerable. They thought they were lucky having lost only three people to the greens, but Mae knew different. Something worse was coming. They continued cautiously on their journey. Mae was looking for birds. Actually she was scanning the sky for a lot of birds. Their group stayed close to coast, heading south. The cluster of tired people knew better, then to ask for clarification from the wizened woman. The old woman had saved their lives. They followed blindly.

Off to the northeast, in the far distance, the nomadic group could see billowing smoke bank the distant horizon. It was the general vicinity of their town. The homeless forlorn assemblage trudged south, the fate of friends and kin unknown.

They didn't have far left to travel. Mae's acute hearing detected the hum of motion detectors—civilization was near.

Mae directed the group to the marina, setting off hidden motion detectors. Ten minutes later the "bird group" cautiously disclosed their previously concealed presence.

This is how she met Dr. Walker, an ornithologist or bird scientist. The doctor's island aviary and labs were ten minutes away by boat. There they studied bird pathology, researching among other things the avian flu.

The bird flu had been high up on the worldwide alert due to the possibility of a global, pandemic threat. The birds were literally going to drop the bomb on mankind—so to speak. The island's scientists tracked avian flu hotspots worldwide, testing the migrating birds as the birds vacationed on the island. The avian flu was such a vanilla virus in retrospect.

The bird island was a fully self-sustained facility—it was beautiful. This west coast research facility was akin to its east coast sister facility, Plum Island. Plum Island was military funded. There they monitored, researched, tested and stored the world's most dangerous contagions, anthrax, being one *of its most lethal. Hence, so nickname Anthrax Island. The east coast facility was funded by WHO, the non-military World Health Organization. The governments of most nations amalgamated to research and monitor the growing avian threat. A global avian flu outbreak could decimate the globes human and bird population in no time. Japan was the major hotspot for the emergence of the avian flu, so it made sense to have a research institute that wasn't far from the shores of the world's densest bird flu epicenter.*

During the reaping, a few fixated scientists stayed to work over the weekend. These few remaining researchers had tried to isolate the virus, using blood samples flown in. They had struggled in vain to distinguish the characteristics of the unknown pathogen. They knew it was contagious; it didn't affect animals and killed within three days of contact. It was found in all body fluids and could be easily contracted. A simple kiss could infect and kill you. They couldn't figure out its geneses. They had no record of the virus on any data base. It was a new pathogen of unknown origin. The scientists were unable to identify and categorize the nemesis that was exterminating mankind.

The island's populace knew it was only a matter of time before their demise would find them. But death didn't come; it somehow overlooked their little island. The greens came instead.

Scientist and support workers could live on the island year round. The island had labs, living quarters, its own water supply and solar powered electricity.

Prior to the reaping, monthly supply runs to the mainland had kept the island provided for. This monthly provision no longer existed. The island and mainland could only be accessed by boat. If the virus was coming to claim the last survivors, they decided it wouldn't take them on an empty stomach.

A small scavenging party of five armed themselves with a couple of flamethrowers and two hand guns. It was to be their first trip made to the mainland.

The small town was home to a lot of Ukrainians. They had forged their own slice of heaven. Home of the largest perogie on the west coast, they were a proud robust people. The townspeople of Belyk, had just thrown their annual perogie fest when the reaping had befallen the domain of man. Generally, the Ukrainian's didn't drink bottled water, but during the perogie fest it was freely distributed by the new mayor. So much for securing future votes—he passively killed his constituents instead.

The scavenging islanders focused on the mainland's well-stocked stores to resupply their depleting stock of goods. The Ukrainian's liked to eat, and supplies were bountiful. Two greens were lounging by a freshly killed deer in the center of town when the islanders pulled up in front of them. The islanders left their stolen trucks idling.

Startled awake by the noise of the trucks, the greens rushed to the source of the disturbance. The islanders were just getting out of their vehicles, laughing about how they'd have to live on frozen perogies for the rest of their lives, when the greens crashed into one of their vehicles.

Stunned, the greens deliberately righted themselves onto their knees and stared at the laughing men. The islanders were surprised into silence mouths hanging open. Glowing green eyes froze them into further paralysis.

Gruffly, the greens stood, shook off their stupor and made to attack the dazed islanders. Dr. Walker pulled the trigger on the flame thrower before he had time to think. Two spires of flame saturated the approaching greens in a blaze of screams. The blazing greens gyrated and screamed. A bullet to each of the greens heads terminated their shrieks of anguish. They collapsed into two fiery heaps. Dr. Walker threw up on his shoes.

Thank God they weren't zombies. He couldn't take zombies. He would need a padded cell if they had been zombies.

They returned to their sterile compound and made efforts to fortify their island against the menacing green mutants. Motion detectors and cameras were hastily set up around the island. To die from a viral infection was one thing—being attacked by a mutant was another. They got more weapons from town. They had barely set up a perimeter on the marina when their newly installed detectors wailed a warning. Movement on the marina!

The islanders idled offshore; knowing their speedboats would give them a chance at out running any land bound greens. Through binoculars they spotted an unexpected sight. An old black woman leaned on a cane alongside a motely group of men woman, children and a grey horse. A big hairy guy with binoculars of his own leaned into the old woman and said something to her. The old woman smiled and waved in their general vicinity.

Mae was part guest, part guinea pig. She didn't mind—her group was safe. The scientist had wanted to catch a green in order to study it. Mae was the next best thing. The scientists were trying to figure out an immunization, perhaps eventually a cure, against the virus. The uninfected islanders could contract the virus at any time, so they decided they would go down fighting. They knew they had lofty hopes, but they had no other option at present.

The search for hope kept their lives structured and ordinary. Everyone had a job. Mae's group was made comfortable and given tasks.

Mae figured out the greens still had a glimmer of humanity buried deep in their psyche. That logic could be penetrated. The sound of laughter infiltrated and stunned their consciousness. The sound caused them to pause, as if it reached in and seized their quintessence. Remarkable—the rabid humans still had souls.

The mountain people were settling into island life. Fortuitously, there were some small mountainous regions on the island. This aspect helped the mountain folk adapt to their new island home.

Mae was optimistically hopeful. She focused within. Yes, the black eyed man was still very foggy.

CHAPTER EIGHTEEN:
The Time of a Little Quiet

"A woman is like a tea bag; you never know how strong it is until it's in hot water."
-Eleanor Roosevelt (1884 - 1962)

"Yes we're fine. No Garrick, this is not a trap. No they are not making me say this. Yes we should come up with a code word. All right we'll see you guys shortly!" Geez, that kid watched more movies then I did. Too funny.

A code word would be a brilliant idea to consider though. Smart kid—who said TV rots the brain? What did the surgeon general know? Scientists, geesh.

The island group had a surplus of boats. After all it was an abandoned marina. Our group loaded up and followed the island's boats.

We must have been quite the vision to anyone observing. Bruno was perched on the bow of the boat, mane flowing in the wind. The king of the beasts was majestic, until Teak pushed herself in front of Bruno. Bruno was no Leo and Teak was no Kate—but you got the picture. We didn't want to surprise anyone, so we all removed our goggles.

We were almost a rainbow with our amber, pink, silver, yellow, orange and blue eyes glowing—pretty. We were cruising across the ocean at a leisurely pace. The island people had informed their people about the new arrivals. We didn't want any accidental panic or shootings. They were being invaded by the infected.

As we entered the compound, I detected the low hum of motion detectors as were on the mainland. The islanders had studied birds, and they needed to be able to track those birds. Utilizing this method of detecting birds, they had simply added a lot more detectors to the island and mainland.

The main compound was wired up with numerous speakers and lights. Our diverse crew followed open-mouthed as we entered civilization, however humble. We were escorted to five large trailers, which were surprisingly modern with comfortable furnishings. We split up roughly according to vehicle: Cory and Adam, Garrick and Bruno, Griff and Christin and, well me the dogs—home sweet homes. Small pleasures are all one can hope for in this new world.

Those in our group who were infected were asked to follow a list of rules.

1. **Don't exchange bodily fluids with humans.**
2. **Don't enter any lab area without an escort.**
3. **Observe standard body fluid precautions. Refer to sec 3b. for details.**
4. **Wear goggles when applicable. Refer to sec 3c. for details**.

They seemed reasonable requests. I mean it was like having Ebola really. We could infect; we could kill. No kissing, no snooping, no sharing stuff. Follow the rules and don't draw attention to the island.

Our hairy counter parts raised a lot of eyebrows. All right; Bruno, raised a lot of eyebrows.

Garrick and Bruno put a show on. Mae would not let Garrick use Bob. In fact, poor Bob had developed an anxious nicker and neck tick when Bruno was around. Bruno eyed Bob with longing. Bob eyed Bruno with trepidation.

Bruno was smart. Garrick had trained him well. There was jumping, rolling, sitting and playing dead. My favorite was that Teak tried to do everything Bruno did. The great lion didn't like sharing the stage. He swiped playfully at an elusive Teak, losing his balance and falling off an overturned boat. The great beast walked to the water's edge like he planned the whole thing. Poor thing—Teak got all the applause.

Thirty five people enjoyed Garrick, Bruno and Teak's performance. It ended up easing people's anxieties.

I wondered if us Varian's could put a show on, we were getting enough attention. People tended to avert their eyes and avoid us directly. The island people gave us furtive glances and talked in serious whispers. The islander's tone wasn't angry or afraid or tense or any other emotion I was expecting. No, they seemed sad. Despair and confusion were etched on all their faces. What did all this mean? The mountain folk on the other hand paid us colored mutants no mind at all. They were probably desensitized to us because of Mae—I think.

I turned from the despondent scene. I needed to see Mae. She had some explaining to do...

I found her trailer with ease—I could smell peppermint. I knocked. "Come in child. Hello Teak and hello Oakley. How are you girls?" They were putty in her hands. Pure delight melted them into the floor.

I entered a roomy trailer as I said. "You got some 'splaining to do Lucy!"

"Oh my, I just loved the, *I love Lucy* show—Desi was such a charmer!" she crooned, grabbing her cheeks and smiling. "Let me get you some tea. Get comfortable please." She gestured to an overstuffed chair.

I got settled, crossing my arms—prepared to interrogate. Mae passed me a steaming cup of tea with a smile. "You tell me. I'll fill in the blanks the best I can," she whispered.

A frown of concentration wiped her smile away as she settled herself into another oversized floral chair.

"Well we got the yellow as you directed—what do you need her for?"

"I don't, the humans do."

"What for?"

"A cure."

"For whom?"

"Everyone, possibly."

I was stunned. My mouth slipped open.

"You mean a cure that could change us back?"

"Possibly." I paused and gulped a hot sip of tea and winced.

"You sent a second string after the yellow!"

"Yes." She chuckled.

"You didn't tell us!" My brows started to furrow. I was fighting to control my frustration.

"I wasn't sure. The boy's mind wasn't made up. I didn't know if he would follow through until you two were gone."

"What happened to the town?"

"Black Eye came."

"Who or what is 'black eye?' Did someone hit someone?" I was getting really exasperated. I wanted to give an old lady a black eye. Instead, I started chewing on my lower lip. She was providing half-assed answers.

Mae sighed deeply and continued. "He's exactly what you're thinking and everything you could imagine. He's a bad man gone terribly wrong, and he's been let loose on a crippled world. He now has the power to follow through with his unscrupulous devices."

She whispered more to herself, "A very bad man…"

Silence in the trailer. Only the dogs panted quietly.

Tick—

The hand of a clock—

Tock—

Cuckoo! Cuckoo!

"Seriously Mae, come on--really!" I burst out of my chair and started to pace.

"Geez, this is all crazy business. I know the world as we know it has ceased to be, but why does it have to have an evil villain?" I pictured Gary Oldman in a dark suit, wringing his hands—with maniacal laughter erupting from his mouth. Damn too much TV. My imagination was really overfed.

I stopped pacing and threw myself back into the overstuffed chair. "What does he want?" I was getting angry. This end of the world crap sucked! I felt as if I'd been on a turbo roller coaster and the end of the ride was nowhere in sight. Okay deep breath. My internal temper tantrum passed, sort of.

"Everything? Nothing...to cleanse the world?" Mae breathed. She continued. "Who's to know what exactly a sad, angry, little man wants." She sipped her hot tea gingerly.

"All I do know is he wants to erase everyone including himself. Ouch burned myself." She patted her lips with her apron. We sat in silence and sipped our peppermint tea. Heat vapours from my tea swirled around my nose. The heat burning inside me was slowly subsiding.

"When? Where is he?" My breath blew the tea's steam into the nothingness.

"He's still far away. My visions of him are muddled at the moment." Mae leaned back in her puffy chair. Her brilliant unseeing eyes stared in my direction.

"What are we going to do?" I huffed. I leaned back too, stunned and angry.

"Don't worry hun, we'll figure it out. I say hope for the best and plan for the worst. We have Jane and Arnold, not to mention the many other colors of the rainbow." She reached over and patted my arm reassuringly, then smiled in my direction. I didn't return a very sincere smile. All the joy had drained from my face. I was angry, frustrated and hungry.

I looked down at the paw I was holding. Teak groaned and rolled onto her back, all four hairy paws stretched into the air.

"What the heck is going on with those hypnotized greens and that whacked out laughter?"

She started to laugh, "I think I have a beautiful laugh!" She held her hand to her chest in mock offense

I reddened a bit. A vein was pulsing in my forehead. I stared straight ahead toward a flowered wall. Taking time to process this new information, I continued to chew on my bottom lip.

Mae was staring in Teak's direction. "Life will always triumph over death. It always finds a way—just look at us!"

I sighed. "We're life triumphing?"

"We're the light and we will sustain life against the dark and death!"

"You sound like Oprah!" I threw up my arms and slumped into the couch, defeated by a hundred year old blind, batty lady.

CHAPTER NINETEEN:
The Darkness Walks Ablaze

"Those things that nature denied the human sight,
she revealed to the human soul."
-Ovid (43 BC - 17 AD)

Ω Ω Ω

The dark roamed the countryside destroying life. Sitting on a Ferrari, he watched a city block burn. The fire could jump and leap, perhaps scorching the city in its entirety.

He liked to burn life as life had burned him. The charred remains of his earthly body had released his life—twice. The man reminisced about his past life before he had been transformed into a God.

Ω Ω Ω

The elderly woman before him was completely ablaze. Her fire dance captivated and lulled his tortured soul. A soothing wave of serenity washed over him, and he relaxed into a trance, hypnotized by the scene playing out in front of him.

The screaming dance turned without warning. The woman's flaming arms found him and enshrouded his astonished inert form. Engulfed in an inferno embrace, the woman and man started dancing

In a torrid tango of red hot flames, fat and skin dripped off their gyrating figures. When his lips caught fire, he screamed.

The medical staff had told him he had died twice and that it was a miracle he had survived thus far. Eighty-percent of his body surface had been melted away. He was a blackened, charred piece of meat, unrecognizable as once being human.

He had no eyelids left. He could see that his body was a contorted pretzel of burnt flesh. A tube was burrowed deep inside his scorched lungs. A beeping machine breathed fire into his lungs with each rasp of its electronic pump.

The hospital staff wasn't optimistic that he'd survive the night. His injuries were just too severe. No family came to visit this man; no person cared to pray for his plight. The burnt man could hear the doctors call him a malignant, sociopathic, narcissist—they had his criminal history in hand.

"Huh? Colorful label." he thought to himself, before the stupouring effect of the drugs pulled him back into nothingness. The team of doctors had told him with a mixture of contempt and pity that he should make peace with his god. The burnt man prayed for death. Which deity he prayed to, he did not know.

During the shadowy night hours, his muffled pleas for death went unheeded. Instead something else was attempting to remove his flesh with a dull hot knife. His escalating agonized screams went unnoticed. The breathing tube stifled his cries of horror. Fire was coursing through his body—God was fire. God was taking him.

His whole essence undulated fire. It had started with his fascination with watching cats burn a howling dance in the moonlight. His passion gradually evolved to people. Dancing ablaze, people tended to scream louder. The screaming was music to his being. The music enriched the macabre dance—it completed his opus.

Fortune smiled down on him often. Once he had several people to burn simultaneously, fireflies pirouetting in the night. He revered the night—it was his canvas, and he was an artist. He was a master creator. His god had granted him further opportunities to create. Fire had cleansed him.

The flame had transformed him into a God. Life renewed, he left the hospital to the mercy of the fire he had set. He had watched it burn and explode throughout the night.

A smile played on his perfect lips. Unbound to man's limitations, he stood and surveyed his domain. Ah, to be a witness to the fire forming his heaven. It burned eternal—the landscape smouldered.

Inspired, he moved on. There were so many blank canvases and so little time. His hand of creation hungered.

Ω Ω Ω

CHAPTER TWENTY:
Bobbing For Apples

"Life is what happens to you
while you're busy making other plans."
-John Lennon (1940 - 1980)

"I was so hungry I could have eaten Bob!" I gnawed helplessly on the cleaned rib of a deer. Mae blanched.

"No it's not Bob! Geez!" He would be too tough and stringy and he'd probably give us gastritis.

We had taken Bruno to the mainland to hunt. The cat was getting proficient in his hunting skills. We often let him lead the expedition. The great cat hadn't disappointed. Remnants of a young buck turned slowly on the spit

It was a striking sunny day about six months after we had arrived on the island, and we were having a grand barbeque with almost everyone on the island in attendance. Grinning sauce-smeared faces surrounded me. These precious moments were how we managed the reality of each day and healed the past. Laughter was the salve for our wounds.

The siren's wail instantly scattered my brain. Reflexively, I tossed my deer rib and jumped to my feet, wiping my sauce-soaked face on my sleeve. BBQ sauce did not instil fear. Damn, did the siren have to be so bone numbingly loud? I swear every time the alarms sounded I peed myself a little. Apparently the GI Jane within was not in charge of controlling my bladder.

In unison all us colors leapt and ran swiftly toward the island's marina. We'd been working on our reaction times, honing our skills and stretching our abilities. The speedboat was loaded with our gear. Bruno wasn't the only one who was becoming a proficient hunter.

Christin, Garrick, Griffin and I were speeding to the coast in our swanky new boat. Our human counterparts hadn't even reached their boat yet. Poor things, we left them the clean-up. But they never seemed to complain—no one enjoyed killing. We thought of anything and everything to circumvent killing the greens, but it was no use. The greens were a threat to humans and wildlife, rabid dogs that hunted relentlessly. We saw no good left in the mutated humans.

There was always a chance the pathogen could find a way to infect the uninfected, so we took precautions for our vulnerable coworkers. The colors tried to do all the wet work and secure the area. The uninfected wore layers of protective garments and handled any contaminated, bodies or body parts as minimally as possible. The greens were once human so we tried to kill them as humanely as possible. We were the bridge between life and death, both for the uninfected and the infected.

The maniacal laughter grew louder as we approached the marina. We thought of changing Mae's recording—it grated the nerves. The mere suggestion caused Mae to recoil in rejection. The old lady was a good actor almost Oscar worthy.

Our marina consistently received visits from greens. We had installed numerous lines of defence. The coast was the first. Motion detectors and cameras detected any movement along the coast for miles.

We all took shifts monitoring the abundant cameras—there were a lot of rabbits and deer out there. Motion detectors were activated by the presence of any activity. Thumper drove us crazy. We were trying to figure out a way to make the detectors more precise—say a hundred pounds and up. Then again Bambi would still be a nuisance.

A camera confirmed a pack of greens. Greens tended to travel in packs. Like minds tend to find each other. Only seldom did a lone green appear on our monitors. Once the presence of one or more colors was confirmed, the recording of laughter was initiated. Then the siren in the compound was triggered.

We hit the mainland running, dispatching the greens easily. They stood frozen, drooling. They were immobile as statues. A big bird could easily poop on them—they were totally captivated by the sound of Mae's laughter. There were three greens, mouths open catching flies. No bird poop—our monitors were efficient and effective. We always reacted quickly to the alarm. We hadn't dared to test the longevity of their sustaining rapture.

The medically clad humans disposed of the dismembered greens into a pit while the colors held the perimeter for our coworkers—safety first. One hundred and seventy two days without an incident, occupational health and safety would be so proud.

The period of time when the motion sensors were disengaged was the time we were all susceptible to an attack. Griff and I were watching the north end of the beach when I decided to ask her about her sensing abilities, curious as a cat I've been spending too much time with Bruno.

"Griff, what's it like? I mean what do you see?" I focused northward. The sun was setting and the stars were starting to poke through the mauve sky. She started to chew on her bottom lip. Hmmm, I wonder where she picked up that habit.

"Imagine a Christmas tree with intermittent blinking lights. The blinking lights flicker on and off, disappearing and reappearing in different spots."

"What made them disappear?" My brow furrowed. I didn't like hearing that colors could disappear. More lower lip chewing. She did this especially when she was contemplative. "Well, I think natural solids. Rock mostly—anything made with rock shields them."

"How far can you sense?"

"Well, it seems far, but I don't have a map in my head. They show up around me. The closer they are, the better I can pinpoint them. It's like standing in the middle of the Christmas tree, like being the trunk."

"What do you see around you now?" I asked.

"Mmmmm, blank spots on the Christmas tree, then lights start to glow and come close together. They just keep moving around the tree, some blinking out, then they go off my grid."

Griff sighed heavily. "Remember that one that jumped out of the drain last week."

"Yes. Sneaky bugger we must have woken it up with the bulldozer!" I remembered the incident.

We were just about done our task of getting rid of two greens, when Adam fired up the bulldozer. I was talking to Garrick when Bruno leapt up and ran to a drain open to the ocean. A green was crawling out a three foot pipe. Garrick and I ran to Bruno. The green was attempting to circle the growling cat. Garrick flew through the air and bounced off a tree then decapitated the green before it realized he had more than an irate cat to deal with.

"Well, I was tracking that one earlier. Then it blinked out—then boom! It felt blinding, when it jumped out into the open. Then it blinked out again when Garrick killed it." Griff seemed lost in the memory.

"Did you have some special sense before the reaping?" I turned in her direction and eyed her ruminating scowl.

More lip chewing ensued. "After the accident, when I got shot in the head, I had great intuition—like really bang on!" Her distress disappeared as she remembered happier times. "My parents used to tease me that I was a human lie detector. My dad and I used to go to the race track once and awhile. I loved the horses!" She was grinning. "My dad asked which horses were the fastest and he'd place bets on my opinion—we won a lot!"

The distress in her young face returned. "We had a lot of fun. I miss my parents." Griff had that faraway look again. She turned and swiped her face. I put my arm casually around her shoulder and stared straight ahead. "You have people now that care about you. It's not the same, I know, but we're here..." I whispered.

She nodded and her gaze drifted down.

"What do you think Garrick's up to?" I scanned the horizon looking for Bruno. The two were never far apart, like me and my dogs.

I caught a glimpse of Griff's face in my periphery. A shade of red was creeping up her neck. "He's probably teaching that old cat of his to hunt." She sniffed snot. Mmmmm, yum.

"Let's go find him. Maybe Teak wants to play bait?" She laughed and reached down to pet Teak's head.

Poor Teak—Bruno took satisfaction in hunting her. Then again, Teak took satisfaction in hunting Bruno's tail. It was a love-hate relationship. I often found the three animals passed out in the sun together—love was blooming.

As Griff and I approached Garrick and Bruno, I caught Bruno eyeing Teak—playful hate. Teak returned a rebuking expression to Bruno. Teak took off, Bruno followed. Teak was fast and smart; she knew how to elude.

We were just about done and we decided to head back to the island. We made sure the islanders were safely speeding away, before we followed.

Just another day in paradise lost.

CHAPTER TWENTY-ONE:
The Purple Rain Cometh

"What does not kill us makes us stronger."
-Friedrich Nietzsche (1844 - 1900)

"Shopping day!" I announced. "Do we have the completed grocery list?"

"Christin has it. He's just making the last rounds." Garrick was smirking. I followed his gaze. Bruno was perched on a picnic table and Teak was under it—Mexican standoff. The dog had to come out sometime. Oakley barked encouragement to Teak—I think. It sounded more like "*chicken!*"

"Is everyone ready to shop?" I asked eyeing the Mexican standoff. Sometimes Teak had a mysterious limp. I knew the cat never meant to hurt her, I just think Teak ran too hard while eluding the king of the beasts. Her old war injury was acting up, I was sure of it. I've watched the three play together, and no one ever yelped—cat or dogs.

Bruno got distracted by Garrick's movement. Teak took advantage of the distraction and scampered out. She pushed on my leg leaning, panting and I think grinning. Bruno did a double take in her direction.

I patted her panting head. "Good girl, you faked him out!" She smiled up at me.

Griff danced up to us grinning. "Hello, when is a girl not ready to shop?"

"Garrick, get that old cat off the table—we eat on that! I don't want to find another fur ball in my dinner!" I yelled in his direction. Geez! Cat hair got into everything. We were adjusting to island living, cat hair and all.

Interrelationships among the island inhabitants were growing sociable, amicable even. I glanced around and saw more hope, rather than despair moulding people's expressions. Still not enough time had passed to heal the deep seated scaring of the reaping. It was like being surrounded by a bunch of Dr. Jekyll's and Mr. Hyde's. Contentment and anguish battled within everyone. Walking the compound any night of the week, you could hear crying behind closed doors. I still didn't want to think about my personal loses and I couldn't focus on the future, so I just stayed in the present.

We hadn't had to dispatch any greens in a few weeks, so it was decided; time to shop.

Griffin informed us of a few greens lurking around the town—sporadic meanderings were all they were.

Christin, Garrick, Griff and I sped across the few miles of open water in the speed boat.

We had a tug and flatbed floater moored at the marina in order to transport whatever goods, supplies or equipment our community needed. We towed ATVs, furniture and all sorts of equipment. In order to transport supplies on the mainland, we used our Rovers, the truck and a cargo van. Scavengers and Acme moving rolled into one.

We had finally finished picking up around three quarters of our needed supplies when Griff piped up on the walkie-talkie.

"I picked up some color activity north of the marina. Do you want to check it out? We have to go that way to pick up the gas"

"How many colors Griff, and what are they doing?"

"Remember no map. They're kind of circling this one area, maybe hunting something."

We turned our vehicles and headed toward the ringing array of colors.

When we arrived, we sat in our idling vehicles and watched five greens going ballistic on a brick building, a bank. They're definitely putting a new spin on robbing a bank. Their lack of ability to procure an opening suggested this was a well-secured bank.

They threw themselves against the windows and doors to no avail. Their violent efforts barely cracked a windowsill.

Griff had joined me in the Rover, our idea of a girl's night out. She passed me the popcorn and rolled down the window. "Those greens really want something in that bank" She said through a mouthful of popcorn. "We should really get going. I'm getting really, really hungry!"

I passed her the popcorn. "You've been eating for the last hour!" I said.

"Those were appetizers. I'm a growing girl." Her incredulous look indicated that this should be an obvious fact. Two mini screams caused Griff to throw her popcorn in the air.

"Damn, what the hell was that?" I grabbed the steering wheel and peered harder at the bank. Enthralled by the greens onslaught on the building, none of us had taken the time to focus on our hearing. A solitary heartbeat was thrumming loudly. The greens had cracked a thick window and were frantically tunnelling through a growing hole. Damn.

Ω Ω Ω

Unfortunately babies enter this new world stillborn every day.

The twins were born with the umbilical cord intertwined around their wee necks. It looked bleak. The doctor quickly cut away the life giving cord that had turned into a noose.

The blue twins were delicately placed onto a warming table in silence. The NICU team functioned as a well-experienced cluster of speed and agility—cleaning out airways, blowing oxygen, administering CPR inserting tubes and stimulating the newborns. No words were uttered.

No heartbeats broke the silence. The team didn't interrupt their rhythm. The blue babies remained lifeless. The medical team didn't waver in their efforts.

The parents were holding each other, their inaudible sobs unnoticed by the medical professionals.

A cacophony of bells and alarms almost concealed two high-pitched trills. The twin's heartbeats joined in the cadence of life. Emma and Oliver had trumped death's call.

Ω Ω Ω

Resonating shrill screams were muffled by the greens excited chortles. The hunting greens were getting closer to their quarry—there was no place for the prey to escape. I could see the greens were drooling.

Trapped, this was the end for the screamers. A green had slipped in through the broken window.

We watched as an explosion of shattered glass burst from the side of the bank. Then a greens gangly body was propelled ass-first through the gaping hole that had been the plate glass window. It hit the sidewalk with a sickly thud—an arrow was sticking out of its forehead.

The remaining four greens intensified their assault. Two of the greens tried to enter the fragmented glass hole at the same time and got stuck. Griff and I raised our bows to stop their entry. The Laurel and Hardy team flew backwards onto the smooth cement, their skulls hitting the ground with a wet smack. Both had matching arrows sticking out of their foreheads. Griff and I simultaneously reconfigured our aim and took out the remaining two gawking greens. We reloaded and held our breath.

I could hear Garrick and Christin breathing twenty-feet away. I ventured a hasty glance in their direction. They had their arrows directed at the door of the bank.

Okay, let's see who's behind door number one. "Hello anyone home? We got rid of your stalkers. Hello?" I bellowed.

The side door cracked open and a rifle introduced itself. "Are you going to try and eat us?" A deep male voice rang out into the still afternoon.

"No we had popcorn already, but Griff is starving, so can we get going?" I wiped the drool from my mouth. I was getting hungry as well.

Two stunned expressions popped out of the door. "Popcorn? You have popcorn?" The two little heads said in unison.

"Actually, I ate it all, but we could make more back at the compound if you like," Griff whispered sheepishly.

"Compound? You have a compound?"

"A lion too." A mischievous grin followed my confession.

The little boy piped up. "Now you're just teasing us!"

"Nope. His name is Bruno. Would I make up an imaginary lion and name it Bruno?"

An expression of awe lit up on the two young teenage faces.

The two kids inched out of the safety of the door frame. "So who might you two be?" I asked as I examined two goggled teens. They looked clean and well taken care off. Both had brunette hair, the young girl's was longer. They couldn't be more then fourteen. They looked to be twins. Wow.

I put my bow down.

"I'm Oliver."

"I'm Emma."

"Oh, so nice to meet you two. Are you guys okay? My name is Sam, and these are my friends!"

They both adjusted their goggles, and I couldn't hear any heartbeats coming from them.

I did hear a string of profanity intermeshed with a heartbeat coming from inside the bank.

Before the twins could answer a tall lanky man with a deep scowl weighted down with a bunch of gear exited the bank. He was cleaning a machete with a rag. "It's about time goddamnit. You took your sweet time showing up. The twins told me they heard others outside for a while now!" The man paused and put away his machete. He slide the lethal blade carefully into a sheath on his hip. "What were you doing playing with your lion and eating popcorn?"

Our accuser was an uninfected human—his heartbeat was strong and fast. The man of about thirty, who had confused hay-coloured hair, glared at us. Well, actually he glared at me.

I glared back. "Well, just the popcorn actually, the lion is back at the compound. The popcorn was tasty though, but don't you hate it when it gets stuck in your teeth?" I said matter of factly. I picked at a molar and checked my nails.

He hesitated for just a moment, then he turned his icy glare on everyone else. "We were almost done for!" He huffed. "We used the last of our ammo getting to this building!" His eyes were dark with fury. I saw the pulse in his neck bounding. If he wasn't careful he was going to blow a gasket and stroke out.

"Oliver had a bow thank goodness—that was the last of the arrows!" He broke off his intensive glare from me and looked down at the boy. I saw his face instantly soften as he regarded the twins.

Protectively he placed his hands on their shoulders. I looked toward Christin and Garrick. They had adjusted their aim on the three newcomers—they didn't waver. I nodded to Christin.

The boys lowered their bows. I returned my attention back to grouchy man. "We didn't know what the greens were hunting!" I said sternly.

"So you just sat back and let the greens entertain you while we were scared out of our minds!" He snapped and continued to scowl at me with black eyes. I stood stock-still and glowered back. "Well actually it was entertaining since we don't have cable anymore! And we left our x-ray vision at home." I smirked and turned to open the Rover's back door.

The man grunted back. "You could have called out!" I tossed my bow into the Rover's back seat.

The man's brows knitted into one long unibrow. I think I saw steam rising from the crown of his unruly hair. Everyone stood in stunned disbelief at the hostile exchange.

I appraised the man's tightening eyes. Nice show of appreciation for saving their miserable lives. The twins looked up at their protector. He stood silent and continued to glower in my direction. I averted my gaze and looked at Griff.

The lanky angry man cleared his throat and curtly muttered. "We have to get out of here, more greens could be around!"

I could see Griff was frowning and her forehead was knotted. She was appraising the area.

Griff sighed. I asked her quietly. "Griff, got anything on your radar?"

"Nope, we're clear. Wait—no, we're good." She trailed off distracted lost in her search. Darn, never a green around when you needed one.

Shaking his head, the man repeated. "We have to get out of here, now!" He snapped. The frustration was not leaving this man's voice.

I returned his scowl. "You need to lower the bass in your voice. We are fine. Griff will let us know if there's trouble!" I said through clenched teeth.

We glared ominously at each other. A Mexican standoff!

"Bane, can we take off our goggles now?" Oliver pulled at Bane's jacket.

A distraction!

"They're making my head hurt again!" he pleaded.

I welcomed the distraction. Bane grinned down at the adolescent, all his anger draining from his face, replaced with a growing brilliant smile. He nodded.

With a sigh of pleasure the twins pulled down their goggles in unison.

"Stupid goggles." Emma groaned.

I commiserated with the young girl. We wore goggles only when we had to.

Two sets of incandescent purple eyes illuminated the afternoon sun. Pretty.

In response to their unveiling, my group pulled down their respected goggles.

A kaleidoscopic of incandescent color surrounded us.

"Wow, now that's something you don't see every day..." Bane broke off his smile; his expression seemed both agonized and surprised. He held a hand up to his eyes.

My icy resolve broke. "You guys want to come with us?"

I pressed on. "The lion is waiting, and we're starving. Are you guy's hungry?"

"Oh Bane, can we go? I'm so sick of rabbit. Just for a visit even, please?" Oliver bargained in a cracking voice.

"Where do you want to take us? Is it safe?" Bane's posture stiffened. This communication thing was challenging, geez. I tried hard not to roll my eyes.

"We don't want to *take* you anywhere. You're *invited* to join us!" I told him, exasperation accenting my invite. My hands went to my hips, preparing to engage in another verbal battle.

Christin strode to Bane's side with his hand extended, breaking the tension between Bane and I. "Hi my name is Christin. This is Sam, Griff and Garrick—pleased to meet you." Ah Christin, ever the diplomat.

Bane's stance softened a miniscule, but he continued to eye me suspiciously.

They grasped hands and smiled, "Hi, I'm Bane. You met the twins. Ahh...pleased to meet you, where are we heading to Christin?"

I huffed and pivoted back to Griff and Garrick. "Let's go get the gas. Christin can load our *guests* into the Rover and take them to the marina!"

Behind me I heard Bane whisper to Christin. "Are we swimming somewhere?"

Christin whispered, "Home."

Ω Ω Ω

Bane had left the state of New York under the cover of night.

It was easier to spot the greens at night. He just avoided any area illuminated by a weird green light.

He had been starving for two days. Apprehensive about entering any towns or cities, he had stayed off the roads and hadn't passed near any houses. Unwelcoming humans were another factor to contend with. It was the end of the world and all bets were off.

When he spotted the ranch, he almost cried, and he wasn't prone to crying. Relief washed over him. Bane appraised the impressive ranch. He scouted out that it had numerous smaller buildings scattered about and a couple of barns. Horses and cattle grazed in an open field. This had been a successful ranch. They must have food stores somewhere.

"Ah, food!" he whispered to himself. "And maybe, if I'm lucky, a vehicle." He ruminated on an uncertain question. Could he personally slaughter and butcher a cow? He was starving. Maybe a small one, he could do it.

Bane's vehicle had been side-lined on the interstate, stuck by a massive pile up. New York had become a stinking war zone. Scattered gangs were fighting the greens. The gangs didn't have a chance.

Gauging the ranch he hunched down near a bush and rubbed his chilled hands while he remembered his exodus from the only home he had known.

The sound of machine guns had pierced the labyrinth of darkened buildings. The city had lost power two days before he left and the city was a pitch-dark mausoleum. The Big apple was starting to stink. There was no running water, heat or power and gangs we're the least of his problems.

Somehow, certain humans had been transformed into green-eyed monsters, which were fast and deadly.

Bane had shot one in the head, not a week ago. It was wearing a dress and looked completely human, except for those weird green glowing eyes. He didn't know if it wanted to kill, eat or do what to him—he'd seen his share of zombie movies. He did not want to become one of them or become dinner.

He didn't try to ask questions. He shot first and ran. Bane decided to abandon his child hood home and make for the country. He had to get out of the city.

Nerves shot, he constantly wrestled with maintaining his sanity. He couldn't dwell on any aspect of the world ending. He had to keep moving. He had to focus on filling his stomach. He started edging closer to the ranch.

In his mind he moved with stealth as he crossed the field. His stomach growling, he tripped in a gopher hole.

He rolled onto his back and clenched his ankle. He hissed "Son of a bit..." and spit out grass.

A mooing cow interrupted him. Three feet from where he was laying a cow eyed him with indignation. He had interrupted her grazing. He laughed at the bovine berating. She apparently didn't like sharing her patch of grass.

He got up and hobbled across the gopher-hole ridden field. The horses gave him a wide berth. He didn't appear dangerous to them, just clumsy. So much for stealth. Who was he kidding? His stomach announced his every position.

A tree helped ease the pain of his throbbing ankle. He scoped out the dark nearby ranch house for green light when he heard laughter in the tree above him.

He looked up. The weight of something heavy landed on his back driving the air out of his lungs in an "Oaffff" sound. His body pushed to the ground he realized he was eating grass again. More laughter added insult to his injury.

"You're not very good at skulking! Your stomach gave you away like a mile ago. Didn't anyone tell you that you should eat before you skulked?"

Great, he was going to be killed by smart asses. He had survived gangs and greens to only be undone by...children's laughter echoed high in the recesses of the tall tree. Well the girl's voice did, the boy's laughter came from his back.

Kids he thought. It sounded like two kids—a girl and boy?

"Uhggg, my ego is bruised. Could you get off my back please?" He groaned.

After a silent moment of contemplation, the pressure on his back abated. Air rushed into his starving lungs, and his stomach growled. He heard a titter of muffled laughter escape from behind cupped hands.

"Would you like something to eat? This is a ranch you know! There's plenty," a young girl's soprano hummed above him.

He heard something land behind him.

Bane rolled over. Two young teens were looking down at his dirty rumpled and defeated form. Twin eye brows cocked up, appraising his humiliated state.

"You need a bath too. You stink" They both reached up and pinched their noses.

My stomach snarled noisily. "I think we should feed him first. He's going to bring the green zombies from miles away." The young girl said to the boy, then with that they headed toward the house.

Bane picked himself up off the grassy knoll and brushed off the remaining bits of his dignity and followed the kids.

The twin's parents had been progressive ranchers. They had embraced modern technology to facilitate the effortless management of the large ranch. Automated timers for feed and water disbursement, electronic gates and fences ran on solar panel which was supported by high tech technology. It was all run by a computer system. The ranch's operation was fully off the grid and as easy to manage as pushing a button.

The house hummed with the sound of electricity, but the twins kept the house dark. A smouldering fire danced in the oversized hearth. Dinner was cooking. Their large walk-in freezer housed a variety of animal carcasses. That was butchered, packaged and labelled. The twins never went hungry. It was, after all, part cattle ranch, part horse ranch. No there were no butchered horses. Heavens to Betsy, they weren't that desperate.

The twins told Bane about the ranch which was set far off from any civilized roadways. The family liked their privacy. Fortunately for the twins, the ranch's location afforded anonymity from curious people or hungry greens. The greens preferred to hunt more challenging game rather than submissive cows.

The green zombies liked the hunt more than the catching. On occasion a cow was found down. It had been killed violently with a chunk or two missing from its hide. The greens either didn't bother with the horses or couldn't catch them.

Too tame of a mark for a fixated and driven green, they mostly ignored the sedate bovine. They preferred the challenge of the hunt, not a TV dinner handed to them. A pacified cow was a convenient meal, if they were hungry. They preferred to search out more stimulating quarry.

The twins survived in relative peace. They learned to dispatch the occasional green when necessary. The trees offered a vantage point for the young predators.

The siblings loved animal shows—they adored jaguars. Emma came up with the idea of using the trees as a vantage point. Greens tended to travel in groups of two or more and were always bigger than the twins. Perched like teen jaguars, they'd drop on the unsuspecting greens and deliver a death blow.

Their dad collected knives, so having weapons of differing sizes and shapes was not an issue. If there were more than two greens, or they got too close to the ranch, the twins would use their father's rifles to end the greens curiosity. Overcoming larger prey on the ground simply became a matter of surprise.

Bane Davidson and the twins continued to live in relative harmony on the ranch for almost four months until the smoke came.

Using a hand to shield his eyes from the glare, Bane tried to gauge the distance of the smoke lingering in the east. It only partially clouded the sun's brilliant rays. In the days to come the smoke's creeping approach thickened the atmosphere around the ranch's pastures.

Bane and the twins decided that waiting out the smoke was out of the question. They unanimously decided that it was time to flee the unrelenting smoky haze and head west. They relieved the horses and cattle of their pastured heaven, opening the gates so they could go as they pleased. The twin's departure from their life long home was a tearful farewell. They slowly watched the ranch dissolve into a murky haze. Turning their heads forward, they rode off into the darkening night on horseback.

They drifted west, ever vigil to the hazards of the road. Bane needed to rest unlike the twins, so they set up camp near a small lake. The campsite was beautiful. Birds and crickets hummed in the backdrop of a pristine lake dotted with budding, rich vegetation. A moose and her baby were slopping up some wet vegetation on the other side of the lake.

For a lingering moment, the New Yorker felt the weight of past circumstances lift from his shoulders.

It was late spring, and Bane wasn't looking forward to an icy swim. The twins had said he was starting to stink, and his odor was overpowering their ability to smell greens. He dove into the fresh icy lake with artificial vigor.

Oh my God, that was cold. He felt his testicles shrivel. The water was fresh and pure. It soothed his parched throat. Water had been a little scarce the last few days. Bane had always hated the artificial taste of manufactured bottled water—it had almost a metallic taste to it. Also, who knew where that stuff was collected from?

The twins laughed with child-like innocence as he came out of the lake, lips blue and teeth chattering. A fire was blazing—the twins were ever the considerate travelling companions.

"Turn the rabbit over, Olive or it'll burn!" Emma relieved Oliver of the spitted rabbit. "Humpff, Boys!" She huffed.

Oh so considerate of their twin stomachs—geesh!

Bane draped himself with a blanket and held his shaking hands to the fire. "Ahhhhhh…sweet heaven. The simple pleasures in life!" Bane sighed.

The twins were absorbed in their squabble. Emma was a better cook, but Oliver was stubborn.

"You guys are going to drop that rabbit into the fire, if you keep grappling for that spit!" He glowered in the twin's direction.

Hunger made his stomach rumble and that rabbit smelled really delicious. Unfortunately, he had to wring its neck earlier. The twins could kill greens without much hesitation, but Emma almost started crying over a caught and wiggling Thumper.

"I can't do it Bane, I know I have to, but I can't." Her quiet sobbing followed.

"It's okay hun, you guys catch them, and I'll fix 'em up for the fire, okay?" Bane did his best to soothe her, rubbing her back. "It's okay hun…"

Bane could hear Oliver behind him. The young man had heaved a sigh of relief. Bane turned slightly and took note of his subtle reaction. His sister's response to killing an animal had spared him the necessity to out himself. Oliver had no taste to harm a helpless animal either. His man hood was intact. Whew.

The twins stopped arguing and turned simultaneously to look at the shaking Bane—pure innocence was wrapped in their expressions. They screamed in harmony.

Bane ducked and rolled and felt something whiz past his head. The twins dropped the rabbit and lunged.

The startled Bane heard a splash as he was tumbling toward the lake. He could see green and purple light in the turbulent water. He leap frogged for his gun, he turned and aimed. He saw only purple light pulsing in the agitated murky lake.

The twins emerged in a waterfall of purple tinted water. "I got him!" Emma was grinning triumphantly.

"No you didn't. I got him. I had him by the neck! I twisted it like a soda pop cap!" Oliver flashed an award-winning grin.

"No, I got my knife buried deep into its eye, just like the spitted rabbit!" Emma was incensed as she twisted her large knife illustrating her point.

The fire behind us flared up, and the rabbit went up in fatty flames.

The twins stopped their bickering and grumbled in perfect unison, "stupid green!"

Bane arched his eyebrow questioningly. Now what are we going to do for dinner? The twins groaned and frowned.

"I'll go get a couple more stinking rabbits." Emma stomped her wet feet into the forest.

"I'll go find the horses!" Oliver jumped to a tree to search out the area. The horses had headed for the hills during the melee.

Bane collapsed in a wet heap of nerves. Wrapped in a blanket cocoon he shook. He was not trembling from the cold. Martin Sheen could keep his *Apocalypse now*.

He lay by the crackling fire for a bit, and then a frozen thought slowly surfaced. He chose to get up. Bane couldn't let the twins see him lose it.

Ω Ω Ω

"Where's your ride?" Christin was opening the back door of the Rover, letting the twins get in.

"Last I'd seen the horses, the greens were getting distracted killing them, or else I don't think we would have made it to the bank!" Bane shrugged. They were good horses, and they had carried the trio far. Bane had actually been quite attached to his little quarter horse, Penelope.

He was a pure city boy and had never sat on a horse before. The little mare had been gentle and easy to control.

He hoped she hadn't suffered.

Christin's voice broke his reverie. "You guys were on horseback? Wow! Really? How's your ass?" Chris's face showed he was impressed.

Bane's face turned smug. "Yes, my callused butt can prove it. It'll be nice to ride in something that doesn't crap every five minutes and has shock absorbers!"

"How come you didn't grab a vehicle?" Chris asked. He told Bane how he took Bob for a ride around the island once. He rubbed his butt while telling the jarring story.

"Just easier I guess. The congestion on the roads and having to get gas…" He looked in the Rover distracted by what he saw. They had it rigged with weapons, lights and new radios.

"Sweet set-up Christin." Bane whistled in appreciation. "I can't take credit. It's Sam's doing. She likes to be prepared and likes her gadgets."

Bane scanned the Rover's interior, appraising and admiring its well-stocked compartment. Guns, crossbow, lights, walkie talkies, knives, pepper spray and a large machete—all had a secure place in the SUV. Bane nodded. Yes, Sam liked her toys, but he realized she was a realist.

CHAPTER TWENTY-TWO:
E ight is E nough

"I am so clever that sometimes I don't
understand a single word I am saying."
-Oscar Wilde (1854 - 1900)

The island compound ran itself, with of course a group effort—no one was really in charge.

The scientist maintained the lab facilities. They were working on something, and they walked around silently excited.

Mae organized the home-stead, the basic day to day chores. Cleaning, feeding, cooking and the sleeping arrangements fell passively to Mae. A tried and true mama, grandma and great grandma, she knew how to organize, maintain and sustain a household.

When questioned about her family, she'd always answer the same way. "How many kids and grandkids did you have Mae?" someone would ask.

She'd chuckle and say, "Too many! I lost count!" And then she'd hobble away ending the conversation.

Mae had exactly fifty direct decedents of her bloodline. Losing her kin was a great lose. She remembered each and every one of them. No one saw her dab her eyes with her apron.

The colors and support workers controlled the security of the island and marina.

Everyone just pitched in to do what was needed. Sam kept the schedule, to make sure everything was covered. The distraction of chores and responsibilities was welcoming to most.

"I don't want to clean the bathroom. It's gross and smells bad!" Emma griped. Chemically malodorous water sloshed over the side of the bucket she was pushing.

Bane was kneeling on the floor, scrubbing a stain. "Suck it up princess; you can't play with Bruno all day. You have to do your part—everyone gets a turn at bathroom duty!"

Exasperated, Bane threw his brush into his smelly bucket and rotated off his knees onto his butt. He eyed his begrudging partner. The twins were still so young, fifteen going on fifty. There was not enough time for them to be kids.

"Damn," he muttered under his breath.

"What? I'm doing it Bane." Emma's purple eyes were shadowed by her brown bangs. She swiped them out of her face with her gloved hand. Bane smiled at Emma and thought to himself. They were such good kids, their parents would have been so proud.

"Okay, lets hurry up and finish, then we'll get Bruno and the dogs and go fishing, all right?" He bobbed for his scrub brush and fished it out of the chemically enhanced water. They both started scrubbing fast.

"All right Bane, but can we bring Sam and Griffin too? Griff wants to show me how she wrestled the shark!" Emma was suddenly mopping furiously and talking animatedly.

Strained patience oozed around his words as he said, "Fine, we can invite Griff and err—Sam to..." He broke off the sentence through clamped teeth. Sam irritated him. He didn't know why. He just avoided her when possible.

Unfortunately, the twins adored her, and she adored them. They'd go off together to "explore" the island. They'd returned dirty and their clothing torn or askew to the compound hours later, laughing at some story or another.

He would grumble, "You be careful. You can't grow back another head—or arm for that matter!

Bane stopped his scrubbing and gawked in Emma's direction. "Can you grow things back?"

"No, we can't grow anything back. I'm not a reptile! Jeez!" She paused in her vicious scrubbing. "Well…at least I don't think we can." She scratched her head. "I'll ask Sam!" She smiled and resumed her scouring.

Yes, Sam knew everything. He was grinding his teeth again. It was a nasty habit he had just recently picked up.

Ten minutes later, having made short work of the communal bathrooms, they headed down to the beach.

"Come on you guys, you can get higher than that." Sam laughed and complained, "Amateurs!"

The twins were wading in the surf tossing each other into the air.

Sam was leaning on Bruno, her legs stretched out on the sandy white beach. The dogs were running up and down the beach chasing terns. Bruno had filled his quota of chasing the elusive birds. He was sprawled out, panting behind Sam. He was her portable back-rest. Sam sighed.

Life is a beach.

"Go in the water Bruno, your hot! Garrick, make him go into the water before he spontaneously combusts into a hairy fireball!" I heaved another sigh. He smelled too. A wet, hot, sandy and salty cat made for a very smelly kitty.

Bruno huffed in response to his name spoken aloud.

"Don't boss Garrick around Sam. It's his lion, he knows what Bruno needs!" Bane snapped at Sam while he stared off into the surf where the twins played.

I could feel my eyes tighten as I considered Bane's languid demeanor. This man had become the Bane of my existence—fine. I said it.

Every time I turned around, he was giving me a hard time. What? What's the problem? I was worried about Bruno! Geez! What, was he jealous or pissed that I was hanging out with the twins? He didn't strike me as an insecure guy! I was always watchful and protective of the twins.

I decided a good eye rolling was called for, so I did my most exaggerated eye roll and aimed it at Bane. Christin would have been so proud. I didn't engage Bane in any hostile banter.

Christin felt it necessary to be an interpreter for the two of us.

"Now, what I think Sam meant to say Bane was…"

"Now Sam, what Bane intended…"

Or, my favourite. "Shut up you two. You're giving me a frigging headache!"

Diplomacy utilized to its fullest.

Garrick got up and called Bruno, "Let's go swimming buddy. It's getting too hot over here!" He gestured for Bruno to follow. Bruno moved so fast he left me sprawled in the sand. I sat up and wiped sand off my face.

"Hahahaha!" Bane sobbed out loud while he wiped tears off his face and held his stomach all in a hapless effort.

In a complete display of lack of grace, he rolled over into a pile of seaweed. Scrambling out of the mess, he attempted to regain his composure. A piece of seaweed was caught in his dishevelled sandy hair.

I returned the loss of dignity and made sure his undignified appearance was noticed. Snorting laughter, I pointed at his head. "You have a friend…"I guffawed. "It appears to be very attached to you."

"Ah! Snake!" Bane squeaked like a little girl and pawed off the seaweed. Dignity—definitely lost.

Bane reddened, glowered at me, stood up and stormed to the water.

Ahh, alone at last. I'm going have to start carrying some sea weed in my pocket. I laid back using my arms as a headrest and started to enjoy a beautiful day.

Ω Ω Ω

Still mortified, Bane dove into the ocean and ducked under the water. He swam briskly as he headed for the twins.

He was petrified of snakes. Once when he was young, he had gone to the zoo with his folks. A Boa had almost killed him.

The thought of it made him shudder.

Bane's dad directed his reluctant son. "Come on Bane, that's it, just drape it over your shoulders. Your mom will take your picture. You'll be king of the jungle!"

Bane had the rather large snake wrapped around his neck. That didn't bother him as much what the snake's tail was doing between his legs. He gave a shutter and stared straight ahead, hoping his mom would get on with the photo shoot.

His mom was busy angling the camera, backing up and twisting the lens, when she tripped over a small goat. There was an unexpected flurry of chaos and mayhem. Everyone nearby was distracted with the goat debauchery. People were trying to help the trampled goat and his mom regain some composure. No one paid any attention to little Bane and the snake.

The boa instantly became startled by the bustle of activity and initiated his instinctual death squeeze. Bane's little body was caught in the middle of the snake's fight or flight response. The snake continued to wrap its powerful coils tightly around Bane's slight seven-year old body. His tiny frame all but disappeared behind the shiny camouflaged rings.

A pile of loops stood stacked with small white runners peeking out from the base of the scaly mound.

A strangled cry escaped Bane's lips, and the snake's body constricted further.

"Oh Lord have mercy!" The snake handler's exclamation of horror, redirected everyone's attention to boy's plight.

Constrictors didn't so much as crush their prey, but rather suffocated them. Every time the snake's victim expelled its breath the snake's body coiled tighter.

Five pairs of hands started pulling at the snake's coils.

"Get it off of him! It's killing him!" his mother repeatedly screamed, hysterical. The crowd's collective strength could only budge a couple layers of the constrictor's strong muscular loops.

The young boy's lips were turning blue, and he was losing consciousness from lack of oxygen.

From his old tattered belt the snake handler pulled out a large knife. He took a deep breath and stuck the knife all the way through the snake's head.

The snake quivered, as its coils slowly fell away from Bane's tiny body. The boy collapsed atop the mass of the dead snake. Bane awoke the next day covered in bruises.

He shuddered at the memory. He hated snakes.

Bane submerged his head and floated in the current not far from the twin's laughter. He thought Sam was so controlling and harsh. He couldn't stop thinking about her, even negative things.

Good thing he was soaking his head.

$$\Omega \; \Omega \; \Omega$$

CHAPTER TWENTY-THREE:
A Green in the Hand Is Worth More Than Two in the Shoe

"An idea that is not dangerous is
unworthy of being called an idea at all."
-Oscar Wilde (1854 - 1900)

"We need a green alive."

Dr. Walker and Ray were seated opposite Christin and I at our kitchen table.

"Can you capture one and bring it to the island?" Ray asked, a big smile playing across his goggled face.

We tried to wear our goggles on the island as often as possible. Our eyes were bright and distracting.

The scene was kind of amusing, witnessing two grown men so excited that they could barely contain themselves. Two kids waiting by the Christmas tree till the parents gave the go ahead to start tearing into the goods.

Without missing a beat, I replied "Absolutely. What do you need the green for?"

They looked at each and smirked. "A cure!" They both chimed.

I was taken aback. "Wha—what?" I stuttered out. My hand reached for my astonished open mouth.

The two scientists sat beaming. "What do you think we were doing, churning butter?" Ray was being sassy.

It was an inside joke. Butter's been a luxury we've been without since, well, the end of the world. Anything fresh or manmade actually— you'd be surprised at what you took for granted.

Of course canned and dried goods remained edible, but fresh dairy products, fruits, vegetables and baked goods were not available.

We made do with homemade bread, a garden, nearby orchards and dried goods—raided from town. We'd often teased the scientists to whip up some butter in their mad scientist laboratory.

Another eloquent stammer escaped my stunned lips. "Err, a cure? For whom? For what? The virus?"

The scientist's grin was quickly replaced with a frown. "Well, it's more like an inoculation. We that haven't been infected are highly susceptible to contracting the virus—in fact we're astounded no one has yet caught it in our group of survivors. It's just a matter of time." Dr. Walker looked me square in my goggled face.

I thought of Bane, and my stomach contracted. "What do you need us to do?"

I sat back in disbelief and listened to their requests.

The following week, we secured the shark cage to the boat, and headed to the marina. We had found a shark cage down the coast in a scuba shop.

I played guinea pig. I had climbed into the cage and did everything I could to get out. Griff, Garrick and Chris had stood by and cheered me on to escape. Suggesting any and every escape mode any of us could come up with. It was an unsettling experience. We fortunately only had to make a few adjustments to the shark cage.

Garrick, Griff, Christin and I landed on the dock and got the vehicles ready.

The twins, Bane and Cory really wanted to come on the hunting expedition, and dissuading them was not easy. It was only after we explained the circumstances, did they stop their laments of protests. It was a dangerous venture and an unnecessary risk to put so many in harm's ways.

Bane was the hold out. "I can take care of myself, and you are not the boss of me Sam!"

Eye rolling ensued. "Honestly Bane, someone needs to be the boss of you. You're acting irresponsible and illogical!"

I continued, his full and attentive glare was rapt on my stern glare. "What if something happened to you—I mean the twins? They well… you can't go. You'll slow us down!"

Pain registered across Bane's face for a moment, before a scowl replaced it. "Fine, have it your way!" He turned and strode off.

Brother, he did that a lot with me. I huffed and stomped in the opposite direction.

I of course *never* reacted in the same childish manner as Bane did.

We left our disgruntled friends, standing immobile with their arms crossed over their sulking chests—speechless.

It would be okay. They'd console one another.

I was going to bribe them when I returned, the twins had requested popcorn. Their stash was getting low—they were fiends for popcorn. A belly full of popcorn would appease their current displeasure at being left behind. I believed in bribery.

I was standing at the front of the boat, the misty sea wind felt refreshing. I was deep in thought.

Why did I let Bane get to me? Stubborn, he always wanted to pick a fight. Honestly, he was such a jerk. I had vocalized this same sentiment to Christin a month or so after Bane had arrived on the island. Chris just smirked and stayed silent, nodding his heading listening attentively without uttering a single word. He often found the floor very interesting during my tirades.

Guys could be so infuriating when they talked, and especially, when they didn't. Men, geez! I rolled my eyes into the wind.

If I kept rolling my eyes, they were going to permanently get stuck that way. I did it so much with Bane. An image of my eyes stuck cockeyed made me frown. Yeah Bane would get a kick out of that.

Once we reached the marina, Griff sat in the Rover deep in concentration. Griff had been watching a small pack of greens for the last hour. She said there erratic movements had grown fixed at the moment.

"What are the greens doing now Griff?" Christin asked.

"The pack is moving off, but one, yes—one—is hanging behind," Griff said after a silent moment.

The young woman sat in the Rover while we started unloading the boat. "Keep an eye on that one Griff" I said while tying off the boat. She rolled her eyes at me. "Dah! I know!"

Such sass!

"Your eyes could get frozen in that position you know?" I said.

We stared at each other. Blink. We started laughing.

I loved Griff. We made each other laugh often. I wasn't by nature bossy—I just knew what had to be done. Formalities associated with proper social interaction were often lost on me.

"Sam you could at least say please." Christine laughed and rolled his eyes. Geez this eye-rolling was contagious.

Christin has been trying to teach me "please" and "thank you." The lessons were being met with hostility on my part.

"It's a given Christin. You know, implied. Honestly, did you know some Inuit cultures don't have a word for please and thank you?" Okay so maybe I made that up. I think they don't have a word for "sorry." However, it sounded truthful enough. Right?

Christin rolled his eyes again and shook his head. "All right boss!" He grinned while staring at the asphalt.

"Uhggg." I turned and walked to the door of the Rover. "Impossible!"

I just analyzed whatever the task was at hand and blurted out what needed to be done. I looked at things as being simple, to the point and logical—just the facts ma'ame, so I conveyed it that way.

I shoved weapons and rope into a bag and thought of Chris's other lessons. We were hanging out in the garden weeding when he informed me that I must like to hear myself talk because I always had something to say. Yeah, thanks Chris.

I told him. "It must be terrible to be you, you poor thing." Christin grinned.

I had guffawed loudly. He had sighed, kicked the dirt, and then walked off snickering.

Great I was impolite and a know it-all. Superb!

Spock would understand. Now there's a man for you, pointy ears, logical and to the point, so what if he was kinda green. I chuckled at a memory of Kirk giving Spock a hard time.

Men I just didn't understand them—they're so from mars!

Griff was guiding us to the southwest grid, which leads to the edge of town. We had the town mapped into a grid system—logical and efficient.

I smelled them before my eyes detected anything. The greens were rancid creatures, bathing was not part of their viral enhancement, unless of course you count running through a passing stream.

The pack was gone, but a solitary green was sprawled out, baking in the sun, legs and arms crossed. The male green was resting his head on a disembowelled brown bear.

The green was sort of asleep. Ah, as cute as a napping baby.

Not!

It was startled awake by our approach. It leapt to its feet and took off. We put four arrows in its pumping legs. It tumbled into a blur of multicolored arrows. The agonized howls of his frustration impeded his attempts to pull out the lodged arrows.

Garrick quickly placed a size ten boot on its chest while Christin stuffed a rag into its mouth. I bound its hands as Griff pulled up the cage. Easy as a rodeo, wrapped, packed and stacked.

Clockwork—tickity boo as my mama used to say.

We decided we wanted our arrows back. The green didn't agree. More howls came from the bound and gagged green as he tried to escape. Thanks to the rag in his mouth, he's cries were muffled this time.

We didn't want to irreparably damage our cargo, nor did we want to alert any nearby greens.

The green continued to thrash about in the cage. I managed to inject a very large dose of horse tranquilizer after we had bound the green. It had no effect. Huh, note to self.

Christen clocked it with the butt of his rifle. Ah, peace at last. Thirty minutes later, we were docked on the island. The green was curled in a corner of its cage, twitching and drooling through the rag. Now that's how I like my men! Kidding—sort of.

A grin played around the corners of my mouth. When a combative, aggressive and verbally abusive patient came into the ER, we *had* to use chemical and physical restraints. I mean they were dangerous to themselves and to the hospital staff—safety first.

When this obnoxious patient did awake sober, they would find that a new, ahh…let's say attachment had been added while they were unconscious. Protruding from their Johnson would be a very large Foley catheter.

Look at your pinky. That's about the girth of the catheter. Stretch your arm out. That was about the length of the rubber tube inserted into the delicate urethra *all* the way to the bladder. Muahaha.

Yep, it's all about patient care. We couldn't have skin break down from them being incontinent of urine. No that would be bad nursing care. Nurses prided themselves on their ability to provide very professional patient care.

I looked at the dazed and drooling green. Yep it was all about managing the unknown variable for possible danger. Whether it was a green or a hostile patient, safety was the priority for all concerned. No I didn't put a catheter in the dazed green, but I wondered if I should. It's been so long since I practiced my nursing skills.

The scientists met us at the docks, wringing their hands in anticipation while concern was engraved in their faces. "Is it all right?" They rubbernecked in the direction of the cage.

"Yes, we're all fine Dr. Walker! Thanks for your concern," I drawled, draping the boat's tie to a moor.

Christin eyed our interaction, grinning. He sure grinned a lot lately.

Ray helped Christin tie off his line. That Ray was always so helpful. I'm glad we adopted him.

Distractedly, Dr. Walker mumbled, "Oh yes, of course. Is your crew—are they all fine?" Sometimes, I think they took our ability to heal for granted.

In general the compound was like a large family, and we colors were the extended family. If there was an attic, that's where they would keep us.

I mean they personally didn't have issues with us colors. We were just walking reminders of the global catastrophe, and we could infect and kill them. They gave us courtesy and respect, but inclusion into the uninfected groups had yet to be forthcoming.

But we colors had our own version of close family ties. What the rest of the family thought of us—well, you know that crazy cousin who should be kept in the attic—had company is all. The islanders smiled a lot but kept their distance and were cautious. We respected their fear.

As a nurse, I treated my mentally unstable patients in a similar manner. Be always respectful, but be cautious—you never knew what would set them off. Kid gloves all the way.

Bane, the twins, Bruno and the dogs came rushing to the boat.

"You got it! Whoop! Nice hunting colors!" Emma wrinkled her nose. "He stinks!"

Bruno leaped onto the top of the shark cage. "Conquered" was written all over his hairy muzzle.

"Garrick get your 'King of the beasts' off our prisoner. If it wakes up—it'll have a heart attack!" I hollered over my shoulder.

He nodded, beaming. He was so proud of his hairy boy. "Come on Bruno. I have a treat for you!" Garrick had skinned the brown bear's hide. A new chew toy for Bruno was rolled up in the front of the boat.

The twins looked jealously at Bruno.

"Did you get it Sam?" Emma's hopeful soprano voice peeped up.

"Ah geez, Emma. We were so busy, and I..." I trailed off as I scratched my head and looked around the boat.

Christin and Bane were leaning against the bobbing boat grinning.

Disappointment overwhelmed Emma's face. "It's okay. It's just popcorn." Sadness drenched her words. Good thing Emma's face was hanging so low that the only thing she saw was the sandy beach. Otherwise she would have seen three grown adults synchronously roll their eyes.

We were graced with such drama in our mist. What an actor. And the Oscar goes to, "Emma, could you and Oliver help us bring up some of our gear? It's up front in two big canvas bags. Oh, and can you check and see if my new sword is locked in its sheath." I absently played with the boat's moorings.

I had traded my machete for a sleek brown-handled samurai sword. It made, dispatching the greens heads as easy as slicing butter in July.

With her head held down, Emma forlornly walked to the front of the boat. "Sure, anything for you Sam..." Her younger brother mirrored her mood as he followed her slow pace.

Geez, you'd think I killed their puppy. I held up my hand to Bane and Christin and counted my fingers down—one...two... three then amplified screams erupted.

"You are such a liar Sam!" Emma jumped to the dock with a smug grin.

"Yeah, but I'm a convincing one, right?" I said smirking.

Emma eyed me suspiciously. "I don't know whether I should smack you or hug you Sam!"

"Yeah, I get that a lot!" I eyed Christin and Bane. They abruptly looked very busy unloading the green.

"Hey Sam, when can we go grocery shopping again? Can we find a sword like yours for me?" She held *her* prized bag of popcorn tightly in her arms.

"Sure, Em, it might not be easy though. I lucked out finding this one!"

I watched Bane and Christin attach a large hook to the shark cage. The green was still out. Christen must have clocked it a good one.

I retrieved my bag and unzipped it. A thing of beauty was nestled on top. We had been out and about in town a couple of weeks ago restocking our depleting dry stores, when we came upon a majestic building, the town's museum.

It was a beautiful brick building nestled amongst flowery grounds. Immense trees surrounded the century old building. I decided immediately it was my favorite place in town.

It didn't house a lot of artifacts, just quality pieces of art and historical artifacts. We walked through the halls, oohing and awing like it was a regular Sunday afternoon.

I saw the sword mounted in a display case when we walked into an exhibition for Japan. I just stood and stared at it. My nose was pressed up to the glass case, exactly like a kid eying a candy display through a store's front window.

Christin drew up beside me and told me to wipe the drool off my mouth. "She is a beauty!" He whispered in reverence.

"Do you think I can have it Christin?" I breathed out softly.

"Why not? I'm sure the original owner would be horrified to see it stuck behind glass for eternity!"

We gaped longingly through the glass window for a few more moments. I had watched the *Last Samurai* and *Kill Bill*. I knew the craftsmanship that went into making one of these swords.

The sword in the display case was in pristine condition. Its silver blade glinted against the stream of sunlight that dared to do battle with its honed steel. The grip had ivory inlay set within brown braided leather.

Its simple beauty exuded integrity and elegance. It was an instrument of an honorable death. The greens had been human once. Even they deserved a little reverence when I decapitated them.

My mind made up, I didn't hesitate. I made short work of dismantling the glass case. My new sword went everywhere with me.

Emma had found the chocolate bars mixed in with the load of popcorn. So through a mouthful of brown heaven, she mumbled, "Okay, Sam. I'm sure we'll find one if it's out there." She continued to be distracted, as she rummaged through her haul of junk food utopia.

I watched her as she froze mid rummage.

"Sam!"

"Yes Emma?" I innocently whispered. I knew she could hear me.

"*Sam?*" The louder utterance was followed by a large gulp.

"Yes Emma, did I not get you enough popcorn?" I inquired sheepishly.

Emma fell to her knees beside the black canvas bag, holding something that caused her to pause and genuflect in veneration.

"You'll have to name her Emma, to connect her to you!" I breathed out quietly.

"She's so beautiful, and she's mineee?" Emma squeaked softly. She stood up and turned toward me.

A single tear lingered mid-drip below her right eye. Respectfully she held her own samurai sword clutched close to her chest.

"Oh Sam, thank you. I'll promise I'll take really good care of her!" She cooed to the sword, a silent contract was exchanged between the sword and the young girl.

"I know, I'll teach you how to sharpen it and clean it." I knew she'd be responsible with the sword. She was the oldest by three seconds.

"Do I get one?" Oliver squeaked.

"No hun." I looked out to the ocean, feigning distraction.

A small moan escaped the young man's lips. His hopeful eyes cast down to his feet.

I couldn't take it. I grinned. "Well, I thought a big buccaneer's sword would suite your personality better. It's in the bag you never thought to open."

I watched his head shoot up and his eyes bug open. He dropped the popcorn-laden bag with a clank and tore it open. Popcorn packs went flying through the air.

"Oh my God Sam. You didn't? It's phenomenal!" Oliver screeched. His voice was changing.

An impressive blade rose in the air. "Arg mate-y. Come about, I mean to board her. ARGGH!" He announced to the boat. He was a born pirate, arg.

I hoped he wasn't planning on boarding any females soon. I reddened at his innocent statement.

He was quickly attaching the belt holder around his waist. The world has changed. The iPhone didn't cut it anymore. It was life or death now and I chose to give the twins every chance at life.

Christin and Bane hauled the greens cage to the lab where they secured it safely away. A walk-in freezer was adapted as a holding cell. The shark cage went into the freezer. We weren't taking any chances. One escaped green could do irretrievable damage—lives could be lost. An around the clock guard was posted outside the freezer—couldn't be too safe.

CHAPTER TWENTY-FOUR:

And then I said, "This wont hurt a bit,"

"To live is the rarest thing in the world.
Most people exist, that is all."
-Oscar Wilde (1854 - 1900)

My trailer was full of people. Mae, Dr. Walker, Christin, Bane, Ray and I mulled about.

Dr. Walker began, "We have to try the vaccine first on a green to see if the virus has a reaction to the inoculation. Then if it's successful as we hope, a human test subject." He stared at his hands and whispered, "We'll need a human volunteer for that."

The room was silent.

"I'll volunteer." Bane's stoic face met the surprised look in my eyes.

"No you won't, that's not fair! I mean, we should have a drawing of some kind." I blustered and glared at Bane.

Bane had a smirk resting on his lips. "Ah Sam, I didn't know you cared," he winked at me.

I inhaled a deep breath and took aim.

Christin was faster. "No. Bane it's better for everyone if we hold a raffle. We're all in this together. Just the scientists need to be exempt." Calmness exuded from Christin demeanor. "That's my vote anyway..." Christin's voice lagged off.

Muttered agreements followed Christin's words.

Bane and I scowled at each other.

"Doc, I'm no epidemiologist but once you are infected with a virus don't you either live or die from the infection, or if you introduced a weakened viral strain, a person could make antibodies against the invading virus?" I asked.

"Yes Sam, like polio or H1N1," Dr. Walker replied slowly.

"Then what good is it to an infected person? Once you got it, you got it. Like HIV or even herpes—you could ease the symptoms but never actually get rid of the virus." My brows were knotted together and my arms were crossed. I stared at Dr. Walker.

"That's true Sam, and we have isolated and weakened the virus much like a polio inoculation, but we added a little of our own recipe to the batch!" He smiled sheepishly.

"What exactly did you add?" I asked.

The doc shuffled his feet and looked at Ray. "Well it's a complicated mixture of antivirals we've been working on." Ray nodded his agreement.

"So let me see if I understand. You have one shot for the uninfected—like the weakened polio virus—and another shot for the infected, right?" I regarded the two scientists. They nodded. "So, that means you need two guinea pigs, an uninfected human and infected color?"

They both looked down at their hands. "Since the virus only infects humans, we have no other choice…but to trial it on a human…" The doc's voice straggled off.

"Guinea pig." I finished his sentence.

"Yes." Ray and the doc said simultaneously, their heads hung lower.

"We have no other way to test it." Ray looked up at me and held my glare. "What would you have us do?"

"Not try!" Pain mingled in his orange incandescent eyes.

I held his glowing eyes as I spoke, "Once I read a quote. It was by John Kennedy I believe. He said, 'Nothing of importance was ever achieved without someone taking a chance." I glanced quickly at Bane. Then I returned my stare to the doc and Ray.

"I guess for something this important we have to take a chance, I suppose. I just wish someone didn't have to gamble with their life."

Everyone in the room nodded.

"So you're going to do two different tests I presume? When?" Christin asked.

I broke my gaze and looked back at Bane with solemn eyes. I quickly turned back to the doc as his quiet voice speared my reverie.

"As soon as we can arrange the lottery, we'll inoculate the green later." Dr. Walker continued to look at his hands. My icy blue eyes held his still-hunched figure.

The doc was dealing with the life or death of someone he knew.

I looked closer at his still form. I could now see the new dark circles under his eyes and the rumpled appearance of his lab coat. He wasn't handling the situation well. The doc was used to dealing with birds, not people.

I felt my posture soften. He was doing the best he could; he was trying to save lives.

Bowing my head, I whispered, "It's okay doc, we'll do what we have to, but we're not forcing anyone into being a guinea pig!" I stated matter-of-factly. No one was going to be forced against their will, cure or no cure. I turned and walked out of the trailer. I felt claustrophobic I needed air.

Not before I heard Bane say, "I'm in!"

I cringed.

Ω Ω Ω

Mae quietly sat in the corner and listened to the scene playing out around her. She wasn't listening to Dr. Walker and the others. She was listening to Sam and Bane's subtle exchange. A smile emerged faintly below her blind eyes.

Ω Ω Ω

I paced up and down the beach. "He never thinks of himself, or the twins—they need him. He's so selfish!" I was venting to Teak and

Oakley. They were immersed in my rant, their heads following my every gesture with rapt attention.

I collapsed on the beach. This was the cue for the dogs to dive in and cover me with kisses.

Giggling, I pushed them aside. "Let's go for a walk, shall we?" They jointly answered the invitation with wagging and wiggling bodies.

We ran the beach at a trot. The stars were out, and they polka dotted the sky with their glinting spectacle. Mother Nature's heavenly tapestry shrouded my dark mood. The Ocean's breeze tickled my face with tiny salty kisses. The mist cooled and calmed the internal conflict brewing in my heart.

"Men. It's a good thing you girls are fixed, you don't have to concern yourself with them." The dogs cocked their heads and gently wagged their tails, listening for further conversation. None came.

I stood transfixed with a thought hanging in my mind, dead in my tracks. I'm fixed. I mean, I could never…Even to kiss an uninfected person…I would. I swallowed hard. I would kill them with the touch of my lips. My hand reached for my lips.

Startled realization dawned on my ignorance. I looked up. So many stars sparkled millions of miles from one another—they were so alone in the darkness.

I turned and headed in the direction of my trailer. The dogs trailed my lone footprints.

Ω Ω Ω

Bane mindlessly chewed his dinner, staring at nothing, yet focused intently on her. She'd been creeping into his thoughts more and more lately. He'd find himself noticing her smile and how it made her eyes glisten an intense molten blue. She'd turn his way and flash her eyes. He'd redden as he realized he was staring and turn away, busying his abashed gaze on anything else.

Her smile stopped him too often. Unable to redirect his path without anyone noticing, he would walk by her wordlessly avoiding looking at her at all. He did his best to avoid Sam, but it wasn't easy. Sam was always with the twins.

Late one evening he had just finished his monitor duty. Exhausted and dirty because he had to help fix a few sensors, he walked into the trailer that he shared with the twins. The three of them were laughing at some of Oliver's earlier antics with his sword.

They had all turned with welcoming smiles when he entered. He saw Sam and hit his head on the door. He felt the blush creep up his neck. "I'll be right back. I need ahh…to soak my head."

He stumbled back out of the trailer entrance, rubbing his forehead. Bane found Bruno's drinking bowl, a rough wooden trough and stuck his head deep into the still water.

A whisper from behind him penetrated the night as he was lifting his throbbing head out of the stagnant water. "If you cut your head, it could get infected—you have no idea what Bruno leaves in there!"

Bane swiftly turned and saw Sam leaning against Garrick's trailer. Her feet and arms were crossed in a relaxed stance. She was smirking. Her eyes blazed fierce molten blue.

His usual dishevelled hair was plastered to his face, water dripped down his back. "Yeah, you're probably right. I should be more careful."

Her face softened as she started toward him. "Let me have a look and see if you cut yourself."

"No I'm fine really!" He attempted to back up, but his head was cupped in her hands before he knew it.

Her swirling blue eyes stared into his. "It's okay I won't hurt you, I have gloves on. See." She held up her latex covered hands. "I always carry a pair."

Bane winced as she gently probed his scalp. Sam noticed the wince and grinned. "Why are guys such big babies when it comes to pain?" She whispered quietly.

Bane stood stock-still afraid to breathe. The pain wasn't the issue. Sam's expert fingers probed deeper into his wet scalp. Her touch felt soothing to him as her fingers massaged his scalp.

An ache the size of Tennessee was growing in between his legs, and it was getting uncomfortable. Bane fidgeted—damn if it wasn't spreading. He backed away from her expert hands and tripped over the trough and fell in.

The loss of his dignity was complete. At least the cold water fixed his discomfort.

Sam's laughter echoed between the two trailers. "Here, let me help you up!" She made to step closer, her hand extended out.

Her eyes intensified liquid blue, and he felt himself stir. "Umm... no thanks. I think I'll sit here awhile. The cold water is, refreshing after a long day and I was pretty...dirty." Bane smiled his most sincere smile at Sam. His discomfort was still growing. Damn. He was going to have to tell Garrick that Bruno deserved fresh *cold* water.

Sam smiled back. "Suit yourself klutz!" She turned and walked away, with the tinkling of her laughter following in her wake.

He splashed the water in frustration, cursing under his breath.

Bane continued to chew his dinner. Damn, thoughts of her kept sneaking up on him. He chewed absently and bit his tongue. He tasted blood. He scowled at the pain.

Her infectious laughter...it all made him very uncomfortable.

Why did he volunteer tonight? Was he crazy? The inoculation could kill him if it didn't work?

Realization slowly spread. He'd be immune from getting infected. He could get lost in her eyes, he could kiss her...

He dropped his head onto the table, adding another lump to his already bruised scalp and groaned.

Ω Ω Ω

Honestly, was he so repulsed that he didn't even want me to touch him? Didn't he know by now that he couldn't get infected from casual touching? I mean, he lives with the twins. Geez!

I sat on the beach most of the night lost in unfruitful musings. I kicked over a mound of sand and headed to my trailer while growling in frustration. I hadn't figured a thing out as to Bane's motives. I stomped into the trailer. Christin was sitting on the couch reading.

I could keep on trying to avoid Bane, but it was awkward. People were noticing.

I ripped open the fridge door. Christin looked up from his book. "What's up with you? Has Bane pissed you off again? Do you want me to adjust him for you?" He asked as he cracked his knuckles and smirked. Very butch, my Christin is.

I snorted while drinking a freshly poured glass of milk. "I think you mean, 'tune him up' Arnold," I choked out while trying to clean my face off.

"Oh…" he murmured.

"No, It's fine, thanks though. He just, ah, doesn't…Umm. The infected thing," I stammered out.

Chris chimed in. "You do know, he lives with two infected?" A grin stole up his innocent face.

""I know. Right! Weird. I don't know what his problem is. My mama used to say avoidance is healthy. But she didn't live on an island." I didn't make eye contact with Christin's gawping smirk and continued to clean myself up as I walked down the hall.

My shirt was a lost cause. I needed to change. "Oh hey, Chris?" I spun around "How are the scientists doing?" I asked.

Christin had been hanging out all hours at the lab. "They injected the green, yesterday. It's just a matter of time. Hurry up and wait, that kind of thing. They're monitoring the impact of the vaccine concoction."

I paused in my cleaning, distracted by a thought.

"We'll get the raffle together within the week." His voice grew distant as I remembered Bane volunteering.

"Sam, are you listening?" Christin was frowning, "Everything all right?" I stared for a moment then walked back to the kitchen.

"Yeah, im fine" I stood in the kitchen glaring at my empty dish. I was going to make something to eat but I lost my appetite. I picked up my empty dish and put it away.

I needed to get out of the trailer. Claustrophobia was setting in again. "I'll talk to you later. Oh, hey—you want to come for a swim? The twins, Garrick, Griff and I are all heading to the beach after chores."

Christin looked toward the lab. "Maybe I wanna see how things are in the lab today." Christin sure liked the lab.

The green paced along the beach. It could smell so many different odors it couldn't identify. The odors made it curious. The interesting smells were coming from the ocean. It entered the water without a conscious thought. It was following its nose and its hunting instincts. The green didn't so much as swim as it walked and waded through the ocean. A shark darted out with its jaws open in an exploratory motion. The green flinched in surprise. The shark veered as the green grabbed its dorsal fin. The shark swam for the open ocean taking the clinging green for a ride. Bored with its inability to stop or kill the shark, the green released his grip. The green bobbed to the surface to get its bearings. It saw waves crash on a rocky beach. It started to swim toward the solid land and dense forest.

I left to finish my chores I needed to string some detectors on the far side of the island. Then it would be swim time.

Garrick, Bruno and the dogs waited by the Jeep. I loaded an armload of sensors into the convertible Jeep. Bruno loved riding in the open Jeep—he was so spoiled.

The dogs and big cat vied for positions. It was like having three hairy, cantankerous kids in the back seat. There was a lot of growling, barking and huffing going on in the back of the Jeep. Garrick and I exchanged looks, simultaneously rolling our eyes— kids! Geesh!

We gave up trying to sort them out. They'd sort it out themselves. We heard a high-pitched cry as we rolled over a deep hole.

We looked back and saw Bruno had sat on Teak. Teak bit Bruno's haunch. Bruno roared and jumped out of the Jeep—he'd prefer to walk. He kept pace with us easy enough, loping along. Teak was leaning over the console, muzzle open, panting. Her smug grin was blowing in the breeze. I swear! Garrick and I laughed. One point to Teak—Bruno zilch!

Oakley was watching Bruno loping beside the Jeep. Jealousy danced in her eyes. Oakley had the legs of a gazelle. She had kicked me in the head enough times, when we wrestled or she wanted more room on the couch.

I slowed down. "Go on Oakley. Go for a run with Bruno. Teak do you wanna go?" There was no moving Teak. She had earned her coveted hard won position—she had incurred the wrath of a great beast's butt.

It was beautiful to see Bruno and Oakley running through the trees. Garrick and I savoured the quiet drive. We drove on in silence. It was a warm sunny day, and we didn't have a care in the world.

Quiet time was scarce. Alone time was even rarer. That was why I loved swimming so much. I could stay submerged for endless periods. It quieted the heavy world. There was always something happening or something needing to be done at the compound.

After a while of quiet, we finally decided to discuss where we should start stringing monitors. We were almost to the other side of the island.

A roar rang out behind us, pulling me out of my thoughts. I slammed on the brakes in time to see Bruno and a green rolling out of the trees behind us. Oakley was fast on their heels, trying to get a purchase on a piece of the green.

We both jumped out of the Jeep as it kept rolling. We sprinted to the struggle. The green was on Bruno's back, its arm locked in a deadly stranglehold around Bruno's hairy mane. He bounced and bucked, but couldn't shake the green lose.

Oakley had jumped and managed to clamp onto the greens upper arm. It howled in rage. It released its grip around Bruno's neck and fell backward onto Oakley. We heard her yelp in pain. Bruno scrambled to turn while we raced past him. Sword and machete in hand, we advanced on the green.

The green held Oakley above its head. It marked us with its glowing eyes as we bore down on its position. Oakley cried out a sickly howl of panic. The green prepared to throw Oakley at us.

I released my sword. It sliced through the air unobtrusively. The deadly sword did not spin nor waver. It sunk deep into the greens chest.

The green maintained its posture for a moment. A surprised expression spreading as it looked down at the foreign object jutting from its chest. The green fell onto its knees, releasing Oakley as it collapsed forward.

Oakley rolled awkwardly, yelping as she fell. Bruno roared behind us, he lunged onto the greens still form. He picked it up and shook it like a ragdoll, smacking it into a nearby tree. A crumpled distorted bloody mess rested at the base of the tree.

Oakley was lying on her side. She tried to get up. Her front right leg hung disjointed. I was beside her in an instant cradling her head while Garrick held her disfigured leg. The beleaguered dog whined quietly.

"It's okay Oakley. Good girl, you saved the big cat." Tears played with my eyelashes. I choked out, "We're gonna get you home and fixed up right as rain." She licked my tears away.

I smelled blood on her breath. "Let's go. Get my sword. Separate the head from that wretched body. I'll carry Oakley. Let's go now!" I hollered as I lifted Oakley and ran to the Jeep. I leaped into the back of the Jeep without jostling the injured Oakley. Teak sniffed her sister and whined. After Garrick and I had jumped out, the Jeep had hit a tree, stopping its progress. The wheels spun slowly in the mud.

I rubbed Oakley's face. "It's gonna be okay girls. We'll be home in a minute," I whispered assuredly to my canine companions.

Garrick jumped into the driver's seat and drove like Mario Andretti. I cushioned Oakley's ride. I could see Bruno racing to catch up. The big cat's conditioning was paying off. We all flew into the center of the compound in a haze of dust.

Christin came running to meet us. "What happened? Oh, jeez Oakley! Sweety!" He rubbed her somber face.

Ω Ω Ω

"It was a green. It somehow got on the island. I don't know how." I grabbed Oakley gently. "Tell him Garrick!" I was breathless, but not from exertion. I felt pain deep in my chest.

I headed to the lab at a trot. Oakley whined quietly in my arms. "Garrick, grab Griff. Get rid of the greens body and do a sweep of the island." I yelled over my shoulder.

"Don't worry about anything Sam. Take care of Oakley!" Garrick answered in a dismayed whisper.

Chris added that he would take the agitated Teak to Mae's.

Bane was just exiting the research facility so opened the doors for me. We held each other's eyes for a brief second. "What the...? Are you okay? What's wrong with Oakley?" His concern was written all over his face. I didn't know he cared about Oakley.

"Can I help?" the bewildered Bane asked.

"Just grab the doors please! I got to get to the lab." I pushed past him. He raced to get by me and open the rest of the doors in my path.

Some lab rat I didn't know his name, dropped his papers in shock at our approach. He stood up and squealed, "You can't bring that animal in here. It's a clean environment!"

His indignant whine was met with Bane's right hook.

Bane smiled and opened the next door. "Thank you," I said and returned his smile.

Dr. Walker was a smart man, so, as we came barreling into the main lab, he had the situation analyzed and logged in under two seconds. "Bring her over here Sam. Tell me what happened!"

I recounted the morning's events, while he worked on assessing Oakley's wounds. Bane paced behind me, glancing nervously over my shoulder.

Oakley's front right leg was shattered. The doc couldn't fix it. "I'll have to take it off near the shoulder. I've never done anything like this before. I don't know if… I don't know how it will end." His voice trailed off. Ray had heard the commotion and came to help.

Dr. Walker turned his attention to Ray, who was now holding an oxygen mask over Oakley's muzzle. They held each other's concerned faces for a moment. The doc nodded to Ray and took over holding the mask. I glanced at Ray as he started darting around the adjacent labs. The maze of labs was separated by glass.

"Ray don't forget the proprofol and morphine." The doc yelled out.

Those drugs meant conscious sedation. I knew what they were going to do. They were going to knock her out and cut off her leg. Oh God, I don't know if I could help. Oakley was like my kid.

I swallowed hard. I steered myself to focus. Oakley needed me. "What do you need? I'm a nurse, I can help."

We worked on Oakley for two hours. She lost her right leg because the bones had been shattered. She groggily awoke from her drug induced stupor curled in my arms wrapped in bandages. We were camped out on Dr. Walker's couch. Bane was asleep in the doc's chair, his head thrown back and snoring. I saw Christin deep in conversation with Ray. Chris was nodding.

Oakley tried to sit up, whining and disorientated. I soothed her distress by whispering softly and stroking her furry head. She laid her head down into my lap and quieted.

Dr. Walker came into the office with a syringe. "Should I give her something to sedate her?" He looked worried.

I shook my head. "Do you have anything for pain? I don't want to knock her out again, but I want to keep her comfortable."

We exchanged anxious glances. "Yeah, sure. Just a second." He turned and left the office.

We spent the next two nerve wracking days on Dr. Walker's couch. We moved only when I thought Oakley might need to relieve herself. A steady IV drip kept her hydrated.

Mae brought me and the dogs some chicken, deer and veggies. Oakley didn't eat anything until the night of the second day. An injured dog that was eating was always a good sign. I heaved a sigh of relief as I watched Oakley nibble on some chicken.

Ω Ω Ω

She was so little when I got her, almost too young to have been weaned from her mother. It was mid-July, and it was a scorching hot month. A friend of mine was sitting beside me in my convertible Jeep. We were heading to the neighbourhood flea market. We both needed a little air-conditioned relief and shopping would be fun too.

We were talking about possible treasures we might find, as we pulled alongside a beaten up old Ford in the market's parking lot. I noticed a guy sitting in the truck bed smoking a cigarette. He noticed us too. "Hey you guys wanna buy a puppy? They're cheap!"

My eyes narrowed. They had puppies put in this heat? Son of a…my thought was interrupted when I heard a gaggle of small whines.

I got out and approached the back of the truck and peered into a cardboard box tucked under the truck. Three pups and an adult dog were curled together in a hairy collection of tiny feet and ears. The mama dog looked like Teak, only white. Interesting. I wondered if they were related. Damn. I didn't want another dog, but they looked so helpless, fuzzy and cute.

Somewhere, somehow I found my resolve. "No, I'm good. I have a dog already. Besides, if I did get another dog I kind of wanted a brown female to hang with my dog!" Okay, that was an illogical statement. I didn't particularly want another dog, brown or likewise—weird.

Smoking man said, "Well we have all black males but…" Just then a well-weathered woman of about fifty drew up to the side of the truck with a little fuzzy *brown* puppy.

"Hey mother do you want to give up that little brown female that your so akin to?" he drawled. His cigarette remained in situ between his lips. A long tail of ash hung precariously on the end of his cancer stick.

"I don't know daddy, I'm kinda partial too her. She's awful quiet, and she has a good temperament about her."

I looked at the brown puppy and could see how dehydrated she was. Her nose was dry and crusty and her breathing was slow and shallow.

"I'll give you fifty bucks for that puppy," I blurted out. I felt panicked as I absorbed the puppy's appearance. The sign had said ten.

"No, no, no. I really like her!" The old weathered woman was lighting a cigarette. She started hacking out what sounded like a lung. I glanced down at the mama dog, "I don't think that puppy is going last the night, just look at it—it's sick. I wouldn't put it with the other pups it might be contagious."

The woman blanched and coughed up another part of her lung onto the puppy. She pulled it away from her and inspected it. The brown puppy's head drooped to the side. The tiny thing was unresponsive to the woman's glowering stare. "Fine, take it. Fifty bucks!" She said as she shoved the puppy into my crossed arms.

"No thanks it's going cost me a lot more to bring it to the vet and have it looked at!" I would have paid her a hundred.

"Daddy I'm just gonna give it to her. I don't want it infecting the other pups." She thrust the lethargic pup at me again. This time I gently scooped the baby away.

"All right mama—whatever you want." His ash fell to the ground.

I looked down at the other pups and mama dog, the mama dog sighed and laid her head over the remaining squirming fur balls. She seemed relieved. I noticed she had food and water by the box.

My confused friend and I jumped in my Jeep and headed to the emergency vet clinic. The brown pup was dehydrated, malnourished and had a really bad case of worms. My vet said that little runt was as tough as wood.

Three days later and a hefty vet bill, the little brown puppy ate anything and everything we put in front of her. I named her Oakley because Oak was the toughest wood I knew.

On day three we decided to move camp to Mae's. Just in case I had to leave Oakley's side, Mae was there to relieve me. Fortunately there wasn't a shortage of volunteers to meet Oakley's every need. Everyone in the camp came by to bring little treats and homemade toys. Oh did she milk it. Literally—she'd hold her one remaining paw up to her head and I could swear if she could talk she would have said "Oh woe is me."

Ω Ω Ω

Geez…You ever see those animal shelter adds on TV that make your heartstrings wrench.

Well, Oakley could have been cast as the star. Chocolate forlorn eyes pressed anyone with a heart to coo while you gently caressed her flattened ears. Her thumping tail showed me just how well she was really doing. Geez she was a good actor. She lapped it up.

During one of the following days, Griff came to see me. "I'm so sorry Sam. I didn't have my attention directed to the western part of the island." She was petting Oakley, not meeting my eyes.

"It's okay Griff. I only decided just the other day to put monitors on that side of the island. Who knew they'd come in from the water? Damn thing must have been chasing a shark or whale or something."

Teak was on my lap. Apparently she wasn't getting enough attention. Oakley must have been giving her acting lessons because a forlorn expression was fixed on her furry face.

Griff's face had a pained expression stamped on her knitted brow. "Yeah but…"

I interrupted. "Yeah but nothing!"

All the colors had made short work of setting up cameras and detectors all around the island. "We're all secure Griff." I'm sorry we didn't think about it sooner and take the necessary precautions." I chewed my bottom lip and paused eyeing Griff who was still focused on Oakley's needs. "I'm sorry we put so much on you hun."

"I can handle it." Her seventeen-year-old chin jutted out defiantly. She looked straight into my eyes.

"I know you can, but you shouldn't have to. We got each other's backs right?" I spoke slow and punctuated.

I didn't want this weight on her young shoulders. "Do you want to help me?" I sighed dramatically. Teak wasn't the only one getting acting lessons from Oakley.

Griff's head shot up. "Yes," she responded without missing a beat. "What do you need?"

I chuckled. "Well…" My expression turned grave. "Oakley really stinks. I think she needs a bath, or Mae's going to kick us outta here!" I stifled a laugh at her serious, nodding expression.

She jumped up, looked one way then the other and back again.

I couldn't restrain myself anymore. "I'm kidding Griff! You really have to lighten up hun. Mae would never kick us out. Geez…If you don't lighten up on yourself, I'm going to make someone put you on bathroom duty for like a month!"

Griff wrinkled her nose. I started laughing at the look of horror that crossed her face. "Come on. Let's go before I figure more ways to torture you." I eased Oakley into my arms.

"Can I carry her? I'll be gentle." Griff asked in a hushed whisper.

The fifty pound dog felt as heavy as a bag of chips in my arms. "Sure, she's probably sick of me lugging her around anyway."

I gently handed Oakley to Griff. I grabbed some fresh bandages. The three of us walked down to the beach. The crippled dog looked exceptionally excited at the prospect of playing in the ocean and the vast sandy beach. Her tail did an excellent propeller imitation.

We stopped walking and I removed Oakley's dressings, under the dog's intense and scrutinizing eyes. The three of us stared at her stump.

I swallowed hard. "I'm going to have to call you Stumpy from now on!" she licked my hand and then her stump. I picked her up and took her into the water.

Oakley's Physiotherapy was progressing well. She swam awkwardly at first, but with me close by she found her rhythm. The daily salt water baths aided in healing her injured leg, while my lavished attention kept her spirits high. Bacteria hated salt. I loved the salt. I loved Oakley.

As the crippled dog regained her strength, she slowly relearned to walk and then progressed to a hopping run. Her gentle eyes still sought encouragement and lots of rubbing. Bruno chased Teak and Oakley chased Bruno—the animal's version of physio.

Things were getting back to normal, minus one leg. That is until a week later, when the scientist announced that the lottery would be the next day.

CHAPTER TWENTY-FIVE:
The Black has a Name

"In any moment of decision, the best thing you can do is the right thing. The next best thing is the wrong thing and the worst thing is to do nothing."
- Theodore Roosevelt (1858 - 1919)

Everyone living in the compound agreed that the testing of the vaccine was a necessity. However, only ten people out of thirty-eight volunteered to be guinea pigs.

The scientist had decided to inoculate the green with their recipe while the lottery's schematics were ironed out. The vaccine didn't kill the green. In fact, the virus inside the green didn't even hiccup at the introduction of the vaccine.

Queue the evil virus's maniacal laughter, echoing into the night. The virus was well ingrained in its established host. Blood tests from the green proved the virus's virulence was as prevalent as ever. Plan B was out the door.

After dinner everyone came to the center of the compound. A table had been erected and a fish bowl sat with the scribbled names of the *volunteers* nestled inside. Some people were sitting at picnic tables or standing near the table. A group of ten people held hands in a cluster. Bane was amongst them. I could see concern and worry marred everyone's faces as they waited for the selection to begin. I stood by Chris and Griff. Garrick and Bruno played off to the side with a few kids.

Ray, Dr. Walker and Mae approached the table where the fishbowl sat.

The doc cleared his throat and spoke loudly to the hushed crowd. "I would like to thank the volunteers for taking this chance at a cure. You may well be saving what remains of humanity from getting infected with this lethal virus."

I heard a few quiet sobs.

Ray stepped closer to Dr. Walker. "If anyone who has volunteered wants to change their minds. Now would be an appropriate time to speak up."

I heard crickets in the growing night.

Mae stepped up. "I will do the drawing since you're all aware I'm as blind as a bat." I heard a few nervous chuckles.

My face remained stoic as I stared at Bane, Cory and Adam in the group of ten.

I held my breath when Mae reached into the glass bowl. She handed the folded paper to Dr. Walker.

The doctor had a bead of sweat on his upper lip as he unfolded the paper.

I closed my eyes and said a silent prayer. Please…

"Adam."

Quiet mutterings peppered the compound.

My eyes popped open and I saw Mae reaching for another folded piece of paper. I looked at Bane. He was staring at me with no fear on his face.

Mae gave the next piece of paper to Ray. It was all happening too slow. I wanted to sprint across the dusty compound and rip the piece of paper from Ray's hands. I grabbed Christin's arm and squeezed.

"Sam. Ouch, you're breaking my arm." I didn't let go.

My eyes hadn't left Bane's.

In my periphery I saw Ray drop the paper, but quickly pick it up and clear his throat.

"Tara."

I exhaled in a great sigh of relief. I didn't know Tara. Chris said she is a support worker for the lab.

Bane dropped his steeled gaze from me and turned to Adam and shook his hand wishing him well.

I turned and left the compound as Dr. Walker announced that the trial would begin tomorrow morning.

I needed to get away. I scooped up Oakley and bid Teak to follow me. My nerves felt shot, my chest hurt and I felt like I wanted to sob. I headed to the docks.

I found my resolve sitting on the metal dock, Teak and Oakley tucked under my arms on either side of me. The gentle crash of the waves hitting the docks slowly started to soothe my fried nerves. I felt relief penetrate my anxiety as I comprehended fully that Bane hadn't been selected. Unfortunately, Adam had been chosen. Guilt reared its ugly head as I realized I felt nothing but joy that Adam and Tara had been picked and not Bane. I was going to go to hell.

Ω Ω Ω

Phillip Poe was growing bored, he hated being bored. He caught the occasional green and lit them on fire—they moved fast when they burned. Their dancing light extinguished so quickly, it was only as exciting as a small firecracker muffled by the wind.

Phillip had no clear direction. He simply moved with the wind. Presently it was taking him west. He left a smoldering trail of ash in his wake.

His black eyes took in the murky haze before him. His path was bland until he painted it with the licking flames of fire.

The dullness of his path caused a deep craving for colour. He adored color. He liked the greens color. It reminded him of the green hue that swayed at the base of his masterpieces.

One night Poe caught a green and absently plucked out one its eyes. Poe then released his captured green, ignoring its scrambled wail. He was fascinated with a fleeting thought.

Could he…he wondered? With one finger he gently scooped and plucked out one of his own eyes and dropped it inattentively to the ground. The empty eye socket burned with absence, he furrowed his brows. Pain wasn't a consequence to him. He had lived with it his whole life.

He inserted the new eye and waited. A vibrant green haze emanated from his right eye. It began to intensify. Pleasing! Oh joy. He clapped his hands together. The light of God was truly growing within. The Almighty must be pleased with his work.

Poe turned and stepped on his old, lifeless black eye. He hummed a toneless tune, put his hands in his pocket and continued to saunter west again. He had a new bounce in his step, for now a green haze illuminated his path, and his spirits felt renewed.

Ω Ω Ω

"Come on Griff, give it a rest. You've been at it for fifteen hours!" Emma whined. She snapped her fingers in front of Griffin's face. Garrick brushed Bruno nearby. The huge cat was actually purring.

"Let her be Em. She's trying to distinguish colors and expand her sensing range!"

Emma kicked the sand. "Dang Garrick. She promised to help me practice my sword fighting techniques!" A squeaky sigh escaped from her pout.

"Maybe later Em. I'll remind her of her promises." Griff popped an eye open and rolled it toward Garrick. He caught the faint movement and smiled. He turned his expression down and suddenly busied his attention on brushing out a tangle of knots in Bruno's mane.

Emma was too engrossed in the sand to notice the change in her friend's behaviours. The young girl abruptly looked up. Her gaze stopped and lingered in the direction of the lab. She wondered how the tests were going.

Ω Ω Ω

The scientists watched the volunteers for symptoms of the virus, measuring everything from urine, blood and vital signs. Seventy hours and no symptoms—the test thus far was a success. The only complaints so far were from Adam, who had a small headache and was bored from being cooped up in the lab for almost three days.

The volunteers were being monitored in a sealed part of the lab. The scientists were taking no chances. They wore level four protective medical gear. Even anthrax couldn't penetrate their suits.

Ray was charting Adam's recent vitals when he noticed that his heart rate was starting to spike. "Gil, hang on man we need you!" Adam shouted in his sleep. He was wrestling with his bed linen.

Ray went to Adam's side and roused him. "Wake up Adam. You're dreaming." He shook Adams shoulder.

Adam sat up and grasped Ray's arms. "Sam, you got to get us out of here—Cory's hurt bad!" he screamed unseeing at Ray.

Ray yelled loudly. "Harley, Harley—help! We have a problem!"

Dr. Walker came running from his office, dropping his coffee midstride to suit up.

Concern was engraved on Harley's face. The lines never eased even when he was sleeping. "What's happening Ray? Is Adam okay?" he yelled back. The doc couldn't get dressed fast enough.

Finally he was stumbling through the two makeshift airlocks. He grabbed Adam's wrist. An aggravated pulse palpated beneath his gloved fingers—Adam was under duress. Ray lifted Adam's eyelids. His eyes were frantically circling in their sockets, searching, unfocused.

Dr. Walker hung his head and whispered through his clenched teeth. "Damn, he's totally infected. Son of a…" He turned to Ray. "Check Tara, quick."

Ray pulled the blanket down from Tara's still form. He shook her and checked her pupils. The young girl was unresponsive to any form of stimuli.

The test had failed. They decided not to prolong the volunteers' suffering, so they chose not to manually assist with their breathing. The two guinea pigs slipped quietly away. They never woke up from their stupor. The compound of survivors burned the bodies that night.

A defeated silence fell over the compound.

Ω Ω Ω

"I don't think...this is a good idea. The people can't take another disappointment again..." I refocused my attention on cooking dinner.

It was Christmas on the coast, and a tentative merriment seeped through the compound's populace. Christin, Ray and Harley were seated at our kitchen table.

After the botched tests, the scientists had kept their heads down and made their presence scarce. When the people of the island encountered the scientists, they greeted them with an array of mixed emotions. The scientists felt it appropriate to bury themselves in their lab and immerse themselves in work.

From the rumpled, hunched figure of Dr. Walker, a low murmur escaped his almost-still lips. "We just need to try a different route. We well...need altered and varied samples."

Christin shrugged his response. "Who knows? Maybe if this works, it'll help. What do you need doc?" Christin continued to be ever the diplomat.

Chris appeared casual, but my keen vision caught the tension in his eyes. He kept eyeing Ray covertly.

My eyes narrowed, and I looked at the three suspiciously. "What is it you actually need?" I asked cautiously. I was ever the pessimist.

Ray cleared his throat. "Blood samples from all the colors. We want to study how the virus managed to mutate your genes."

The room grew silent.

I shrugged. "Sure, I'll talk to the others—" Three heads popped up simultaneously.

Two fatigued faces smiled. "Thanks Sam."

"On one condition."

The two scientists did a double take. Dr. Walker spoke up first. "Sure, of course. Whatever you need."

I took a deep breath and let out a long sigh. "Under no circumstances do you let anyone know anything, until you have something concrete." The people might lynch the scientists if they suspected another vaccine trial was amiss.

And so it went. All the colors gave blood samples, and the scientists hunkered down with the goods. They had shiny new and dangerous toys to occupy themselves with.

I kind of missed the snow and the changing seasons. The west coast weather remained constant, much like our lives at the moment. The colors exchanged weapons for Christmas. Sentimental fools we were.

Christin's absence in the trailer grew more frequent. "Where have you been hiding Christin? I never see you anymore." I straightened up my new pile of weapons. It was cleaning and repair day.

He looked sheepishly towards the window. "Oh you know, helping out at the lab." He gathered fresh clothes into a bag. He shrugged. "You know. Staying busy and stuff." He turned back to his hunting and gathering mission.

My eyes either rolled or narrowed when it came to Christin lately. They now narrowed. "No I don't know. There's something you're not telling me Christin! Dish!"

I imagined maybe that the scientists were making headway in their investigation of our infected genes.

So I was surprised when Chris blurted out, "It's Ray!" Chris sat down on the couch in a huff.

I looked at him with alarm. "What about Ray, is he all right?"

He brought his hands to his face. With exasperation he voiced his concerns. "No, yes—he's fine. It's just…he likes me, and I like him, but he's obsessed with finding a vaccine. He and Dr. Walker can't forgive themselves. And well, he's killing himself trying to find a cure!"

My eyebrows rose in surprise. I didn't see that one coming.

Christin being gay wasn't a shock, but Ray and Christin together was. In retrospect it was so obvious. Geez, Mae wasn't the only one that was as blind as a bat.

I recovered quickly and closed my gaping mouth.

Christin didn't notice my astonished expression. His face was still in his hands. "He and Harley feel so bad about the failed trial. They're relentless. I think old Harley is going to keel over trying to keep up with Ray!"

Chris removed his hands and stared at the lifeless TV. "They're trying to find a life-saving inoculation, and I'm worried about my boyfriend. Selfish I know." Christin frowned.

I looked at my clasped hands, ruminating. "I think Ray needs to take a step back from his work to get a fresh perspective, and I doubt he'll do that voluntarily!" I smiled a devilish grin.

Christin looked at me with a blank expression, a growing smile spread into a conspirator's smirk as he absorbed my mood. "What did you have in mind?" he asked.

The colors were responsible for security, so I delegated.

I told Christin and Ray to cruise down the coast in a small yacht to scout our surrounding areas. I convincingly professed it was a very important aspect to maintain our secure site.

Ray was not impressed I made him go. "Listen Ray, in case of emergency, all colors need to be familiar with the security of the island, and you have been shirking your share! It's only fair and safe to have you go as well. It should only take you guys a couple of weeks."

"What do you mean two weeks? I can't be gone that long!" Ray and I squared off toe to toe. We both had our hands on our hips. We were two immovable objects that glared at each other. I'm sure we could stand that way for days.

I scowled at him.

"Fine, I'll go." He snarled. He turned and stalked off.

Harley was standing behind Ray. He heaved a sigh of relief as Ray departed. Poor thing needed a break too.

"Why can't I go? I've been on a boat before. I'd make a great first mate!" Oliver was passing gear and supplies to Garrick.

The boat swayed gently in the waves. Christin's head popped up from the galley. Concern was awash on his face.

I smirked in Christin's direction and winked. "Ah Olli, you can't go I need you!" I said with fake sincerity.

Lying was becoming second nature for me now. Garrick ogled me suspiciously. I averted my gaze from his penetrating stare.

"Really Sam? Why? What did you have in mind?" Eagerness crept into Oliver's voice.

I racked my brain, "Umm…" I paused after tossing Garrick a bag.

Christin's voice jumped in from deep in the cabin. "You have to go to town for that thing you told me about—remember Sam?"

Oliver eyed me sceptically. "What thing?" He screwed up his face in confusion.

Damn smart kid didn't miss a thing.

Garrick quickly interjected, "It's a surprise runt! You don't want to wreck the surprise?" He then winked at me—his mama didn't raise no fool.

"Oh all right, I'll wait." The young man conceded defeat.

I heard a breathy sigh from inside the cabin.

Fortunately, the surprise came a week later. We were doing our usual supply run when it found us. I almost ran it over. A little, black hairy lump ambled dazedly onto the road after it had fallen off a nearby curb.

Oliver screamed for us to stop. I did immediately, and the following cargo truck rear-ended us.

I smacked my head on the windshield and was rubbing it. "Damn Olli, you scared the crap out of me!" I was speaking to an empty back seat.

"He's under the Rover!" Emma informed me and pointed down and out the passenger window. Oliver popped up beside Emma, a beaming smile exploding on his face. He had a fuzzy wiggling black mass in his hands.

I was shocked. "That thing almost became a skid mark!" I stammered. Now I'm not one to advocate or encourage *kids* to raise wild animals, but then again, Oliver wasn't a regular kid. Oliver was almost as fast as me and was as strong as Garrick.

We inadvertently welcomed our newest member to the island. Good thing Oliver was fast, agile and healed quickly.

When startled the cub thought poor Oliver was a tree and ran up the boy's body. The bear's claws marked up and down his arms and legs.

"Oliver, get that cub outta Mae's flowers—she's worked hard on them!" I was watching the black cub, roll in Mae's flower bed, kicking petunias and daisies up in the air.

"Skid, get out of there you monster!" Oliver chased the uncooperative, mischievous cub out of the flowerbed. Ollie accidentally stomped the remaining flowers down while trying to get a grip on the squirming crying bear.

"Sorry!" he yelled back.

He gave chase to the fleeing cub. The bear groaned and Oliver laughed. "Get back here you little monster!"

During the weeks that followed, Garrick helped Oliver begin Skid's training. Geez, what a name!

The bear had the attention span of a gnat. Oliver and Skid became inseparable especially at dinnertime. The bear transformed into Einstein when food was in his vicinity. He would perform any deed the boys dreamed up for popcorn! Oliver, it seemed, had found his soul mate.

Life at the compound advanced gently. We needed some gentleness. Almost forty percent of a person's day was habit. We all had developed new habits to fill our day. We planted the back of the compound with seeds scavenged from town. The sun-enriched soil enabled us to reap a bountiful harvest of vegetables.

Canned foods were growing bland to our taste buds. All our palettes craved freshness, especially if it wasn't a protein. Fresh meat wasn't an issue. We hunted every other day.

Fresh fruit was a luxury, fresh veggies, well, unimaginable. We had found the occasional apple tree and orange tree, but we weren't really near any orchards. Thank God for the garden. In the past we had taken so much for granted. We used to be able to walk into a grocery store and purchase whatever our hearts desired. How I missed the convenience stores.

Tonight we decided a group barbeque was called for. We had just harvested a batch of corn and one of the guys had figured out how to make butter. Who needed scientists? We had a cow and fresh butter.

Old Trixie the cow was absconded from a field where she lazily grazed not far from town. We had been tracking a pack of greens when we happened upon her. The colors had grown restless and bored, so we had decided that passively waiting for the greens to show up was over.

We were going after them. I organized a hunting schedule to correlate with the recon of the surrounding area and supply runs.

The colors were geared up for some activity. We always went as a group—safety in numbers. Packs of greens had been getting smaller and scarcer. The last winter must have been hard on them. During the cooler months of winter, we had come across frozen and emaciated corpses—green popsicles. We burned them.

The colors had discussed doing more extensive scouting for survivors, but the security of the island was more of a priority. The incident where the green found the island made us all nervous. We didn't want to leave the island and its inhabitants vulnerable. So we kept our scouting close to home.

We shucked corn, and spit a hollowed out deer, we had oranges for desert. That's if Skid left us any. Lions, tigers and bears—the compound housed an animal farm, geesh. We just needed a tiger—Emma was asking for a pet, oh my! It'd been two weeks since Christin and Ray had left for the coast, they were due back today.

I was shucking a husk off a corncob. "Hey Griff?"

"Yeah?" She was distracted. She and Oliver were racing, husking corn in turbo mode.

"Do you see Christin and Ray anywhere?" She paused her speedy shucking and focused her attention elsewhere.

Click.

She refocused and resumed her shucking. "Nope, nothing. A couple greens north of here though."

"Have you been able to distinguish colors yet?" I asked.

"Nope. Just dots on the radar." She frowned. "I'm looking for the boys in the water. I don't think it's normal for a green to go into the water, unless I suppose it's drawn by something."

"Huh" I narrowed my eyes. Christin wouldn't be tardy. He knew I'd worry.

I caught Bane staring at me. He didn't miss the exchange. His eyes were constricted in concern. We had been more cordial since the Oakley injury incident. We were almost friendly—almost.

I pulled my eyes away from Bane's intense stare and looked at Griffin.

"After dinner I think we should go for a drive. Griff, Garrick, you in?" I asked.

"Maybe they got distracted," Garrick uttered under his breath and chuckled.

"No, Ray would want to get back as soon as his sentence was up. I told them a week down the coast and another week back, and to not go any farther." I spoke in a monotone, staring at Mae's trampled flowers.

A bad feeling started to take shape in my stomach. "Come on." I jumped up before the feeling could paralyze me with fear.

A racket followed behind me, chairs falling in a clamber. Bane and a gaggle of colors followed me.

I turned on my heels and the gaggle ran into each other.

"Listen, I think Christin and Ray are in trouble. Go collect our gear. I have to talk to Mae." I directed the gaggle who nodded in unison then banged into each other as they tried to go their separate ways.

"Hurry!" My voice rose with my tightening nerves. I turned and headed toward Mae's trailer.

I found Mae getting up from the ground. A salad on the floor surrounded her.

"Oh Mae, are you okay?" I rushed to her side and helped her up. "Don't fuss now child, you have to go find Christin and Ray. The black has arrived on the coast." She was pushing me out the door.

"Wait, I—what's 'the black'?" I held her hands in mine.

She looked me straight in the eyes, even though she was blind. "Sam, you know what the black is! It's hate, envy, pain and death rolled up in a color, if you call black a color." She was incensed. "Hurry, he needs your help!" She gave me a final push.

I stood at Mae's door, dumbfounded. She said he, not them. Teak's whine at my side provoked my attention. I looked down at my hairy girls. They were staring up at me with expectant faces.

I ushered the two reluctant dogs into Mae's trailer. "You stay with Mae girls—she needs you." I groaned. This wasn't going to end well.

I don't know what trouble awaited us. It seemed prudent to bring only colors. I felt responsible for the compound's safety. It superseded all concerns, even someone's ego. Bane had asserted that I "was not the boss of him. And that he could do as he pleased."

I then asserted my impatience and decked him. I left him unconscious. More than half of the island's security staff would be far away. We couldn't leave the island vulnerable.

Cory had been training members of the compound on the virtues of being armed. He knew his weaponry and set up numerous nests of fifty calibre rifles on the beach that surrounded the island. The compound now housed and was surrounded by many lines of defensive. Bane needed to stay and help Cory and the twins keep the island safe. The twins both assessed my mood as I told them to talk to Cory about the island's security. They nodded quietly eyes huge with fear.

"You guys will be all right. Cory is a tough soldier. Could you take Bane to his trailer—please." I asked. Christin would be so proud. I said *please.* The sick feeling in my stomach was growing.

The twins scurried to the unconscious Bane and took him in the direction of his trailer. "Oh and get some ice from the lab for his face." I yelled in the direction of their fast retreating forms.

Griff and Garrick came with me. We sped south down the coast in two Rovers. "Can you see anything Griff?" I struggled to control my tone. I was driving at break neck speeds. I stole a quick glance at Griff.

She had her eyes closed and was frowning. "I'm trying to look for two colors, hang on!" She gritted her teeth.

"Look for a single color." I said, emotionless. I stared straight ahead and focused on the road.

"What? What do you mean?" Her eyes popped open in astonishment.

"Just focus on one Griff. A color that is alone. " I grimaced. If one of them was alive, it would be because colors weren't around him.

We drove south down the coast for hours, into the dawn. If we stayed near the shoreline we had to stumble into them, even if they were on the water.

"I have something. It's weak. Keep driving straight." Griff was excited. She had a blip.

CHAPTER TWENTY-SIX:
Death Becomes Him

"Darkness cannot drive out darkness; only light can do that.
Hate cannot drive out hate; only love can do that."
-Martin Luther King, Jr. (1929 - 1968)

Christin and Ray were heading home. They'd explored the coast line for almost two weeks, looking for signs of life and green movement. They had spotted random greens that seemed oblivious to the passing boat or its passengers.

They had no close encounters. The boys had a restful trip. Once, that is, Ray finally released some of his obsessive nattering. Ray was confused about his work and how he didn't understand Sam's rational for sending him on this 'security' trip. Chris and Ray travelled well together and soon fell into an easy routine.

They were almost home, only a day or less to go. The sailors decided not to arrive home empty handed. They would hunt. They were hoping to nab a wild hog—eating venison was getting old. Ray was Jonsing for pork ribs. His mouth watered at the thought.

"We should head in over there." Ray pointed to a deserted wooded area. Forty feet up a rocky embankment a grassy knoll and trees swayed in the breeze. "I can smell them!"

Christin looked at the cliff face with scepticism. "Really? What about the cliff?"

"Come on my delicate flower, we can jump and climb!" The wind was picking up, his voice carried easily to Christin.

Chris could see Ray's mind was set. It made Christin happy to see Ray relaxing and wanting to explore and have fun.

They both had needed the trip. Since the reaping neither had been able to stop and absorb the enormity of the past events. They both had lost people they cared about. A year was not sufficient enough time to process the atrociousness of the life altering happenings. Their existence had changed radically. After some time they decided to embrace the new world together. The future was too intangible to imagine, so they eased their grief with moments of peace granted to them. They were living in the moment. Christin smiled and felt his heart swell. He was happy and content.

They boarded the small boat that they had been towing and drove it to the rocky cliff base. The boys stood and appraised the jutting cliff face. It didn't seem as immense or treacherous when viewed from out on the sea.

"You first, Mr. Explorer!" Christin gestured with his chin, his eyes squinting as he continued to scan the cliff face.

Ray chuckled and a playful grin spread across his face. "Race you?" The suggestion barely out of his mouth, Ray leapt ten feet up the imposing rocky face.

"Cheater!" Christin laughed and jumped a few feet above Ray's position. His hold wasn't as sure as Ray's. His grip crumbled beneath his hands.

"Damn!" he cursed as he plummeted fifteen feet. He heard snorted laughter from above as he fell. "That'll teach you to overreach!"

Concern for Chris, sobered Ray's snort quickly. "You okay Christin?"

Christin was brushing the sand that had ingrained itself into one of his palms. "I'm fine!"

"You screamed like a little girl. You probably scared the hogs away!" Another snort came from above Chris's head.

"I did no such thing. Your snorting has probably enticed them—a mating call for any wayward hog in the area!" Christin picked at the gravel buried in his palm and chuckled to himself.

Another snort bounced down from above.

"You should have that looked at. Your snort could be a symptom of a medical condition!" It was Christin who snorted this time.

"You find yourself very amusing, don't you?" A huff from above carried down the rocky face. Ray was climbing higher.

Chris chuckled to himself. "Only at your expense. Wait up!" He yelled up the side of the cliff.

Ray was almost to the top. Christin tried a few jumps to catch up. Christin's recent plummet to the bottom of the rock-strewn base had tempered the rapidity of his ascension. His palms were already healed, but he didn't want to fall again and have Ray see him pick up his dignity.

Christin heard Ray's triumphant call from above. "Made it Ma! Top of the world!" Ray was facing out to sea, his arms outstretched in a victorious salutation.

"Show off!" Chris said smirking.

"Christin?" His name was whispered from above.

"Yes Ray?"

Nothing. "What, are you so full of your gloating that you can't answer me?" He was almost to the top.

No response.

Christin reached for the grassy ledge. "Give me a hand you fool." A rock was jabbing his side.

Ray's orange eyes flared above Christin. Depending on the circumstances we kept our goggles on. Our eyes were very bright, distracting and could draw unwanted attention. "Put your goggles back on. You're blinding me!" Christin adored Ray's incandescent orange eyes.

Something large grazed Christin's shoulder. "What are you playing at? If I fell from this height…!" Chris climbed up the last leg of the ledge.

Ray's dazzling orange eyes remained ablaze. "It could damage you—maybe even kill you! Can you fly boy?" A deep, callous voice whispered from behind Ray's orange eyes.

"Ray?" Christin held his hand up to shade his own from Ray's bright eyes. A questioning look appropriated Chris's face.

"Ray is not here right now, but you could leave a message." A massive weight lodged itself into Christin's chest and he felt himself thrown into empty air.

"Ray?" he called out and reached out to emptiness. The wind muffled his strangled cry as he plummeted once again to the rocky beach floor.

This time he was about forty feet up.

The landing splayed him on his back. Stars exploded in his vision. Disorientated he realized he couldn't move or feel his legs. In fact, Christin couldn't move his body at all. He did manage a weak turn of his head.

Slowly the blast of stars receded from his vision. He forced his dimming sight to focus. Lying a few feet from him Ray's body was haphazardly strewn like a pretzel. His head was missing.

Christin felt darkness start to take him. He welcomed the numbing embrace of nothingness, rather than face the aching pain in his heart. The last thought that passed through Christin's mind was sickening horror that someone could sadistically kill Ray. Chris tried in vain to reach toward Ray, but darkness stole over him.

Ω Ω Ω

"A color is at the bottom of the cliff, straight down there!" Griff was pointing as she simultaneously opened the Rover's door and jumped out.

"Wait!" I yelled.

Griff was out of the Rover before it had come to a complete stop. I wasn't concerned that Griff would hurt herself physically but what she might see over the side of the cliff.

Griff shrieked. She was looking, over the edge. "Sam!"

I leaped to her side in one bound. I braced myself mentally, and, clasping Griff's shoulders, I looked down.

Christin's body was sprawled chaotically, in a collection of wrong angles. Ray was headless a few feet away.

Garrick's hand fell on my shoulder. "I'll go down." His calm voice and steadying grip didn't penetrate the explosion of pain radiating in my chest.

Christin was dead. Ray was dead. We were too late to...

I stood in my horror, the taste of blood on my tongue. I stared at Christin's still form for what felt like an eternity.

Tick!

Then Christin's hand twitched. My eyes bulged with disbelief.

Alive.

My God, he was alive still. Did I imagine that movement? Did I will it perhaps?

"Griff!" I uttered breathlessly.

"Yes, I saw it too."

"Stay here and watch our backs!" I hollered.

I jumped.

I've never jumped from such an overwhelming height. I felt my knees absorb the shock of the impact and I rolled.

I ignored the jagged rocks piercing my back. The pain cleared my head. I moved and looked down. I had Christin's blood-encrusted head cradled in my hands already.

"Christin, hun I'm here," I whispered urgently.

I checked his eyes. Dim yet beautiful amber light met my probing scrutiny. He didn't respond. I assessed his injuries.

He had two broken legs, a broken wrist, a broken upper arm and discoloration on his abdomen. He probably had internal bleeding. Three of the fractures were open. I had no idea what his spine looked like—I left my x-ray vision at home. Could he heal from this? I had to try. I had to help the virus's healing process.

"Griff, Garrick—I need you two to go and find me something to splint his legs and arms with. Then make something to carry him on! And stay together!" I barked up the cliff.

I softened my voice. "Hurry, I don't know how much time he has…!" No time for pleasantries. Christin could give me a lecture later. I steered my mind for what I had to do.

I scanned the beach for any assailants and saw Ray's headless body. I gritted my teeth.

I laid Christin's head gingerly on my jacket and crawled to Ray. His lifeless, headless body didn't even seep blood. My gaze spun three hundred and sixty degrees.

I spotted his head floating in the surf—bobbing eyeless. Sockets filled with white bubbly foam. I swallowed hard. Oh god Ray. I had to hold myself together; otherwise I'd be no good for Christin.

The kids were fast. They kneeled quietly beside me, gear in hand. They both looked sadly at Ray's remains.

I steadied myself with a deep breath. "I have to help the healing process, if it's even possible. I don't kn…" My voice cut off by the crash of the surf.

"What do you need us to do?" Griff's anxious voice whispered.

"I'm going to straighten out his fractures and dress them, and then I need you to splint them. I'll show you, okay?"

Griff and Garrick nodded mutely.

"He might scream. That might even be a good sign, all right?"

Another unified nod followed. "Screaming is good." Griff said. She did not look convinced.

"We'll do his legs first." I showed them how I wanted the splints applied.

Realigning a broken bone in the hospital was done with painkillers, sedating medication, a respiratory therapist, two doctors, a nurse and an orthopedic technician. During which time the patient's vital signs were carefully monitored in a clean controlled environment.

I had two frightened kids, some wood and lashing. Confident was not a word I'd use right now. I prayed the virus would be anal retentive in its healing capabilities.

Thank goodness for super strength. As a regular human I would never have been able to pull on Christin's right leg with the bone protruding up like a tent on his thigh. The femur and thigh muscle was the densest and strongest parts of the body. The tenting flesh disappeared, and the kids quickly applied the splint. I pulled on his left leg. The bone sticking out the top of his lower leg disappeared beneath the torn flesh and the kids applied another splint while I held the bone in place.

What a team. I smiled encouragingly at the kids. They returned nervous smiles. I pulled on his wrist and heard a crunching noise. Another deformity disappeared. I pulled on his upper arm and it reduced smoothly to its former state. Christin didn't scream once.

We straightened his whole body out and rolled him onto the makeshift stretcher. It was sort of spinal precautions. If a patient presented with possible spinal injuries, we would put a stiff collar on them and do what's called a log roll. We tried to keep the patient straight as a log, while rolling them. This prevented further damage to a delicate spinal column. Any medical professional would have cringed at our treatment of Christin's spinal precautions.

I ran my hand down his spine and felt many bony protuberances. Every fiber in my medically-educated mind vied with what I was about to do. I pushed on the bulges. I heard bone grind against bone—or was that my teeth?

Christen moaned quietly. I was afraid to hope. We covered him and carried him to the Rover, taking the longer route around the rock face this time

We drove fast. No faceless assailants pursued us. I scanned the horizon. A smoky haze drifted in from the east. I peered quickly into the back of the Rover.

Griff hovered idly over Christin's still form. There was nothing else we could do for Christin. We had to get him home. Griff checked his eyes periodically. They glowed dull amber.

Garrick had Ray's remains in a tarp strapped to the other Rover's roof. He had carried him wordlessly across the beach. We couldn't leave him. If Chris made it, he would need closure.

We travelled in silence, too afraid to break the spell of hope. Driving non-stop, we reached the compound by mid-evening.

We took Christin to our trailer. He was home.

I was reassessing Christin's wounds when Mae came in. "Thank God you found him in time. I wasn't sure if you could..." her incomplete sentence hung in the air—unfinished.

"How bad is he?"

I just stared at her, the silence between us overwhelming.

"Oh my dear, will he?" Her blind gaze redirected away from what remained of Christin.

"Why didn't you see this sooner?" I glared in her direction. Her head drooped; a defeated abashed expression crossed her face. "Child, I'm sorry. I don't have much control over the visions. They come to me when they reckon. I'm so, sorry child." Her face fell into her hands.

I felt guilty for directing my anger toward Mae. My quilt, however, was not sufficient enough to allow me to relieve Mae of hers.

I refocused my attention on Christin's wounds. The jagged open lacerations were already healing. The discoloration that marred his skin was fading. He remained unconscious, but his amber eyes grew steadily brighter. I continued to hope.

A nursing instructor told me a story about hope once. She said it's like a tube of toothpaste there's always a little left in the tube. Even when it seemed hopeless, there'd always be a little hope left. I squeezed my arms tightly around my chest.

Ω Ω Ω

Mr. Phillip Poe was having a fabulous time. He was going to burn the world—life was a dream.

He loved explosions. Phillip would set up a timer, find an auspicious location with a panoramic view and then settle in for the show.

He had so much to burn, and oh so much time. There were no obstacles or interferences. The world was wide open so he could manifest his creations.

He was the Creator, the Master, he was the Hand of God and he was hungry for more.

"Made it Ma! Top of the world!"

Phillip turned to the sound of another human being. A man was standing at the edge of a cliff, his arms stretched out above his head. A warm orange glow radiated around him.

"Show off!" A voice echoed up the cliff.

Phillip hadn't really noticed the other voice. He was staring, mesmerized by the radiating orange light in front of him. A prime fire color danced in front of Phillip. The yelling man turned as Philip gasped a sigh of release.

"Christin?" the orange whispered. Shock choked off further articulation. Poe had the man around the throat. The orange fought amateurishly.

Poe turned his head ever so slightly as he heard. "Yes, Ray!" come up from below his feet.

Phillip twisted his wrist slightly and the wiggling body in his hand went limp.

The night was still aglow in orange. Mr. Poe tugged his green eyes out smoothly and then felt for the man's eyes. One at a time he plucked them like plump cherries. He slid them into their new home. His eye sockets prickled then his vision transformed from blackness to a brilliant orange hue in a matter of seconds.

The remnants lying at his feet were ripped apart. He separated the head from the body as easily as ripping a cooked chicken wing from its breast.

"What, are you so full of your gloating that you can't answer me?"

Phillip felt overwhelmed with joy. He was becoming his dream—he was becoming fire. He looked down at the ant that broke his reverie.

"Give me a hand you fool."

He'd get more than that. He'd get a taste of heaven.

"Put your goggles back on. You're blinding me!"

He kicked Ray's headless torso over the cliff.

"What are you playing at? If I fell from this height…!"

He saw amber light emerge from the edge of the cliff. He thought to himself, yum another pretty color—amber.

Hmm.

It was only a boring amber. His newly claimed incandescent orange eyes engulfed the insignificant amber before him. It was time to dispose of this annoyance.

"It could damage you—maybe even kill you! Can you fly boy?"

Phillip kicked out with his right foot. It landed solidly mid-chest on the amber-eyed man.

"Ray!" the man screamed. Poe watched as the annoying ant became a firefly, albeit a boring firefly in Poe's standards. The amber drifted out into the moonlight and then dropped.

Poe kicked the head over the edge.

With the demise of the firefly—boredom stole over him, he turned and walked away. Like a bird with a shiny new object, the brilliant, dancing orange mesmerized him.

He was evolving. Heaven was coming through him now.

The dark man laughed loudly, full of joy. He didn't see the pack of greens following him.

Ω Ω Ω

"Christin hun, can you wake up for me, please?" I whispered close to his ear. "He's not waking up Teak!" My dogs wouldn't leave Christin's side voluntarily. It had been two days since we got home. Christin has had almost the whole compound come to check on him. I kept a constant vigil. People brought me what was necessary.

Christin's obvious outside wounds had all but healed. His eyes were incandescent and vibrant. His heartbeat had beaten four times in two days and he breathed on occasion. But he hadn't budged a finger or uttered a sound. He was broken inside and not just physiologically.

We burned Ray's body and buried him. A small ceremony followed. Harley looked deflated.

I didn't leave my friend's side and Bane didn't leave my side. He still nursed the black eye I had given to him a few days ago.

Bane was not impressed by my assault. We hadn't spoken much since the incident. But his presence was soothing. I often caught him watching me—waiting for a chance to repay me? The problem with that theory was that, well, he hadn't looked angry. He genuinely looked relieved when I made a simple request of him, acknowledged his presence or just allowed him to be in the same room as myself.

Bane was presently sequestered in Christin's chair, his neck crooked at an odd angle.

"Bane? Bane?" I touched his cheek gently. He jumped off the chair dazed, knocking me down as he stood.

I landed smack on my…

"Christin, is he okay? What are you doing on the floor Sam?"

"Oh, I don't know, checking for dust bunnies. The dogs have been shedding a lot lately." I rubbed my butt and grimaced.

"What?" He wasn't as mentally awake as he was physically. He looked around the room a little dazed.

"Sorry, I was dreaming" His hands went to his crotch as a blush crept up his neck. "I'll be right back!" He strode to the door before I could get a word out.

I flattened myself out on the floor. "Honestly. Oh, for the love of God." I sighed.

Beige. I think I'll paint the ceiling beige.

Ω Ω Ω

Bane had been dreaming of Sam's lips caressing his, when she called his name.

He dunked his head in Bruno's drinking bowl. He was going to have to get himself one of these. This couldn't be sanitary. He returned to the trailer shaking his wet head.

Sam was leaning over Christin, checking his eyes.

"How is he?" he asked shyly.

"He's the same, no change. I don't know how long he can go on like this?" Sam's face looked troubled.

"Yeah, but you guys have that healing ability, right?"

Sam looked Bane directly in the eyes. He felt his loins quiver.

"He has to eat, or else he'll slip away." She said. He felt himself slipping away, lost in her molten blue eyes.

Bane pried his gaze from Sam's letting them rest safely on Christin's still shape.

He had to get control of himself. Now was not the time to be having teenage boy fantasies. Guilt punched him in the stomach. His face sobered into deep concern for Christin's well-being. Losing him would hurt Sam deeply. He didn't want anything to hurt Sam.

Ω Ω Ω

Sam felt stricken. He couldn't even meet my gaze.

"Will you keep an eye on him? I have to go talk to the doc for a minute. To see if he has any ideas on how to get food into him."

Bane scratched his wet head and nodded. "Sure."

I glanced back at Christin then turned and headed for the door. I strode across the compound to the lab. The doc was hunched over a microscope, so engrossed he didn't notice my silent entry.

The automatic door slid silently behind me. "Doc?"

He jumped and almost fell off his stool.

He looked tired, unshaven and rumpled. The doctor had not taken Ray's death well. He wasn't alone in his grief. While my heart rarely beat, a constant ache reminded me I still had a heart—and it was breaking.

"Oh, Sam, ah…sorry you startled me! I'll never get used to how silent you colors can move. How nice to see you! How is Christin? Any improvements, any changes?" He righted his stool and straightened his crooked glasses. He turned his full attention to me.

"I think he's stabilized, and he has healed physically." I paused and chewed on my lower lip. "I'm worried. He needs to eat, or he'll slip into a…" I hung my head.

Dr. Walker finished my sentence. "A coma and die…yes, I know. Ray and I discussed the colors various abilities and needs." He rubbed the stubble on his chin and pondered the dilemma.

We had tried an intravenous the day before on him, to no avail. Christin's body had pushed the catheter out of his arm in mere minutes.

"Well. I suppose we could stick a tube down his throat, and force feed him." Dr. Walker suggested.

I had done countless nasogastric tube placements in my life. Usually the procedure was for someone with a bowel obstruction or to administer medications to an unconscious patient. It is as barbaric as it sounds.

Dr. Walker looked hopeful. "I mean, I see no other option. I have tubing. Mae could whip you something up to put down tube." Pureed venison and vegetables came to mind. Yum. I could almost hear Christin whining.

I was chewing on that thought when the doc yelled, "Sam, the alarm!"

"What?" I was re-emerging from my thought cloud.

I heard a deep constant droning in the background. The insistent alarm continued. "Oh shit!"

I turned and dashed to the doors. I was too fast and landed on my back. Huh solid glass doors. That was going to leave a mark. I rubbed my forehead and heard a chuckle behind me.

I twisted and glared at the doc. "Really?"

His smiling face immediately sobered. "Sorry Sam, I'm tired." His face started to take on a pinkish tint.

"It's okay." I got up and sprinted. I waited cautiously for each sealed door to open to my graceful exit.

The compound was organized chaos. Everyone knew what their roles were.

I met Griffin mid-way into the main compound. She was tying her hair back. "There are six of them at the marina!" She mumbled around her hair tie.

I looked in the direction of the marina, "You, me and Garrick. Let's go!"

I could hear the steady stream of laughter in my head. "They're already at the boat waiting for us. Are you sure you want to go Sam? I think we could handle it."

"They? We?" I spoke curtly. I didn't want to be slowed down today. I needed to get back to Christin and feed him. But I was also responsible for the security of the islanders. An ache in my stomach started to expand. I couldn't let anyone else get hurt. I wouldn't.

"Cory. He insisted on coming. It'll be safe for him won't it?" She turned her worried expression to the docks.

"I'm sure it'll be fine Griff. Let's hurry. Your right, Christin needs me."

We took flight racing to the docks, kicking up a dust trail in our wake. This time there were no glass doors to impede my sprint.

Ω Ω Ω

Bane was starving. The venison stew he was cooking smelled delicious.

"Thanks Bane."

"Wha…?" He started at his name and turned around.

"Christin?"

Christin was standing in front of him.

Smiling, Christin whispered, "Sorry Bane," again. Christin cold cocked Bane just as he was beginning to turn from his cooking dinner. A relieved smile evaporated as his limp body hit the floor. Chris scratched the two hairy girls behind their ears as they stood by his legs wagging their tails. He directed them to stay by Bane. They panted happily and stayed. He ate Bane's stew hurriedly. He was starving and had things to do.

Ω Ω Ω

I stood back and let Garrick, Cory and Griffin finish the pack of greens. Bruno was lying in the truck bed. I scratched him behind his ears and listened to the big cat purr. It was a peaceful moment. Bruno's purring usually affected me like a dose of valium. Today I had immunity to that valium. Garrick approached the truck. Bruno huffed a few times—-hello. The big cat appeared to be in a little bit of ecstasy.

I was lost in my worry.

"Everything here is taken care of Sam. Cory is almost finished burying them. We should get going, right?" He was reloading his bow. I looked over toward the six smoking bodies just as the dozer pushed them into a hole.

"Yes, we should hurry. I have a bad feeling—something seems off. It's weird. I've been getting this feeling when trouble was coming." Garrick just looked up at me with a quizzical expression.

"What kind of feeling? What do you mean?" He asked.

"A feeling of unease… something is bothering me now. I don't know how to explain it… let's go."

Ten minutes later we sped across the open water. My sense of foreboding grew progressively stronger with each strike of the boat hitting a wave.

Before the boat was even near the dock, I leapt twenty-feet and ran to my trailer full tilt. Griff was on my heels. I didn't sense Christin.

I fell through the trailer's open door. Christin's bed was empty. I heard a heartbeat. I turned and saw Bane spread out on the kitchen floor. Two hairy guards were nestled beside his still body.

"Bane!" I shouted and rushed to his side. My careful hands checked him for external injuries. A large goose egg resided on his right temple and both his eyes were black. He groaned and opened his eyes. I cradled his head in my hands and moved his dishevelled hair out of his eyes.

His blinking eyes regarded my concerned expression. "Hello beautiful." He breathed a sigh of relief and smiled a drunken grin.

"Wow, how hard were you hit?" I smiled at his crooked grin.

He reached out to touch my face.

"You have a concussion Bane, lie still." It came out in a soft whisper.

"Who hit you?" I knew the answer before I believed it.

"Christin did. Is he okay? My head is pretty hard, so he must be hurt." He started to laugh at his own joke. A grimace broke his laughter, as he reached for his head. "Ahh, geez, he must really be hurt, ouch…!"

I touched the hematoma and small laceration on his temple. He grimaced again.

"Ouch, that hurts."

"Baby." I smiled down at him.

"Bully." He half grinned and half grimaced back up at me. "I seem to get a lot of head injuries around you!"

Ω Ω Ω

Bane turned to stare up at Sam's molten troubled eyes, and he felt his groin stir. Ah geez, not now.

He tried to sit up, but a wave of nausea and dizziness washed over him. He fell back into Sam's lap.

"Going somewhere, *baby?*"

"Bruno's watering dish, to soak my head. Ugh it hurts, but I don't think I can stand, let alone walk yet."

"Shall I carry you?"

"Ah…no. That's okay. Can I just lie here for a minute, and get some ice, please?"

Sam turned to Griff, who was now standing at the door.

Vying emotions played on her expression. In the end, Griff managed to smirk and look troubled all at once.

"Griff, can you get Bane some ice please?"

"Did you just say please?" She released a small grin. "Sure, it's in the lab. I'll be a minute!" And with that she was gone.

"What happened?" Sam asked as she stroked Bane's throbbing head.

"Christin woke up when I was cooking, apologized and then clocked me. He's not here?" Bane tried to sit up again, almost instantly falling back into Sam's lap. "Ugh!" Bane groaned.

"Lay still you fool or you'll throw up on both of us!" Sam whispered. Her voice was less firm than the command warranted.

Sam's soothing hand caressed his furrowed brows. Her hands were cool and soft. He relaxed into Sam's lap as his eyes closed slowly. Soft breathing followed.

Ω Ω Ω

I cautiously picked Bane up and placed him on my bed, covering him. I listened to his steady heartbeat. I stroked his forehead, lingering

258

a moment too long. Bane's hand reached up and gingerly took my hand in his. Bane started snoring lightly, while he held tight to my hand. I remained by his side.

It's an old myth that those with a head injury shouldn't be allowed to sleep. The brain, when traumatized, needed rest. Decreasing stressful stimuli is imperative for the brain injured. When we had a head injured patient, we lowered the lights and kept our procedures to a minimum. We needed to assess the patient for changing neurological signs, but let the patient rest as much as possible. They were often medically induced into a coma.

Let the patient rest, but assess often, a head injured care mantra.

I had just assessed Bane's neurological state: pupil size, check. Breathing was spontaneous and easy, check. Able to move limbs independently, check.

I turned my attention to Griff, who had just returned with the ice. The task of finding Christin was now a priority. "Griff can you see him anywhere?"

Griffin concentrated hard. She sat on Sam's floor, petting Oakley absently.

Bane had finally released my hand, but I remained close to him. He was still safely asleep, snoring loudly. "No, I can only see a few greens milling about, no solitary figures."

"Keep looking Griff." I exhaled deeply.

Where are you Christin?

Ω Ω Ω

Christin awoke to the delicious smell of spiced venison stew. He was home and in his bed alone. His gut wrenched with his last memory— Ray.

Ray's headless, grotesquely displayed body had lain feet from his grasp. His hand was outstretched on the rocky beach, motionlessly beckoning for Christin.

Christin attempted to will his frozen body to move. Common unconsciousness stole his last vision of Ray. There was nothing common in the grief and anger that now assaulted Christin's whole being. He had to find the man that had stolen Ray's life and his eyes.

Chris had dispatched his caregiver easily enough. He was not going to put anyone in harm's way.

Anger propelled him into action. While he felt mentally and emotionally weakened, the rage coursing through him made him feel physically like the *Terminator*.

He ate the stew over Bane's somewhat still body. The rise and fall of Bane's chest hypnotized Christin's focus. He blinked and formed a plan. He would cut the thief's head off and feed it to some hogs. Chris grinned and wiped a dribble of stew from his smooth chin. Sam had taken good care of him.

Chris needed a boat. He quickly grabbed his gear and headed for the dock.

No one saw his swift covert departure.

Ω Ω Ω

The cameras revealed that Christin absconded from the island, in a small boat, aiming the small skiff down the coast. I saw the resolve chiselled in Christin's face. He was going to kill someone or something. We had to help him.

Griff's continued to concentrate. "Maybe we should just head back to where we…ah, found them?" She popped one eye open, sneaking a peek at my reaction—subtle.

I narrowed my eyes. "Can you see anything down there?"

"No, I can't see that far. Maybe if we were closer…" Both eyes were open now. Hope exuded from her face. Griff adored Christin. He had rescued her. She owed him her life. Griff was anxious to do something, anything. "What do you want to do Sam?"

260

I chewed on my bottom lip, considering the undertaking at hand. "Your right Griff. We should head in the same direction Christin headed in. Get Garrick. Let's go." I whispered.

I decided the dogs should stay with Mae. They were battle worn enough. I spoke with Cory and the twins. I also decided they were to stay and maintain security of the compound. The twins put up a colossal argument. I was not feeling very democratic.

"We're ready Sam." Oliver looked frustrated.

"We can handle ourselves." They each chimed in.

I reasoned with them—we needed them here to secure our home.

"Your job here is a very important one. The safety of the compound is in your hands." Cory was trying not to smirk. He was a strong man.

"Okay Sam. We'll take care of the island. I mean, well… Cory can't do it all by himself." Emma held her head up just missing Cory clear the growing smirk off his face. The subdued smirk threatened to burst into an episode of laughter. See a strong man.

The twins couldn't hide their pouting as Garrick, Griff and I prepared for the hunting expedition. Bruno was coming—he insisted. Pacing around the group, the great cat felt our mounting anxiety. I couldn't deck an impatient lion, but the thought crossed my mind.

"Bruno, stop pacing. You're driving me crazy!"

Bane was striding toward the dock, a bag in hand, a gun slung over his shoulder. I rolled my eyes. Really, does everyone want to get killed around here?

"You can deck me again Sam—but as soon as I wake up, I'll follow you!" I braced myself for an argument and pointed my eyes at a rumpled Bane.

"Bane it's too dangerous. I don't even know what we're up against! You could get hurt!"

He rolled his eyes toward Bruno. "A mortal lion can come though?"

Honestly, really! "Hello, he has teeth and claws!"

I eyed Bruno. He had finally settled. He was nestled on the boat, chewing on one of his large claws.

Bane pulled a rather lethal looking gun from around his back—Cory's M 40 sniper rifle. I asked Cory about it. It was a standard sniper rifle in the marines.

"I have this." He patted his new toy. "I have claws!" He whispered lovingly to his new friend stroking the barrel.

I gave him an exaggerated eye roll. My eyes were really going to get stuck that way.

"Fine, but if you die, I'll kill you!" I scowled and pointed at his chest.

A throaty laugh escaped from Bane's chest. "Deal! Let's go!"

An hour later we had the truck and Rover flying down the coast at tandem speeds. Night lurked on the smoky horizon when we parked at the scene of the crime.

Silence met our footfalls as we made our way to the edge of the cliff. Christin's escape vehicle was nestled on the rocky beach, swaying gently in the waves.

"There's green activity in the town about a mile from here. I don't see any single colors around." I could tell she was distracted. The memory of Christin's rescue was surely replaying in her mind.

"All right, let's go and check out the town." I turned from my own replaying of those horrid memories.

CHAPTER TWENTY-SEVEN:
The Greens Rapture

"Life is very interesting…
In the end, some of your greatest pains
become your greatest strengths."
-Drew Barrymore (1975 - 2012)

A small rural town jutted up amongst fallen trees, a pit stop on a person's journey, not a destination. A few abandoned buildings stood in the twilight. The very deserted town had probably been on the brink of becoming a ghost town before the reaping. The American economy had hit rock bottom in the days prior to the end of the world. The Bush administration had drained the American economy dry. Poor Obama had fought valiantly—but in vain—to save the American way of life. The reaping ended just about everyone's way of life.

Faint movement to Christin's left caught his eye. It was only a dog that had gone feral. Its eyes crazed in fear, the canine skirted the town's bland boundaries.

Christin smelled greens. The greens odor was spiced with a dank burnt stench. Laughter in the distance accompanied the source of the odor. He redirected his pursuit.

Ω Ω Ω

Poe had adopted an entourage. He now had five fans to be exact. They had followed him unobtrusively for miles, simply watching him, mouths hanging open.

In the past he found the greens no less than a pack of wild dogs. The dogs had a new ball. He was the ball. He laughed at the image of a shiny red ball bouncing—it had his face on it.

The greens paused, mid step and stared in his direction. Poe chortled out another peal of laughter at their dumb slacken expressions.

Hmmm, what to do with his onlookers? Poe had never played well with others.

A rather large arrow skimmed his right brow. A slice of pain made him turn abruptly from his frozen stupor. Recovering quickly he spun toward the arrow's source.

The pack of greens had turned their attention as well. Their eyes contracted. Something threatened their shiny new toy. The pack crouched and surveyed the area. Their greens' eyes fell on a solitary figure standing by a derelict truck. They attacked the distraction.

Poe watched amused. Huh, go figure—new bodyguards.

Ω Ω Ω

Christin had no problem tracking his quarry. He simply followed the smell. The odor was becoming more poignant—five greens and his assailant. Huddled in the heart of the desolate town the greens stared at a man with his back to them.

The man was laughing as he turned toward Christin's hidden direction. Christin's anger seethed. The man's eyes glowed orange.

The released arrow flew sure until, at the last moment its, target turned to walk away from the greens.

"Dam it." Christin was now looking at a pack of pissed off greens.

They crouched getting ready to attack. He lunged into the forest behind him. They were fast on his heels. Christin was no fool, he knew he was outnumbered.

The greens were well fed and fast. They tracked his swift getaway easily. As Christin leaped from tree to tree, he realized with trepidation that the pack matched his bounds. Mid-flight from one great tree to another he flew, until a weight around his chest sent him hurdling to the ground.

He laid spread eagled on the ground with a green wrapped around his chest. Both in-flight passengers were stupefied by the abrupt landing. Unfortunately, the remainder of the approaching pack was not.

They set upon his motionless body in less than a human heartbeat. Christin had no heartbeat to match the tempo to which his body was being ripped apart. He thrashed and kicked in vain. Each green had a limb and they were pulling him apart limb by limb. Christin pulled with all his strength. It couldn't end this way, he had to destroy the man who had killed Ray.

With every ounce of his strength he pulled the greens closer. He managed to head butt one which released his right arm. He swung and hit a green square in the nose, which caused the green to release his other arm. He fell to the ground hitting his head, while the two remaining greens continued to clasp his legs in steel grips. Chris tried to do a sit-up to get at the two greens, but the green that had tackled him in the trees seized his head. The greens that he had hit a moment ago grabbed his flailing arms. Then they all pulled.

His guttural scream escaped into the forest.

Christin's parting thought as he left this celestial plane was of his two loves. Sam—he was going to miss her—and Ray, who he was going to join. He smiled as his head was ripped from his body.

Ω Ω Ω

Christin? I felt a jagged pain in my chest. I almost drove off the gravel road.

"Sam are you okay?" Griff's hand was on my shaking shoulder.

I barely managed to bring the Rover to a complete stop before grief overwhelmed my shaking body. "I felt. Christin leave." I choked out. I had my head resting against my hands, which were presently gripping the steering wheel. I could almost feel the wheel bend under my vise grip.

"What do you mean leave?" A slight panic tinged Griff's words. I stuttered, without releasing my death grip, "I think he's dead Griff!"

Bane and Garrick's concerned faces appeared suddenly beside me.

"What's going on?" Bane asked worried.

"Are you guys okay?"

They saw our stricken faces, and then scanned our vicinity. Alert to danger.

"It's Christin. I felt him leave…" I couldn't finish.

"What?" Bane's incredulous expression mirrored all of our faces.

"We have to go. Hurry!" I sped off before they could ask any more questions. I left them in a cloud of dust.

"Where are you going Sam?"

"We're not far. I felt him. It's not far." I could barely speak.

"What do you mean you felt him Sam?" I could tell Griff was cynical. So was I.

"I have no idea what I'm talking about. Just go with it. Trust me while I'm trusting this… ah, feeling."

"Okay Sam. I'll always trust you."

"Thanks Griff. You can have me committed when we get back." I whispered as I focused on the feeling.

"You and me both." She said.

"Here." We pulled over and got out of the Rover. Garrick and Bane pulled up behind us. I grabbed my gear and Griff followed suit.

"Sam I don't see any colors in the area." Griff whispered.

I paused at the edge of the forest. "I know we're too late." I breathed deeply and coughed. A smoky rotting odor filled my nose. I breathed in again and concentrated focusing on my memory of Christin's smell.

We found what was left of Christin scattered in a grove of trees. I collapsed clenching his hand. It was ten feet from his body. I hung my head feeling empty.

Our group wordlessly gathered his remains. I laid beside him rocking myself quietly.

An hour passed before I sat up. Griff, Garrick and Bane sat circling Christin and me. Quietly I swallowed the choking ache in my throat.

"Griff are there any colors around?" I asked softly.

Griff had her head hung and her eyes closed. "No. Nothing."

It was quiet. A few birds chirped and the wind rustled the leaves. I smelled that pungent smoky odor again. The wind was coming from the north.

"Come on. I have an idea. Griff you're driving. Garrick can you please wrap Christin up and put him on the roof of the Rover?"

"Sure Sam." They both answered at the same time.

We needed to end the creature responsible for decimating our hearts.

Ω Ω Ω

Mr. Poe's followers resumed their ever-watchful vigil. The greens awaited in anticipation for Poe's beguiling laughter. They hovered around Poe's periphery, birds awaiting a crumb.

Poe decided to continue along the coastal route and head north. The setting sun sparkling on the sea pleased him. He needed to continue his work. The newly acquired eyes were dimming. The adopted additions never seemed to last long. Pity, he enjoyed the brilliant orange gleam.

Poe's body rejected the foreign tissue. The specimens couldn't handle his great revelations. He craved a flawless example to match his greatness and to light his way to glorious Divinity.

Ω Ω Ω

Sam's group followed the scent north. Their quarry was on the move and heading in the direction of their home. Anxiety riddled Sam's body.

Ω Ω Ω

Mae was feeding the dogs. Actually she was standing as lookout. Skid was always trying to steal their dinner. Oakley would have none of the cub's stealing antics. She'd playfully pounce on the baby bear, pinning the fuzzy mewling monster with one paw. She licked Skid's face and returned to her dinner. Skid decided that if he couldn't have Oakley's dinner, her tail was fair game. Oakley ignored the distraction and wolfed down her dinner Skid took a chomp on Oakley's tail. Oakley yelped and growled at her assailant. Skid impishly pawed at Oakley's growling muzzle—a face wash by Oakley quickly ensued. Skid didn't stand a chance. Oakley was a born mama.

Mae just rocked in her chair entertained by the animals' display of affection. Who knew that one day she would be sitting on an island, engrossed in the drama of a three legged dog mothering a baby bear? Ah, the universe had a strange and warped sense of humor. The peace of the moment stole over her. She smiled and rocked.

A curtain of darkness descended over her mind's eye. He was coming. This dark man was hungry for a color. Mae shuddered. Mae stood up on shaky legs. She had to warn the others.

How would she warn Sam? Her old wrinkly lips pursed into a small smile. Sam knew. And she was coming home. Mae hastily ambled in the direction she knew she'd find Cory.

Ω Ω Ω

Mr. Poe had smelt them for the last hour. A waft of color carried on the sea air. It was coming from the northwest.

His orange gaze was wavering. It was time to pick up his pace. He moved with lightening certainty. His destiny awaited him. Poe's followers trailed after him, augmented numbers of greens followed his laughter.

Ω Ω Ω

It was a lot faster heading home then the trip down the coast was. We pulled into the marina slowly. Something was wrong, it was too quiet. We eased to our dock and got out of the Rover. I stared up at the speakers that had been torn from their mounts.

My stomach dropped to the ground. The island was in danger.

We hurriedly loaded onto the speedboat, tense with fear; our faces were statues against the gamut of the assaulting water. Revelations of our home's fate strained our resolve.

Our approach to the island's dock was met with silence and the absence of movement. I smelled gunpowder in the air. The compound was deserted.

The silence was pierced by the crack of a .50 calibre retort echoing from the center of the island. We reacted quickly, sprinting towards the origin of the sound. Bane attempted to follow in the island's Jeep, which he had snagged from the docks. He quickly fell behind.

He had to stay on the road, he couldn't swing through the trees and jump over any obstacle.

An abandoned nuclear test bunker made of reinforced cinder block and steel was almost buried by the growth of trees. The government had planned on testing detonations of nuclear weapons off the coast of the island in the early 1900's. The idea was quashed over concern that prevailing winds would bring poisonous fallout onto the coastal line. The coast made money—greed won out over experimentation.

Years later the shelter had remained intact. Forged with man's strongest resources—it stood the test of time.

"Griff, can you see anything?" Griff was having a hard time focusing after seeing Christin's remains left in a horrifying state. The vision eclipsed her ability to think straight.

"Griff, I don't mean to sound insensitive, but the twin's—need us… where…?"

Griff focused intensely. "Yes… Thank goodness. I see a teeming amount of green activity by the old shelter. I don't see two colors together though. The twins could be anywhere!" We were speaking at a dead run.

I lifted the walkie-talkie to my mouth. "Bane, head to the old bunker. Find a tree and introduce your little friend to some greens would you? Oh and be careful, Griff says there is a lot of green activity."

"My pleasure! I'll see you there—be safe! Over." he replied in a heated tone.

"Garrick, head in from the south side. Griffin, head from the north side. I'll head straight in!"

They responded in unison. "Shouldn't we stay together?"

"I know we're going to be out numbered if we split up, but they'll be distracted by a multidirectional assault!" I clicked the walkie-talkie, I wanted Bane to hear the plan. I had been hanging around Cory and he'd been sharing some of his military tactics with me. I was a very keen student.

I smiled in their direction and picked up my pace. They both smirked. They looked like they were game for a little diverting.

"Anyone have any other ideas?" I breathed deeply, attempting to calm my brewing anger. My adopted family and friends were in trouble.

"Wait until you hear my first shot before you engage the greens!" Bane instructed via the walkie-talkie.

I grinned. "Yes princess!" I countered into my radio.

I heard "bully" come from the radio, as I veered off from Garrick and Griff's speeding profiles.

Diverging in three different swift trajectories, we flew eagerly to our targets while a hairy beast roared behind the fluttering dust and leaf tails.

Ω Ω Ω

Mae was holding the dogs. They growled and strained at the pounding that reverberated throughout the shelter. The greens were assaulting the shelter with all the vigor of a wrecking ball. The shelter was withstanding the onslaught.

Cory and the twins were positioned with rifles at the shelter's view holes, firing intermittent rounds off into the night. The greens were avoiding their line of sight.

Thirty or so people hunkered down in the fifty square foot room. They could only wait for the end. They clung to each other in desperation, jerking with each rifle shot while squeezing tighter as the blitz on their shelter continued.

A shot rang out in the distance—help had arrived.

Mae smiled. *She's here. Thank the heavens.*

Ω Ω Ω

Poe sat back against a tree and let the greens do all the heavy lifting. He focused on his nails and yawned. Finding the island had been a simple matter of following his nose.

The laughing speakers had been a distraction for his followers, so he dispatched the disruptive noise. Poe and his followers took to the water. The seawater eased the burning in his eyes.

When he and the greens walked up the beach, he was disappointed that the island initially appeared deserted. A small fire pit located in the center of a compound released lazy smoke into the evening sky. He inhaled deeply and found the sweet scent of his destiny. Why did fate make him toil so hard? It should be as easy as the sun setting on the horizon.

Creating greatness could be so tedious. Poe looked up with surprise when he heard a foreign gun report echo in the night.

Ω Ω Ω

Bane had mastered climbing trees when he fled New York. Greens didn't bother looking up when they were in pursuit of more interesting prey.

He didn't need the night scope on his rifle—the greens lite up like a sensor beep on a radar screen. The outside of the shelter was deluged with green pulsating light. A soft orange light hung near the tree line not far from his perch. He took aim in its direction, but a large tree blocked his shot. He turned instead and set his sights on the melee of greens that had encircled the shelter. Fish in a barrel—he opened fire.

He spotted blue, silver and yellow streaks of light racing from different trajectories toward the shelter.

Green lights extinguished in the wake of the three approaching colors. Bane smiled and kept shooting.

Ω Ω Ω

I used my cross bow at the onset of the attack, switching to my sword in a smooth fluid motion. Decapitation was an efficient method of termination. It was like reaping hay with a honed scythe. The swing of my arm felt no resistance as I dispatched copious numbers of greens. So many in fact, I actually lost count. Where did they all come from?

I heard Bane's rifle retort bounce in the dense forest.

"Sam." Bane's voice pierced my warrior cry as I decapitated a female green. She was wearing the remnants of her Sunday best. It looked like a nun's habit. Oh geez, I am so going to hell.

"I grabbed the walkie, "Yes Bane. I'm a little busy here." I sliced through an advancing green with one hand. I loved my sword.

"I don't know what to make of it, but I see a couple of orange lights on my twelve o'clock. I'm at your two o'clock."

I quickly scanned an imaginary clock. I saw Bane's rifle flare as a green coming up beside me suddenly flew three feet in the air backwards. I waved in Bane's direction.

I looked for twelve o'clock. A couple of dim orange lights flickered beside a large tree. I started toward the flickering orange lights as I glanced in Griff and Garrick's direction.

The area surrounding them was clearing of green lights. Bruno was dispatching greens, head first. His massive jaws clamped down on a greens head and tossed it like a rag doll, separating its head from the body.

I grinned. Such an efficient boy, Garrick had worked so hard with him building up his confidence. I knew Garrick was keeping an eye on him—he must be so proud.

The greens we're thinning—time to find my primary target. I searched the perimeter for the orange glow again. I had lost sight of the dull orange spheres, when I checked on my partners' status. I turned slowly scanning the heavily wooded area. I startled when I saw two bouncing orange lights rapidly approaching my position.

$$\Omega \ \Omega \ \Omega$$

Blue eyes—he must have them. They must be his.

Poe saw an array of beautiful colors. He was overwhelmed with need. But the sight of the molten blue orbs caused his first stirrings of love. He had to possess those eyes. In a split second upon seeing them, they had become the pivotal point to his existence. His God had delivered the tool to fulfill his fate.

Poe strode toward his destiny. A weight fell on his shoulders, and he flicked it off like an annoying fly. Poe peered down at the movement at his feet. A dishevelled man was trying to get up; a rifle was clenched in his hands.

Huh. Damn things were falling out of trees now, how boring.

Poe made to stride forward, but something was now wrapped around his back and neck. Damn pests, he made to grab it. Instead it bit him.

"Go away, I'm busy!" He yanked at the interruption and threw it fifteen feet.

"Bane!" resounded from afar.

He refocused his attention on the blue.

Ω Ω Ω

I saw Bane attempt to wrestle the black shadow. I watched helplessly as he was hurtled through the air. I yelled his name and ran to him— damn greens were in my way. The sword made short work of the barrier.

I spun in search of the orange orbs. Almost fully turned around, two glowing orange eyes pulsed two inches in front of my face. I stumbled back surprised, and tripped over the remains of a headless green. The dark man advanced. I was up to my knees in dead greens.

I tried to right myself, as the man launched himself on top of me. His weight crushed me to the ground. The dark man's fetid breath caressed my neck. I lurched to push at the dead weight—he had me pinned. I was trapped. I realized in that horrific moment I didn't have the strength to maneuver or push his bulk off of me.

I gagged at the overwhelming smell of him. The odor of burnt garbage oozed off of him. My gag was stifled as his massive hands closed around my throat. He grunted to bring our faces together. I saw greed overwhelm his facial features. I panicked and brought my knee up and slammed it into his groin. Ahh—once again the power of the hairy testicles.

The wanton desire exposed on the man's face—disappeared in a flash. A grimace of immense pain distorted the man's desires. I pushed the dead weight off my crushed frame. My throat was on fire. I held fast to my burning neck. I could see that the man was curled up in a fetal position, groaning beside me. He was holding fast to his groin.

Beatrice. My sword was lying two feet from my fetal position. I made to crawl toward her.

"I believe you have my eyes!" The man loomed over me. I rolled onto my back to face my assailant. He had one of his hands cupped to his crotch with a strained expression engraved into his forehead. He was barely able to maintain a erect stance. I stared at the comical scene. This *man* before me was not a depiction of evil incarnate. Instead, he was a depiction of a rumpled, dirty, smelly psycho that was holding his Johnson.

I started laughing; I couldn't help it. I'd snapped. In that moment my life flashed before my eyes.

I flipped the sign in my head. Closing time.

The overwhelming grief my life had encompassed thus far seeped through my every pore. Laughing hysterically, while rolling on the ground was my coping mechanism—my release valve. The pressure had finally caused me to pop.

The man paused with his head cocked to one side. Anger was beginning to overtake his stunned face "How dare you laug…" A green blur swarmed him, making him disappear.

Click. Just like that he was gone. Extinguished, like flicking a light switch off.

Tears streamed down my face. I turned my head slightly in time to see the pack of greens ripping the dark man to pieces. The pack then whirled in one fluid motion and looked in my direction. A fresh burst of laughter escaped as I returned their stare. They were unmoving and dumbfounded.

I couldn't take anymore, I continued to laugh hysterically and curled tighter into a ball. The stretched elastic band that had been my sanity had finally snapped.

The world dying, Adam and Ray dying, Christin dying, and now my own life…I started sobbing.

A beautiful purple haze shrouded my tear soaked vision.

Ethel, Emma's sword, so named after her mother—sliced diagonally though the dumbfounded greens. The remaining advancing pack was decapitated by Oliver's sword, Fred, so named after his father. Yes Fred and Ethel, polish farmers slash ranchers.

I violently cried throughout the quiet pandemonium. I was done. Stick a fork in me.

I dimly saw Bane's concerned face hovering over me. "Sam? Sam? Are you all right? Sam!" His voice was alarmed.

I just kept laughing and crying. He finally shook me. I stopped laughing but kept crying.

The ache of my grief reverberated within the hollow walls of my soul. Bits of the ache ebbed out with each released tear.

Bane cradled me in his arms and took me to the Jeep. The dogs found me in the passenger's seat and covered me in kisses. I quietly sobbed and hiccupped all the while. The Jeep bounced along the cratered dirt road.

The compound was still deserted. Bane was holding me in his arms, rocking me gently. We were curled on my bed.

The room was dark. A soft hum rumbled deep in Bane's chest. He was humming a song to me. My dogs were nestled on either side of me. I stared blankly at the wall. My breath caught in my throat in stuttered sighs. I was cried out. The well of grief was dry.

I felt heat rise from Bane's close body. Temperature wise, he was very hot.

"Bane?" I whispered.

"Yes, Sam," he whispered back.

"Are you all right?" I paused. "I smell blood."

"I'm fine, a little cold though. Can I grab your blanket?"

"You're really hot!"

"Yes I know. I'm glad you finally figured that out!" He chuckled at his mock arrogance.

"No you fool. Your body temperature feels really warm. Are you hurt?" I turned to look up at him.

His face looked flush and he had a layer of sweat on his forehead. A trickle of dried blood was on his chin. "Your chin, it's bleeding!"

"It's not mine. At least I don't think so!" He reached for his chin.

"Whose is it…?" The possible answer didn't allow me to finish the sentence.

But I knew. "The dark man's?" I whispered. I didn't want to speak it out loud.

"Yes, I bit him. I know. It sounds like a girl fight maneuver, but it was all I could do—to slow him down. He was going for you and I ran out of bullets." He said this through clenched teeth.

"Bane, I think…"

"I know Sam."

"You're infected Bane. We have to go to the lab, now!" I sat up quickly and eyed Bane.

"You know it's no use Sam. Ray and Harley have been… I mean had been working on something, but nothing was finished." He murmured.

"I would rather die with you in my arms. Not in a cold sterile lab." He hugged himself. His shaking was getting stronger.

I smacked him on the chest, "You're not going to die unless I kill you, remember?" I was mad at his cavalier attitude.

"Ouch. Bully!" He rubbed his chest.

I grabbed his arm and pulled. "Come on princess, we're going to the lab. Don't make me throw you over my shoulder. You know I can!"

People were starting to trickle back into the compound. We said our cursory hellos but kept moving forward.

With each step, Bane was requiring more of my assistance to walk. I dragged him half-conscious into the lab.

The lab was still equipped with a few stretchers, ever since the scientists' fateful trial of a vaccine.

I laid Bane down on a stretcher carefully, then I went and retrieved intravenous supplies and started a line.

Harley walked into the lab, the swoosh of the automatic doors announced his arrival. He hurried over to the stretcher. I looked up and we exchanged concerned expressions. "Is he hurt, what happened?" His hand reached for Bane's wrist.

I stopped him before he could touch Bane. "He's infected. He bit the dark man!"

"Oh shit! But that was only a few hours ago. How is he showing symptoms already?" Harley was a scientist, that's for sure.

"I don't know. Maybe the virus is really virulent in our blood stream?"

"Yes, maybe that's why the vaccine didn't work—it was too strong." Harley thought about his vaccine.

Typically, vaccines are a weakened form of the organism. Which are then introduced into the body. Infected with the weakened virus, it stimulates our body's immune system to initiate production of antibodies against a weak enemy. Hence, our body could build immunity without acquiring a full blown infection.

Dr. Walker's head bobbed as he tried to make connections. Absently he said, "If we really weaken it, that might…the one we tried was still too strong for the body to…"

"Harley focus. Bane is sick." I snapped.

"Yes, I'm sorry Sam." He gave me his full attention.

"How? How can we help Bane?" I didn't mean to sound impatient.

"What about the vaccine Doc?"

"No it won't help he's already infected."

"Is there nothing we can do for him?" I snapped.

He ignored my tone and stood there rubbing his stubbly chin and scratching his head. I wondered if he could act anymore more cliché. Here stood a (sort of mad) scientist, contemplating a disconcerting dilemma, all the while stroking his chin. Queue diabolical music and lightening.

Bane started screaming. Okay that works.

I almost fell off the stretcher; instead I threw myself onto Bane's thrashing body.

"I'm sorry Sam." Dr. Walker's head hung in defeat.

I silently cursed. He couldn't die.

As the hours passed I wrestled Bane's frenzied physical torment, I realized something else might be happening to Bane.

Dawning realization almost made me smile—he was being transformed. My heart wrenched for him. I remembered Lucifer's locker, I knew he was going through horrendous torture. All I could do was hold him safe in my arms until he made it through.

In between Bane's bouts of howling, I saw Garrick and Griff come into the room. Their glances caught my distraught expression.

The island I was informed—in between Bane's screams, was presently secure from threat. Garrick and a few islanders had gone to the marina and replaced the speakers. Griff had worked with Cory in locating and disposing of any green stragglers. Griff advised me that we were clear of green activity for miles and that the dead greens remains were being disposed of as we spoke.

Harley tried in vain to administer various sedating medications to Bane—to no avail. All I could do was continue to physically restrain him so he wouldn't harm himself.

Hours after his agonized turmoil commenced, Bane's painful cries slowly began to recede.

Bane was covered in perspiration. His breathing was becoming slower and more irregular. My head was resting on his chest when I heard his heart stop and not resume.

I gently ran my fingers through his damp hair and looked up at his peaceful face. "Bane? I'm here. You're going to be okay," I said in a mumbled whisper.

His eyes remained closed. His body was still. The intense heat of his body was waning. We laid in this quiet embrace for another hour.

Bane's heart thumped once more.

I lifted my head off of his chest and looked at his still expression. He took a deep breath.

"Bane, are you awake?" I sighed expectantly.

"Bully. You held me down." He spoke softly with his eyes closed as he wrapped his arms around me.

"Are you all right?" I pushed myself off his chest and out of his embrace. I could see he was smiling.

"I am starving" He reached for me and pulled me down so that we were face to face. Bane opened his eyes and stared lovingly into my molten blue eyes.

"Bane your eyes!" I gasped and stared. Incandescent eyes the color of chocolate swirled in front of me.

His hand found the back of my head and pulled my lips to his. An ache overwhelmed my body as I felt his groin swell. I lost myself in the kiss. Our kisses couldn't get us close enough or allow us to sink deep enough into each other. My breath caught in my throat as I felt him grow harder beneath my hips.

"Excuse me. Ah..." Harley was clearing his throat.

We ignored him. I pulled my lips from Bane's insistent mouth and sought his neck. I glided my lips down his neck. I heard him moan.

"Excuse me...Um Sam."

I pulled my lips away just long enough to say. "Yes, Harley?" My multitasking skills remained intact since my response to the doctor didn't distract me from my task at hand.

"I assume you want to be informed of the state of the island?"

Bane had his hand gently tangled in my hair. His other hand was pulling my hips into his.

"No not really" I gasped.

"There are cameras in here." Harley murmured. He was shuffling his feet uncomfortably. Bane and I paused. We exchanged smiles and looked into each other's eyes. We both shrugged. To be continued. I marked the page with a deep kiss, and with remorse pushed myself from Bane's enveloping embrace.

I turned a brilliant smile on Harley. He looked abashed. "Sorry!" he said.

"It's okay Harley. What's going on?"

Harley found the floor tiles very interesting, "We're burning the greens and burying them, our security is up and running and one of your dogs peed in my lab," he muttered while he continued to stare at the floor tiles. He was such a gentleman.

In other words what he meant was, "Everything is fine, get out of my lab and take your hairy counterparts with you."

I laughed. "All right Harley, sorry! We are leaving." I turned my attention back to Bane. He had his arms behind his head and was quietly whistling while he focused on the ceiling tiles.

"Fuzzy white bunnies?" I asked raising one eyebrow at Bane's deflated groin.

"No grandma in her two piece" He wiggled his eyebrows and guffawed.

I looked at the dogs. "Sorry girls for keeping you penned up in here." Teak sneezed and stretched. I was forgiven.

I grabbed my new Cheshire cat and yanked on his hand. "Come on, you stink, and we need to eat!"

"Bully!'

"Princess"

Our laughter followed us out of the lab.

Chapter Twenty-Eight:
Fuzzy White Bunnies

"Every beauty which is seen here below by persons of perception resembles more than anything else that celestial source from where we all come…."
-Michelangelo (1475 - 1564)

We walked out into the deserted compound holding hands. The night sky was laced with stars and music. We followed our noses to Mae's place. A fire was roaring outside Mae's trailer, surrounded by our family. I saw similar fires interspersed throughout the circling trailers.

A cacophony of music played into the night. The time for mourning and celebration weighed heavily on everyone. It was a bittersweet moment.

Bane kissed me and said he was going to shower. I didn't release his hand.

"They need you. It's okay, we have time." His molten brown eyes captured my heart. It beat once. We laughed together.

He kissed my neck softly and let go of my hand, then turned and strode toward his trailer.

I walked into a circle of chairs that held the people I cared about the most. Six grinning faces welcomed me. Mae passed me some venison steak and corn. "Thanks Mae!"

"You eat up child. You're going to need your strength." She stood with her arms across her bosom, grinning in my general direction.

"What?" I focused on my plate. Then I looked around the fire. Everybody appeared a little dazed. The last few days had been so overwhelming.

Garrick was chewing the remnants of venison off a bone. "So, Bane's going be okay Sam? I didn't know he had died before!"

I swallowed a juicy chunk of steak. "I'm sure he needs time to process what's happened to him. I didn't know he had died either. We never talked about it."

I played with the food on my plate. We never really talked, Bane and I, but then again I never really opened up to anyone. Except Christin. I felt my chest start to ache. The next piece of steak went down my throat as a hard lump. I chewed absently. I needed to resolve the issue of not opening up.

"Is everyone okay?" I asked to no one in particular.

I looked around the group as everyone nodded. The nodding didn't erase the sadness I knew lurked there.

Emma was petting Bruno and answered quietly. "Yes. I think we'll be okay. It was both frightening and thrilling. Now I know why you tried to keep us out of it."

"Yes well, you guys proved you can handle yourselves and you two protected the island like ninja warriors." I paused until Oliver and Emma both looked at me. "And you saved my life. Thank-you."

They both grinned and their chests puffed up proudly.

"No, this doesn't mean you get out of doing bathroom duty." They groaned and their chest deflated a little. "But I will increase your security duties."

Their chests reflated.

I smiled and turned to Mae.

"Mae, do you know how I sensed Christin's passing?"

Mae had taken her place in her rocker. She stopped her rhythmic rocking.

Mae frowned, then answered. "You know what you are child."

"What? No, I don't. I haven't a clue!" I glared balefully in her direction.

She grinned to herself and straightened her cane. "You have an extra ability like Griff and me." Her pink swirling eyes somehow looked directly at me and she said, "You're an empath!"

Griff, Garrick, the twins, Cory and I, all uttered in unison. "A what?"

Mae laughed out loud. "Oh children, we have so much to learn about ourselves, and so much time to do it!"

"But Mae, what does that mean?" I stammered, still stunned.

"You can feel the emotions of others sweetheart!" My jaw hung open. I was really speechless. I just stared in her direction flabbergasted.

I looked around the fire. Everyone was just as speechless.

"No I can't. It's only happened a few times, and I didn't have any say in the matter. It just happened. I can't control these so called *special abilities*." I frowned at Mae. She could be as clear as mud sometimes.

"Child." She began. I could see I was trying her patience like she was trying mine. "This is all so new. You're raw. Your empathetic ability was triggered by a few intense situations. People you care about will be the easiest to feel. As you increase your understanding of this ability, so will your capacity to read and feel anyone."

"What kinda ability is that? I have a hard enough time figuring out my own emotions. Now I have to be tuned to everyone else's?" Frustration wasn't just creeping out it; rather it was really rearing its ugly head.

Mae just smiled and rocked. I really wanted to throttle that little old lady.

"Sam. You have to give it time."

"This must be hell, because the idea of being able to feel what other people are feeling sounds like torture." I put my plate on the ground and Teak went for it.

"No girl. You had yours and you're getting fat." She wasn't, but I liked giving her a hard time.

"Imagine if you could almost read someone's mind Sam, or you knew when someone was in trouble. Wouldn't that be useful?" The mean old blind woman smiled again and started rocking.

I paused just as I was about to respond and shut my mouth, while I leaned back in my chair.

Well yes, that kind of ability could be useful.

"You could sense danger." She said as she leaned over to coax Teak and Oakley to take the two bones she was offering. There wasn't a lot of coaxing needed.

A tumble of random thoughts and questions battled in my head.

"It's okay child. We'll figure it out. You don't need to fret none."

"How do you know this stuff Mae? Did you get a manual and I didn't?"

"No hun." She chuckled quietly. "How do I do what I do? How does Griff? You must have had great empathy in you—you did become a nurse. I bet you were a good one too. I'm sure you were very intuitive to your patient's needs. Almost tuned to their emotional needs I'd say." She chuckled louder and rubbed Teak's full belly.

I didn't know what to say, so I didn't say anything at all. I stared into the fire as did everyone else.

Bane jumped into my head. I hopped up. "I'll bring Bane a plate of food. He must be starving. I'll be back."

Ω Ω Ω

Bane walked to his trailer, feeling implausibly perfect. His hearing, smell and vision were impeccable. It was overwhelming. He needed a moment alone to collect and ground himself.

He peeled his sweat-encrusted clothes off and turned on the shower. He looked into the mirror. Glowing eyes stared back at him. He stepped back quickly and fell through the wall.

As he brushed off the dust from the drywall he made to push himself up. Instead he flew into the ceiling. He landed sharply on the bathroom counter, catching his chin on the way down. He rolled off the counter and hit his head on the toilet.

He groaned and then laughed. He used the toilet as a purchase to ground himself. The room was steaming up. He wiped the mirror. He didn't feel high or wired, he just felt clear.

His chin was discolored and bleeding. Actually the bleeding had already stopped and a scab was forming.

"Wow!" He scratched the scab away. At least he wouldn't have to use pieces of toilet paper anymore for those shaving nicks.

Huh…

His face was smooth, and his laugh and stress lines were gone. Bane's hair remained dishevelled, coated with a light sprinkling of drywall dust. The rest of his body was relatively unchanged. However, the scar on the left side of his chest, where a broken piece of rib had once pierced his skin, was gone. There was no more reminder of the snake that had tried to kill him.

He stared into the reflection of his swirling eyes. The snake, oh damn. His mother had said the incident had *almost* killed him. Had he died for a moment and no one told him? It seemed an important piece of information regarding his life. Someone should have informed him. He shook his head at the irony. Death had given him life.

The mirror had fogged over again. A brown light illuminated the bathroom. He stepped into the hot shower. Ah… that felt good. He lathered his gently muscled body, enjoying the soothing spray of the shower.

He heard someone enter the trailer and paused in his lathering. He smelled her then. Sweat oranges. Sam.

His groin swelled, responding to the thought of her. He listened and heard something drop to the floor outside the shower.

Sam's hand reached into the shower and moved the curtain aside.

"Hi" she murmured "I think I smell too. Do you mind sharing the hot water?" Sam's cool body grazed past Bane. She ducked under the cascade of hot water.

Stuttering he said, "Ah…ah…no." He stood with his hands covering his swollen groin, while he openly stared. He quickly shut his mouth. Water caressed her smooth muscled body, rippling over her firm breasts. Bane reached out to the wall to brace a moment of dizziness that washed over him. He felt an intense ache ripple up his body. It was not an unpleasant ache.

"Could you wash my back? It's been ages since I had anyone wash it." She said casually.

Bane squeezed the bar of soap in his hand. It shot straight up and dented the ceiling. They both laughed a little nervously.

"Let me get that for you." Sam bent over and grazed his stiffness with her hip. A moan escaped his lips.

"You okay?" She handed the soap back to him, a mischievous grin played on her lips.

Bane cleared his throat. "Turn," he directed her with a twirling motion of his hand. He looked very serious. Sam complied and leaned her hands against the front of the shower.

Bane lathered up the soap. He gently massaged Sam's shoulders, back and buttocks in a smooth firm rhythm.

Sam moaned and gently pushed into him. His lathered hands slid to her front.

Bane was nothing if not a perfectionist—work, work, work.

He moved his soapy hands down her abdomen then gradually worked his way up to her small, firm breasts. Sam moaned again as a floodgate of butterflies was released and danced in her stomach. She pushed deeper into his chest.

A deep groan slipped from Bane's lips. He leaned into her neck, breathing out warm air. He felt her tremble. His tongue and lips feathered down to her shoulder.

Sam reached back between his hard legs and caressed his substantial hard bulge. Her hand was soapy, so her caresses were slippery and slow.

Velvet caresses made Bane gasped warm air onto Sam's neck. "Oh God," he growled as he wrapped his arm tightly around Sam's waist pulling her closer to him.

His soapy hand slid down to her taunt stomach then slipped gently between her firm soft legs. She welcomed his caress with warmth and moistness.

Sam sighed and shivered. She pushed back deeper into his slick body while she gently directed him into her. She enveloped his throbbing hardness fully, snuggly—a perfect fit.

His breath caught in his throat and he moaned "Sam."

"I know." Sam breathed out hard.

Bane's fingers tenderly spread her folds then rhythmically began to caresses her. He felt himself throb and grow even harder as he pushed deeper into Sam. Heaven couldn't be better. He felt Sam tighten around the euphoric pulse emanating from his groin as he slipped in and out of her heated moistness.

Overwhelming pleasure met each of his thrusts as she pulled him in deeper and deeper. Their breathing became frantic and irregular. They moved rhythmically, lost in each other's hunger—two dancers who had become one.

Gasping in elated ecstasy, he struggled to pull her even closer as he felt her warmth explode and pulse around him. He slipped further into her as she cried out his name.

"Oh Bane."

Waves of desire cascaded through his body, as he released into her throbbing and contracting embrace. He held her tight against him as he remained absorbed in her throbbing heat. Their bodies pulsed in harmony.

Sam released a heavy sigh, as a small chuckle escaped from deep in her chest and murmured. "Hallelujah. I can breathe again." Bane chuckled.

"Are you hungry yet? You must be starving." Sam pressed against Bane as warm water flowed over her. He had his arms wrapped tightly around her.

Gently he withdrew from inside her and softly kissed her neck while he whispered, "Yes, I'm starving."

He tuned her forward to face him and kissed her deeply. He pressed her body into the wall, as she wrapped her arms around his neck. Their bodies were still soapy and slid smoothly over each other. Nuzzling her neck with his teeth and tongue, he savored the taste of her. Sam moaned, a carousel of emotions washed over her.

Bane's body responded with a throbbing stiffness as her smooth abdomen moved against him. Their kisses were deep and wet. He gently slipped one of her leg's up around his waist and very slowly bordered her warm recesses. Taking his time, he teased as he held back from fully entering her lush heat. Sam attempted to pull him into her—he held her shaking body back. Just a hint of his hardness touched her quivering succulent opening. They gasped together as his mouth found hers. Their moans were stifled as their kisses became more zealous. Bane pulled Sam's other leg over his hip. He pulled away from her kiss and looked deep into her eyes. Sam slowly opened her eyes—blue molten lava singed his heart. He allowed himself to smoothly slide deep into her warm folds, while he watched her inhale in pleasure. Her heart beat a single thump as their bodies drew together in an intense slow heated cadence. Their breath came out in ragged gasps as they surged and surged in a torrent of rapturous bliss together.

They slid down the wall as one. Panting and grinning. Sam had her head on Bane's chest as the shower washed over them. The water had long since cooled—neither noticed.

Sam traced patterns on Bane's chest connecting the water droplets. "I guess the virus helps with stamina." A little guttural chuckle snuck out of Sam.

Bane smiled and inflated his chest. "A drug company would kill for the secrets harboured in the virus." He laughed.

"I can see their ads now—*if it doesn't kill you, it'll keep you harder.*" He snickered an exaggerated guffaw.

With a velvety kiss, Sam lifted herself from Bane's taunt body. "You must have food, or you'll be no good to me!" She laughed and extended her hand toward Bane's superb body.

"They'll find us pruned and shrivelled up with grins on our faces." Sam kissed his chest.

"Yes I feel like a Cheshire cat that just ate the canary." Bane grinned and his stomach growled.

Bane jumped up and pulled Sam into his arms." You have no idea how good I want to be for you bully!" Then he planted a deep wet kiss on her lips. Bane felt himself respond to her welcoming warm mouth.

He looked down. "Mercy, I have no control around you!"

Sam noticed his condition and grinned. Mischief danced in her eyes. Her mouth slid down his chest. He didn't resist but braced his waning stance.

Bane groaned, as Sam glided her hands down his back while tracing her tongue over his hard abdomen. "Oh save me." He pulled the shower curtain out of the wall and tossed it aside, as her warm mouth languished attention on his *"condition."* Sam's mouth was insistent; he arched and cried out a throaty moan as he released in a shuddering spasm of pleasure.

"For the love of...Mercy already! I don't think you can kill me, but I may slip into a deep coma of happiness." He collapsed slowly to the floor. Sam's waiting arms found him.

In a silky voice Sam whispered. "This was unexpected." Her head again rested on Bane's chest.

"Yes, to say the least." Bane sighed while he ran his fingers through Sam's hair.

"Since the reaping, it's been nothing but a series of overwhelming circumstances. I've been at the mercy of the fates." Sam frowned and felt distracted. She quickly appraised Bane's face.

His face was smooth. He was patiently listening as he traced her jawline.

"Come on, let's get dressed, I'm presently at the mercy of my stomach, and I have plans for you princess!" Sam pulled Bane with her.

He smiled up at her. "Bully." His heart was at her mercy—fate had brought them together.

CHAPTER TWENTY-NINE:
Milk and Cookies

"An individual has not started living until he can rise above the narrow confines of his individualistic concerns to the broader concerns of all humanity."
-Martin Luther King, Jr. (1929 - 1968)

Time marched on, dragging the seasons with it. It was the beginning of a new summer and life was blossoming on the island. A young mountain couple had just welcomed the first birth in our group since the reaping. They named her Hope. The community was healing from the global devastation—I was healing from my personal devastation. I still missed my friend. Time moved easily, as a comfortable routine in the community evolved. The compound became a home. We all became a family of thirty-six. We reaped what we sowed. Our home became a haven of gentle survival. Greens continued to visit our marina town, and we continued to dispatch them as easily as a matter of habit now. Occurrences with the greens became scarce, only about once a month was it needed for us to dispatch to the marina. We scavenged supplies from the town, grew fresh produce, collected pigs, chickens and cows and we hunted for fresh game once a week.

There was always activity bustling in the compound. Mae and her committee of women had taken it upon themselves—to warm up the compound's sterile atmosphere. Small trees, bushes, and flowers dotted the boundaries of the compound. Trailers were pushed together to add more footage to dwellings.

The colors converted from security detail to furniture movers periodically. We brought couches, sofas and chairs to the island. The uninfected, never ventured to the main land—it was still just too dangerous and unpredictable to risk it. The infected took it upon themselves to retrieve any necessary goods while running security checks.

Our latest project was to clear the town of corpses, remove blocking vehicles and scout out potential supplies. We used a dump truck and our bare hands. We tried not to think of the lives the bodies had left behind. It was dirty mind-numbing work. We prevailed with each other's support.

None of us we're religious, yet we took the time to be respectful as we buried the bodies and marked the graves with white boulders. We burned and buried them in mass graves deep enough that the remains wouldn't be disturbed by any unwanted attention.

I stood by and watched as Bane threw gasoline into the pit.

"Light it up Bane. All is clear!" Garrick yelled from the bulldozer.

A thought began to take shape as I watched Bane light a match in slow motion. "Bane wait!" I lunged toward him, but I was too late—he was mid toss.

He dropped the flammable cocktail he had lit in a stunted lob. "Damn, Sam. I almost became deep fried!" Bane was stepping back from the mini bonfire glowing in front of him. "What's up?" he checked himself for flames.

"The smoke. I just realized it could be a massive signal to someone!" I was beside him checking him for flames as well.

He stopped padding himself down and looked up at the last pit. It was still smoking grey plumes of smoke that were rising into the clear blue sky. "You think there are still survivors out there? That would be a good thing then, wouldn't it, if they saw the smoke?" he asked, confused.

I followed his gaze, "sure if they're good survivors, I suppose. What about other colors—remember the black-eyed man?"

The black eyed stranger had long since been burned and buried on the island, as had Christin and Ray.

My heart lurched at the memory. We had tried to position Christin's remains, wondering if the virus could heal him. We waited an agonized week while being tortured between feelings of sadness and apprehension. We didn't want to lose Christin but we were concerned about the state of his mind if he was reanimated. Seven days later, his remains were as lifeless as when we found him. We burned and buried him beside Ray.

I missed my friend.

All the members of the island came to show their respect. Christin was loved. Whenever a thought of Christin passed through my mind, it still caused a deep ache in my chest.

I looked at Bane, and my heart swelled, if anything ever happened to him... I averted my eyes and looked east. A frown creased my brow.

"Sam?" Bane reached out and wrapped his arms around me. "If we get visitors, we'll figure it out," he whispered into my ear.

"I know princess. I just don't want to lose anyone else is all." I flipped him over on his back. "Flame!"

He groaned.

"I'm sure a saw a flicker." I pointed earnestly to his feet. "Really! I swear!" I said stifling a smirk.

He did not look convinced. Bizarre, I was so sure.

"Help me up!" He reached up. I took his hand, and he pulled me down onto his chest. "Flame!" he whispered into my ear. A spirited smile played on his lips.

I smacked his chest and guffawed at his blatant lie.

"Wow bully, thank goodness you were there to save me." He did not stifle his smirk.

"Glad I could be of assistance, wouldn't want you to burn up princess! You are getting kind of hot!" I kissed his neck.

A shadow descended over our entangled forms.

"Ah...excuse me Sam." A lot of throat clearing followed.

"Yes, Garrick, how may I assist you?" I didn't take my eyes from Banes. He and I exchanged mischievous glances.

"That's the last of them. Do you want me to burn them? Bane here looks like he's—um—having a problem with the...*ah* fire." Garrick was a gentleman and turned his gaze to the pit.

Bane indeed had a problem. I could feel it growing under my hips. But he didn't have a problem with fire. I felt heat flow between us.

"Fluffy white bunnies," I mumbled into his ear.

"Nope. I think I'm going to need visuals of grandma in her two piece!" He groaned as I got off of him.

I could hear Garrick snickering quietly to himself.

Garrick had his own problems. Griffin and he had just moved into their own trailer. We're all just trailer park trash—our mommas would be rolling in their graves.

"Let's just bury them. I'm thinking the smoke might bring unwanted attention!" I adjusted Beatrice my sword, who was usually slung over my shoulder—she was wrapped around my neck. I looked east again.

Garrick mimicked my frown and followed my gaze east. He then turned and strode over to the idling bulldozer. "Hey Griff, you can get started on this last bit. I'll get the boulder!" The dozer roared to life, burying the past.

That night we all sat around the fire, sipping hot chocolate and discussed the possibility of visitors.

"Our security system is sound. We should be okay as far as knowing if any trouble is coming our way!" I blew on my cup. A steady stream of sweet vapor encircled my vision. I could drink the concoction down in one gulp, but I'd end up with blisters down my gullet.

In between mouthfuls of popcorn Oliver mumbled, "What about the good guys? What if someone needs help?" He was a good boy, generous with everything except his popcorn.

Skid sat behind Ollie, pawing at the boy's head, hoping for a waylaid kernel to fall his way. The bear eyed each handful that entered into the boy's mouth with coveting intensity.

He looked almost, pathetic—he must have been hanging around Oakley and gotten some acting tips.

Skid had already devoured three batches of popcorn. He was a fiend for popcorn. He was now a year old, well-fed adolescent black bear with an insatiable appetite. Ollie and Skid were best friends—the bear worshiped him.

"Yeah, you're right Ollie. We're pretty well set up here." I looked down at the base of my chair. Teak and Oakley were sprawled out beside it, satiated from the evening's BBQ. Oakley had a large bone wedged protectively, between her fake leg and hairy paw.

Bane and Harley had engineered a prosthetic leg for Oakley. Poor thing had originally hated it, but the two men had eventually perfected the mechanics of the fake limb.

She bore the burden of their tinkering and adjustments with kisses. My bionic dog. She now tolerated the appendage. It eased her awkward bouncing gait. Oakley could manage well enough on three legs. I only affixed the artificial one, to give her shoulders a break.

"Maybe we should go on short sweeps and see if anyone is around or needs help?" Emma was curled up on a blanket leaning on Bruno with Garrick nestled beside the two. The big cat was presently passed out and snoring. His big rear leg twitched. Dreaming of his hunt today, I'm sure.

I grinned and blew on my drink. "We could go on day trips. I don't want to leave the compound vulnerable for very long though."

"We could go in a team of four and leave two colors behind. I mean our people are armed and Cory knows how to handle himself," Bane said, scratching Teaks sleeping form.

Teak and Bane were becoming fast friends. If she wasn't with me, she was shadowing Bane. When we had changed the living arrangements, Teak wouldn't let Bane in the bed. He insisted on sleeping on the floor the first night. Teak had glared at him through the twilight hours.

The next morning I found them curled up on the floor together. Oakley and I had stepped over their tangled forms. I swear Teak was grinning.

We had pushed two trailers together, so all of us had room. The twins were a package deal that came with Bane. Forget nuclear family, we were a viral family.

"What do you mean youngling by "leave two"? Am I chopped liver? Humph!" Mae banged her cane to the ground to make her point.

All the animals responded by jumping up, alert to trouble. A few growls ensued.

Griff was flipped off of Bruno as he roared and shook his mane.

Skid intensified his furry grip on Oliver's head. "Ouch Skid, you got my nose!" Ollie whined.

Bane looked down at his hands. "Well Mae, you're so busy and important to the people, that I thought you had better things to, ah do!" I saw redness creep up his neck.

"Good save." I laughed, and everyone resettled. Mae was smiling at the discomfort she had created.

"Yes, your right Bane, I am very busy. I think day trips would be a necessary reprieve and would alleviate our concerns."

Sometimes Mae talked like a hillbilly, and other times like now, she spoke eloquently, as if she'd been schooled in university. I realized I knew very little about this enigmatic woman.

Mae stared unseeingly into the fire. "There are people out there. *That* I'm sure of. We just gotta weed out the bad ones!"

Garrick laughed and said, "Bruno could be a good weed whacker." We joined him in his laughter.

For the first exploration Griff, Bane, Garrick and I loaded our gear and decided to head straight east. The twins we're not pleased at their exclusion, but we conquered their arguments with assurances of popcorn and participation in the next trip.

They we're tough little negotiators.

We decided to take two vehicles again, in case one broke down. The route we decided on consisted of back roads, primarily because we wanted to start in rural towns. We agreed that our goal was to be gone for only two days, max.

The boys took the truck, and we girls took the Rover. I wanted to utilize Griff's tracking skill.

The walkie-talkies got well used. We passed a few burned out towns we didn't even bother entering. Griff pointed out a herd of zebras grazing in a farmer's field. Bruno stood up in the back of the truck when we passed them. We could only wonder where they came from.

Griff sensed a few greens sporadically on our drive. They were a dying breed. They only had base survival skills; they lived in the moment. They didn't seek shelter or protection from the elements. They didn't hole up in permanent lodging. So, exposure to varying climate changes froze many of the greens as they slumbered. We had found numerous greens decaying in the open. Griff's gift left little to chance or guessing—she was focused.

Our heightened senses didn't detect any uninfected human activity. We scanned for environmental disturbances, which a common human might create. Fresh tire tracks, pilfered stores, smoke from a chimney, noise even—any hint of activity. Unaffected humans, as it turned out, were very uncommon.

Bane and Garrick's truck drove ahead of us. We couldn't see anything except their taillights. The dust and dark made it impossible to distinguish even their expired plate. So much for our super vision.

We had switched places to accommodate Bruno. The big cat was tired of eating our dust. An open truck bed did not always translate into fresh air.

The truck's taillight unexpectedly flamed an intense red. We almost ended up on Bruno's hairy lap. The truck had stopped abruptly. The lion was pissed—im sure he ate a little of the truck bed.

Anxiously Griff and I climbed out to meet Garrick and Bane. "What's going on?" I asked.

Bane answered with a worried expression. "I think we hit something!"

Garrick was reassuring Bruno.

It was pitch dark out, except for our headlights. I removed my goggles, everyone one else followed suit. The night lit up like a carousel—minus the music. There was a cloud of dust surrounding us. I scanned the perimeter. The dust made it difficult to see no more than five feet in front of us. Enhanced vision or not, the dust made it difficult to even make out each other.

Armed we split up slowly, listening for movement in the cloud of dust.

Bane yelled from the driver's side of the truck. "Over here. There's something on the ground." Whatever it was, it wasn't a green—Griff hadn't sensed any colors in the vicinity and no green haze pierced the night.

We inched forward slowly. It could be a wounded animal.

Brush was covering it, so we couldn't make out a shape. It smelled… human! I dashed to the hidden form and pushed the brush aside.

A young teenage girl was curled in a fetal position. She was moaning and holding her stomach. Her eyes opened, and she screamed. I reached out to comfort her. She passed out.

She was light as a feather. I carried her still form to the Rover. Griff opened the back door.

"I must have hit her with the truck. Is she going to be okay?" Garrick looked concerned.

I was too busy checking the young girl for injuries to answer.

"Grab that blanket Griff!" The girl's body was bruised with old discolorations; her pelvis seemed stable; her stomach wasn't rigid; she could have internal bleeding. I just didn't know for sure. I checked her head and neck—no obvious deformities.

The girl looked to be about seventeen. I assessed a little closer. The adolescent appeared well fed. Her clothing was only a little dirty, and her long brown hair was tied back.

"We should put our goggles back on, in case she wakes up and it freaks her out or gives her a heart attack." I fit my goggles back on my face.

"Is she going be okay?" Bane was tucking the blanket around the girl.

I looked up and surveyed our surroundings. No obvious movement caught my eye. "Griff, any color activity around?" I asked, concerned something had been chasing the girl.

"I thought I sensed something earlier, but it was faint. Umm... nope nothing." She was doing her usual scrunchy face. I didn't know what to do for the girl. I had nothing really useful—I needed a cat scan or x-ray and possibly a surgeon. Something to see what was going on inside her.

I could hear the girl's heart strumming quickly. Too quick. "I think she's going into shock—bleeding internally" I groaned. I felt helpless.

"Griff make a fire! Let's warm her up. I don't know what else to do." I almost felt like crying. Bane put his arm around my shoulders. He could hear the distress in my voice. I reached in under the blankets and palpated her abdomen. It was becoming rigid. Damn, damn, damn...

"Let's make her comfortable at least. Grab those blankets Bane! I got her." I lifted her gently. Her head lolled on my shoulder. She remained unconscious.

Griff and Garrick had built a roaring fire. Bane made a soft nest out of our blankets. I placed her gingerly in the center of the makeshift bed and quickly covered her still form.

We had a first aide pack, so I started an intravenous on her. She didn't seem distressed so I didn't give her any medications.

We sat and waited.

I cradled her head in my lap and stroked her hair. I murmured gently, "It's okay little one, I got you, and you're not alone. You're safe." I continued repeating this statement into the quiet night.

The young girl died in my arms just before the morning sun blinked over the horizon. She never regained consciousness.

Garrick's shoulders were hunched over, his face in his hands. "I killed our first contact." His voice cracked under the strain. He was desperately trying to hold it together. Griff put her arms around his hunched form. Bruno head butted his back.

I was angry as I stared into the fire. "No, something tried to kill her. We just put her out of her misery." I explained to the group that there were many old bruises marring the girl's body.

Everyone in the group wore scowls of anger.

"Let's go find whoever, or whatever hurt this little girl," Garrick hissed through clenched teeth. Everyone nodded their agreement.

We buried the beaten and abused girl as the sun was rising red. Silent promises of revenge were left unspoken.

CHAPTER THIRTY:
The Devil Wears a Plaid Grey Suit

"Ambition is the last refuge of the failure."
-Oscar Wilde (1854 - 1900)

We smelled them, before we saw them. Cows— approximately fifty of them. Mae would love to get her hands on that herd. We pulled alongside the pasture.

These cows had been tended to. They were clean, well fed and milked. The bovines appeared unfazed by our presence.

The walkie-talkie buzzed to life. "Do you see the smoke rising south of us?" Garrick asked.

Griff and I both craned our necks and peered toward the horizon. Five or so piping trails of smoke rose into the sky.

I clicked the walkie-talkie to life. "Yes!" How do you want to do this guys?"

"Griff do you see any colors around?" Garrick asked through the radio.

She concentrated. "Yeah, miles away on the northern periphery, a couple not really moving much."

"We're clear of colors," I said into the radio.

"How about you and Bane go in? We'll hang back just in case..." He didn't finish.

"Sounds good Garrick. Give us an hour. Get your butt over here Bane!" I laughed. We stopped the vehicles. Bane came bounding out of the truck.

Griff took the dogs with her. I didn't want to have to worry about them.

Bane's eyes we're alight with excitement. "Put your goggles back on princess. We don't want to freak any one out." I was adjusting mine to cover my eyes.

"Yes bully." He kissed me quick. My lips lingered in the air, alone. Humpff!

Even after a year of being with him—I craved him too much.

"We'll check back within an hour. If you don't hear from us, send in the posse!"

Garrick's laughing voice came through the walkie-talkie. "All right I'll send Bruno in for lunch!"

We drove the Rover along a wired fence for about a mile until we came to a locked gate. I pried it easily.

I opened the gate, while Bane moved through the threshold. "Let's go say hi to our neighbours, shall we?" I grinned at Bane. "We forgot the welcome basket and pot-roast," he said.

I patted my cross bow, and he patted his shotgun. We had brought other house warming gifts just in case.

The gravel road we drove on twisted through a grove of trees. The trees protected a small open breadth of land filled with ten modest houses—cabins really. A rock-strewn stream ran the length of houses. Apple trees dappled the back drop, and laundry waved in the breeze. The smell of humanity rippled with the wind.

It was a beautiful little alcove, well maintained. We saw doors shutting in our wake. Not very welcoming, maybe we should have brought a casserole. I felt a pit in my stomach.

We pulled into the center of the alcove that was surrounded by cabins, and killed the engine. Silence greeted us. I noticed a few birds chirping in the distance, while a shutter banged in the soft breeze.

Various curtains were gently pushed aside. Our keen eyesight caught everything. Regular human eyes attempted to evaluate us covertly. I heard heartbeats.

"Bane do you…?"

A door to our right burst open interrupting me. The sudden activity caused us to draw our weapons. A man of above average height carrying a strong muscular build emerged with his hands up; a smile was painted on his face.

His eyes blazed a yellowish-green. "Hello, friends!" He walked toward us. Bane and I both narrowed our eyes. "Welcome to our humble abode. I am unarmed. Please lower your weapons!" he said through his smile.

We didn't adjust our aim—I immediately disliked him.

He stopped and scratched his head. Stalemate. "My name is Tony Stevenson, and this is my family compound." He bowed and gestured to the surrounding cabins.

Tony turned to the closed cabins. "Ladies and kids!" Doors eased open slowly. Hesitantly the women and a few children eased through the doors. Nervous eyes looked toward us apprehensively.

I scanned the area, focusing on heartbeats and any hidden sounds. Like the cocking of a gun. We were alone with this crew of nervous survivors.

Ten sets of eyes stared at us. The spectators were conservatively dressed, but clean and well fed. Seven woman and three children

Bane and I exchanged stoic looks and lowered our weapons.

I hit the walkie-talkie button twice, signalling that we found people. I pushed and held the button down, indicating that Griff and Garrick were to wait for our signal.

I turned and smiled. "Well hello neighbors!" We exited the Rover, weapons in hand.

Tony extended his hand to invite us into his home. "Won't you join us for some tea?"

We introduced ourselves to Tony and entered his home. The women and children did not follow.

The cabin was rustic and homey. A blazing fire sat in the hearth. Shelves filled with various types of books lined the walls. Handmade blankets were strewn on the furniture. A second floor loft bedroom faced the front door.

"Nice cozy place you have here Tony." I was taking in the comfortable ambience. It definitely had a woman's touch, but I didn't feel comfortable.

The front door opened slightly and a young girl of twenty slipped in, heading to the kitchen. A black eye and angry split lip caught my attention. I saw her pouring water into a large metal teapot. Tea, as Tony promised.

"Please have a seat." He gestured to a couch by the fire. "We have much to discuss." he watched me with his fiery eyes. I could feel his eyes crawl over my body. His stare made me feel like I needed a shower.

Bane gestured to Tony's mouth. "You have a little something there, you might want to...."

Tony wiped his mouth and looked abashed—caught in the act of coveting.

Bane sat unusually close to me on the couch—possessive. Men, always needing to pee on their territory—geez, some things never change. I actually didn't mind it in this case. This guy gave me the heebee-jeebees.

The young woman came out of the kitchen and set a pot of tea in front of us. She poured three cups.

"Won't you join us?" I looked closer at the girl.

My assessment had been wrong. She was fifteen tops. Faded bruises discolored her cheeks. She glanced quickly at Tony and then back to me. "No thank you. I had my tea a little earlier."

She backed away, tray in hand, into the kitchen.

Was she scared of us, or Tony? I narrowed my eyes and sipped my tea. Both probably. My back ached with tension. Bane absently rubbed my shoulder.

Warm apple cider enveloped my taste buds. Huh, delicious,

"Amazing," I said. Surprised by the delicious flavor, I took another sip.

"Yes. We have a press in the barn and an abundance of apples. There's a grove not far back from the houses." He smiled. "I prefer tea though. The cider is too sweet." he murmured into his cup.

"So, how did you end up in this little oasis, Tony?" I attempted to keep suspicion out of my voice. I removed my goggles.

Tony gasped and almost dropped his cup in his lap. "Your eyes are beautiful!" He rubbed a growing stain on the crotch of his pants. "Damn, hot!"

I stifled a chuckle.

A small sharp crash came from the kitchen, followed by a yelp. The young girl came stumbling through the kitchen door.

"I'm so sorry, it slipped! I'm so sorry!" The young girl's voice wavered.

Tony looked up and I saw quilt pass over his face.

He smiled and continued to stare at me.

Click.

Tony tore his hungry gaze from my direction as he swiftly dashed to the girl's side. He held her petite shaking hand. "It's okay Kelly, I have other plates," he cooed, while caressing her hand.

Kelly started to shake harder. Taking a deep breath, Kelly pulled her hand away and wiped it on her shirt.

"I'll get a broom." She turned and was out the door in a shaking flurry.

Tony looked down at the floor, "I guess cookies are out of the question?" He turned and resumed his seat in an old leather chair.

The cookies were left to the floor.

"So where were we? Ah yes—how did I come by here, right?" He crunched up his face. "Where to begin?

Ω Ω Ω

Tony came up from the south. New Orleans had become a stinking cesspool of decomposing bodies amidst the stifling humid heat. Katrina all over again, times one hundred.

He couldn't stand the cloying, putrid stagnation any longer. The rancid wind encouraged Tony to find a fresh place with civilized people.

He wandered the barren wasteland, devoid of humanity, for months. Tony decided to head west. He had never seen the ocean before, and he wanted to wash away the past.

After a few negative run-ins with the green-eyes he chose to avoid their kind. They were no better than wild animals. Actually he preferred the wild dogs. At least they had a sense of community.

Ω Ω Ω

He breathed deeply. "I found the women and children at a Mennonite community. I managed to convince them to join me and to head out west.

Their home had been under constant siege by green-eyed creatures— they were barely holding on. The sickness took most of their colony, and the green-eyes were picking at what was left.

"No men I see." I spoke softly, but my eyes remained contracted.

He looked sideways, toward his front window. "Nope, just us."

"That's sad," Bane mused and eyed Tony closer.

Tony looked uncomfortable. He kept crossing and uncrossing his legs.

"It's unfortunate, yes. So many, ah…people dead and you can't get close to anyone. That's got to be lonely," I mumbled. Tony looked very uncomfortable as he continued to cross and uncross his legs and adjusted his buttoned shirt.

His attention snapped in my direction when I spoke.

His eyes narrowed. "It's nice having the company. They're lovely people. We have a little community here, and I keep them safe." He gaze moved back to the window.

I felt a dark ache in the pit of my stomach. It was starting to grow.

I squeezed Bane's knee. "Well, we best get going. We want to check a few towns out before it gets too dark. We wouldn't want to hit anything on the road. Bane are you ready hun?" I stood up and reached out for Bane's hand.

He looked at me quizzically. "Yes dear." Confusion was written all over his fake smile.

Tony was already striding to the door, opening it before we could change our minds. Don't let the door hit you on the way out!

Two women were standing in the open doorway with a basket in hand, ready to knock. They appeared startled, but they recovered quickly.

Fake smiles appeared on their stunned faces. "Ah, hello. Kelly felt so bad about the cookies, so we brought some fresh ones over!"

Tony stood at the open door way, full of fake pride. "Yes, and feel free to stop by again when you're in the area." He took the basket from the older of the two women and handed it to me. He didn't take his eyes off the two women.

"Thank you so much. It'll be great to have fresh baked cookies again—it's been so long" I smiled and went to shake their hands.

Tony swept his arm out to allow Bane and me room to exit his home. The stunned women were swept aside with his arm.

"Okay then, thanks for your hospitality. Nice meeting you, take care of..." Bane had my back and was propelling me forward.

Bane knew I was lying. Mae prided herself on her vast baking skills. He had sensed danger as well. We waved with fake smiles and drove off with a plume of dust trailing after us.

"What the hell was that?" Bane spoke through clenched teeth.

"I don't know, but something was definitely wrong. I could feel it!" I sighed. You didn't need ESP to see the wrongness in that state of affairs.

We rendezvoused with Garrick and Griff, and explained what we had just encountered. Their expressions of concern mirrored ours.

"Cookie?" I offered them the basket.

Ω Ω Ω

"Damn," Tony muttered to himself over and over, while slamming his clenched fist into his open palm.

He went down to his cement encased-basement. His man cave he called it. He started pacing, mumbling under his breath. Tomorrow he was going to infect Kelly. Maybe she'd be the one to survive. He was running out of potential choices.

Tony had easily dispatched the men, and placed most of the children in captivity locked in a storm cellar not far from the compound.

Damn brats, they always needed something. He had thought of dispatching the children right away, but they were a good motivator in keeping the women in line.

He tried changing one woman a month. All eight had succumbed to the illness. His groin stirred as he remembered the means in which he infected the women. He managed to get a few days of usefulness out of them before they died quietly in his bed.

Those beautiful blue eyes he mused. He didn't know the virus made colors in such vivid beautiful varieties—yum. He wiped the drool off his bottom lip. Her partner had hung pretty close, but he could fix that.

He pondered, maybe he could track them. Or maybe better yet— they'd come back. Perhaps he'd prepare something in anticipation of their return—brilliant idea.

His last brilliant idea had almost gotten him killed. Well, technically it had.

Before the reaping, he had decided to mix crack cocaine and methamphetamines. He had overdosed, barely making it to the hospital where he had collapsed in front of the emergency department, as his heart raced like a locomotive. People had actually walked over his prone body splayed on the road. The hospital had revived him twice. He had circled and entered the darkness of everlasting oblivion. Something was waiting for him. He shivered at the memory.

After his near death incident Tony entered rehab. The death defying event gave him strength to finish his stint in rehab. His boss concerned for his star employee, encouraged him to take a vacation before hitting the ground running.

Tony was their top stock broker. Even when Tony functioned at his worse, he still raked bales of money in for the firm. New York City was his stomping grounds. He often referred to it as his hunting grounds.

He had been vacationing down in New Orleans when the sickness started. He didn't see the harm in using drugs and alcohol recreationally. He could temper his habit. He could keep it clean and be a professional. Rehab had been a breeze.

New Orleans was a haven for anything. And anything was exactly what Tony was up for. Within a day of his vacation, he had been too drunk and stoned to notice people dropping around him.

When the transformation took Tony, he thought he had been in the midst of a bad drug trip. Unable to stand upright, he collapsed in an old cemetery. Hell was upon him and he was unable to pay the ferry man. His screams went unheeded in the dying city.

Tony was not a good person. His talent laid in bilking the elderly out of their savings. It's been said that psychopaths can function in society by being stock-brokers.

A cutthroat business, it perhaps kept his own murderous urges at bay. The ruthless business dealings could satiate a closeted blood thirst, just enough to keep people like him from slipping over the edge into active psychotic behaviour.

Tony didn't have to kill anyone. His analytical mind devastated his customer's hopes, dreams, income and future. As a businessman, he ruined his clientele. It was all legal.

Most of his customers completed the physical aspect of killing themselves. It was just business, nothing personal for Tony.

He was a shark in the financial seas. It was easy and legal. Tony slept well most nights, except when he was flying chemically high.

Miraculously, he had survived death yet again. Alone, altered and hungry, he wound his way through the humid, deserted streets of New Orleans. Aghast at the state of the city and the world, he roamed aimlessly for days.

There were rotting bloated corpses strewn everywhere. He had to leave the city. Tony thought he might be trapped in a drug-induced coma, purgatory or even hell. Confusion and panic propelled him out of the city of sin. He needed serenity, peace, food and fresh water.

He stopped at an abandoned news station seeking any information—only to find more rotting bodies and newspapers strewn on the floor. Fumbling with a newspaper, the plight of the world's atrocities leaped out at him.

"The End of the World!"

"Killer Virus!"

Tony gagged on his own spit. Not a drop of religion or spirituality flowed in him, but he felt the need to praise someone. "Praise Jesus. I'm not in hell. I can still change things." Tony felt like Ebenezer Scrooge on Christmas morning.

He regarded the news room. The sight of bodies in varying states of decomposition didn't distress his psyche any more. Instead, it was the smell that caused him distress.

Tony had high cleanliness standards and this city was not meeting them. A man of expensive taste that lived well, he was reluctant to leave the lavish stinking city.

He chose a black beast of a hummer to be his ride. He might as well travel in style. Tony loved luxury, and so with a heavy heart he drove away from the rotting city.

The city was a congested labyrinth of cars and debris. He literately had to push himself out of the city. The huge black beast made an excellent dozer but his slow progress convinced him to take to the back roads.

A day later as he was driving through the country, Tony spotted a community of farms busy with activity. People. He missed human contact.

The people turned out to be a Mennonite's colony. He was in hell. They took him in, but segregated him from their women. They didn't know what to make of this…man.

Devil or saint? The elders counselled with one another to decide Tony's fate. Tony laid in wait, assessing the situation.

This businessman had always been a multi-tasker. He had already eye-fondled most of the young women while appearing sublime and humble. Tony was a very good salesman. Part of his expertise entailed acting. The community was innocent of his worldly ways and didn't realize they had let a fox into the henhouse.

Tony was a white-collar worker who had soft hands and no realistic skills—he was little help to the men. Instead, the men assigned him woman's duties. He didn't mind. The women weren't close but were near. He was given out of the way vocations to keep him busy. Simple tasks filled his days, like folding laundry, gardening or picking people up from the fields. Restless and bored, the mind numbing work was becoming loathsome to his needs.

Late one evening Tony stole into Heather's cabin, and he attempted to force himself on her. She was only seventeen.

The elders were up in arms. They brusquely located their rich stash of shotguns and rifles and angrily escorted him off their property at gun point. The men made it clear he was not welcome any longer. A few God-fearing members wanted to shoot the devil on the spot, but the majority over ruled.

They were not murderers, even in this dark time. They removed his cache of weapons, allowing him to leave with his Hummer.

"But I was in love! Show mercy" Tony had half-heartedly pleaded. He had kept his hidden strength a secret. He had allowed them to exile him.

Later that evening while he sat on a ridge overlooking the community, he watched patiently—assessing his prey.

Five armed sentries made rounds. They took the threat of his possible return seriously. Amateur farmers, they knew how to plant, but not how to plot. All his life Tony had been a plotter.

Maneuvering his way to the compound stealthily, he hunted in silence. He took the first sentry by the throat, his skull easily crushed like a ripe melon. A beating heart beat no more.

A thick knife wordlessly slipped into the skull of the second man— he was barely old enough to grow whiskers.

The third man stood under a tree and collapsed beneath Tony's weight. His six and a half foot frame trounced the surprised man. His stunned expression made Tony chuckle. The knife went through the guard's throat. Blood spurted, ruining Tony's sporty garb. He'd have to get someone to clean that. It could stain.

The fourth had turned as Tony maneuvered behind him. Face-to-face the sentry had time to inhale—once. Tony grabbed the sentry's head and twisted.

Gurgled gasps escaped the young man's twisted mouth. Huh, head twisting was an exceptional means to conclude someone's life—not messy at all. He enjoyed learning new things. Challenging himself was his favorite thing in life. He was driven. Tony felt invincible, untouchable—the bullet that hit him in the shoulder spun him to the ground.

From his vulnerable position laying face first on the ground, Tony heard the pounding heartbeat of the fifth man above him. Without a second thought he levitated himself four feet off the ground with a simple push of his legs and arms.

He swung midair and kicked the gun from the guard's hands. Tony found his footing and gracefully reached out and grabbed the guard's neck. The guard's startled response did manage to catch Tony square in the nose with the palm of his hand. Tony saw stars.

Tony twisted his hands tighter as they encircled the guard's neck. Snap, crackle and pop. That sound reminded Tony, that he was hungry. He dropped the weightless body with its head hanging at an odd angle, then turned and plodded to the first house, whistling. His shoulder was healing, as he grabbed his nose and squeezed it back into alignment. He had to look pretty for the women. He was hungry.

The first house that he came upon held a couple of frightened women; he had one warm up some delicious stew while he satisfied his other needs with the other younger one. He pistol whipped the two women into unconsciousness before he left to be neighbourly.

The next structure, housed an old lady and an elderly man. Double the cracking and popping.

Tony was trying to regulate his excitement. It had been so long since he had so much fun. He glanced at his shoulder wound. The bleeding had eased to a scant dribble and a scab was now forming. He flexed his arm and only felt a small twinge. He was pleased with his ability to heal so quickly. However, the bullet might still be inside, it might blemish his skin. He strode on—he'd have to rectify that.

In total, he found thirty adults, about eight kids and a baby—minus the seven adults he had already killed. Armed with numerous hand guns and two rifles he separated the men from the women, then the women from the children. Dispatching the men in groups of twos, proved to be most efficient, and efficacy was an important trait to foster within oneself.

Tony delegated a few men to dig ditches before he shot them in the head. He wasn't a savage—of course he would bury them. Delegation was also a healthy attribute to possess in a leader.

The thirteen remaining woman covered the graves, muttering prayers and sobbing in grief.

The colony remained home for Tony and his harem of women, until smoke was spotted breaking over the rise to the east one morning.

The women were well on their way to conforming to Tony's leadership. The meek women were not above attempting to poison Tony—he could smell it before he ingested it. He took the offender to his bed. Exceptional and repeated bouts of discipline followed.

The remaining women buried the woman's eight-year old son beside his mother. No further attempts at poisoning Tony were made.

If only he could turn one of these women. He was going to run out of test subjects soon.

The fast approach of smoke and fire on the horizon escalated the group's imminent haste to depart the farming community. The women quietly sobbed as they packed up trucks with cows and supplies and with heavy hearts they headed west.

The convoy found "Apple Haven Resort" a few days later. They set up residence and made it their home. They tolerated Tony's leadership, partially for protection from the greens and partially because he held the children in captive in an unknown location. This kept the women in servitude.

Ω Ω Ω

The stockbroker continued his pacing while he contemplated his next step.

Moving was out of the question, he was set up in this little meadow. He also hoped the blue would come back.

Tony's mouth salivated as he paused in his manic pacing. He'd like the opportunity to convince her to be his mate. Those molten blue eyes made his loins quiver with anticipation.

"Kelly!" he bellowed up to the door. "I need you now!"

The door squeaked open, and Kelly stuck her head in. "Yes Mr. Stevenson, what do you need sir?"

"Please call me Tony. I need you to help me with something." He cooed his suggestion.

Kelly swallowed hard. "Yes Mr. Stevenson, what do you need?" Tony was at her side, holding her hand as he closed the door.

He smiled his most charming smile. "Well, you know I have your little brother—and he's safe of course! I was wondering if there was any reason I should bring him home?" He posed the question in his most sultry unbusinesslike tone.

"Oh Tony that would be fantastic. He could be very helpful around the settlement. He's growing so fast. I imagine he's getting very strong!" she sang in a breathless barrage of pleas.

Tony approached Kelly and took her face in his hands. He gently kissed her neck.

Kelly froze rigid as a statue. "But Tony, I'll die if you…you touch me too close!"

315

"Sometimes you just have to take a chance for those you love," he whispered into her ear ever so softly.

"If something happens to me, will…will you let him go?" she beseeched him. Tears caught in her eyelashes.

"Of course little one. Do not be afraid, I'll be gentle!" He started to unbutton her blouse. Kelly stood bravely and stared into the fire. Her brother was only five.

Ω Ω Ω

"So what should we do? We can't leave them, what sh—what the hell is this?" Griff pulled out a piece of paper from a cookie she was nibbling.

She held out the piece of crumpled paper to me as she resumed her mindless chewing.

"These are delicious? We have to rescue them just to get the recipe!"

I unravelled the grease soaked piece of paper. My keen vision was needed to make out the message.

PLEASE HELP. HE PLANS TO KILL US ALL
AND HE HAS OUR CHILDREN.

I grinned menacingly. "Of course we will rescue them. An excellent cookie recipe should not be wasted."

Everyone grinned.

"What's the plan Stan?" Garrick had Bruno by his side.

"How well do Bruno and Griff get along?" I asked the both of them. I wiggled my eyebrows.

"Fantastic, he loves her and obeys Griff better than me most times!" He looked over to Griff and winked.

A mouthful of cookies sprayed out of Griff's mouth. "Ibit 'is poo, he woves me!"

We all laughed at Griff. "I think I understood that. All right this is the plan!"

Ω Ω Ω

Griff and Bruno walked from the gate. Bane headed directly for the grove of trees and I raced around the grove of trees to come up from the rear.

I could see everyone in the compound had spotted Bruno. Extreme fear possessed them. Shrieking and dashing commenced. The community of women cleared the communal area in five seconds.

Griff and Bruno waded into the center of town casually. They stopped in the middle of the settlement. Griff stroked Bruno's mane and leaned on him, one foot crossed over the other.

"Is anyone home? I need to be adopted. I have a cat though—anyone have allergies?" She smiled a cat-ate-the-canary grin.

Tony's door flew open. His shirt was open and his belt was undone. Geez we must of interrupted something. Kelly stood hanging out the door, her dress half hanging off her body. Fear fixed on her brow.

Damn, she was just a baby still, an innocent. Griff tried not to narrow her eyes.

Tony's initial panicked expression turned hungry as he focused on Griff's goggled eyes. A not so-subtle protrusion from his groin made it difficult for Tony to zip up his pants.

Griff wondered if Skid would like a chew toy...Hmf, nah. It would most likely make him sick. The poor bear would need a tetanus shot for sure.

No treat for Skid. Griff would have to settle for a new hacky sack. She'd give it to the next green she found.

"You've been a naughty boy, hurting helpless women Mister. I'm here to take their place." Griff narrowed her eyes and winked.

Tony was fixing his greasy hair while attempting to buckle his pants. A sly grin was starting to form on his mouth. Tony gave up on his tight pants and started buttoning his shirt.

"Well hello little lady. Uh…is that lion safe?" He eyed Bruno nervously. Bruno sat quietly cleaning his very long sharp nails.

"It depends really. Say if someone wanted to hurt me or my friends— or say even a helpless woman. Well, he doesn't particularly like that." She sighed and resumed cleaning her own nails.

"Friends?" He quickly scanned the area. "Where? I would ah… never?" He bustled, while rubber necking the settlement.

Griff eyed Tony. His growth was decreasing. Pity, the green would be disappointed with such a small toy.

"Bruno and I think it's time you left. You have worn out your welcome. Leave this instant, and we may let you live." Her nails were a mess.

"I said now! Running should commence—and do up your pants. You could lose an eye with that thing!" She looked up and removed her goggles.

Tony gulped and professed. "But…but you're the one I've been looking for. I've been waiting for you. I…I need you!" Then he lifted his arms to embrace her.

Griff glared at Tony and whispered, "You need to be neutered." She pointed her small pocket knife in Tony's direction.

Tony dropped his arms and chuckled. "Are you going teach me a lesson little one?" His smarmy gawffs cut off, as his hand reached toward his back.

Garrick jumped out of the nearest tree. He uncoiled himself from his landing and walked straight toward Griff. Anger was threading its way through his expression.

He removed his goggles mid-stride, and pointed them at Tony. "There's nothing here for you." He leaned in and kissed Griff while he released his stretchy goggles. They hit Tony in the head.

Griff turned her attention back to Tony. "We think you're a very bad man Tony. Time for you to pay the piper. We found the girl." A mischievous grin spread across Griff's face.

"Theresa? But I…How did you? When?" A sob escaped from Tony's throat. He crouched and shot up into the air, aiming for his roof. Sam met his jump midway and kicked him backwards. Bruno leapt and caught him mid-chest.

In a tumble of dust and screams, Tony attempted to push Bruno's clamped jaws off of him. Tony screamed like a school girl and tried to punch Bruno.

The great cat readjusted his bite, picking the flailing screaming Tony up by the neck, and then shaking him like a new play toy, slamming him head first into the dusty ground.

Ω Ω Ω

Bane approached from the grove of apple trees, munching on a juicy apple. He tossed one to Garrick and Griff.

I waved the offer of an apple off. "Are you done trying to hurt the lion? Because he can go on for hours." Garrick said as apple juice spilled onto his chin.

Bane wiggled an apple in front of me. I smiled and took a bite of his.

"Eat your own apple—bully." I smiled. His eyes gleamed liquid chocolate in return. I took an apple out of his pocket.

"Children, the task at hand. What should we do with the monster?" Griff was getting bored, she wanted the monster ended.

I cleared my throat and looked at the battered bleeding chew toy in Bruno's mouth.

"Excuse me ladies, hello? We need your assistance. We won't harm you!" I yelled out to encircling cabins.

Doors began to slowly ease open.

Women wearing mixed expressions poked their heads out. Stunned relief was the prevailing emotion.

"What should we do with him?" I asked the women before returning my focus on the drool-soaked rapist.

A tiny voice from Tony's doorway whispered, "The children?" She hid in the shadows.

"Kelly? What kids?" I grimaced.

"Brothers, sisters, the children. He hid them somewhere." The young woman gripped the top of her dress tighter and stepped out into the sunlight.

I stiffened when I saw her bruised and bleeding face.

Bane's face turned serious. "I'll go have a sniff around. Be right back." With a quick kiss he was gone.

"Garrick follow him—two noses are better than one." He looked concerned for a moment, and then nodded toward Griff.

She nodded. She had this.

He gave Tony a hairy eyeball, then turned and followed Bane.

"So Tony, where are the kids?" I asked ever so nicely. Christin's diplomacy sort of rubbed off. I smiled warmly.

Griff did a double take at me then walked over to Tony and kicked him in the head. Good cop, bad cop.

"Wake up slime ball, Sam is talking to you about something important!"

She scratched Bruno behind the ear and he purred. Griff then returned to peeling her apple using her pocket knife I had given her for Christmas. Damn apple skin always got stuck in her teeth.

"Maybe we should skin him before we let Bruno finish him. Bits of him might get stuck in Bruno's teeth—it'll be nasty business getting him out of Bruno's molars." I grinned at her concern for Bruno's oral health.

"Good idea Griff. You want to start or shall I?"

Her hard gaze turned to concern. "Nah, It's all right. Garrick has floss and has been brushing Bruno's teeth with a scrub brush. I think he could tolerate a little skin."

Tony groaned and coughed up blood. "Please, no more. I'll go in peace!"

Griff said, "Down" to Bruno.

The lion dropped Tony onto his face.

Tony moaned and coughed up more blood.

Hmmm, a negotiation. Tick...Nah.

Griff's foot came down hard on Tony's chest. A spray of blood arced all over Tony's silk shirt.

Tony coughed in ragged gasps of breath. "All right already, the kids are holed up in a storm cellar behind the apple orchard. They're fine."

Griff motioned with her hand.

Bruno nosed Tony's head and clamped down. Tony screamed like a five year-old girl. "Please...no more. Please!" His screams were kind of muffled by Bruno's tongue.

"How many people did you kill Tony? How many women did you scar? How much pain have you caused? Don't you think you deserve a little in return?" Griff was getting angry.

"He's starting to drool on me *please*!" he pleaded from Bruno's clenched jaws.

"You are a selfish, superficial little man." Griff made another hand sign at Bruno. The lion released Tony.

The lion made a disgusted look—a surprising human expression as he licked his lips like he was trying to get a bad taste out of his mouth.

"Man up Tony. It's just a little gingivitis. Garrick's been working hard on alleviating that issue!"

Tony made to stand up. Bruno fiercely grabbed him by the midsection. Tony screamed again and Bruno growled.

Ω Ω Ω

I heard shaky, teetering laughter behind me. The women had found their voice and were coming closer.

The monster wasn't as scary in the light—not to mention hanging out of a lion's mouth.

"What would you have us do with him ladies?"

The women huddled close to one another.

"Should we let him go, maim him permanently or kill him?"

Hushed silence met my inquiry.

"Pleaseeee!" Tony wailed.

"Quiet Tony. We're talking" I scowled in his (flailing) direction.

"End his foul existence—he doesn't deserve to breath. Don't feed him to the lion though. He's rotten. It might cause the lion harm or indigestion." Kelly hissed through clenched teeth.

The meek young woman held her head down, ashamed of her outburst. I could see a black eye swelling.

Griff and I burst out laughing at her surge of defiance. Now that's what I'm talking about. She still had a little fight left in her. The rest of the woman seemed shaken and speechless.

"Indigestion? Well, you have spoken. Worm bait he shall be—his ashes anyway!" I smiled at the girl's courage. She returned a weak smile.

An older woman stepped forward, toward Kelly. "We are a God-loving people, and I'm sure he is in cahoots with the devil or is the devil himself. Who may have come to walk among us common people. Be the hand of God. I think he would want that monster gone." She skirted away from Tony and embraced Kelly as the girl collapsed in the elder's arms.

"Hmm, hand of god. No I don't think so. But I will be his middle finger." I said and turned to look at the women.

"Ladies, you might want to turn away." No one turned.

Griff wordlessly directed Bruno to release his toy. Tony dropped in a crumpled drool-soaked heap.

He made to stand but only managed an unsteady half bow.

"Please don—" he whined and reached for his gun.

Damn, gun.

He aimed the gun at my head.

I nodded to Griff and I threw her Beatrice in a swift fluid motion.

With one fell swoop Tony's head was severed from his body then rolled a few feet like an uneven bowling ball. I kept Beatrice very sharp. Tony death reflex squeezed the trigger of his hidden gun.

I ducked and rolled and felt the bullet graze my cheek.

Griff yelled my name but it was drowned out by the sound of small feet and cries of "mommy" streaming from the grove of trees.

"I'm all right Griff." I felt a wet trickle slip down my cheek.

The women turned from the macabre scene. Released from their captor's imprisonment, they ran to their little ones. Their joyous tears clashed with their heavy hearts.

Garrick and Bane followed the kids with large grins on their faces.

Bane saw that I was bleeding and rushed to my side.

"Are you all right Sam?"

"Yes, I'm fine. Don't fuss. We got careless."

"Do you know what fine stands for?" he asked a smirk growing over his concerned expression.

"No, but I bet your going to tell me."

"Freaked out, insecure, neurotic and emotional."

I rolled my eyes. "Yep, that about sums my life up."

"And I adore every fine thing about you."

"You are a masochist Bane."

"Yep, that about sums up my life."

We laughed while we both eyed the end of Tony Stevenson.

Bruno lounged by the remnants of Tony's headless corpse.

Griff and Garrick were smiling at us. It felt good to do something right.

"Let's get rid of the garbage. We don't want him to infect anyone or for Bruno to get a piece of Tony stuck in an incisor." I said. Griff nodded toward Garrick. "We cleaned house, how about you two taking out the garbage?"

The boys both rolled their eyes. Griff and I laughed and as Bane and Garrick grabbed Tony's remains. They dragged them to the pasture.

The cows were unperturbed by the burning and digging activities.

Griff and I went to check on the women. An exuberant reunion greeted us.

Our group was invited to a beef barbeque. We were all starving and readily accepted. The women knew how to make butter. We had found heaven.

Over the feast the women took turns filling in their story where our assumptions failed. We were horrified for them—such pain and sadness. They had lived in fear for almost a year. Tony was a psychopathic, murdering rapist with a god complex—there's always one. In our case we kept running into little men with big complexes.

"I really would have liked to have fed his penis to a green. Damn." Griff said as she was gnawing on a steak bone.

"At least the greens have a reason for their behavior. Would you really want to torture the poor things? Haven't they been tortured enough?" Bane grinned at Griff.

She paused in her chewing. "Yeah your right Bane, we shouldn't torture the poor greens. Even they don't deserve to be exposed to his rot. I hate bullies."

The women thought the grove was beautiful—if it had been under different circumstances. Now they were all too keen to leave this grim reminder of the hell they had endured. They wanted a fresh beginning.

They were excited at the prospect of joining the island compound. We all pitched in to get their trucks fixed while Bruno babysat.

At first the women were nervous about the children's close interaction with a grown lion, especially after witnessing how he treated Tony. After various, tentative approaches, aided of course by Bruno's pathetic demeanor—rolling on his back, legs lounging in the air while purring—the women relented.

Eight children climbed, rode, pulled, petted, kissed and laughed at the magnificent lion. Bruno appeared to be in heaven.

He added new hairless members to his pack. Teak and Oakley were thrilled with the reprieve from Bruno's attention. The dogs got plenty of affection from the kids and parents alike. Love unrepressed coursed through the apple orchard.

A convoy of cows, trucks and a lion headed west into the sunset—to a place we called home.

CHAPTER THIRTY-ONE:
The Beginning

"A jug fills drop by drop."
-Buddha (403 BC - 483 BC)

The new additions were made welcome. They were astonished by our home. Most had never seen the ocean, and so a few got seasick on the journey across the water. But there grins remained intact throughout the voyage.

Mae knew we were coming and had already organized a feast. Her sight was so temperamental.

The women stayed together, overwhelmed by the warm welcome.

Cory took them aside to show them their new homes. They still seemed nervous around us colors. Go figure.

It took about a week before I heard them laughing with other members of the compound.

"Time heals almost all child. Don't you fret none. They'll be okay!" Mae was in her rocker looking like she was watching me. I waved my hand in front of her eyes. She didn't notice.

"It horrifies me what people are capable of!" disgust emphasized my words.

"Yes, but look at what good they're capable of too! You kids saved them folks. Easy as pie!" She started rocking.

I held my head down. I was thinking of the young girl that died in my arms. Theresa. The Mennonite woman said she was next to become Tony's companion, she had fled into the breaking dawn hoping to escape from Tony's affections. The women had been saddened to hear of her plight.

"Not all of them though." I sighed, frustrated.

"You do what you can child. You're a nurse, you know that! Now don't make me angry, I'll come after you with my cane and give you a good whooping!" She laughed and kept rocking.

I grinned while I visualized blind Mae chasing me with her cane held high. "We gotta go out again. I'm sure there are others." My gaze turned to look across the marina.

Smirking, Mae continued. "Ain't that the truth? You'll save who you're supposed to. Nothing more, nothing less. Don't you worry none child. You'll always do your best—you may even find more help!"

I eyed the wizened woman sceptically, "All right Oprah." I heaved another sigh. "But will that be enough?"

I shook my head and headed to the beach.

The dogs and I sat on the beach. The cool ocean air mussed my hair. I absently brushed some out my eyes. I groaned deeply. The wind carried my breath away.

"SAM, SAM!" I turned and saw Griffin swiftly approaching where I sat. The alarm on her face registered in me and I felt a surge of panic. I stood up quickly.

She was by my side instantly. "Sam, oh my God Sam." Griff grabbed me by both my arms.

My stomach lurched. "What Griff, is it Bane?" He and Garrick had gone out on a foraging trip.

"No, it's a color!"

I breathed a sigh of relief. "Okay, we'll get everyone together and—"

The young beautiful girl interrupted me mid-sentence. "No it's not just a color—it's a yellow!"

"What? How? Since when…? Ah, since when can you distinguish colors?" I stammered, aghast and amazed.

"I can't Sam. I don't know. But…but I see it, and it's coming from the west. It's not far!"

Holding each other, we both turned toward the west and gawked at open water.

I slammed my mouth shut and steadied myself. "Go get the twins and Cory. Meet me on the west side of the island. It'll be all right, okay?"

Griffin's panicked eyes searched mine for a moment. "Okay Sam, we'll meet you," she breathed out quietly. She did not look convinced.

Griff took off in the direction of the compound. I grabbed the island's Jeep and headed to the western region of the island.

The dogs and I stood on a small embankment overlooking the calm ocean and scanned the distant horizon.

Click. Time to live or time to die. The world and I have changed.

Tick. The hand of a clock drives the fate of my very soul.

I choose to adapt and smash that damn clock.

I glowered. Off in the distance I distinguished the mast of a ship enmeshed in yellow luminosity.

I was not prey.

Click.

"I find hope in the darkest of days, and focus in the brightest. I do not judge the universe."
-Dalai Lama (1935 - 2012)

-Acknowledgements-
Ж

I am grateful to all the people that made this book possible.

My ninja editor Laura Carlson, who shared her experience and knowledge sprinkled with tremendous patience to educate me on the writing process. My best friend Jill Corbett, who has the patience of a God as she encouraged me to follow my dream, while she endured countless hours of conversation about the trials and tribulations of writing a book. The patience and support of my co-workers at the Royal Alex hospital--and yes I'm going to keep nursing. Vanessa C your suggestions for the book rocked, you are brilliant. I thank my hairy counter parts—Teak, Oakley and Bruno for their forgiveness when their walks were late and all their love bombs when I was frustrated. I especially want to thank my readers who shared in the adventure. Thank you for coming on this journey with me.

P. L Jones

CPSIA information can be obtained at www.ICGtesting.com
Printed in the USA
LVOW101240201012

303660LV00005B/5/P